THE LAST VILLAGE

R M HUGHES

ISBN 978-1-718-19337-6

Independently Published

R. M. Hughes
50 Ronald Avenue
Llandudno Junction
United Kingdom
LL31 9EY

CONTENTS

For Wendy, my wife, best friend and soul mate.

ONE

It was night on the North Wales coast when lightning erupted above a mountain pointing out into the Irish Sea. Dazzling energy streaked to the horizon in a straight line, then back and to, back and to. It arced without pause, as though ancient gods had short-circuited this small corner of Earth to the heavens.

Thunder deep-drummed but this was no ordinary storm. With a speed that was more magic than nature, clouds materialised and grew into fat cumulonimbus. They squirmed as though tortured by the bolts of electricity tearing through them.

While below it all: a sleeping village, yellow-lit streets, house interiors all in darkness. Except for one…

Here a window pulsed red as the first raindrops popped and tapped against glass. And there was movement within: the shape of a man hurried to a computer screen flashing a red alarm.

The rain became torrential. Water spilled from gutters along the side of the house. A drain gurgled and plonked as liquid displaced air in its hollows.

Now the man emerged from the front door. He wore zip-up motorcycle boots that were not zipped. Pyjama bottoms stuck out from beneath his trousers. Booted feet scurried and flapped, loose buckles jingling in the downpour to a 4x4 on the driveway.

In the air over the mountain, that sequence of lightning made its journey out to sea yet again, thunder resonating like stomach punches.

At the same time, the 4x4 headlights illuminated daggers of rain and the vehicle pulled out onto the road. It turned towards the village centre and the mountain beyond.

On a steep forestry track, water did not so much drip but fall in sheets from the pine trees. And the dirt road itself gave off a noise like gravel being poured as the rain blasted into it.

The 4x4 ploughed through all this uphill, spraying muddy water in high arcs towards the trees either side. It slowed as it approached a security gate. This opened on its own, rattling behind a bold sign on a razor-wire-topped fence in the headlights:

GOVERNMENT PROPERTY
KEEP OUT
HIGH VOLTAGE
DANGER OF DEATH

Behind rows of trees inside, the compound was lit by a single halogen lamp fixed above a steel door in a rock face. Nearby, rain hammered a tarpaulin covering a gas canister cage next to an electrical transformer.

The 4x4 came to a mushy halt and the driver's door swung open. Flapping zipper boots, sodden pyjama bottoms and trousers emerged first. Lightning flickered, thunder boomed and some sort of fluorescence tinged the boots as they touched down into a puddle. The man ran to the steel door.

Naked light bulbs illuminated a tunnel inside the mountain. Its walls were lined with red brick and rust-stained concrete. In places, bare rock stuck out like forgotten tumours.

One part above a workbench was lined with aged plywood, upon which posters from the Second World War trumpeted mildewed messages about security, *Mum's the Word*, *Walls Have Ears*, alongside a 1947 calendar showing the month of September with half its dates crossed out in purple crayon.

On the workbench itself, somewhat incongruously, laptops displaying bar charts overlooked two men lying unconscious on the floor.

Zip-up boots arrived between them, now actually zipped up. He paused here, peering down at the men from beneath the hood of a silvery suit pulled on over his soaked clothes and pyjamas.

He then hurried along the tunnel towards an arch at its end. This opened into a rock-hewn chamber about the size of a tennis court.

One side in there was a mess of antique purple cables and electrical service boards, dusty switches and fuses. The opposite wall housed modern equivalents with digital read-outs and shock warning symbols.

A thick cable snaked from here to a junction box in the furthest wall, next to which was a bricked-up arch.

This barrier to somewhere deeper was in the initial stages of being demolished, rather haphazardly it seemed. There were scars left by missing bricks in its face layer. A steel bar stuck out of it, issuing a constant electrical arc into a man lying either dead or unconscious on the floor.

The man in the silvery suit approached this scene. He picked up a lump hammer from beside the prostrate figure then struck the steel bar sideways. A second blow caused it to fall with the sharp clang of metal against concrete. The electrical arc ceased immediately.

Outside, above the mountain and its neighbouring village, the lightning also ceased, the last peal of thunder echoing in a diminuendo into the distance.

-o-

During daylight with fingers of sunshine poking through clouds, the village and its long-dormant harbour looked vaguely normal.

Seagulls were noisier and more numerous than its visible inhabitants. Most of the birds were gliding over the sea. A minority landed on the disintegrating timber pier at the end of a short sea wall.

Inland, streets were disturbed by occasional vehicles, including a yellow minibus that had *Children Crossing* symbols on its rear.

The overlooking mountain seemed peaceful if unattractive. The rocky part poked out into the sea, slopes and escarpments scarred by the mine workings of past centuries.

Its inland body was covered in spruce pine. The geometrical

border of the trees heralded that this was man's work employing nature, not the industry of nature itself, even if it did hide most of the mountain's scars.

The newest insult was pristine white. Tucked in on the exposed ridgeline below one of the mountain's lateral cliffs, the dishes of a communications tower provided a proud and taller counterpoint to the greenery of the pines.

When the sun reached its midday zenith, a faded *Amharfarn* sign greeting visitors to the village was passed by a roaring mess of a vehicle.

The *Jones Bros* bus spewed white smoke, crunching gears as it slowed. Its passenger door opened with some reluctance at a bus stop.

Here the driver watched a trim, prim, mature woman, her city clothes somewhat dishevelled as she supervised a duel between her suitcase and the incompletely opened door. When she finally made landfall, the same driver waved a cheerful farewell.

The city woman flinched as the bus roared off, leaving her in a cloud of exhaust. She saw it veer into a triangular turning area just ahead. And as it manoeuvred to go back in the direction from whence it had come, the woman pulled a scrap of paper from her coat pocket.

She eyed a scribbled map before setting off towards the village, wheeled suitcase bumping along noisily behind her as she towed it.

A mud-splashed 4x4 stood on the driveway at the front of one of two large detached houses on the outer edge of Amharfarn.

The dwelling's neighbouring twin sported a B&B sign in a bay window. An overlooking window at the side of this framed a man with grey hair. He was adjusting a pair of tripod-mounted binoculars but glanced at the woman as she trawled her suitcase up the drive next door.

Inside the B&B, the man with the binoculars turned to speak to his wife who was busily dusting an antique bureau.

"They have another visitor," the man said.

Wife, domesticated and rather larger than her husband, moved to the bay window and shifted a net curtain aside with practised fingertips. "Another guest more like... a woman this time."

4

Oblivious to this judgement, the city woman awaited a response to the bell push.

The man who opened the door was wearing fresh zip-up motorcycle boots, neatly fastened and buckled up, respectable work trousers and a white shirt covering his barrel of a chest. Blue eyes peered from beneath a balding head. They stared at the woman as his lips stayed in a position that was neither a smile nor a sneer.

"Miss Norton, I presume..." He was softly spoken, a gentle North Wales accent.

"Yes... I'm Emily..."

The man's gaze did not alter. His eyes remained fixed on hers. "You seem to have travelled far. How was the weather during your journey?"

"Oh, of course," the city woman said. "Not as humid as Bangladesh."

"Nor as dark as Portugal," the man said. "I wonder how much the idiot who comes up with these passphrases gets paid."

"Not nearly enough I suspect. Am I allowed to come in?"

He moved aside in the doorway. "Enter, Miss Norton, please do, and welcome to our safe house. I am Lock, by the way."

Lock watched with something akin to ambivalence as Emily Norton oversaw another duel, this time between her suitcase and the doorstep.

"Leave the case by the stairs," he told her without making any move to help. "Missus Evans will prepare your room when she returns."

"Thank you."

"The office is through here."

She followed him into a lounge: faded rugs, laptop-strewn tables between ancient armchairs and a sofa. An enormous grandfather clock ticked alongside solid French doors in the middle wall. Norton took it all in with a hint of dismay in her eyes.

Lock faced her. "Tea, coffee?"

"Tea would be nice."

He moved to the French doors and touched the handle before hesitating and dropping his hand. "Before we join the others, is there anything you want to ask me?"

She shrugged. "We got our Security Service passwords out of the way. What about the other thing?"

Only now did Lock give the faintest of smiles. "Ah, Circus. We are all Circus in this house, including Missus Evans who will return later. I am sure you and she will get along nicely."

"And the incident last night... Have there been any side effects?"

"One man dead from electrocution, but no other side effects."

Just then the grandfather clock hammered the half-hour with an out-of-tune version of the first eight notes of the Big Ben theme.

With a disdainful glance at the clock, Emily Norton said, "The nineteen forty-five incident report suggested it may have caused some impaired judgement locally. How about this time?"

Lock raised his eyebrows. "Impaired judgement? Have you looked at the world lately?"

She allowed him a grudging, quiet chuckle. "Accepted. Still, it's something to watch out for."

Lock nodded and opened the French doors. Beyond them in a kitchen just as old-fashioned and decrepitly furnished as the office, two men were seated at a dining table. Younger than Lock, they were both in their early thirties, studious and a little nervous-looking. One held a banana he was about to peel.

"So far," Lock said as he looked at this man, "nobody is acting more ape-like than is usual."

The man heard this and returned his banana to a bowl of fruit in the table centre.

Lock introduced them. "Emily Norton... Doctor Banes... Doctor Hardcastle..."

As both stood to shake her hand, Norton said, "Nice to meet you. I'm sorry for your loss." She then offered her hand to Lock.

There was some puzzlement from the three men at first, then Lock twigged. "Ah, Shakespeare-Smith, we didn't know him too well." As though dismissing the subject, Lock moved to an age-faded worktop and sink by the window.

"Us two and Smith only arrived four days ago," Banes explained to Norton. "We were just getting to know each other when he was killed. Still, it's very sad."

"I feel sorry for his family," Hardcastle chipped in, "if he has family."

"And the body?" Emily Norton asked.

Lock tilted a kettle to pour into a mug. "Clean-up section from Manchester took it this morning. Quite dignified actually... I laid him out before rigor set in. They came to the compound in a white van, but they had a nice coffin for him. He was treated with some dignity and respect."

"Did they want to know what happened?" Norton asked. "The clean-up guys, I mean."

Lock gestured with a dismissive hand. "Silent types, they didn't see anything inside. I moved the body to the entrance before they arrived. They asked no questions, just did their job." He now gazed at Norton as though conducting an appraisal.

She shifted her eyes around the kitchen in response. Her hands trembled slightly as she sat down at the table.

"Circus has thrown you in at the deep end," Lock told her. "But try to keep cool. You're not alone here."

"I know," she agreed. "But all this is a bit disconcerting. I have to produce a report and fake evidence that doesn't get us all tortured and killed by our own government."

Hardcastle offered Norton a smile. "Welcome to frontline Circus," he told her cheerfully. "All for one and one for all, as Shaky used to say before he got zapped."

"Shaky?" Norton queried, puzzled.

"He means Shakespeare-Smith, the man who was killed," Lock explained as he placed a mug on the table in front of her. "Have a nice cup of tea while we talk you through it."

-o-

7

Hands in his hoodie pockets, a young male walked along the pavement from the village centre. There was a cough from beneath the hood as he headed towards the detached houses.

He glanced around, rather like a soldier in enemy territory. Yet his eyes, though bloodshot from lack of sleep, seemed intelligent and sensitive. As he approached, he noticed that the 4x4 in the driveway of Lock's house was splashed with dried mud.

Inside the B&B next door, the woman hurried to a ringing phone and lifted the receiver. "Ellis residence... Mair Ellis speaking."

Mr Ellis entered the lounge. He saw she had got to the phone, so went over to the side window where he kept his binoculars and tripod.

"Yes, it is," Mair Ellis told whoever was calling. "We can also offer an evening meal as well, in our dining room... Yes."

Mr Ellis smiled at her official tone and accent. He glanced out of his favourite window, but then reacted quickly when he saw his wife gesturing to him. "Let me check our reservations diary..." she was saying. He reached into his jacket pocket and moved to her side. He gave her his pen, then a scrap of paper from another pocket.

Thus armed, Mair Ellis addressed the phone. "Can you repeat the date, please? Well, that's actually today, but we do have a vacancy. For how long? And the gentleman's name, please? Could you spell it?" She listened as she wrote, then said, "That's fine, I can spell Jones no problem... That's a firm booking then, thank you... Goodbye."

She put the phone receiver down. "We have our first booking in years, Wyn," she told her husband excitedly.

Wyn Ellis seemed genuinely pleased for her. "Congratulations." He gave her a quick hug before retrieving his pen from her hand. Looking out through the bay window, he noticed the young man wearing a hoodie turning up the drive next door.

Mair Ellis noticed him as well but continued expressing her thoughts with enthusiasm. "The dot-com really works. This Caycey Jones is a mature American from Texas. The travel agent got our details from the dot-com. He's already on his way. We'll have to do some shopping, steaks and French fries, things Americans eat."

8

Emily Norton placed her mug on the worktop next to the sink and looked out through the window. "Trouble is, this incident will have blipped on the radar of just about every intelligence agency on the planet."

She noticed something and leaned forward for a better view. The young man wearing a hoodie approached a large shed at the bottom of the rear garden. He held a key in his hand.

"A rather furtive-looking youth is going into your shed," Norton observed.

"That will be Kyle. Does the gardening and a few odd jobs for me," Lock explained. "He's clueless about what we really are here. This is a close-knit community, so we'll know straight away if any strangers start poking their noses around."

Norton returned to the table and sat down. "How can you differentiate between operatives and tourists?"

Banes and Hardcastle glanced at Lock, who smiled. "Wait till you see the village proper. Amharfarn is no tourist destination I can tell you. We are well off that map."

She took this in with some evident scepticism. "Diplomatically, the reassurance from Five to the Foreign Office seems to have been accepted by most governments so far, secretly of course."

"A natural event story won't wash at all," Banes put in.

Lock leaned forward over the table. "Circus is handling the cover story for diplomatic backchannel purposes."

"Good," Norton acknowledged, "but first I have to debrief you. How I concoct my report to make it believable to Five is our immediate problem. They want my initial report today. Did you take photographs?"

-o-

Kyle was seated on a fold-out garden chair in the shed. He finished rolling a joint before placing his stash behind some roof slates leaning up against the timber wall behind him.

The rest of the shed was filled with junk, together with the ubiquitous lawn mower, strimmer, various spades, forks and other gardening tools. Three mountain bikes were suspended from ceiling beams in the furthest corner.

He lit and took a deep pull from the joint, before reaching into a pocket for a mobile phone. *Yack yack yack... Yack yack yack.* It was at his ear for a moment before he spoke.

"Yo, bro, wassup?" His accent was very North Wales.

Inside the safe house kitchen, Emily Norton studied photographs at the table, with Banes, Hardcastle and Lock passing them around for sombre reflection at the same time: Shakespeare-Smith, dead, lying on the floor of the underground chamber, but now apparently alongside the modern circuit boards and controls. One photograph clearly showed a *Danger! High Voltage* sign in the same shot.

"You positioned him well, I must say," Norton commented. "It should work." She fixed her eyes on Lock, but the man seemed distracted.

"I'd better go and see Kyle," he said, rising from the table.

"We need to go up to the compound," Norton warned. "Walk through the cover story."

"Did you bring boots?"

"Of course."

"I suggest you put them on then," Lock said with a grunt. He let himself out through the back door.

Norton raised her eyebrows.

Hardcastle noticed this and grinned at her as he handed a photograph to Banes. "You'll get used to him, don't worry. Are you in charge here now, Miss Norton?"

Norton smiled but addressed both scientists in a serious tone. "We have to get a few things straight. It's exactly like before. As far as Five is concerned, Shakespeare-Smith was in charge of the test.

I'm his replacement. We all protect the cover story Five needs to be given. As far as *reality* is concerned, we are all Circus and Lock is in charge. We all protect the cover for that and obey his orders."

"Understood," Banes acknowledged. Hardcastle merely shrugged and reached for a banana in the bowl of fruit.

In the garden shed, Kyle continued on his phone. "I'm not giving her any more money to snort it up her nose. I'm really finished with her this time. She cleaned me out..." He glanced up to see Lock appear at the shed door. "Dude, have to go." Kyle disconnected the call and looked around for somewhere to dispose of his now dead joint.

Lock's tone was relaxed. "Put it in the bin in a plastic bag as usual."

"Sorry, Mister Lock, just needed to take the edge off."

Lock leaned against the doorframe. "I heard some of your conversation. Are you having problems with Sharon again?"

"I moved out," Kyle answered.

"I'm sorry to hear that."

"She was behind with the rent, so I gave her all my money. But she didn't pay the rent... Put it all up her nose."

"Cocaine?" Lock said the word with distaste.

"Yeh, it's evil what it's done to her. Now she's in debt to the Scousers and she told them I can pay them."

"Are they after you?"

Kyle considered the question. He glanced at the floor, then at Lock, but answered without looking the man in the eye. "I don't know, I don't think so. Anyway, I've left her."

"Back with your gran?"

Kyle nodded. "Yeh."

Lock's tone was fatherly, sympathy evident in his voice. "I know you care about Sharon, but if she's an addict, you can't help her. She will just harm you both if you try. Keep your cannabis stash here. If you must smoke it occasionally, smoke it here. But stay away from trouble. And that means Sharon and especially those Scousers."

Kyle seemed relieved at this. "Understood, absolutely understood. You got more antiques coming soon, Mister Lock?"

11

"Not just yet, but there is something new I want you to do."

"Sure, anything for you, Mister Lock."

"I want you to keep an eye out for strangers arriving in the village."

Kyle's eyes widened. "Five-Oh?"

"No, not police, I want to know about any strangers walking about, and especially any strangers asking questions."

"Why, Mister Lock? Are they Antiques Feds or something?"

Lock smiled at this. "Nothing serious really, possibly competitors in my antiques hobby. Doesn't matter why. If you see or hear about strangers, you phone me. Quiet. Make sure nobody hears you, okay?"

"Sure, Mister Lock," Kyle agreed.

-o-

High above them, a transatlantic airliner gleamed as it drew vapour trails against the rarefied atmosphere.

In first class, an African American gentleman, mature and rather overweight, was alone in a window seat. He was deep into his iPad and had a pair of wired earphones stuck in his ears. A male voice choir sang Cwm Rhondda directly into his eardrums.

On the iPad itself, in black and white, the 1941 movie How Green Was My Valley displayed an army of singing coal miners as they marched through a weird Hollywood version of a Welsh mining village.

A stewardess leaned over and tapped his shoulder. The man removed his earplugs. The choir was replaced by the quiet hum of the aircraft cabin. He smiled at the uniformed woman.

"Mister Jones, we're not far from Manchester now," she told him. "If you look out the window, we're just off the North Wales coast."

Jones did as she suggested, then looked back at her, still smiling. "Thank you, ma'am, it looks very pretty." His voice was deep bass and resonant as he pointed to his iPad. "I'm watching my favourite movie. Really looking forward to Wales, the singing in the pubs and chapels, British Bobbies, red phone boxes and small automobiles."

The uniformed woman smiled and nodded a bit knowingly. "Let me know if you need anything," she said, before moving down the aisle to the next passenger.

Jones plugged the tiny earphones back into his ears and gazed through the window at the mountains below.

-o-

Kyle was on his hands and knees, weeding the front garden border at the safe house when he saw Lock and the others come out. They all headed for the 4x4.

"Kyle," Lock said. "This is Miss Norton."

Kyle issued a friendly nod and wave to the woman.

Norton acknowledged it with a restrained smile.

Lock continued to address Kyle as the others climbed into the 4x4. "Mister Shakespeare-Smith had to go home. Miss Norton is here instead of him."

"Okay," Kyle said. He returned to weeding, then raised his eyebrows and shrugged as the 4x4 drove out onto the road. It headed in the direction of the village.

-o-

The Manchester Airport terminal was a noisy drudge of activity, the air tinged by a faint smell of paraffin.

At the car hire compound, a woman with a clipboard stepped back from a Jaguar. Jones was seated behind the wheel. He was leaning over an open CD case on the passenger seat, where he quickly made his selection. The player swallowed this, but Jones hit the stop button before any sound was produced. He then touched the engine start.

The car hire lady waved casually as he drove off towards the compound exit.

-o-

The entrance chamber flooded with daylight when the steel door was opened from outside. Lock and Emily Norton entered.

Lock flicked light switches. "This is the only modernised part of what we have here," he told Norton. "Lockers there. Choose one if you want. Shower room and toilet through that door there."

A row of head-height lockers stood against one neatly hewn rock wall. The adjacent face sported a rack of miners' helmets, and alongside that, a charger with a dozen or so lamp batteries plugged into terminals.

Lock pointed to an open-frame steel dresser. Inside this, silvery jackets and over-trousers were hanging in a row. "EMF suits. We'll need them when the operation gets properly underway."

Norton felt one of the suit sleeves. She had some distaste in her expression but shook it off when Banes and Hardcastle came in. They were carrying aluminium cases.

Lock beckoned Norton to follow him into the tunnel workspace. Daylight was replaced by the yellow glow of low wattage and naked light bulbs.

Emily Norton seemed fascinated by the propaganda posters and 1947 calendar above a row of laptops on a bench. "Did they leave any notes or records from that period?"

Banes and Hardcastle both turned to face Lock, apparently just as interested in an answer to that question.

Lock shook his head as he moved on. "Nothing, just scraps of paper, shopping lists, doodles. One of them was a lousy but prodigious cartoonist."

In the electronics chamber, Norton approached the partly dismantled, walled-up arch where Shakespeare-Smith had met his end in an arc of strange electricity. She tapped the brickwork. Its face layer was partly missing, edges jagged. The next layer was still intact. She stepped back carefully to avoid tripping over loose bricks on the floor. "Tell me about this and what your orders are from Circus."

Lock faced her. "As you know, as far as Five and just about everyone else in government is concerned, that passage is taboo, the wall is taboo. If they saw what we have begun, MI6 would torture and kill us. Circus orders are to open it up, report what we find beyond it and await further instructions."

Emily Norton sighed. "So, my report needs to be convincing enough to make sure they don't drop a spot inspection on us."

"Not just your report," Lock said. "Circus responsibility as well. It's as much their job as ours to make sure nobody is motivated to pay us a proper visit."

"Five will expect photographs with my report, complete coverage…" Norton pointed at a junction box immediately adjacent to the sealed-off arch, where the thick cable was plugged in. "I'll need close-ups of the terminal seals on that as well, with the serial numbers clearly visible."

"We have that covered," Lock said.

Hardcastle stepped forward. "We took complete photo coverage before Shaky started hacking away, the seals, everything. I can put it all through your camera and date-time stamp it" – he checked his watch – "using the time as of now."

"Is your camera discrete from the Five systems?" Norton asked.

"Of course," Hardcastle answered. "I'll match the embedding to make sure what you send appears to be from your camera."

Lock approached the loose bricks on the chamber floor. "Did they give you my phoned report before sending you here?" He glanced at Norton.

"No, sent me mostly blind, apart from telling me you were running a planned test when one of you was electrocuted and killed. Plus, the fact the geomagnetic standing wave here grew rapidly at the exact same time. What *did* you report?"

Lock went down on his haunches and started moving and stacking the loose bricks. "Exactly what you just said."

"How did you explain the sudden increase in standing wave energy?"

"I didn't, except that we didn't cause it."

Norton looked perplexed. "But you did, didn't you? The Circus protocol?"

Banes came over and helped Lock shift bricks into stacks. Lock remained silent.

"They're going to want a cause for the standing wave peak from me," Norton said.

"And you're not going to give them one," Lock told her.

"But you did cause it."

"Of course we did. But you are going to report that the surge must have been triggered by an unknown external event."

Norton turned to Banes and glanced at Hardcastle who was joining in with the brick stacking. She stepped out of their way. "Exactly what were you two doing when the incident started?"

"Five's protocol is entirely passive," Banes answered. "It was designed to monitor for any coherence in the existing standing wave, and…"

"And that's what you say we were doing," Lock chipped in.

"But we were running the active series for Circus," Banes continued, "on the precise resonance setting ordered by Circus. A low yield increase in energy was what we expected. We didn't expect it to suddenly escalate or Shakespeare-Smith to get killed by a fluke resonance in a steel bar. We were lucky we only got stunned."

"So how do I explain the not-so-low yield electromagnetic standing wave that's put a bullseye on this place on every secret intelligence map on the planet?" Norton demanded.

"You don't," Lock answered. "Circus has it covered."

Norton frowned. "How?"

"All you need to do in your report is find nothing here and conclude an external cause, source unknown."

"And if they don't buy that?"

"They will. They already have the external data that will confirm our cover story."

"How external?" Norton asked.

"Submarine maybe," Hardcastle said. "That's the only external event that could explain it. Submarine deploys its ULF array in the vicinity."

"In breach of the forty-seven treaty?" Norton rebuked. "No navy in the world would risk that."

Lock stood up, wiping brick and mortar dust off his hands. "Stop guessing, all of you. Circus has been planning this for years. Having

16

an external cause of a higher order standing wave is the only way we could ever pull it off. The only unplanned thing that happened here is that Shakespeare-Smith got killed."

"So, we stick to the script," Norton said, nodding sceptically. "Has Circus actually got a submarine?"

"Stick to the script," Lock reminded her. "And stick to what Five ordered you to do." He pointed at the modern electronics rack. "I assume they want data from all the monitors?"

"Yes they do," Norton confirmed.

"Better start laundering it then," Lock said, then gestured to Banes and Hardcastle. "You two help her."

The two men opened their instrument cases. Norton stared worriedly at the electronics rack.

Lock carried on stacking bricks as though he had no concerns at all.

-o-

Caycey Jones smiled as his hired Jaguar purred comfortably at 70mph. Up ahead, a steel overbridge sported a *Croeso, Welcome, Cymru, Wales* sign, red dragon proud above the words.

He now pressed the CD play button on the dashboard.

Paul Robeson's basso profundo voice followed an orchestral introduction. From beyond the grave, Robeson was singing the Welsh National Anthem in English.

Jones sighed. "Civilisation."

-o-

Kyle was still weeding the front garden when the 4x4 returned to the driveway. He stood up, brushing weed leaves and blades of grass from his gloves.

The young man watched as they climbed out of the vehicle. Lock came around its front towards him.

Lock took only a cursory glance at the flower beds. "Very good. You can pack up and go home now. Same time tomorrow. Same job,

17

eyes open, in the front here, okay?" Lock possessed that fatherly tone as he spoke.

"Okay," Kyle answered. He noticed how busy and in a hurry some of the others were.

Hardcastle opened the front door to the house. Norton and Lock followed him inside, leaving the door open.

Banes leaned up against the 4x4 and lit a cigarette. "Want one, Kyle?"

Kyle picked up a bin bag and trowel from the lawn. "No thanks, Doctor Banes."

After he had put the weeds in the wheelie bin by the side of the house, stowed the trowel in the shed and locked it, Kyle returned to the front. Banes had finished his cigarette and was struggling to lift three instrument cases at the same time from the ground by the 4x4.

"Let me give you a hand," Kyle offered.

"Very kind of you," Banes said. He allowed the younger man to take the third case.

Kyle carried this as far as the porch where he put it down. Banes was already returning to the vehicle for another load.

"Any more?" Kyle asked him.

"No, you go home. I'll be a little while yet."

-o-

A compact black car with twin exhausts revved noisily to a halt by the faded *Amharfarn* sign. The vehicle's windows were tinted dark. A gangsta beat boomed loud from the high output sound system built into its interior.

Alone inside, the driver was a brutish-looking man in his late twenties, his head shaved with a designer pattern. As the engine idled, he peered angrily over the steering wheel.

In the distance, he saw Kyle coming out from the safe house driveway and turning in the direction of the village centre.

Kyle had Walkman phones plugged into his ears as he whistled something tuneless. He glanced back briefly at Banes who was still at it, now apparently bringing instrument cases out of the house to

18

put back into the 4x4. Kyle shrugged with disinterested puzzlement as he walked.

Some distance up ahead of him, he spotted a diminutive, forty-something woman wearing a red jacket and carrying shopping bags. She was coming from the village in his direction. Kyle was lifting a hand to wave a greeting to her when the black compact screeched to a halt beside him.

Startled and with a look of horror, Kyle ripped the phones out of his ears as he twisted around, sprinting immediately back towards the safe house.

Revving loudly, gangsta music still thumping, the black compact commenced making a rapid three-point turn.

On his final manoeuvre and as he floored the pedal, the head-shaven brute saw Kyle veer and sprint into the same driveway where he had originally spotted him.

When Banes emerged from the open front door, Kyle had already made it up the side of the house.

Kyle swerved past a garage and across the back lawn, dodged around the shed and vaulted over the rear fence. The open sand dunes behind it sloped down towards the sea a moderate distance away. He was gone.

Banes reached the 4x4, where his attention was taken up by the black compact screeching to a halt on the road outside. He watched as its driver got out of the now silent car. The brutal-looking man marched towards him with the angry stare of a crazed predator.

"Can I help you?" Banes asked him nervously.

But instead of answering, the predatory man grabbed his arm. "Where is he?" The man's accent was heavily Liverpool, a Scouser.

"Get off me," Banes protested, clawing at the man's grip. "Where's who?"

"Shut the fuck up."

The brute now marched the cowed and barely resisting Banes to the still open front door and inside the safe house.

Lock and Emily Norton were seated at the kitchen table. Norton was connecting cables to instruments brought from the underground spaces on the mountain. Hardcastle was standing at the sink, watching a kettle boiling noisily like a steam engine to one side of it. It clicked off at the same moment Banes was propelled into the kitchen.

Norton looked up, alarmed. The Scouser occupied the French doorway. He waved a pistol so they could all see it, before pointing it first at Norton's face, then at Lock, who stood up and backed away.

Banes now had his back to the worktop, leaning on it with a look of horror, next to an equally stunned Hardcastle.

"Where is he?" the Scouser shouted. He glanced around, then moved along the inner wall of the kitchen and faced out from a corner, still threatening with the gun.

Lock spoke calmly but with a stern tone. "Young man, I don't know who you are looking for, but—"

"Shut the fuck up," the Scouser warned. "Where is he?"

Now Lock began edging forward. The handgun was immediately pointed at his face.

Lock halted. "Where is who?" he asked, voice still low and calm. Behind him, Hardcastle allowed his forefinger to reach under the worktop edge.

"Pinko," the Scouser shouted, as though dealing with an idiot. "I saw him come in here. Where is he?" The brute now swung his gun towards the French doorway as a rustle of plastic against canvas pre-announced the arrival of a small woman. Wearing a red jacket and carrying shopping bags, she breezed into the kitchen. The gun tracked her as she headed straight for the worktop without looking at the intruder.

"Hello, hello, hello," the woman announced cheerfully in a broad North Wales accent. She dumped her bags on the worktop.

"Who the fuck are *you*?" the astounded Scouser demanded, his gun aimed at her back. "Who *are* you people and where's Pinko?" But the woman ignored him, despite his loud voice.

Lock took a bold step forward as he asked, "Who is Pinko?"

The Scouser swung the gun again and took a step forward to aim at Lock. This caused Norton to cower in her seat at the table.

There was a sound like a cheap and aged Christmas cracker being pulled, accompanied by the instant appearance of a small black hole

20

slightly left of centre in the brute's forehead. He crumpled to the floor with a spurt of blood from the hole.

Norton remained frozen for only a fraction of a second, before twisting around in her chair in time to see the small woman lowering a pistol, with an enormous silencer fitted to it, held expertly with both hands.

Lock sounded surprised but he spoke in a normal volume. "Why on earth did you do that?" he asked the small woman. Banes and Hardcastle stared at her. They seemed frozen.

The woman, however, moved to the still form on the floor near Norton's feet. Fixed on this woman with a gun, Norton's eyes suggested she was watching the predator that was about to devour her.

"You pressed the panic button," the small woman said. "Clear ringtone on my mobile. He had a gun on you."

"I didn't press the panic button," Lock retorted. "Who pressed the panic button?"

Hardcastle raised a feeble hand. "I did. This one here, under the worktop."

"The panic button is only for an existential threat," Lock told him in the quiet tone a teacher might use to advise a child of a spelling mistake. In contrast to his voice, Lock's eyes were piercing.

"Well he did have a gun," Banes said, his voice trembling.

"And I felt existentially threatened," Hardcastle added, then breathed deeply. "That gun... I've never seen one before, not like that."

"But that didn't mean he was going to use it," Lock said. "Even if the gun was real, which it isn't."

The small woman lowered her gun in one hand as she leaned over the Scouser's body to pick up his. She looked at it quickly before dropping it and returning her attention to the body. Her own gun was returned to both hands where she kept it ready to fire again. "It's a fake alright," she announced. "Why didn't you tell me?"

Lock's eyes were wide. "I didn't know the panic button had been tripped."

"But you saw my tactics?"

21

"I thought you were just distracting him. I was about to convince him, physically if necessary, to leave. He's just a druggie. I think he was after Kyle."

"And I thought *you* were distracting him so I could take the shot," the woman concluded in a satisfied tone. "The front door was wide open when I arrived, back hatch on the car as well. We seem to have forgotten all our security protocols, don't we?"

Still rigid in her chair, eyes glancing away from the woman with the silenced pistol to the bloody hole in the dead Scouser's forehead, Emily Norton now spoke. Her voice was high-pitched, warbling slightly. "I'm not really a field officer. Does this sort of thing happen often here?"

The small woman lowered her gun. "You must be Emily Norton," she said cheerfully, offering her right hand for the customary greeting. "I'm Gwenda Evans. It's so nice to meet you."

Norton viewed the hand as though it was a new and terrible threat. She did not move to accept it with hers.

"Nothing like this has ever happened before," Lock announced.

As the others tried to digest this, Gwenda Evans gently patted Norton on the head. Norton flinched at this, then relaxed, but only a little. Gwenda turned her attention to the Scouser, cuckooing down to place two fingers against the side of his neck.

"Not since Chile, for me," Gwenda said as she now began going through the dead man's pockets. "That was for Circus, but he was a real nasty, one of Pinochet's exterminators. This one though... Well, he *was* a druggie thug, but it is a shame."

Lock paced back and forth in a small arc. "We have to dispose of him quickly."

Gwenda Evans held up a key fob she had found in the Scouser's pockets. "There's his car as well. And you need to text London with the accidental alarm code."

"Damn, yes," Lock said, pulling a mobile from his trouser pocket. He immediately thumbed it. "See if you can find identification on him." He turned to Hardcastle. "Go down to the cellar. There's a row of big cardboard boxes in the far corner. They're full of body bags. Bring one, please."

"What about one of the boxes as well," Gwenda suggested. She placed some of the contents of the Scouser's pockets on the table in front of Norton: a mobile phone, bag of weed, a Rizla packet and a lighter. "We have to get him out of the house."

"Too much like a coffin," Lock said. "It would probably split as well." He paced quickly into the adjoining office where he turned to the oversized grandfather clock.

Banes followed him, watching Lock as the man opened the clock's solid winding door and pondered the swinging, loudly clunking pendulum inside. Lock reached in, interrupting the pendulum, and tapped the rear panel with his knuckles. It sounded like solid wood.

In the kitchen, Gwenda Evans added a driver's licence, a crushed cigarette pack and some banknotes to the items on the table in front of Emily Norton, and then patted her on the head again. This time, the city woman did not flinch quite as much.

Pointing at Banes when he returned to the kitchen with Lock, Gwenda said, "Be a dear and fetch two big towels from the airing cupboard upstairs. Two of the older ones, please."

Banes hurried away.

Hardcastle returned to the kitchen with a body bag, then stood there holding it awkwardly.

Lock leaned on the table shaking his head with an expression of disbelief. "Fifteen years I've been here," he said quietly to Norton. "Never once have I had to harm anyone in that time. This operation is only four days old. I have shipped off one man in a coffin and now there's a dead body in my kitchen."

"He must have been after Kyle," Gwenda Evans said. "But Kyle must have run around the back of the house. Probably went over the fence towards the beach."

Lock nodded, eyes still tinged with disbelief,

Banes arrived back in a hurry. He handed two towels to Gwenda. She began wrapping the dead Scouser's bloody head with one of them. She spoke quietly to Norton as she did this. "When did you last go on a covert mission?"

"Never," Norton responded. "I'm a scientist, like Shakespeare-Smith."

"Well that's alright," Gwenda said. "Get his details for me, dear, and the SIM from his mobile phone if you don't mind." She looked over at Lock. "So how *are* we going to dispose of this?"

But Lock was tapping digits into his mobile phone. He was answered almost immediately.

"Maldwyn? It's Andy Lock… Is your flatbed truck available right now? Great. I need an electric hammer as well… Just for a day… Hundred and seventy quid's a bit steep, but okay. Can you deliver it? Straight away, please."

Lock lowered his phone.

At the table, Emily Norton got a result on one of the laptops. "Mister Damien Miller," she announced. "He's got form."

Gwenda paid attention.

"String of convictions," Norton continued. "Supply of Class A drugs. Murder charge reduced to manslaughter, for which he got five years, reduced to eighteen months. There's an arrest warrant out for him, breach of bail and probation, two charges of GBH. Nice man."

Lock nodded at this. "We're getting rid of him right now, and his car. This is what we are going to do."

-o-

Caycey Jones's deep voice hummed along with the music of a choir. They were singing a Welsh hymn from a CD as Jones drove along the potholed road and passed the *Amharfarn* sign. Joining in with the choir's triumphal amens, he pulled the Jaguar up to the kerb outside the B&B.

"You have reached your destination," the satnav announced.

Jones switched off the engine and the CD player before getting out. The American inhaled, relishing the sea air. It was coming in with quite a breeze, blowing a few leaves and a plastic cup along the pavement. He stretched a bit, taking in his surroundings, before getting a suitcase from the trunk of the car.

Gwenda Evans came out of the safe house, leaving the front door

24

open. She paused, briefly looking back into the house before hurrying along the drive. She had passed between the 4x4 and the lawn and was about to move around a large flatbed truck, now reverse-parked on the drive between the 4x4 and the street, when she first spotted Jones. He was beginning to tow his suitcase along the driveway to the B&B next door.

Jones saw the woman widen her eyes. He tapped the side of his forehead in a gentlemanly salute, a broad smile accompanying this gesture.

Gwenda hesitated, composed herself by gripping the canvas shopping bag she was carrying more tightly with one hand, before returning the greeting by waving the key fob she held in the other. She uttered a nervous "Hi," which somehow transformed into a meaningless "Hah," before hurrying past the flatbed truck.

Jones raised his eyebrows as he watched her. The breeze blew in a folded leaflet, litter, which landed close to his feet. Still surprised by the woman's behaviour, he dutifully picked up the litter with a cursory glance at its imagery and text.

Holding this with one hand and adjusting his grip on the suitcase with the other, he saw the woman getting into an untidily parked black compact with dark tinted windows.

He had taken a few more steps along the drive when his thoughts were interrupted by the roar of twin exhausts, accompanied by the loud *boom boom* of gangsta music. Jones hesitated, then looked back at the car. It now commenced a three-point turn as the gangsta chanted "huh-huh-huh motherfu—" before that sound was killed.

As the car roared off, Jones now noticed some grunting sounds from the doorway of the house next door. Three men and a woman appeared to be hauling out a very large and apparently heavy grandfather clock.

Politely, Jones averted his gaze and approached the B&B, where he prodded the doorbell. As he waited, the sound of muted clock chimes clanking in a tuneless and disorderly fashion prompted him to look in that direction again. The B&B door opened as he did so.

25

Two of the four people with the clock noticed him at the same time, gaping in evident disbelief as they rested the top end of the clock on the tail of the flatbed.

Mair Ellis briefly took in the man on her doorstep, saw the leaflet in his hand, before her attention was drawn to more chimes from next door. They were sliding the clock on its back onto the flatbed. She viewed this activity then returned her focus to Jones, who smiled at her.

"I'm sorry," Mair Ellis said. "I have the greatest respect for your faith, but not today. I'm expecting a visitor." She closed the door in his face.

Stunned, Jones turned to look at the people next door. The older man was up on the flatbed, playing out load straps to one of the two younger men. A woman dressed for a city, except for her black army boots, was standing at the end of the truck looking back at him. Emily Norton waved a feebly self-conscious greeting towards him, lips moving soundlessly.

Jones rang the doorbell again. When Mair Ellis answered almost immediately, Jones spoke rapidly to avoid interruption. "I am sorry to disturb you again, but perhaps I have the wrong address. My travel agent has booked a room for me with a Missus Ellis. Do you know her?"

Mair Ellis was immediately mortified. "Oh dear God, I am so sorry. I thought you were a Jehovah's Witness. You must be Mister Jones." Her attention switched irritably to the sound of the truck roaring into life, followed by the 4x4 engine start.

"They seem busy next door," Jones commented with a smile.

"Please come in, please, I am so sorry," Mair Ellis said, her hands moving up and down in front of her as though undecided about her guest's suitcase, which he was now lifting.

She stood aside to allow Jones to cross the threshold. Mair then glared at the truck as it drove out, followed by the 4x4, before closing the door.

The woman looked at her guest's suitcase again, then inclined her head sideways towards the stairs in the hallway. "Wyn, Wyn," she shouted in a high-pitched voice. It sounded like a small dog barking.

The American's eyes widened and he stepped back a bit.

"My husband, Wyn," Mair Ellis explained when she saw his response. "I am so sorry. I must have seemed so rude."

"Not at all," Caycey Jones reassured her.

"He probably has his headphones on," she said, then inclined her head once more. "Wyn, Wyn," she barked towards the staircase, before seamlessly switching to a gushing, presentational voice. "Please come and sit down in our reception lounge until my husband can show you to your room."

Jones was ushered thus into a room off the hallway.

-o-

With her feet on dusty compound ground on the mountain, Gwenda Evans sat on the open back of the dead Scouser's compact.

She had parked it slightly off the internal track, behind a couple of pines and the ruins of a building from the distant past. She rose when she heard the flatbed truck approach.

This pulled to a halt in the open part of the compound yard, its front end pointing towards the steel door in the rock face. The 4x4 followed but halted short before manoeuvring to turn around. Banes and Hardcastle got out of it.

Lock and Emily Norton climbed down from the truck cabin. "Reverse it to the back of this," Lock told Gwenda. She hurried away.

Equally in a hurry, Norton headed down the access lane, her army boots scraping against the ash and quarry waste surface.

Lock, Banes and Hardcastle climbed onto the truck's cargo deck and began loosening the load straps securing the grandfather clock.

With its rear hatch still open, Gwenda reversed the compact. The car's twin exhausts roared, the hatch door rocked, chippings popped, and its brakes squealed when it halted at the truck's rear.

27

Norton reached a position where she could see the closed security gate between the trees. She stared in that direction for a couple of seconds, then turned and gave a thumbs-up to the others.

Seeing this, Lock said "Okay" to Banes and Hardcastle. They reached into the open door of the prone grandfather clock and started lifting out the body bag. Lock joined them, pulling on the heavier middle part. They put it down briefly on the deck before carrying it to the rear, where Gwenda was ready with some blue plastic sheeting.

Banes and Hardcastle jumped down and turned to pull feet-first. Lock grunted as he pushed from above, then awkwardly got to the ground while he was still holding the upper torso. The three men then swung the body into the compact, where it landed with a fleshy thump.

Gwenda covered it with blue plastic sheeting then slammed the rear hatch shut. "Did you see that man who arrived at Mair and Wyn's next door?" she asked Lock.

-o-

At the B&B, Caycey Jones was seated on a sofa in the reception lounge, finishing off a cup of tea. Mair and Wyn Ellis occupied a matching sofa opposite, where they held cups and saucers from the same Willow Pattern set as their guest's.

"The room is lovely," Jones said. "The whole house is a credit to you."

"You're very kind," Mair Ellis told the American. "We want you to feel at home during your stay with us."

"I am *actually* in Wales," Jones announced in a deep voice. He put his cup and saucer down on a coffee table between the two sofas. "I've imagined this for many years. Now it's real."

"We've left some brochures in your room," Wyn Ellis said. "Places to visit."

Jones nodded. "Thank you, but I think I'm going to be spending most of my time in Amharfarn. Am I pronouncing it right?"

28

Mair Ellis pronounced it correctly for him. "The f is pronounced like a v," she explained.

"It's a beautiful language," Jones said, smiling.

"There isn't really much to see here," Wyn Ellis said, "but we are in easy reach of all the tourist spots."

The American acknowledged this with another of his wide smiles. "Well, this is a sort of pilgrimage for me. My great-great-great-grandfather was born on a farm here in Amharfarn."

"Really," Mair Ellis said with some surprise.

"He was Idwal Caradoc Jones," Jones told her. "The family lost their farm when a mining company bought it off their landlord. He worked in the mine for a while before migrating to America."

"Amazing," Wyn Ellis said with genuine interest.

Jones nodded and continued in an affectionate tone. "He fell in love with my great-great-great-grandmother, and had the courage, loyalty and fortitude to marry her at a time such unions were severely frowned upon." He smiled. "So here I am. I think I owe him to pay my respects to his place of origin."

"Do you know the name of the farm?" Wyn Ellis asked. He rose from the sofa and went to the antique bureau.

"Wurn Batch," Jones answered.

"Ah, that might be Wern Bach," Wyn acknowledged, now deep into one of the bureau drawers. "It doesn't ring a bell, but I have a copy of an old map from the nineteenth century here."

"Is there anyone by the name of Jones in the village?" Caycey Jones asked Mair Ellis.

She almost laughed but prevented it. "I'm afraid Jones is a very popular name in Wales."

Wyn Ellis spread a map on a table between the sofas and the bay window. The others joined him, Caycey Jones leaning over it with ardent interest.

"Here it is," Wyn said, pointing to a spot on the map. "I've passed it dozens of times. Quite a nice walk up there. Most of the mountain has been used for forestry for many years now."

"Is the farmhouse still there?" Jones asked.

"Just a ruin," Wyn answered. "The walls are mostly intact, but the roof has gone and there's a tree growing out of it."

"Even so, it will be fantastic to pay a visit and take some photos," Jones said. "I think that's what I will do tomorrow."

Wyn Ellis marked the map with a felt tip, then folded and handed it to the American. "Take this. I've marked the farm for you. It's a lovely walk."

"But your map?"

"I can get another copy easily. Keep it, a souvenir for you."

"That is so kind," Jones said, holding the map as though it was treasure. "But speaking of nice walks, I think I could do with stretching my legs. Is it far to the ocean?"

-o-

The compact was followed closely by the 4x4 along the forestry road on the mountain. The lead car took a turn onto a tight track descending into an area of older, taller pine trees. There was grass in the centre of this track. Both cars reduced speed.

Further in, they took another turn. Vegetation scraped the sides of the vehicles; the centre grass grew wider and thicker.

Within a couple of hundred yards, it was difficult to define a track at all. The trees were very tall here, their lower foliage widely spanned, interconnecting and embracing the branches of neighbouring trees. The lead car scraped a boulder before correcting its course.

They eventually arrived at a rough clearing. Its centre was dominated by an aged circle of security fence, together with a gate. Saplings grew here and there, together with scrub, which grew thicker towards the circling wall of pine forest.

Gwenda Evans got out of the compact. The 4x4 behind it turned to one side, snapping a few saplings as it came to a halt.

They all moved in an organised, pre-planned manner, without speaking. Emily Norton headed to one side. Hardcastle went in the other direction where the vegetation was thicker. Banes headed back up the ill-defined track for some distance, before coming to a halt and glancing back. He then stood in that position, on watch.

From a bunch of keys, Lock found one that opened the padlock chaining the gate. A faded sign warned *Disused Mineshaft, Danger, Keep Out.*

After receiving prompt signals from all three lookouts, it took some kicking and pushing against weeds and vegetation to get the gate moving. Finally, Lock and Gwenda joined forces to lift it over some mining waste.

Inside, a circular fence, composed of wooden posts and square mesh sheep wire, surrounded a deep shaft. Sunlight cast a beam onto a sheer rock side below.

Lock used wire cutters to cut away a section of fencing. Gwenda opened the compact door and leaned inside. The car moved slightly on the incline as its handbrake was released.

She and Lock then went to the back of the car, hunched over it and pushed. It rolled easily between the fence posts and swiftly launched itself into the mineshaft.

They listened to the diminishing sounds of the car crunching against the sides as it careened and plummeted out of sight into darkness.

Water ran along a drainage tunnel deep below. The feeble twilight provided by the small eye of daylight at the head of the shaft seemed to be blinking erratically as something approached.

The compact slammed into the rock bed with an abrupt and final sound of metals compressing rapidly and shattering safety glass. A terminal velocity was instantly decelerated by unyielding rock beneath shallow water.

Something liquid spilled from the misshapen wreck, adding to the gentle noise of water running into the drainage tunnel.

On the surface, Gwenda finally spoke. "Do you think we should say a few words?"

Lock grunted ironically. He began returning the square mesh fencing to its original position. "Do you think that will help?"

"Not really," Gwenda answered, handing Lock a pair of heavy-duty pliers. "But this is his grave now, sort of."

Lock shrugged and held the pliers with both hands below his waistline. "Rest in peace," he announced in a sombre tone. "May you never be disturbed."

"Amen," Gwenda agreed.

-o-

Caycey Jones was wearing a fawn double-breasted raincoat as he took his first evening walk in Wales. The seaside air was cool and breezy.

The road from the B&B to the village itself stretched a moderate distance. A few semi-detached bungalows dotted both sides before it reached a narrow, humped bridge. Jones paused halfway over this. He raised his camera. A row of miners' cottages was adorned with hanging baskets of flowers. They formed a quaintly aesthetic backdrop to a small river. He took a picture.

The road then meandered a short distance before he came to another bridge. Jones crossed it and took in the sudden view of what looked mostly like a scrap yard. Half the dusty interior was parked up by two Jones Bros buses, a row of vans and a cabin office. A couple of wrecked and scavenged buses added to the mess of scrapped cars littering the other side of the yard.

Further on, he passed a village shop. It also served as post office and cafe. A grimy red letter box stood outside it. Jones seemed disappointed to see that the neighbouring chapel had *For Sale* signs emblazoned over its stone frontage. A couple of locals idling on the side of the road issued friendly greetings, which he acknowledged with natural ease as he passed them.

A group of teenage hoodies he encountered a little further on seemed especially pleased to see him. "Yo, bro," they called out in a scattered, uncoordinated chorus.

In return, he raised a hand and issued his own similar greeting, a little unnaturally and with some surprise in his eyes. Immensely satisfied with this, the teenagers moved on, chatting conspiratorially in Welsh with hushed voices.

He took a fork in the road, where a rusted fingerpost sign drooped as it pointed to *The Beach*.

The narrow lane passed between cottages then sloped upwards before curving on the level. Along here, a high walled area concealed a building revealed only by its roof. A big man stood facing outward by a closed door built into the wall.

Dressed in a grimy boiler suit, this man's face seemed even dirtier. It was plastered with coal dust bound to his skin with sweat. White rings circled his eyes. A cigarette smoked to its stump was stuck in the corner of his mouth.

The man barely moved his head, but his eyes tracked Jones as he passed. "*Ish a shishe ayy arr a waak,*" the man said from unmoving lips, although the wagging cigarette stump signalled they were moving slightly. He then became animated, tilting his head around as though hunting for the source of what he himself had uttered. "Bet you couldn't tell where that came from?" he called to Jones.

Disbelief tinged the American's eyes as he walked on, picking up his pace in response. The lane now hair-pinned downwards. It brought him to a point where it finally curved back again on a rocky outcrop towards a parking area. This overlooked a small harbour.

A sea wall curved across the tiny bay. It terminated with a timber landing pier that was fenced off and posted with danger signs.

Below the parking area, a few locals, mostly young women with babies in pushchairs, were congregated around a shabby-looking bench. Jones halted here, before beginning to negotiate a path winding down and away to the left of the sea wall. Ahead, cliffs grew steeper and stretched out to sea where they formed the mountain's outer end. He marvelled at the waves breaking into the cliffs with white explosions.

Nearer to him, two young boys were arguing on a strip of sanded beach where a culvert cut into solid rock. Water flowed out of this and streamed into the sea.

The boys argued loudly in Welsh, but Jones recognised the word *petrol* repeated a couple of times by one of them. As if to prove his point, this boy produced a box of matches, struck one and threw it into the stream as the match was still igniting.

33

Yellow flames immediately spread along the surface, moving both inward to the culvert and spreading out a short distance on the sea itself.

The boys turned and ran, escaping uphill past Jones on the zigzag path.

With a dropped jaw, Jones took in the bewildering sight of fire on the water, then looked over his shoulder up the slope behind him. The young mothers up there had their mobile phones aimed to catch the action as they jabbered excitedly.

The fire on the sea was short-lived, whatever had fuelled it devoured quickly by the flames. Jones now noticed something inland, high up the side of the forested part of the mountain. In the distance, a faint but perfect smoke ring seemed to be rising from the thick blanket of pines.

"So, this is Wales," Jones announced quietly to himself.

-o-

The sun dropped below the horizon. Street lights flickered into life. First pink, then gradually reverting to their familiar yellow, they drew their snaking shape of the village in the dusk.

An owl hooted from pines overlooking the compound on the mountain. Something scurried through the undergrowth alongside a drainage ditch.

Underground, beyond the closed steel door, the deafening sound of an electric hammer echoed in the tunnel.

Emily Norton and Gwenda Evans were seated on rickety folding chairs at the workbench. Norton typed furiously into a laptop, her forehead wrinkled into a frown that accompanied the noise. Gwenda watched three monitors. Their bar charts hovered in amber territory.

In the adjacent chamber, Lock was wearing a miner's helmet, goggles and ear defenders. He attacked the bricked-up arch with the electric hammer. Dust billowed. Lock then stepped back to allow a similarly attired Banes to remove newly loosened bricks. The man handed them to Hardcastle, who was building neat stacks to one side.

Another dose of the hammer freed up a larger section. Lock put

34

the machine down. "Stand clear," he shouted to Banes. He then reached and pulled at the brickwork, keeping his legs out of the way as the section tilted outwards and fell with a crump.

A quarter of the arch was now open, a rough oval shape. Lock leaned through it. His helmet lamp illuminated only dust in the dark air. "Bit more," he yelled to the other two men, before lifting the hammer and placing its chisel bit against the brickwork. The rattling, nerve-shredding noise filled the underground spaces once more.

At the workbench, Emily Norton finally sat back in her flimsy chair as the noise stopped. "My report is done," she told Gwenda, then slid her laptop over so that the woman could look at it.

Lock's voice reached them from the other chamber.

"Why is he shouting?" Norton asked.

"Ear defenders," Gwenda answered as she studied the laptop screen. "The others are wearing them as well, so they probably can't understand a word he's saying."

The cacophony re-erupted. Norton put her fingers in her ears. Gwenda continued her study of the report, apparently with no concern about the noise. When silence returned, Gwenda slid the laptop back to Norton and said, "Looks fine to me."

Lock appeared from the chamber. "We're ready to go through," he announced in a normal voice, ear defenders now held in one hand. He was covered in dust. There were streaks in his goggles where he had wiped some of it away. "How's the report to Five coming along?" From behind him, there was a faint sound of bricks being stacked.

Norton vacated her chair and gestured at the laptop. "It's ready to send. Needs your eyes on it first."

Brushing dust from his clothing, Lock sat down. He rapidly scanned the contents of the screen before standing up again. "Send it," he said.

The other two men now appeared. Banes took off his helmet, allowing it to hang by the lamp cable over his shoulder, then lifted his goggles. Hardcastle was going through a similar procedure as he tried to brush dust off his clothing at the same time.

"Dust is starting to settle," Banes announced.

Each of the five was wearing a hooded suit when they stepped in turn through the partly reopened arch. The hoods were clipped over miners' helmets, making them look as though they had misshapen heads under the material.

Gwenda Evans, the shortest of them, needed some help from Hardcastle to get over the still intact brickwork at the foot of the hole.

They found themselves in what was clearly an old miners' tunnel.

Lock carried a handlamp. He pointed this at a thick cable, which came through the rock and ran along the tunnel floor.

Banes and Hardcastle carried an instrument case apiece. Behind them, Emily Norton wielded a handheld device. Norton appeared nervous and uncomfortable as she took in her surroundings. The rock sides were stained with mould and growths of crystallised minerals. Water dripped from stalactites in the tunnel crown. And an intermittently puddled floor was scarred with the sleeper marks of a long since removed narrow gauge rail track.

Lock's handlamp illuminated the way ahead as they walked. Its beam swung, following rock contours, revealing the fact that the tunnel sloped downwards, and picking out the thick cable following the side wall. He now switched it off. Their eyes adjusted to the glow from only miners' lamps, beams mobile on the walls and ceiling as they walked silently in single file.

The incline grew steeper as they descended. Norton's nervous expression did not subside. Ahead of her, Gwenda maintained an air of determination with her eyes fixed on Lock in the lead. Hardcastle appeared nonchalant, tired, and only vaguely interested in where he was placing his booted feet. It was Banes who glanced back, saw that Norton was lagging slightly, and waited for her. She smiled when he allowed her to pass with an encouraging sweep of his arm.

They arrived at a gallery where miners in the past had excavated upwards and outwards. Rusted steel ladders were fixed to the steeper parts of this. Lock did not allow them time to pause. He pressed ahead.

The tunnel and the cable continued beyond the gallery, still descending but also now angling to the left for some time until they arrived at a fork. A rotting timber contraption constructed from pit props blocked the right fork, a rusted sign attached to it. Only one word embossed at the top of the sign was decipherable: *Danger*. The cable crossed here into the left fork.

This tunnel curved on the level for a while before bending right. It then descended steeply.

After several minutes, Lock switched on the powerful handlamp and played its beam ahead. In the distance, it looked as though there had been another rockfall. As they approached, it became clear that whoever had tunnelled here had broken through into another area.

The sides and ceiling near the breach had been quarried to create space. Age-blackened but solid concrete formed a level patch of floor. Rusted eye bolts protruded either side of an equally rusted steel plate in the concrete. The miners' tunnel beyond this was blocked with rocks.

To the side of the concrete, the breach itself was elliptically shaped, tall and wide enough for a truck to pass through. Lock's handlamp did not illuminate any detail, just a dull ring of light in there.

They approached. Inside, there was a perfectly smooth tubular bore, much bigger than the miners' tunnel, and it was lined with a black, glassy material that was poor at reflecting light.

The new tunnel sloped downwards to the right of the breach. Another rockfall blocked the upward side, the rocks forming a tight but untidy barrier, interspersed with broken shards of the black material.

Lock took them through.

Hardcastle stooped to examine one of the shards with a gloved hand. It was as thick as his arm and sharply square along its edges. He set down his case, took out a small hammer, then used this to strike at the shard. It caused no damage. "Looks like glass, but I doubt it," Hardcastle said. "It's extremely tough." He switched his attention to the floor instead. His helmet lamp illuminated small shards of the black material in among dust and stones that had been swept close to the cave-in. There were brush marks in the dust.

But Lock was more interested in making progress. He aimed his handlamp; the new tunnel sloped downwards. They seemed to be in a massive underground pipe. The thick cable snaked into this from the miners' tunnel and continued along the floor into an unseen distance.

Hardcastle slid a small shard into a plastic envelope.

"We need to keep moving," Lock told him.

Hardcastle placed the sample in his case and snapped the lid shut. He appeared keen to move on.

Norton was in less of a hurry. She studied the instrument in her hand. "If there's a collapse this end, what's the risk it might collapse again while we are down here?"

Lock pointed at the cable. "Our wartime colleagues seemed to have been alright."

"We are about fifteen to thirty metres below sea level," Norton said as she continued reading her instrument, "but still under the mountain, about two hundred metres in from the coast. If this tunnel continues at the same angle in the same direction, we will soon be under the sea. Who on Earth built this thing?"

"Not the miners, that's for sure," Banes answered. He was gazing up at the perfectly curved ceiling. "It's about twelve metres in diameter," he added, "and it looks precision machined."

"Let's stop guessing and see if we can find some answers further in," Lock said. "Time is tight." He started walking ahead. The others followed. Norton did so with some obvious reluctance.

Lock kept lighting up the handlamp at intervals and aiming it into the distance. Each time he did so, the result was a featureless, seemingly endless tube.

Eventually, there was something different ahead. At first, it appeared as a circle of darkness, which grew bigger as they approached. It was as though the tubular underground construction opened out into empty space.

When they reached it, they found themselves walking out onto a

38

wide landing in a void of darkness. There was a stairway with open edges going downwards directly in front. It was constructed from the same glassy black material.

Neither their miners' lamps nor Lock's handlamp could pick out any features, either below, to their sides, or above them. The lamp beam showed as a dull circular glow only on surfaces at nearer distances. The stairs descended to somewhere unseen.

The thick cable dutifully curved out from the tunnel behind them. It followed the right-hand outer edge of the stairs into the dark.

Lock lit a flare. They all gasped. In the dazzling magnesium brilliance, they could see the enormity of what they had walked into. Above them, and above a space that could have housed a cathedral, a huge silvery, metallic coil attached to the ceiling ran continuously in a straight line. Two others ran along the walls either side.

It was another tunnel. Rectangular, it extended to a distance that was impenetrable even for the flare.

"Who on Earth built this?" Norton demanded in a hushed voice.

Ignoring her, Lock squinted and peered downwards. "Below," he said calmly. "There's something on the steps."

The flare sputtered out before they reached the object. Lock lit up the handlamp. A figure was sprawled lifeless on the edge of the steps. It was wearing a strange suit of loose and disconnected pieces of armour. A skull grinned toothily from a simple, featureless helmet.

Lock moved carefully to the edge above the skeleton and shone the handlamp downwards. "Keep away from the sides," he warned. "There's one heck of a drop."

Below him, Banes opened his case on the same step as the skeleton.

Gwenda Evans crouched near, keeping away from the drop, but watching his actions with keen eyes.

Banes put on a pair of plastic gloves, then used a scalpel and Petri dish to scrape some bone from the skeleton's lower arm. Parts of it disintegrated into dust. "It's been here a very long time," he said, sealing the sample and putting it in the case. "He was about six-foot tall, but this armour stuff…" Holding another Petri dish, he now tried

39

to scrape what looked like a shin guard lying loose on the step. "It's not metal and it doesn't seem to have had anything to keep it secured to his body or limbs. Looks more like it was enclosed in some sort of suit he was wearing."

"Bring a small part of it," Lock instructed.

Banes put the shin guard in a plastic bag.

Norton watched, her eyes taking in the skeleton with a mixture of distaste and curiosity.

"Bits of it are missing," Gwenda pointed out. "He's got a piece of armour for his right upper arm. The one on the left has gone. But look at his feet, what's left of them. Looks like someone pulled off his boots and most of his foot bones at the same time."

"Maybe our wartime colleagues took samples," Hardcastle said as he leaned over inquisitively, "but look at the chest piece, those holes and channels."

"Could be decorative," Banes suggested.

"I don't think so," Hardcastle said. "They look a lot like they—"

"Stop speculating," Lock interrupted. He shone the handlamp downwards. "We need to move on. I think there's something else down there."

They progressed down the steps.

At the bottom, eight bicycles stood upright on a rack fashioned onto a metal-framed base. The cable curved behind this from the foot of the steps and headed for the tunnel wall at a thirty-degree angle.

Lock and the others approached the bicycles. They were all identical, black, with black mudguards, wheels badly corroded.

Banes prodded a perished tyre.

Lock shone his lamp along the tunnel. It revealed nothing. "What does the Doppler give you here?" he asked Norton.

She held up her instrument, pointed it in the same direction and thumbed a button. The device whined like a flashgun charging, then clicked rapidly.

"This tunnel is about ten miles long," Norton said as she read the small screen.

"And our position?" Lock prompted.

"We are definitely below the seabed," she answered. "And there's a slight downward gradient ahead."

"Evidently our destination, whatever it is, was too far to walk for our wartime colleagues," Lock said, now approaching the bicycles. "But these are no good to us."

"Couldn't we fix them up?" Hardcastle suggested. "Bring parts?"

Lock shook his head. He gripped the end bike's handlebars and pulled. The machine seemed glued to the rack. He then kicked one of the forks attached to the front wheel. It immediately snapped, spraying flakes of rust and paint dust. The front of the bike collapsed onto the wheel.

Hardcastle shrugged and stepped away. He noticed Norton was still studying her instrument. "Ten miles, are you sure?"

Norton held the small screen towards him so he could read it, then both flinched when they heard a pop and fizz, accompanied by an explosion of light. Lock had lit another flare. He threw it along the tunnel.

It revealed little more than they had seen from the top of the steps: a huge, perfectly rectangular tunnel lined with glassy black material. Three cylindrical coils stretched along its walls and ceiling to an unseen destination.

Hardcastle shook his head and whispered to himself. "Who built this place?" But he was a little too loud and they all heard him.

Lock seemed to snap a bit then, his voice rising above his normal calm. "All of you," he announced. "I don't want to hear that question again." He then stared at Emily Norton. "You too, Miss Norton. Think about it. What if I was to ask you about the circumstances and reasons you were recruited by Circus?"

"I would say I am forbidden to answer you."

"Exactly," Lock agreed. "So stop asking questions for which you already have a pretty good idea of the potential answers. We have an important job to do and we all know why we are doing it."

Along the tunnel floor, the magnesium flare sputtered out. Five yellow beams from helmet lamps probed the fog of smoke it left behind.

41

TWO

The morning sun sent forks of gold onto the row of terraced cottages facing one of the small rivers in Amharfarn. Here, a bumblebee droned. It hovered at a hanging basket before landing on a blue flower.

Kyle was still asleep in bed in one of the cottages. A games console hand controller rested at an angle on the pillow next to his face.

On the wall facing the foot of his bed, a flat-screen TV flashed a white light in standby mode. The console on the chest of drawers below it flashed similarly. Clothes were heaped on chairs either side.

Someone knocked softly at the bedroom door. A woman's voice called equally softly from the other side. "Kyle... Kyle darling... Breakfast is nearly ready." She sounded old.

Kyle stirred and groaned.

Bleary-eyed but dressed, Kyle ate at a table in the kitchen area of an open-plan ground floor. The elderly lady wearing a pink dressing gown put down a teapot before seating herself with a smile by her own breakfast.

She was gently spoken, the lilt of her local accent more pronounced than most. She also spoke with kindness and affection in her tone. "You should get to sleep earlier instead of playing those computer games all night." It did not sound like a lecture.

"I know," Kyle accepted. "Time just flies though, Gran."

"You always called me Nain when you were younger," Gran told him, her eyes attentive but kind.

"Nain, sorry," Kyle apologised. He did so with the ease of unconcerned familiarity. "This breakfast is good, really good."

Gran then began speaking in Welsh but was interrupted by the *yack yack yack* ring tone from Kyle's mobile. Gran reverted to English. "Early for a phone call," she said as her grandson reached for his pocket.

Yack yack yack.

Kyle answered it. He sat upright, eyes widening into calm alert. "Mister Lock... Good morning... Sure, I can work right away..." He frowned then as he listened. "A bike trailer? Never seen one... No, none of my friends, but I could ask Ventriloquist Jack for you. He's always got stuff or can make things... No, sorry, I don't know his phone number... Okay, Mister Lock, I'll go see him right now... Yeh, I'll phone you straight away..."

Kyle disconnected the call, put his mobile on the table and stared at it.

"Andy Lock keeping you busy then?" Gran asked him.

"Yeh. Interesting stuff though."

"Not *too* interesting, I hope. Is he still paying you well?"

Kyle answered this with enthusiasm. "Every month, straight into the bank, same amount, even when he hasn't got much work for me. Do you think Ventriloquist Jack will be up by now?"

"I would think so," Gran answered. "But you don't call Mister Thomas that to his face, do you?"

"Never," Kyle said. He started to rise from the table. "Mister Thomas always."

"Wait a minute," Gran said. "Finish your breakfast. You need food in your belly if you're going to be working."

Kyle obeyed, picking up his knife and fork and carefully holding them with the proper etiquette. He ate in a hurry.

Gran ate as well, her eyes beginning to calculate something. "I know Andy Lock has always been kind to you since your mum and dad... Even so, the government has all that money they promised for you to go to college." Pausing, she looked quizzically at her grandson. "Now you are finally finished with that Sharon."

"Maybe next year," Kyle said. "But college, you know, it's full of stoners, druggies… More stoners there than here."

"I'm just thinking about your future. When you lived at the house Andy Lock is at now, with your mum and dad…"

"I don't remember it much."

"Well you did, and your mum and dad did the same kind of work as Andy Lock."

"It's just telecoms, Nain," Kyle warned with a hint of irritability. "Mister Lock is not a spy. Mum and dad weren't spies either."

"I've never said they were," Gran told him. "But they *were* secret, for the government. So is Andy Lock. I don't want anything to happen to you."

Kyle loaded the last pieces of fried bread, bacon and egg white from the plate onto his fork and stuffed it in one go into his mouth. He then stood up and grabbed his phone from the table, speaking as he chewed. There was no anger in his voice. "It was an accident. Their boat capsized. Mister Lock never lets me go out on the boat with him."

"Well, don't ever," Gran said.

"I have to go," Kyle told her. "But, Nain, I don't remember much about mum and dad, only that they were nice to me. You've been my mum and Mister Lock has been sort of like my dad since I can remember. I'm not going to let him down, or you."

Gran seemed to accept this. Kyle went to the coat hooks by the front door and reached for his hoodie. Gran blinked as though holding back a tear as she watched him.

"Great breakfast," Kyle said as he opened the door. "I love you lots, Nain, see you later."

"Love you lots too, son," she answered as he went out.

-o-

Lock put away his mobile phone. He pressed a button on the security panel next to the closed steel door in the rock face, then walked the short distance to the 4x4.

Early morning sunlight did not penetrate the tall forestry surrounding this place. The compound still seemed dark and gloomy as Lock climbed into the driver's seat.

Emily Norton watched him from the front passenger side. "What did Circus Control have to say?"

"No reply, I'll ring again later," Lock answered. "Kyle is going to try to get us a bike trailer."

Norton's next question was not directed at anyone in particular. "How much equipment will we be taking to our destination down there?"

Lock ignored her, pressed the start button and put the 4x4 in gear. He drove between the banks of pine trees either side of the track curving down towards the security gate. Norton looked over her shoulder at Hardcastle and Banes in the back. Gwenda Evans next to them had her eyes fixed, staring out of a side window.

It was Banes who answered. He leaned forward. "Two equipment boxes at least. A trailer could save us a lot of time."

"And it could cost us a lot of time getting it to the bottom of those stairs," Lock said a little grumpily. He thumbed the remote controller to open the security gate ahead.

Both Banes and Hardcastle nodded at this. "But worth having if we can get one," Hardcastle said, "if we have ten miles to shift stuff along that big tunnel."

"Which we won't know until I get more information from Control," Lock explained as the car passed through the gate. "They insist on giving out information in instalments."

"Understandable though," Emily Norton said.

"Hah," Lock grunted. He then sighed and mellowed. "I think we could all do with some sleep."

-o-

Caycey Jones dabbed his lips with a linen serviette. He was seated alone in the B&B dining room. He rose and then went through the hallway to the long room Mrs Ellis had told him was her reception lounge.

46

Wyn Ellis turned away from his binoculars by the side window where they were mounted permanently, it seemed, on their tripod. "Was breakfast alright?" he asked Jones.

"Delicious," Jones responded. "Best breakfast I have had in a long time. Please give my compliments to the chef."

"That's very kind of you. Mair's gone shopping to Caernarfon in the car. I'll tell her when she gets back."

Jones nodded, taking in his host's position by the window. "That's a fine pair of binoculars you have there."

Wyn Ellis gestured enthusiastically at them. "Carl Zeiss, they're old, but still the best I have ever seen. Have a look if you want."

Graciously, Jones approached the tripod as the other man stepped aside.

"I imagine you are an expert on optical devices, given your professional background," Wyn Ellis said.

Jones put his eyes to the binoculars. "NASA was a long time ago." He was looking at a clearly magnified area of the forested part of the mountain. Some sort of fence was visible near a track. "But I was never in optics. I worked in advanced concepts." He stepped back from the tripod, pointing through the window. "According to the map you gave me, that's roughly where I am headed this morning."

"The old farm is a bit further up than those small buildings. Did you see them?"

"Saw something," Jones answered casually. "Couldn't make out any buildings though."

"That's government," Wyn Ellis said. "The people next door are contractors. They work up there... telecoms. When you see the fork up to a security gate, keep left and follow the main track up to the brow of the hill. You'll come to the old farmhouse about four hundred yards beyond that. It's along a sort of dip to the next brow."

Jones nodded with a slight chuckle. "Thank you." He tapped the binoculars. "Visual reconnaissance prior to my walk. I appreciate it."

-o-

Kyle approached an arched doorway in a wall edging the narrow road to the beach. He looked at the black-and-white painted metal nameplate as though he had never seen it before: *Ponderosa*. There was a bell push below it.

Taking a deep breath, Kyle pressed this. There was no sound of a bell or chime. He inclined his head and listened, then checked his watch and waited.

A seagull squawked somewhere above him, others joining it for a time. He was about to press the button again when the door opened, squeaking on its hinges.

Ventriloquist Jack's boiler suit was pristine clean this morning, as was his face. Fixed eyes took in Kyle with a hint of suspicion before nonsensical sounds emitted from unmoving lips. *"Ore da hyle."* The man then moved his head, as though startled and hunting for the source of the sound he himself had made.

Kyle went along with it and turned around, searching, his expression a picture of exaggerated amazement. "Who was that?" he demanded at a deserted landscape. He then faced the man and grinned.

Ventriloquist Jack smiled with pride. "That was me. Where did you think it came from?"

"No idea, Mister Thomas," Kyle answered.

"You're having me on, aren't you?" the man said, but with good humour. "What do you want?"

"A bike trailer," Kyle told him. "It's for Mister Lock."

Ventriloquist Jack frowned. He narrowed his lips as though he was about to perform his voice trickery again, then seemed to change his mind. "Come in," he invited an astounded Kyle.

The young man had the air of someone entering forbidden territory as he stepped through the doorway.

By village standards, the yard was huge. A wide, squat bungalow occupied the centre of an area of sloping ground surrounded by high walls.

It had clearly been a formal garden in the past. But the lawns and borders were now overgrown with weeds and couch grass, which also encroached onto the narrow paths interlacing them.

A series of timber sheds, crates, and what looked like a workshop leaned up against the high wall separating and concealing the yard from the road.

Ventriloquist Jack led Kyle along the path alongside these, the young man observing piles of junk and scrap metal between them with interest.

A sun-bleached fibreglass dinghy was propped upside-down against a rusted oven range. Next to them, a bronze Welsh mountain pony with a damaged nose was caked in pale-green oxidisation.

It was the heaps of coal further down that had Kyle nodding to himself as though in answer to an internal question. But his eyes widened when he saw a polished steel contraption near the coal. It was in a wooden shelter surrounded by coal dust. Hydraulic pipes and electrical cables ran from this to a shed.

Ventriloquist Jack glanced at Kyle as they passed it. "What do you think that is?" he asked, pointing at the object.

"Looks like a crucible," Kyle answered. "You trying to make diamonds, Mister Thomas?"

The man laughed. "Out of coal?"

"No," Kyle agreed. "You would need pure graphite to make diamonds."

"Good boy," Ventriloquist Jack said. "I do know that. I have a doctorate." But there was no explanation for the tons of coal or crucible as they walked on.

They arrived at a squat barn of a construction. It was made up of old railway sleepers and timber panels painted dark green.

"Wait here," Jack instructed. He opened a double-leaf door and went inside.

Kyle did as he was told, looking upwards now at the front of the bungalow. This faced north towards the sea. The driveway ran to a vehicular door in the lower wall of the property. A pickup truck was parked on the drive, chrome and paintwork gleaming in the morning sunshine.

He could hear Ventriloquist Jack's grunts and the shifting of metals and thrown junk from inside the shanty building.

Jack came out backwards, pulling something that honked and

hooted like a dog's toy, *whaffft*. The man gripped the handlebars of an ornate, man-sized and gaudily coloured tricycle as he pulled the contraption out into daylight. It was towing a trailer, over which rotated a partly tinplate mechanical dervish. This had a wooden clown's head, complete with a three-point hat and bells.

The once brightly painted face was flaked and chipped to an almost non-existence of features. And the child-sized clown's legless torso was connected somehow to the trailer axle, which gave it a slow rotation as the wheels were turned.

Kyle pursed his lips doubtfully.

"Ta-dah," Ventriloquist Jack celebrated in his imitation of a fanfare. He gestured with both hands at the strange machine. "What do you think?"

"Not sure if it's exactly what Mister Lock has in mind," Kyle told him in a carefully polite tone.

"Well, you could remove the clown," the man said. "Then you will have a perfectly usable trailer." He wheeled the tricycle and trailer forward a bit more onto the path. The clown made a jerky half rotation as something honked airily with a loud, dysfunctional *whaffft* from somewhere underneath it.

"I'll inflate the tyres and then you're good to go, fifty quid," Ventriloquist Jack announced. He smiled and gestured with open arms at the contraption as though offering the bargain of the century.

"I'm not sure," Kyle answered.

"Why don't you phone Andy Lock?" the man suggested. "He might be able to use the trailer on another bike. I can talk to him as well if you want."

-o-

Caycey Jones tapped *send* in the e-mail dialogue box, before shutting down his iPad and placing it on the bed. He rose from the adjacent chair and opened a wardrobe. His room had a pink carpet and a tiny walk-in bathroom. Jones threw his suitcase onto the bed and used a key to open its latches.

50

A grey backpack, a pair of boots and a bright red mountaineering jacket joined the other items on the bed before Jones dug deeper into his suitcase.

Downstairs and dressed for the outdoors, he issued his quick "goodbye" and "see you later" niceties to Wyn Ellis, who was watching daytime TV in the lounge.

The American welcomed the morning sea air on the B&B porch, tugged one of the backpack straps onto his shoulder, then began along the driveway towards the road.

From somewhere in the near distance, a strange repeated honking sound was getting closer.

Jones took a quick look around his hired Jaguar parked on the side of the road, then shifted his attention as that sound grew louder. Someone was frantically pedalling a strange contraption in his direction. *Whaffft... honk... whaffft... whaffft... whaffft... honk...*

The American raised the corners of his mouth a tweak, then passed the driveway next door as he started heading towards the village. He hesitated as the cyclist drew closer.

Kyle was finding it difficult to pedal the tricycle. There was some sort of intermittent resistance built into the axle mechanism in the trailer. The clown figure spun around and hooted as he pedalled, but then it paused until something in the mechanism clunked to make it spin another half rotation. Each time it clunked, the trailer bounced and acted like a suddenly applied and released brake for the axle, which then transmitted those forces to the tricycle.

Head over the handlebars, Kyle rocked back and to in an involuntary rhythm as he pedalled furiously in return for very little speed. *Whaffft... clunk.... whaffft... clunk... whaffft... honk...*

Now he spotted Jones. Surprised and off-guard, Kyle said "Yo" in a breathless greeting, then turned the tricycle onto the safe house driveway.

The clown seemed to grin at Jones with what was left of its painted face. Its arms lifted into a partial shrug as it made its next spin. *Whaffft... honk...*

"Good morning," Jones responded, face creasing. He halted and watched the contraption as it was pedalled up the drive.

A bedroom curtain moved aside at the upper front of the house. Jones saw a woman's face appear. Her hair was wrapped in a towel.

Gripping her dressing gown collar, Gwenda Evans spotted Jones looking up at her and swiftly closed the curtain again.

With a wry smile, Jones turned towards the village.

-o-

Lock came out of the back door and halted. Incredulity swept across his face when he saw the contraption. Kyle was still sitting on the tricycle, stooped over the handlebars, getting his breath back. The mechanical clown seemed to be staring at Lock.

Hardcastle appeared in the doorway, wearing a white dressing gown above bare legs. "What was all that honking?" He then pointed, grinning widely. "*What* the hell is *that*?"

"Mister Thomas wouldn't let me dismantle the clown," Kyle explained, "but, Mister Lock, I saw a brother on the road outside."

Lock finally took his eyes off the clown. "A brother?"

"A big man. He was going towards the village."

"Oh, we know about him. He's a tourist staying next door."

"Cool," Kyle said, getting off the tricycle. "I told you it was a bit strange," he added, patting the seat. "But the trailer is good if we can get the clown and other junk off of it."

Lock stooped over the machine, running his hand over the curved tow bar connecting the trailer to a hinged bracket below the tricycle seat. "Looks like it might connect to an ordinary bike," he said to Kyle. "See if you can pull it apart."

Kyle shrugged. "Will do, Mister Lock. Plenty of tools in the shed."

-o-

The junction of the potholed country lane from the westernmost side of the village centre had a dead-end T sign tilting out of a hedge on its corner. From there, the narrow road climbed gently inland, running parallel to the mountain through sloping farmland.

A grass-munching heifer glared wide-eyed over a hedge at Caycey Jones as its metal-tagged ear flicked away at a cloud of flies.

Jones grinned and took a deep breath as he walked. The heifer issued a loud *moo*. Others answered it from a distance.

There was grass in the centre of the narrow tarmac and frequent potholes in the wheel tracks either side of it. The American avoided the outer edges of the lane. They dropped into drainage ditches that gurgled and plopped with fast-running water in the quiet of the morning.

Up ahead, a farmhouse stood close to the road, roof slates glistening in the sunshine.

Jones saw an old man with grey hair leaning over an agricultural gate facing the lane, but his attention was diverted to the farmhouse itself as he approached. Something was painted on the front stone wall of the house. It was faded and barely discernible in an untidy script:

RESIDENCE
OF THE
KING OF WALES

"Good morning, friend," the old man greeted Jones, looking him up and down. "Can I interest you in a television?"

Puzzled but remaining polite, Caycey Jones approached the gate.

Behind the old man was a battered trellis table with three ancient cathode ray tube TV sets arranged on it. Their dead screens were green and rounded. A portable aerial stood on one of them, cable dangling loosely over the side, bent twin antennae looking like the feelers of some drunken insect.

A black-and-white sheepdog sat under the table, observing the newcomer with interest.

"Good morning, sir," Jones responded. "Is this your farm?"

"You're American," the old man commented. He wiped a hand on his trousers before offering it. "I am Hefin Gwynedd."

Jones shook his hand. "Jones… Caycey Jones."

"Railwayman, are you?"

53

"Uh, no," Jones answered.

"How about a television then?"

Jones shook his head. "If you don't mind me saying, though I don't personally need a TV, those are a bit old." He pointed at the sets on the table. "Televisions these days are LCD or LED."

"And look at the rubbish they churn out," Hefin Gwynedd argued. "These are much better."

"It's all digital now, so I doubt you could get a signal on them," Jones said, beginning to back away.

"But you can here in Amharfarn," the old man said with a twinkle in his eye. "Only yesterday I was watching Gilligan's Island on the set I have indoors."

"That was a great show," Jones told him with a chuckle. "It was nice meeting you."

"You should smoke a pipe," Hefin Gwynedd suggested. "It would look good on you." The dog now came out from under the table and approached the gate, tail wagging.

"I'll consider it very seriously," Jones answered politely, still trying to edge away.

"My family was on this farm long before the Romans came," the old man told him.

Now Caycey Jones seemed genuinely interested. He planted his feet and listened.

"Later, the Normans arrived and told them our farm belonged to *their* baron," Hefin Gwynedd continued. "Changed their names for them and made them pay rent and taxes. Then later the local lord wanted to sell it from under their feet, but they bought the title themselves from the treasures our family ancestors left behind."

"Really," Jones said. "You must know this mountain well."

"My great-great-grandfather dug it up somewhere on the farm. Gold coins, Phoenician, Egyptian, Roman, Celtic, all sorts. There was something here they all wanted."

"Do you still farm?" Jones asked.

"Oh no," Hefin Gwynedd answered as though in horror at the thought. "My father stopped that, rented all the fields out to the other farmers nearby." He pulled a fist out of his trouser pocket and opened it up to show Jones some small, misshapen black coins. "These are Roman, silver. All that's left of the treasure that was hidden in the house."

Jones peered at these and then saw the dog was watching him. "Nice dog, is he a pedigree?"

"Nah, this is Pero, Welsh sheepdog, pure mongrels all," Hefin replied, before issuing an instruction to the dog. "Pero, salute the man."

The dog stared at its master in response to this, then reluctantly lifted a front paw halfway to its head.

Jones chuckled.

"How about a television?" the old man asked. "It was the mountain that drew the Romans and everyone else here. My televisions are tuned to it. Mountain's been talking to me all my life."

-o-

Sparks crackled and flew as a carbon arc-welding terminal rapidly cut through a steel rod with a gear at its end. Something clattered to the ground as it separated. A gloved hand loosened the gear from its larger cogged counterpart on the axle.

Lock lifted the front of the welder's helm he was wearing, disconnected the crocodile teeth of an electrical cable from the axle and stood up.

The trailer was on its side, the clown figure now lying forlornly beside it on the driveway near the open garage to the rear of the safe house.

Kyle stepped forward to drag the clown further out of the way. Now fully dressed, Hardcastle righted the trailer onto its wheels and pulled it back and forth a couple of times with its curved tow bar. The wheels turned easily. The trailer tilted forward when he let it go. Kyle studied the trailer before moving to the nearby tricycle, which was already missing its seat.

"I'll get one of the mountain bikes from the shed," Lock announced.

Hardcastle grinned. "How's that bracket?" he asked Kyle.

The younger man held a spanner against a rusted hinge bracket on the cylinder where the tricycle seat belonged. He began straining against an equally rusted bolt. "Tough, but I'll get it," Kyle answered.

Wyn Ellis watched them at an oblique angle through the side window of the B&B next door. The phone rang. Reluctantly, he left the latest entertainment from next door to answer it.

"Good morning, Ellis residence... She's not available right now but I can take a booking... We do have a double room available. It has single beds and en-suite bathroom... Two Japanese ladies, how nice... Do they have any special dietary needs?"

-o-

Caycey Jones breathed heavily as he reached the top of a steep stretch of forestry road. The compacted dirt, dust and stony track split two ways below cliffs quarried into the mountainside.

Jones walked over to a boulder near a stack of rotting timber. Trees towered over from above a clay and rock cliff behind it. A shallow canyon ran downhill from here, its track barely discernible from the grass and small bushes along it. The sound of a hidden waterfall came from somewhere in that direction.

Jones sat on the boulder and sighed, clearly enjoying himself. He looked around as he opened his backpack. Even from this height, there was nothing but trees and sky to be seen in every direction. He drank from a plastic water bottle, then lifted his camera.

Jones looked up at the sky, where he saw two birds of prey circling lazily at a height, then took off his jacket and tied it by its arms around his waist. With a look of determination, he rose from the boulder and returned to the main track, where he contemplated the descending canyon and the sound of the waterfall.

A dragonfly zoomed towards him a couple of feet off the ground. Its body was a rainbow of colours. It stopped close and hovered as Jones fumbled for his camera. The insect swerved and darted at the trees, before racing back towards the unseen waterfall.

Jones turned in the other direction. Another steep stretch of dirt forestry road faced him.

He seemed like a man who at last believed he was getting somewhere when he later paused to look back. The sea, as well as part of the village, was now visible between the tops of some of the trees. He continued walking. A grassy lane branched off the main track a little further up the steep incline.

Upon reaching this, through his camera, Jones was able to make out a tall security gate, together with the razor wire topping it and part of an equally tall fence, but little else. Trees shrouded anything beyond that. The camera clicked.

He then panned upward and to the right where the mountain ridge arched, dipped and glowered in bare, jagged rock in a series of cliff faces.

Along this, closer to the sea, white domes faced outwards in multiple directions from a communications tower tucked under a lateral cliff.

Jones snapped that with his camera before continuing upwards on the main track.

Behind him, a larger part of Amharfarn could now be seen over some of the pines.

-o-

Wyn Ellis took his eyes away from the binoculars as Mair breezed into the lounge. "That's the shopping done," Mair announced. "What are you watching up there now?"

"I was keeping an eye out for Caycey Jones," Wyn answered. "Just spotted him. He's got a red jacket. We've had another booking."

"Really?" Mair Ellis responded. She started taking her summer coat off. "The dot-com is really pulling them in. What are the details? Have you written it down?"

"On the pad by the phone, two Japanese ladies, they're arriving tomorrow. They want to share a room, so I told the agent the room with two single beds."

57

"Japanese," Mair Ellis repeated to herself. "What do they eat?"

"Perhaps they might like to try what we eat in this country."

Mair Ellis's coat was now halted in a half off position. "But aren't they all vegetarian or something, the Japanese?"

Wyn Ellis shrugged. "I think they eat raw fish and a lot of noodles."

"Did you ask if they had any special dietary needs?"

"Yes, but the answer was no, whatever we have going."

Now Mair Ellis's coat got fully pulled back on. "I'll have to go back to Caernarfon and get more shopping," she said, then pointed at the tripod and binoculars. "Don't you think you'd better put that away while we have guests?"

Wyn Ellis frowned. "I don't see what harm it does. Mister Jones enjoyed looking through it."

"But Japanese ladies might think you are a pervert or something," Mair Ellis countered.

"They love cameras and binoculars," Wyn responded.

"Did the agent tell you that?"

"No, Japanese generally. Nikon, Pentax, Japan are world leaders in optical equipment. I'll bet there are tripods, telescopes and all sorts set up in every room in their houses."

Mair Ellis sighed. "Well as long as you don't talk about your UFOs and strange lights to any of our guests. You promised you wouldn't."

"And I won't," Wyn Ellis said. "But maybe that's why they are coming here, now that we are on the web."

"Nonsense," Mair Ellis retorted as she went out of the room.

-o-

Caycey Jones stepped carefully over a ditch of running water next to a piped culvert running under the forestry road. He trod down some brambles and weeds in front of him then stepped precariously onto a boulder hidden in the undergrowth. Some sort of flying insect made a soft burring sound close to his ear. He swatted it away.

The ruined farmhouse was surrounded in undergrowth and bushes. A pine tree occupied part of its roofless interior.

The sun did not reach here next to the dip in the road along the side of the mountain. Beyond the ruin, the dusty track headed between trees for another brow, which took it towards another steep bank of contrasting, sunlit trees rising towards a mountain ridge.

Jones reached an empty stone-framed window, grunting quietly as one of his booted feet slipped between two hidden rocks. His clothes were now covered in fluffy, hooked seeds.

He aimed his camera through the window and snapped, the flash triggering automatically. Slates cracked under his feet as he struggled further along the wall.

-o-

At the safe house, Lock tightened the seat bolts on a mountain bike outside the garage.

Hardcastle and Kyle watched him, Hardcastle smoking a cigarette, Kyle leaning over for a closer look.

Lock now gripped the bike seat with both hands and strained downwards to test it. "You can hook the trailer up now," he told Kyle.

The young man grabbed the tow bar and drew the trailer closer to the bike. He slipped a hook affair over the eye bolt connected to a bracket under the seat, then tightened a grip which closed a hinge onto the grooved point of the hook.

The three of them studied the trailer. It now stood with its front end held off the ground by the tow bar connected to the bike.

"Not quite level," Hardcastle observed. "But it will do if we can strap stuff onto it."

"Bungees," Lock said. "They'll attach easily to the sides."

"You want me to try riding it?" Kyle asked.

"I think Mister Hardcastle had better do that," Lock answered.

"Why me?" Hardcastle protested, stubbing his cigarette out on the ground.

"Because the trailer is your idea," Lock told him with a thin smile. "Can you ride a bike?"

Hardcastle stepped up to the machine and studied it. "I did plenty of mountain biking when I was in college. Was pretty good at it."

"Then you'll be good with this," Lock said.

"You going mountain biking with a trailer?" Kyle asked innocently as he watched Hardcastle swing a leg over the crossbar. Neither of the two men answered this.

Hardcastle launched the machine and upped himself onto the seat, riding it slowly along the drive with a slight wobble of the front wheel. He brought the bike and trailer to a halt within a short distance. "It will do nicely," he called back to Lock.

"We're just looking at ways to move equipment around easier up to the telecoms mast from the compound," Lock told Kyle. He then checked his watch. "Okay," he said in a business-like manner. "Let's get the trailer into the back of the car."

-o-

Caycey Jones managed to get around to the first window space along the wall that was furthest away from the forestry road.

Midges swarmed around his face. He swatted at them and spat when one got into his mouth. He glared through the window space, his booted feet crunching against broken glass.

As well as a pine tree growing in there, the interior of the farmhouse ruin was a mess of rotted eaves timbers, bushes, weeds and broken roofing slates. A partial raft of the upper floor tilted downwards from somewhere on the inner side of the wall. It was a skeleton of decayed joists, and hanging battens decorated with rust-blistered nail heads.

The camera flashgun illuminated it all briefly twice. Jones then aimed at the exterior of the house wall, taking a couple of shots of its lichen, moss and vegetation-scarred masonry.

With a deep, quiet groan, Jones then began the struggle of reversing his path, stepping carefully onto the wild plants and bushes he had flattened to get here, a hand leaning up against the wall of the

60

ruin as he negotiated the unseen rocks and other hazards beneath his feet.

-o-

Lock yawned and wiped a hand across his eyes as he drove the 4x4 alone up the forestry track.

He slowed almost to a halt when a fox ran out ahead of the vehicle, then gunned the engine as the animal disappeared safely into the forest.

The 4x4 climbed comfortably, tyres popping loose chippings. Two bikes rocked like war feathers on its roof rack.

Lock swung the car onto the branching track with practised ease, one hand already reaching for the remote controller. But then his head lifted, eyes alert, and he put his hand back on the steering wheel. Up ahead, someone wearing a red jacket was standing in front of the security gate.

Caycey Jones was bent over, plucking fluffy hook seeds from his clothing as the 4x4 approached. He straightened up when it came to a halt, the driver window opening with a hum.

"Good morning, sir," Jones said cheerfully. He lifted his backpack and stepped closer to the car.

"Are you lost?" Lock asked through the open window.

Jones shook his head. "No, I was just curious about what's beyond this gate." He reached into his pack and pulled out a card envelope, put the pack on the ground by the car, then slid out a glossy black-and-white print from the envelope. "Have a look at this."

After a studied gaze into the man's unflinching, smiling eyes, Lock switched off the engine and reluctantly accepted the photograph. In the glare of a flash exposure, two men wearing 1940s suits were posed either side of an intact, bricked-up archway that Lock had partly demolished only hours earlier inside the mountain. He shook his head, looked at Jones and smiled. "Interesting I'm sure, but it means nothing to me."

61

"I'm pretty certain it does," Jones told him. "The gentleman on the left is Bill Donovan, Director of the CIA when it was taken two years after the war. The guy on the right was one of yours."

"Wow," Lock said, still smiling. "That's really interesting, but it still means nothing to me." He handed back the photograph.

"It was taken in there," Jones said, pointing through the security gate. He then held up the photograph so it faced Lock.

Lock made a play of studying it again. He also managed to look baffled. "I don't think so. It looks like it was taken underground. There's nothing like that here, just storage, all above ground."

"Let's introduce ourselves properly," Jones said. "You are Commander Andrew Morris Lock, an officer in the so-called Section Five of Her Majesty's Security Service. I am Caycey Jones, an officer in the Central Intelligence Agency of the United States."

Lock pondered this. His expression changed to something that was neither a smile nor a sneer. "I am sure you mean well, sir, but I honestly haven't got a clue what you are talking about. I'm just a contractor. I maintain communications equipment, all of it above ground."

"It's very simple," Jones told him. "All my agency wants is verification that the incident two nights ago was not deliberate. A photograph of you and I standing by that bricked-up arch would help greatly."

"Mister Jones," Lock answered in a low voice, "I have tried to be polite to you. I think you have perhaps come to the wrong place."

The American shrugged. "Then perhaps I should get in touch with your government. But that would bring a whole mess of trouble down on your head, wouldn't it?"

Lock stared into the other man's eyes. They were cold, none of the earlier friendliness apparent there now.

Then Jones spoke very softly. "Do dragonflies attack frogs in these parts?"

Lock sighed. His body seemed to sag as though tension had been released. "Only certain types," he answered, "when the north winds come from the east. You'd better get in the car."

Jones nodded graciously and stooped to lift his pack. When he straightened up with a slight groan, he looked at Lock, wagged a finger, and said, "On the subject of Circus, you and your crew seem to have a *real* one on the go around here."

Lock waited for the big man to walk around the front of the car and get into the passenger seat. Jones did this with some huffing and puffing as he finally placed his backpack on his knees.

"Circus Control didn't warn me to expect you," Lock said. He started the engine and the security gate rattled open.

"And they didn't answer the encrypted voicemail you left this morning," Jones told him. "Until now. *I* am your control officer."

The 4x4 moved up to the wider compound area and came to a halt a few yards away from the transformer. The two men made no immediate move to get out of the vehicle.

"You have no idea what I have had to do to maintain my cover," Jones told Lock inside the car when the engine was switched off.

"What *is* your cover? We'll all need to be briefed."

"Researching my family tree," Jones told him with a smile.

"Here?"

"That's the easy part. I *do* have an ancestor from Wales and I *have* always been interested in this country, especially the singing, just not this part of it. The only lie is that I am partly descended from a family who lived on a farm up the road a bit from where we are now."

Lock absorbed this for a moment. "I've got to get the bikes inside. Then I could show you around if you want."

"That's essential," Jones agreed. They got out of the car.

Jones watched as Lock stood on an open car door sill and unclipped one of the bikes on the roof rack. He helped him lower it to the ground. "By the way," he told Lock, "I'm going to need one of these. Better make it a sturdy one."

-o-

Kyle was fixing an inner tube puncture by the side of an upturned bike on the lawn when Emily Norton came out from the kitchen door.

63

"Where is everybody?" Norton called out.

"Sleeping, I think," Kyle answered in a hushed voice. "Mister Lock has gone out in the car."

Norton approached. She looked down at the bare wheel lying on the grass next to a metal bowl of water, then at Kyle who was squinting up at her in the sunlight. "Mending a puncture?" she asked conversationally.

"There's no spare inner tubes, Miss Norton," Kyle answered.

"You can call me Emily," Norton said. "You're a very polite young man, I must say."

"Mister Lock took two of the bikes and the trailer up the mountain," Kyle told her.

"This is a man's bike," Norton observed, looking at the presently one-wheeled machine balanced upside-down on its seat and handlebars. She went to the open shed door and peered inside. "Did Mister Lock tell you we also need two ladies' bikes?"

"Yeh," Kyle answered as he now inflated the inner tube with a bicycle pump. "Ventriloquist Jack has loads of bikes. I'm going to fetch them when I finish this."

"*Ventriloquist* Jack?"

Kyle plunged the patched part of the inflated inner tube into the bowl of water. "That's what everyone in the village calls him. Mister Thomas is his real name."

"I could help you fetch the bikes when you are ready," Norton offered.

"Cool," Kyle accepted. "Mister Thomas thinks he can throw his voice. That's how he got his nickname, but—"

The *yack yack yack* of his mobile phone interrupted Kyle. He lifted it from his pocket. "Mister Lock..." Kyle listened. "Sure, will do." He looked up at Emily Norton and disconnected the call. "He needs another man's bike now." Kyle's voice possessed a tinge of surprise.

Norton raised her eyebrows then hastily relaxed her face. "Well, you can never have too many bikes. It's always good to have a few spares."

Kyle shrugged then dabbed at the wet part of the inner tube with a cloth. "Cool," he said with apparent disinterest.

-o-

Caycey Jones took in the wartime posters as he wheeled one of the bikes behind Lock, who was pulling the trailer.

"You can put it over there," Lock said, pointing to the 1940s disused equipment side of the electronics chamber. "Use the foot stand please."

Jones did this before he approached the half-demolished inner archway. He ran a hand down the exposed brick edges forming what was left of the wall, then glanced through the opening into the darkness beyond.

"I *will* need to send a photo of you and me by this as it looked before you opened it up," he told Lock.

"Then we'll have to photoshop it," Lock answered as he started towards the exit.

"They would spot that immediately," Jones said. "But not to worry, we've got a plan for this. It's just a matter of bringing forward what we were going to do anyway." He glared at Lock. "Whose body did you have in that grandfather clock?"

Lock pushed the trailer to one side and then shrugged. "We've got a cover story for that."

"Well I hope it's a good one." Jones now approached the modern electronics and studied the instrument displays. "What are you doing with the excess created by the standing wave?"

"National Grid is taking it, putting a few wind farms on idle I expect."

"And the incident the other night?"

"Low demand on the grid and too much, too sudden anyway. It discharged into the stratosphere and God knows where else lightning connects to out there."

"Whose body did you have in that clock?" Jones repeated quietly.

-o-

Kyle and Emily Norton approached the doorway in the tall wall along the lane to the beach.

Norton took in the *Ponderosa* nameplate with a smile. She nudged Kyle and pointed at it. "Bonanza," she whispered with a conspiratorial grin.

Kyle's eyes widened at this as he appraised her expression. "Cool," he responded with evident puzzlement, then prodded the doorbell.

"Ben Cartwright, Hoss and then there was Little Jo," Norton continued as they waited. "Daddy always watched Bonanza on video tapes when I was little. I'd forgotten that. He so loved Bonanza."

The door opened with a squeal from its hinges. Ventriloquist Jack's eyes quickly took in Kyle before fixing on Emily Norton. His lips, maintaining a fixed slit, barely moved. "*Who daa we ha here?*" he asked in a high-pitched voice.

Startled, Norton twisted around, hunting for the source of it. She looked genuinely stunned. Kyle's jaw stayed in a dropped position as he watched her. Norton then faced Ventriloquist Jack. "That wasn't *you*, was it?"

"It was indeed," the man answered, looking at her appreciatively. "Are you a friend of Andy Lock's?"

"Just a colleague," Norton answered. "I'm here for a few weeks."

"Where did you think it was coming from?" he asked her.

"I don't know," Norton said. Her hand described a short arc in a direction away from him. "All around it seemed."

The man smiled at this and gazed into her eyes. "I'm Jack Thomas," he said.

"Emily," Norton told him a little nervously.

Whites showing, Kyle's eyes alternated between the two of them. There was a puzzled wrinkle across his forehead.

"Please come in," Ventriloquist Jack invited, glancing also at Kyle before turning into the yard and waving him to follow as well.

They were led briskly past the sheds, piles of coal and the crucible to the shanty barn of a building. Three bicycles were leaned up against the railway sleeper part of its wall.

There was a large standard man's bike with thick tyres and a normal woman's bike behind it. Behind that was a smallish pink chopper, its banana seat foreshadowed by pink-and-white plastic tassels hanging from the grips of its cow-horn handlebars.

Norton pointed at it. "This one looks the ideal size for Missus Evans."

"I've inflated the tyres and oiled the cogs and chains," Ventriloquist Jack announced, then looked at Norton and tapped the saddle of the conventional ladies' bike. "Would you like to try this for size?"

"It'll be fine," she answered. "Interesting place you have here."

"I'm an inventor," the man told her. "Come and have a look at this." He went around the barn, beckoning Norton and Kyle to follow him to the driveway below the bungalow. The pickup truck standing there glinted with pristine paintwork and chrome trim.

"Never seen you drive this, Mister Thomas," Kyle commented.

"I haven't been out in it yet," Ventriloquist Jack said. "Still got adjustments to make to the generator." He opened the driver door and climbed in. "Have a listen to this."

Something clicked under the vehicle; a starter motor *yah yahed* a few times, then a low turbine sound accompanied a hiss of steam from a vertical chrome exhaust sticking up behind the cab.

With the driver door still open, the vehicle then moved forward silently a few yards. It halted before reversing back up the incline.

"Electric hybrid?" Kyle asked as the man climbed out. The steam hissed for a few seconds before it ceased.

Ventriloquist Jack's eyes glinted, his lips drawn into a slit. "*Hyshoshen atter esheshic.*"

Emily Norton moved as though she was going to look behind her, but then grinned and wagged a finger at the man. "That was you again, wasn't it? You're not storing liquid hydrogen in that, surely?"

Jack patted the side of his prize vehicle. "Tank is full of water. The generator ignites hydrogen direct from vapour. It will be more efficient when I build a condenser into the exhaust system."

"You should patent it, Mister Thomas," Kyle said dubiously.

Ventriloquist Jack shook his head. "They wouldn't let me if I tried. Anyway, it gives me something to do and saves me a lot of money in the house. I have a unit in there as well."

Emily Norton digested this, her eyes tinged with what looked like admiration for the man. "Well, we'd better get these bikes moved," she prompted.

"I'll ride one of them round for you," Ventriloquist Jack offered.

Hearing this, Kyle hurried around the side of the shanty barn.

He was already seated with one foot on the ground on the man's bike when the others arrived, not so much chatting, more Ventriloquist Jack practising his act and Emily Norton answering the individual bits of hissed nonsense Kyle could hear.

"This is a very special lady," Jack told Kyle, who merely nodded in agreement.

Emily Norton blushed. "Not true."

"It is. Not everyone can hear me when I throw my voice."

"I hear you fine, Mister Thomas," Kyle said helpfully.

Ventriloquist Jack grinned as he looked at the young man. "That's not the voice I'm talking about."

-o-

Mair Ellis turned the car into the driveway at the B&B. She got out as three cyclists approached along the road from the village. Kyle was the first to freewheel to a halt by the garage next door. "Yo, Missus Ellis," he called out.

Mair Ellis merely said "Kyle" in response as she saw Norton freewheeling along the same driveway. The city woman was followed a few seconds later by Ventriloquist Jack pedalling furiously, knees angled outwards on what looked like a girl's pink chopper from the 80s.

"*Ishush, shuh shi shishus,*" Ventriloquist Jack called out, waving gleefully.

Ignoring him, Mair Ellis frowned. She opened the car boot and took out two shopping bags.

Wyn Ellis was at the binoculars window when she came into the lounge. "They've got some sort of bike thing on the go next door," Wyn told her.

"I noticed," Mair said.

"Andy Lock has already taken two bikes up the mountain. I think he had a trailer in the back of the car as well."

"Maybe you should ask them to tone it down a bit," Mair Ellis suggested, clear irritation in her voice.

"But they're not actually doing anything wrong."

"It's unseemly with us getting guests and all."

"I'm not worried about that," Wyn Ellis said, "but I do think we will have to report it."

"Report what and to whom?" Mair Ellis dismissed, about to turn for the door to the hallway. She then noticed her husband was looking very seriously at her. "No… surely not… after all these years?"

"I think we do," Wyn Ellis said sombrely.

"But the cause has been dead for years."

"Not any more."

"Then just keep sending your e-mails to the UFO websites. They always publish them. If Centre is still monitoring them, they'll pick it up there as usual."

"Nobody's going to publish a report of bicycle sightings."

Mair Ellis groaned exasperatedly. "Because it is of no importance. We have a good life here and there is nothing going on next door or up on that damned mountain."

"And Caycey Jones?"

"Researching his family tree."

"I've been keeping watch," Wyn Ellis said, pointing to his binoculars. "When he came back in this direction, he took the turn to the compound. Andy Lock has arrived there since with two bikes and a trailer. No sign of Jones coming back down. And now more bikes just arrived next door."

"But it's nothing," Mair Ellis insisted.

Wyn went to the antique bureau, opened a drawer and pulled out a folded magazine. He handed it to Mair. "Postman delivered it while

69

you were out. Personals, column two, third one down. It's the book code. It gave me a YouTube channel."

"And?"

Now Wyn Ellis lifted a laptop from a coffee table and tapped the touchpad. He pointed the screen towards her.

It had a caption: *Dolphins Attack Fishing Boat in Irish Sea.* A still cartoon depicted three smiling dolphins jumping over a boat. From the laptop speaker, the first eight chords of an orchestral version of the Beatles' Yellow Submarine repeated over and over.

Mair Ellis sat down on the sofa. "I don't believe it, after all these years." She looked horrified. "That's our activation code."

"I'm afraid so," Wyn Ellis said gently. "That's Moscow saying they want to talk to us. I already sent the e-mail. I'm going to the rendezvous point in Liverpool tomorrow."

-o-

Lock and Caycey Jones were in the underground work tunnel. Lock sketched a map on a sheet of crumpled paper by the side of one of the laptops.

Jones leaned over the workbench. "How far did you go along that tunnel?" he asked, pointing at the crude map.

"We walked for about twenty minutes before turning back," Lock answered. "It just goes on and on."

"In fact, there's a passageway at right angles about five miles in from the bottom of the stairs," Jones said, taking Lock's ballpoint pen. He drew a couple of lines on the paper. "The device is somewhere along this, but I have no idea how far it goes, or what else we should expect to find down there. The bikes and the trailer are going to be essential."

"We'll need to work in shifts," Lock said.

"I agree, but our logistics problems are complicated because of the incident. The attention created means moving stuff and people is going to be harder to do covertly."

"I have a lease on an old service station on the main road to Caernarfon," Lock said. "We can accumulate supplies there and use it to transfer you up here. There's plenty of room for your car." He looked at Jones. "Do you want to take a walk to where the ancient stuff starts now?"

Jones shook his head. "I'll see it soon enough tonight. What do you know about my hosts next door?"

Lock shrugged with some surprise. "Mair and Wyn? They've lived here for years. He was a primary school headmaster. Mair Ellis taught domestic science, cookery, that sort of thing. I think she wrote some books as well."

"The male is kind of nosy," Jones said. "He has binoculars trained on this part of the mountain."

"Oh, I know," Lock agreed. "He's a UFO buff. Thinks he saw one hovering over the village."

"And *did* he see a UFO hovering over the village?"

Lock shook his head. "It was years ago, in the nineties. He wrote to the local papers. Some fishermen saw something as well. He told me he reported it and that the RAF told him it was a NATO refuelling exercise."

"Why did he tell *you* about it?" Jones asked.

"It was just after I moved into the house, after my predecessors, you know… I mentioned the binoculars in that window to him, casually. He opened up about UFOs, scalar rays and all sorts of crazy stuff. Kind of got used to being next door to a nosy neighbour who thinks I'm doing top secret work for the government."

"Which you are."

Lock laughed. "Half the village thinks I am doing secret stuff. The other half knows there was something going on here during the war. Some of them are old enough to have signed the Official Secrets Act from when the navy was here on the ground in full force. Nobody talks to strangers about the mountain, or about me. They're all preoccupied with living from one week to the next and paying their rent and mortgages."

"Still, it's a lot of talk between themselves and quite a few eyes," Jones said seriously.

71

Lock laughed again, gently this time. "You need to understand this village. Most of us had you down as CIA as soon as we clapped eyes on you."

Jones seemed surprised. "Really?"

"Really," Lock said with a knowing smile. "After September the eleventh, one of the bus drivers reported an Arab with blue eyes taking photos of the communications mast from his bus."

"To you?"

"Yes, to me. Special Branch picked him up in Bangor the following day. He wasn't Arab, he was Israeli and he had a diplomatic passport, so they let him go."

"Do they always report that sort of thing to you?"

Lock shrugged. "It's very rare there's anything for them to report. We're not exactly a tourist destination, but some of them, yes, the bus drivers especially when we do get visitors. If you stayed here long enough for them to get to know you, they'd likely nickname you Jones the Spy."

Jones took this in, nodding his head slowly. "Is it possible then that one or two of your fellow villagers *are* actually spies?"

Lock took a breath to speak then hesitated as though this was the first occasion he had considered such a question.

"I'm not trying to trigger paranoia," Jones cautioned, "but a little bit of it right now is kind of wise."

-o-

Hardcastle was seated with a mug in his hand on a fold-out garden chair on the rear lawn. Banes sat a short distance away, yawning as Kyle carried gardening equipment out of the shed.

Gwenda Evans came out of the house behind them, looking slightly dishevelled. She was frowning.

"Sleep well?" Banes asked her.

"So-so," she answered. "Andy just phoned from his mobile. You'd better come inside."

The two men rose. Kyle changed direction.

72

"Not you, dear," Gwenda told him. "Just carry on as normal with the gardening."

"Cool," Kyle said. He changed direction again and headed around the side of the house to the front garden.

Hardcastle and Banes leaned against the worktop in the kitchen. Gwenda Evans faced them. "Our Circus Control officer is actually here," she told them. "It's the man we've been seeing next door."

Hardcastle groaned. "The guy who saw us with the clock?"

"Yes indeed," Gwenda answered uncomfortably. "He's up at the compound with Andy now. He's been briefed about the druggie. We're going up there as planned tonight, but we've got to sort out a few things before then."

-o-

Mair Ellis peered nervously out of the side window and spotted Kyle. He was busy weeding at the front garden next door. She turned her eyes to the binoculars and squinted. An irritable hiss came from between her teeth as she adjusted the width.

When she put her face to them this time, the eyepieces were too narrow. She hissed louder and kicked at the tripod, swiftly grabbing it before it toppled over.

Now Mair heard the front door being unlocked. She stepped away from the tripod, leaving it with a slight lean.

Caycey Jones appeared in the lounge doorway.

Mair greeted him with a rushed, syrupy voice. "Hello, Mister Jones, did you enjoy your walk?" A significant amount of the upper whites of her eyes was visible. They did not blink as she looked at him. She also appeared slightly out of breath and her cheeks glowed red.

"It was very nice," Jones answered. "I found the old farmhouse."

"Fantastic," Mair Ellis said, bringing her hands together in a loud clap, with which she seemed to startle herself.

Jones tilted his head back a fraction in response to this. "I'm just going to take a shower," he said.

73

"Will you require an evening meal today?" the woman asked him, voice still in syrupy mode.

"Actually no," Jones answered, keeping *his* voice sounding just about normal. "I'm driving to Bala to meet some friends. They've rented a house there. I'll be back sometime tomorrow."

"Well, your room will *still* be here," Mair said with exaggerated cheeriness.

"Thank you," Jones responded. He turned away and headed for the hallway, raising his eyebrows. As he climbed the stairs, Mair's voice reached him, this time in a high-pitched call from somewhere at the back of the house.

It was a repeated "*Wyn... Wyn...*" She sounded like a small dog barking.

-o-

When the sun dipped below the horizon, it was already dark in the shaded compound on the forested part of the mountain. The light was on above the closed steel door in the rock face.

This illuminated the rear of a parked, rusty-white transit van. It had *Jones Bros. Van, Bus & Truck Hire* on its side. Small bats swooped in and out of a swarm of flying insects attracted to the light.

Banes and Hardcastle were part way down the long flight of steps in the giant tunnel underground. Their miners' lamps barely illuminated the glassy black material. Silvery EMF suits squeaked and rustled as they moved.

Hardcastle had the trailer. He was guiding it in reverse with the tow bar below him. The wheels took each step down at the same time as his feet took theirs.

Behind him, Banes carried two aluminium cases. He stopped occasionally to put them down. Both men carried heavy rucksacks on their backs.

"Do you want to swap?" Hardcastle called to him as he paused with the trailer wheels resting on a step. A gap had opened between the two men.

"No, keep going," Banes answered. He looked at the dusty skeleton lying on the step below him. "Can't be far now. Can you see the bottom?"

"Just about," Hardcastle responded.

The cycle rack was now devoid of its previous occupants of rusted Second World War bicycles. They were piled untidily away to its side. Two modern mountain bikes stood in the end of the rack. A pair of identical rucksacks leaned upright against each other in front of them on the floor.

Hardcastle wheeled the trailer over and set down the heavy rucksack from his back. He then climbed upwards on the stairway to take the cases off Banes, who handed them over with some relief.

On reaching the bottom, Banes took off his silvery gloves and began opening his rucksack.

Hardcastle checked his watch. "An hour and twenty minutes," he announced.

"Not bad for two trips," Banes said as he pulled a modern lighting unit and cable from the rucksack. "We've been quicker than I thought."

Hardcastle followed the thick cable. It veered at an angle from the bottom of the stairway. He was not far beyond the bicycle rack when he found what he was looking for. "There's a joint here," he called out.

Banes looked up. "Too close, maybe. Find the next one."

Hardcastle continued walking away for a few seconds then halted, the glow of his miner's' lamp the only thing visible to his companion. "How about here?"

Banes stuck a thumb in the air. "Looks good."

When he hunched down, Hardcastle's helmet lamp illuminated a solid joint in the thick cable. Banes approached and handed him a two-pronged plug on the end of an orange cable.

Hardcastle slid this into a metal receiver in the thick joint. Both men backed away to where the lighting unit rested on the floor, then stood there contemplating it.

"You want to switch it on?" Banes asked.

"If it was going to blow the cable, it would have done it already," Hardcastle answered.

"Even so, that big cable has been here for over seventy years."

"Real heavy-duty though," Hardcastle said. "It must have taken them ages to haul it all down here."

"They probably had plenty of manpower," Banes told him. "Maybe four men carrying each section." Banes then leaned over, prodded a switch on the unit and turned his face away.

It clicked uneventfully into life. Sudden and brilliant light illuminated a large area, including quite a length of the silvery coils running along the sides and ceiling of the tunnel.

"It seems our base camp is now established," Hardcastle announced in a satisfied voice. He gazed around, wonderment in his eyes.

Now that more of it was visible, the enormity of the stairway towering upward, and the gigantic space within which it was enclosed, seemed almost Biblical.

-o-

Inland, the winding main road was barely lit by a clouded moon. The Jaguar car extinguished its headlights as it came around a gentle bend. It then immediately pulled across the otherwise deserted stretch of highway and onto a ramp sloping up to some dark, squat buildings. An overgrown lane took it around the rear.

Two figures waited in an unlit vehicle entry to the largest of the buildings. One swung a lamp to beckon the car inside. The other pulled rapidly on the chains to close the roller door behind it.

Caycey Jones wound down his window. A handlamp lit his face. Lock leaned towards him. "Put it over there in that bay."

Jones saw a faded sign on a wall facing an inspection pit. He steered the car's wheels onto the wooden boards either side of it, switched off and got out.

In the lamplight, he made out the small woman he had tried to greet politely when he first arrived at the B&B. She was standing by the 4x4.

76

"Missus Evans," Jones said as he approached, rucksack in his hands.

Gwenda Evans nodded to him. "There's a blanket in the back. You'll need to stay under it until I tell you that it's safe." She took the rucksack off him.

Jones towered above her. He looked at her face in the dim light. "I hear you're a crack shot," he said.

"It's part of my job," Gwenda answered without pride or shame. "When and *only* when needed."

"Let's hope it won't be from here on in." Jones then turned to Emily Norton. He shook her hand before climbing into the 4x4.

The roller door rattled open in the dim moonlight, the 4x4 pulling out immediately with no lights. It halted as the door rattled back to its closed position. There was a click as this was locked from inside.

A normal door opened a short distance along the outer wall. Emily Norton came out and locked it behind her. She sprinted to the front passenger side of the car.

The 4x4 moved past the rear of the building. It stopped at the top of the ramp. One set of car headlights raced along the highway below. As red tail lights passed out of sight around a bend, the 4x4 pulled out, headlights flaring into life as it joined the main road and accelerated rapidly in the other direction.

-o-

Kyle took off his trainers and socks and sat on the bed. The games console was going through its boot-up routine. Still wearing his tracksuit, he rolled over and picked up the hand controller. The flat-screen TV beeped as his console dashboard appeared on it.

Face relaxed, the young man thumbed control levers on the pad to move the highlight around the screen. It halted when there was a loud knocking at the door downstairs. Kyle looked at his watch, frowned and hurriedly got to his feet.

He opened his bedroom door a crack and listened to Gran unlocking the front door below.

"Is Pinko there?" a male voice demanded. The accent was Liverpool, a Scouser.

Downstairs, Gran squinted at a young man wearing a black hoodie at her doorstep. "Nobody by that name here," Gran told him.

There was a sound of bare feet hurrying down the stairs behind her. Kyle appeared. "It's okay, Nain. I'll deal with it."

"It's very late," Gran protested to the figure at the door. Kyle ushered her away. She hovered near the stairs.

"What do you want?" Kyle asked the Scouser.

"Have you seen Jampox?"

"He'd kill you if he heard you calling him that," Kyle answered. "But no, haven't seen him for a while." His face managed to conceal the lie.

"You were on the list," the Scouser said.

"Not me," Kyle said. "I don't owe anything."

"Shaz texted you had the money."

Kyle shrugged. "No, I'm finished with her. I wouldn't give her any more stuff if I was you." He leaned out through the door frame and saw another man, who was stooped with hands in pockets along the path to the road.

"You sure you never saw Jampox yesterday?" the first Scouser asked.

"Definitely. I would remember seeing him. Who was with him?"

"He was on his own."

"Wow," Kyle said.

"Yeh," the Scouser acknowledged. "But all along the coast, they saw him."

"You asked the others here?" Kyle asked. "You must have a few punters in the village."

The Scouser considered this, then glanced around and lowered his voice. "You need anything?"

"No thanks," Kyle said. "I don't do that stuff."

"Okay," the Scouser said and abruptly walked off.

Kyle leaned out, listening.

"I tell you," the other Scouser hissed in a whisper as the dealers paired up along the path, "he's fucked off to Ireland with the car and the money."

Kyle closed the door and faced Gran.

"Trouble?" she asked.

"No, nothing, Nain."

"Well stay away from that Sharon," she said. "*She* must have told them where you were."

"They won't be back," Kyle said. "Honest, I don't do drugs."

Gran watched him as he went up the stairs.

-o-

Banes and Hardcastle were sitting on the bottom step underground when they heard faint voices from above.

In the brilliant glare from the lighting unit behind the bicycle rack, the four distant figures coming down the stairway looked like astronauts in their silvery suits, astronauts wheeling bicycles, which tilted and bobbed with each downward step the individuals took.

Caycey Jones groaned when he reached the bottom. He put his bike down on its side. Elevated by one of the pedals, the rear wheel spun slowly, making clicking sounds.

"Doctors Hardcastle and Banes," Lock said, pointing at them individually. "This is Caycey Jones, our Circus Control officer."

Both younger men seemed eager to greet him, but Jones was busy taking the rucksack off his back. Lock helped him.

Gwenda Evans wheeled her pink chopper to the bicycle rack, contemplated the latter briefly, before hiking the small bike onto its own foot stand where it leaned over in her loosely balancing hands. It toppled with a clatter when she let it go. She did not seem concerned by this. Lock stared at her but said nothing.

Jones sat down on the second from bottom step of the stairway. Frowning, he rubbed the lower part of his back.

Emily Norton seemed to have no trouble putting her bike down noiselessly and easing off her rucksack, which she placed on the ground next to it.

"Backpacks and bikes don't mix," Jones said.

"It's actually worse when you ride them," Hardcastle told him. "Frame digs like hell into your back."

"It's because we are all carrying a lot of water," Lock said. "You can unpack and leave most of it here. And drink some here if you need to before we move on. We'll carry one litre each."

"Racks," Banes announced. "We should have fitted carry racks to the bikes. Why didn't we think of it?"

"You can bring a couple down with you next time," Lock told him, "since it's your idea." He then noticed Jones seemed to be struggling to get to his feet. Lock moved to help him up.

"Thank you," Jones said. He plucked at the silvery hood clipped over his helmet. "Are these suits really necessary?"

"I don't know," Lock answered. He opened a rucksack and took out a pack of supermarket water. "Circus instructions say we wear them down here if the electromagnetic standing wave goes beyond yellow. It's still in the amber, so we're wearing them."

Jones gazed around and up at the tunnel ceiling. "My my," he said softly, almost to himself. "I wasn't prepared for the sheer scale of it."

Gwenda Evans studied him as she took a noisy swig of water over by the bike rack. "Excuse me, sir," she called out. "We need to fit your bike to you before we start riding them."

"What do you mean?" Jones asked her.

"The handlebars need to be high enough so you can keep your back straight." She looked at Hardcastle. "You did bring some tools, I hope?"

"Of course," Hardcastle said.

Lock nodded at the pair of them before going over and studying the trailer attached to one of the mountain bikes. He patted the two silvery cases bungee-strapped on top of it.

Behind him, Jones was now sitting on his bike as Hardcastle adjusted its handlebars. Lock took a deep breath and headed for his own bike.

Tyres squeaked as six cyclists pedalled and freewheeled along the tunnel's glassy surface, their lights illuminating very little ahead of them. Even the heavy-duty cable running along the side was difficult to see. It was as though they were cycling into a black void.

Riding at a moderate speed, Hardcastle was in front, his bike towing the trailer quite easily. This now had a rucksack bungee-fastened on top of the two metal cases.

Jones was close behind him, his front wheel wobbling slightly as he kept balance and pedalled. The others followed at various gaps.

Behind them now, a diminishing coin of light, the lit area at the foot of the stairway.

None of the group attempted to speak as they rode.

Hardcastle almost missed what they were looking for. "Whoa," he shouted, voice echoing as he applied his brakes. There was a small entrance in the tunnel wall. Old bikes were leaned against the side near it.

Jones veered and wobbled to avoid Hardcastle, but he managed to get a foot down as his rear wheel locked and skidded. In the same movement, he hopped off the bike, allowing it to drop to the floor. Jones hissed as he lowered the rucksack painfully from his back.

The others halted without incident.

"Sorry," Hardcastle said to Jones. "I wasn't watching the cable."

"I was too close," Jones admitted, his helmet lamp now pointed at the opening in the tunnel side. It illuminated very little.

Lock was already approaching the trailer. He unhooked the bungees and took the rucksack off the cases, opening it immediately.

Gwenda Evans pedalled her pink chopper closer to watch him. Lock followed the heavy cable. He found a metal joint and stooped down. A lighting unit flared into life.

A look of relief crossed some of their faces, but not Emily Norton's. She looked pale under her helmet and hood. Her eyes narrowed with some apprehension when Lock aimed the unit directly at the opening. It was a passageway, wide enough for three or four people to walk alongside each other.

"There's space to ride if we need to," Lock called out. He moved closer, dragging the thin supply cable with him. He aimed the light down the passageway. "Sir," he called to Jones. "It opens out in there… forty feet at the most."

"The rest of you wait here," Caycey Jones told the others. Nursing his back, he headed towards Lock.

"You okay?" Lock asked him.

"I'm fine, pulled something coming down those stairs. Let's have a look."

The passage ceiling was not much higher than a house hallway. As they progressed, light from the unit behind them ceased to illuminate anything up ahead, though they could see that the passage opened out. The thick cable on the floor turned away at the threshold.

They arrived and halted. Jones took a deep breath. Their helmet lamps probed. It was a chamber about the size of a small dining room. Trellis tables were lined up on one side. They were cluttered with yellowed papers, ancient radios and electrical equipment. Wooden chairs faced them; one was occupied.

A motionless figure sat facing one of the radios. It was wearing a peaked black hat. Two other figures were sprawled untidily on the floor.

Jones walked in, approached the chair and leaned over it. The black hat was being worn by a skeleton whose face was still partly covered in a dry, parchment-like skin. Teeth grinned lifelessly from naked jaw bones.

It was wearing a naval uniform, which Jones studied, especially the hat badges. A silver eagle hovered above gold leaves circling a bullseye. The eagle was clutching a small swastika.

Lock stooped over to examine one of the skeletons on the floor. It was also wearing a uniform. "This one was Royal Navy," Lock observed. "Petty Officer."

"This one wasn't," Jones told him.

Lock went over. His miner's lamp illuminated the badges. "Second World War Kriegsmarine Officer," Lock said with a frown. He then took hold of its shoulders and pushed the skeleton slightly away from the back of the chair. A dirty white patch was stitched to the back of the jacket. This seemed to satisfy Lock. "Prisoner of war."

There were two other doorways, one of them in the wall opposite.

The thick cable curved through there, but Jones went to the side opening first.

This chamber had six camping beds arranged along one wall. Two rows of rusted jerry cans were lined up neatly along the other. Piles of papers and some suitcases were stacked along the far wall, as well as a heap of folded blankets.

"No bodies in here," Jones observed. Flinching from pain in his back, he leaned over one of the camping beds and patted its canvas. Dust billowed from it. He then struck it harder with his gloved hand. This time the canvas tore immediately.

Lock watched from the doorway as Jones then tapped one of the rusty jerry cans with his boot. The hollow noise this produced suggested it was empty.

Jones returned to the first chamber and headed for the furthest doorway. "Shouldn't it reek to high heaven in here?"

"You would have thought so," Lock answered.

The American went through. Lock followed.

The third chamber was slightly bigger than the others. Its back wall housed a closed door constructed from silvery metal. Both side walls had coils running along them.

The cable from the surface was connected to a metal distributor, from which three thinner cables extended. One was attached with a giant crocodile clip to a coil on the wall.

Opposite, the collapsed figure of a man wearing some sort of diving suit and brass helmet was sprawled over a skeleton wearing a white coat. Another crocodile clip and cable lay beside them.

The third cable, on closer inspection by Jones, was resting with its prongs separated by less than an inch from a receiver in the distributor box. The cable snaked from here to the closed door. Jones followed it. "Looks like the door cut it," he said. The cable was neatly severed at the frame where silver metal blended seamlessly into the glassy black of the wall beside it.

The door itself was smooth and featureless. Jones patted it with a gloved hand. "Our objective is on the other side of this," he told Lock.

THREE

A drowsy Kyle was propped up against the headboard on his bed. The bedroom was lit only by the TV screen on the wall opposite.

His eyes were almost closed when the TV beeped and his thumb reflexively tapped a button on the controller in his hands. He was suddenly alert and pressed more buttons. A couple of beeps later he said "Yo" into the flimsy microphone attached to his headset. "You're late coming on... Yeh, the Scousers came *here* as well, to my *gran's*..." Kyle narrowed his eyes. "No, I haven't seen Jampox in weeks. How about you?"

On the screen, the game Kyle had left on pause shut down. The highlighter moved around the dashboard menu as he fiddled with the control sticks. This stopped as he listened.

"I don't want anything to do with the stuff," Kyle responded, "or with the Scousers, but did *you* see Jampox?"

The look of concern grew on Kyle's face as he listened. "Did you hear anything about where he might have gone?"

A frown crinkled his forehead when he heard the answer.

-o-

Deep underground, Hardcastle waited impatiently in the lighting unit glare near the new passageway entrance. He squinted as he tried to see what was going on in there. Banes did the same from a short distance away.

Emily Norton was seated on the glassy floor near her bike, which was lying on its side.

85

Gwenda approached. "You alright, dear?"

"I'm fine," Norton answered. Her face seemed small and drawn below her helmet and EMF suit hood.

"It's okay to feel scared, you know," Gwenda soothed as she studied the woman.

"Is it?" Norton asked. "How about you? You don't seem frightened of anything."

"Oh I am..." Gwenda began, but their attention was diverted when Lock's voice sounded out. He reappeared at the passage entrance.

"Leave the bikes," he called. "Just bring the primary gear and your packs."

Gwenda helped Norton to her feet. Norton's face was full of apprehension but she managed to smile, if a little nervously, at the other woman.

Inside the first chamber, Caycey Jones examined the dials on the Second World War radio transmitters positioned along the trellis tables. His helmet beam played over them one by one. He moved carefully without touching them, sliding a couple of folding chairs out of the way.

He approached the final radio and turned to the skeleton seated in front of it. Empty eye sockets stared at him from under the German naval officer's hat.

"Please excuse me," Jones said. He groaned quietly from back pain as he lifted the seat with the officer still in it and set it down a couple of feet away. The skull seemed to nod as he completed this.

Hardcastle and Banes entered carrying their equipment cases. "Wow," Hardcastle said.

Banes pointed a finger. "Is that a German?" Two helmet lights converged on it. Teeth grinned from a lipless mouth.

Jones faced the younger men. "Study these transmitters. I think they have something to do with opening *this* through here..." He moved to the doorway in the far end.

Banes and Hardcastle put their cases down and followed him. When they reached the next chamber, their attention was drawn to the additional corpses in there. Both were particularly interested in the prone figure dressed in what looked like a diving suit, complete with brass helmet.

Watching them, Jones pointed at the silvery door at the far end. "Over there."

"You want that opened?" Hardcastle asked.

"Affirmative," Jones answered.

Gwenda Evans and Emily Norton arrived in the other chamber, the latter crinkling her nose when she saw the skeletons. Gwenda quickly assessed the situation and turned her attention to her companion. Norton's face looked pale in the lamplight.

Jones came back, followed by the other two men. He looked at Norton. "I want you to examine these and see if you can determine any obvious cause of death." He gestured at the skeletons.

"I'll try," Norton said. She looked uncomfortable with the idea.

"I'll help you," Gwenda told her.

Banes and Hardcastle jostled as they moved their cases closer to the trellis tables. They glared at each other when the cases collided. Banes shrugged and stood aside.

Hardcastle leaned over a table and tilted one of the transmitters in the beam from his helmet lamp. "Valves are all blown," he announced as he looked inside. He then examined a smaller device connected to the set with thin wires, before ducking under the table itself. His helmet beam revealed some papers on the floor. He grabbed them and stood up.

Banes hunched over the middle transmitter, studying its dials. His lips moved silently, conducting mental arithmetic. He approached the furthest set and took in the dials there. After further arithmetic, employing animated lips and a few nods of the head, he said, "It's Pi."

Hardcastle glanced at him then at Jones, who was watching them. Hardcastle had a sheaf of yellowed papers in his gloved hand. "That's what these notes say," he told them.

Banes leaned over to look. "Really?"

"They were also using binary," Hardcastle said. "Three side bands, two sets of eight bits. Primitive... It must have taken them weeks." He pulled up one of the folding chairs and sat down.

Banes dragged another one and sat close to him. Hardcastle rested the papers against the trellis table so both men could read them.

Lock came in from the big tunnel. He carried two rucksacks, which he set down against a wall. He looked around, noting what the others were doing, before joining Jones at the next doorway.

"No gunshot wounds, no scorching," Gwenda called out from where she was crouched beside one of the skeletons.

"None of them carried firearms," Norton added. "There's no immediately obvious cause of death."

"I think it's safe to say we are looking at one of the effects of the nineteen forty-five incident," Lock said.

"I agree," Jones said as he again nursed his lower back. "They were tickling the dragon's tail."

"Isn't that more nuclear fission?" Hardcastle suggested, lifting his head from the yellowed papers.

Jones smiled thinly. "You're right. I misappropriated the metaphor. Are you getting anywhere?"

Banes pointed at the old equipment stretched out along the trellis tables. "Looks like these transmitters were nothing to do with their *event*, but they were being used to do a lot more than just open and close the door in there."

Hardcastle nodded in agreement. "Which apparently they managed to do as well it seems. Open that door, I mean."

"Can you duplicate it?" Lock asked.

"I think so," Hardcastle answered. He stood and lifted one of the metal cases. There was no room for it on the trellis tables so he balanced it on one of the chairs. The case wobbled as he unfastened its lid.

"Leave them to it," Jones told Lock, gesturing for him to follow into the next chamber.

Once they were in there, Caycey Jones ran a gloved hand over the edges of the silvery door.

Lock crouched over the diving suit skeleton, examining a lattice of thin copper wires stitched to its cloth. There were black scorch marks alongside the wires running down one of the sleeves.

"There's no visible joint or crack in this," Jones said as he examined the door. "Incredible precision engineering."

"I believe this man was electrocuted," Lock said.

"Looks that way," Jones agreed. "They pumped high voltage into something down here and got taken by surprise when it pumped high voltage right back at them."

Lock nodded. "As well as creating a geophysical standing wave, which killed anyone too close to its source."

"Obviously," Jones concurred.

"Madness."

"Which is nothing new," Jones said. He stepped away from the door and contemplated the skeletal corpses. "But you have to remember the mindset of the British at that time. They handed over most of their nuclear programme materials to the Americans, who had convinced them wrongly that the Nazis were close to building a bomb. Promises to share weren't kept by the US Army, so the Brits pursued what they were really advanced with at that time. Developing information technology and using it to try to decode what was down here."

"In the hope they could use it as a weapon," Lock said.

"Evidently," Jones agreed, "until they realised that its use was far more dangerous than any number of atomic bombs."

"So, two years later they bricked it up."

Jones chuckled drily. "The world bricked up a lot more than this in nineteen forty-seven. What little was left of the age of reason by that time finally died when the Cuckoos came out of the closet."

Gwenda Evans and Emily Norton appeared at the middle door. They hesitated on the threshold. Jones beckoned them to come in.

Gwenda held up a piece of paper. "I found this on the German officer."

Emily Norton gazed at the skeletons in this room and then at the silvery door. She seemed to find the door more disturbing than the skeletons. "Who built this place?" she whispered.

Hearing her, Lock shot a slightly worried look at Jones, who noticed as he accepted the paper from Gwenda. Jones also noticed Emily Norton's face. Eyes wide, she was staring at the closed door.

"It's okay," Jones told Norton. "After all, we are actually down here in this remarkable place. Such questions are natural." He then looked at the paper Gwenda had given him, assessing it rapidly. "If my German serves me correctly, this is a translation of part of the Bhagavad Gita." He handed it back. "Seems our German officer was as romantically inclined as Oppenheimer."

"Oppenheimer?" Gwenda queried as she looked at the neat Gothic script in her helmet light.

"The atomic bomb project in the forties," Lock told her. "Oppenheimer supposedly quoted 'I am become death' when it actually worked."

"You would like to know who built this?" Jones asked Norton. His tone was kind, patient.

"Vishnu, I presume," Norton answered with nervous humour. "Or was it Krishna? I never read that sort of thing."

Jones smiled thinly. "The skeleton on the stairway... Did anyone think to run a radio spectrum on a bone sample?"

"We did," Lock answered. "But we concluded the portable machine we have is probably faulty. According to that, it's over twelve thousand years old."

"Could be much older," Jones said as he looked at Norton. "*Who* built this place is probably the wrong question. *When* is initially more to the point."

Norton glanced at the closed door. "Twelve thousand years screws the history books. But this place, this thing, I don't know..."

"This is hard for all of us," Gwenda told Norton. "We all knew the impossible was in fact real, but actually being down here still gets to you."

"Are you alright?" Lock asked Norton. His eyes showed concern.

Norton looked around with wide eyes. "Sort of just hit me. All my instincts suggest this place is utterly forbidden to us, not just because of the obvious, that our so-called government, the deep and empowered version of it will torture and kill us if they find us out, but... I don't know... as a species. Does that make sense?" She looked nervously at Jones.

Jones bowed his head slightly. "You've been thrown in at the deep end but try to remember why you joined Circus."

"And am forbidden to speak about," Norton challenged in a soft voice, "even to my fellow double agents?"

"For good reason," Lock said.

Jones nodded thoughtfully. "Since we are all risking not just our own lives, but those of countless others without their consent, we must remember one very important fact. Those who constructed this place are not our enemies. They are, in the final analysis, our only hope against the Cuckoos." Jones then shifted his eyes from Norton's and looked expectantly beyond her. She turned to see who was there.

Banes stood in the doorway. He spoke in a dry tone. "For me personally, when I was recruited, I was horrified by the idea we might not be descended from apes after all." His eyes were fixed on Lock's. "Apes as ancestors seemed like a better deal, don't you think?"

"That's enough," Lock warned. "Aren't you supposed to be opening this door?"

"We're ready to try a couple of routines," Banes said, eyes now focussed on Jones. "But you need to come and look at something first, sir."

Jones moved immediately. "What's up?"

"We're not absolutely certain," Banes answered. "But we think something is trying to establish a dialogue with our laptop."

On the trellis table, the laptop screen displayed red text in a small window: *Firewall Warning, Intrusion Detected*.

Another window showed an updating firewall log: *Intrusion Detected, Unknown Source*, followed by *Intrusion Blocked*, constantly repeating itself. A scrolling list showed the date and time of each event to the second. Hardcastle was seated watching it with fixed eyes.

"Is this laptop wireless enabled?" Jones asked as he leaned over.

"Definitely not," Hardcastle answered. "And there's no TCP or IP activity. But that's not the only strange thing," he added, clicking on a minimised window on the taskbar.

The window expanded. *Monitor detected*, it warned, and below that: *Compiling*, followed by a progress bar.

"Is something taking control of this computer?" Jones asked.

"Maybe trying to," Hardcastle answered. "I don't know. I've seen a lot of hack routines, but this looks nothing like any of them."

The others were now crowded behind Banes and Hardcastle. Emily Norton inadvertently rested her hand on the German skeleton's shoulder. She grimaced as she quickly withdrew it.

"Can you turn it off?" Lock demanded in a low voice to Hardcastle.

"Sure," Hardcastle answered, "but I won't be able to open that door if I do." He held up a small black device. "This is the equivalent of a few thousand of the transmitters these guys used. If I don't network the laptop to it, there's no way I can duplicate the transmissions they used to control stuff down here."

Banes held up a sheaf of papers. "This officer worked on something for the Germans during the war. Apparently, some procedures came out of that and they used them here."

Jones took the papers, but Hardcastle tapped his arm and pointed at the laptop. "This progress bar is nearly complete. Do I switch off?"

"Yes, switch off now," Jones told him.

Hardcastle pressed the power button. Nothing happened. He pressed it again. He then lifted the laptop and looked underneath it. "I'll have to take the battery out," he said with a touch of alarm in his voice.

"Too late," Banes announced as the progress bar completed.

At the same time, a rectangular glow appeared on the glassy black wall above and behind the trellis table. It coalesced into bright colours then came into focus.

Six pairs of stunned eyes stared at it.

"Interesting," Jones said.

The laptop display was now duplicated with perfect clarity in home cinema size on the wall. This glowing rectangle provided more light in the chamber than their helmet lamps. On it, another dialogue box appeared: *New Programs Detected*. Three new symbols materialised at the same time.

"What are *they*?" Jones asked.

"Those are mine," Hardcastle said, "simple routines extracted from the notes I found." He pointed at the display on the wall. "Top one is lights, apparently. Next one is environment. Control of the door is below that. I suggest we try the lights first."

Jones frowned. "Can any of this be detected above ground?"

"Not unless it's imparted somehow into the standing wave," Hardcastle said.

"Amazing," Banes said as he compared the display on the wall to the laptop. "Smart material…"

Norton opened her rucksack and took out an instrument. After studying its screen, she handed it to Jones.

"It's scanning for any obvious coherencies in the standing wave," Norton told him, "but nothing detected other than the wave itself."

Jones looked at it, considered the data, then handed the device back to Norton. "Keep an eye on it while we figure this out." He turned to the others. "I just realised something. Anyone notice lighting units or lamps being used by these wartime guys?"

"The one in the diving suit had a handlamp," Lock answered as he looked around this chamber, "but come to think of it, no."

"I just assumed they took their stuff out of here before bricking it up," Banes said. "There were no lamps on their bikes either."

"Well, they didn't work in the dark," Jones observed. "And they didn't retrieve the bodies. Just left them here and bricked up the surface entrance two years later." He pointed at the screen. "Try the lights routine."

"I'll need to network to the transmitter," Hardcastle warned, lifting the small black device again.

"Why not launch the routine without it," Banes suggested. "Laptop seems to be talking to that wall just fine without a radio." He pointed at the magnified version of the laptop display glowing there.

Hardcastle shrugged. Gloved fingers tapped at keys. Immediately, it was as though daylight had broken through from above. The ceiling now glowed white. Apart from the rectangle of mirrored laptop display, the walls glowed with a dull green. The floor had turned from glassy black into a pattern of pale blues. Helmet lights were now barely discernible, relegated to a dim yellow in the light now flooding the chamber.

They were speechless, except for the most diminutive member of their group. "I wasn't expecting that," Gwenda Evans said, smiling in the artificial light. She looked at Norton.

A little of the tension had gone from Norton's face.

"Now try the door routine," Jones told Hardcastle.

The scientist pressed keys. There was a faint humming sound from the other chamber.

"Okay," Jones said. "It seems we're in."

Norton looked at Gwenda and took a deep breath.

-o-

It was an immense circular chamber. A green wall enclosed it, supporting a dome that glowed with white light. Three metallic devices stood in the centre. Positioned triangularly, these looked like massive cannons with their barrels pointed downwards from tower-shaped mounts.

Jones led a group of now five people, while Banes stayed back at the entrance. Following a cable on the floor, the group headed towards a table and some chairs that were roughly halfway to the centre.

Hardcastle gazed around but particularly upwards. The ceiling rose beyond cathedral height in its centre.

Norton's eyes were drawn to something over to the left. It looked as though blankets had been thrown over heaps of bones. A mix of blankets, exposed skeletons and dust littered the blue floor in a curving line towards the centre.

Lock walked at the group's rear. He glanced back at the entrance and saw Banes standing there. "Stay on the other side of that threshold," Lock shouted, voice echoing.

"I am," Banes shouted back, then he moved out of sight.

It took the group nearly four minutes to reach the table.

Gwenda Evans was the first to put down her rucksack. She helped Jones with his. "How big do you reckon this place is?" Jones asked.

"Don't ask me," Gwenda answered. "I need a telescopic sight and a target to judge distances."

"Half a mile across, maybe more," Hardcastle guessed.

Lock gazed upwards. "And the ceiling, how high?"

"Don't know," Jones answered. "But those devices in the centre, whatever they are, must be about thirty to forty metres tall."

"Big then," Gwenda said.

"Yep," Jones agreed. He pointed towards the cannon-like objects, then at the cable that continued to the centre. "First thing is to disconnect that cable." He gestured to Hardcastle and Lock. "What do you make of how they wired it?"

Both men turned to assess the green wall circling the chamber. A silvery coil dipped in and out of recesses halfway up it. They seemed to be connected all the way around to terminals either side and above the entrance.

"I have no idea," Hardcastle said. He pointed at the cannon-like objects. "If those got power from the original construction of this place, it must have been from somewhere below the floor. We might find an answer in all those papers back there."

Jones shook his head. "It can wait, but we must avoid duplicating what the wartime guys did, so their cable has to be disconnected."

Lock lifted his rucksack. "Hardcastle, you're with me."

"Watch out for induced current," Jones warned. "That severed cable is still plenty long enough to pick it up in here."

"Absolutely," Hardcastle agreed.

The two men headed towards the centre.

Gwenda and Norton approached Jones at the table. There were two folding chairs, one of which was lying on its side.

On the table itself were three rows of metal boxes, each

containing complex, clock-like mechanisms fashioned from wheels and cogs, together with numerical dials. These were wired to each other. More wires extended from each box to a wartime radio transmitter.

"What do you make of this?" Jones asked the two women.

Norton studied it all briefly before she shrugged. "Looks a bit like a Turing machine, maybe. Small scale though."

"But maybe more complex," Jones said. He looked at Gwenda.

She shrugged. "Don't ask me. I'm security... guns and that sort of thing."

"I think the wartime guys might have detected something and were trying to communicate with it," Jones said. He pointed at a chair lying on its side. "They also left in a hurry."

Gwenda and Norton watched him open his rucksack. As he began pulling out coiled wires, Jones said, "Why don't you two check those over there?" He pointed towards the line of blankets, bones and skeletons.

Norton sighed heavily enough for Jones to hear her, but she followed Gwenda in that direction.

Lock and Hardcastle reached the foot of the closest cannon-like device. It towered above them. A short distance away, one of the skeletons was wearing a helmet and what looked like armour parts.

Hardcastle pointed at it. "Twelve thousand years ago... Who were they, and what do you think happened to them?"

"Let's get this clip," Lock said. He pulled a pair of gloves from his rucksack.

Hardcastle opened his and rummaged until he found a similar pair. "Aren't you even a bit curious?"

"Of course," Lock answered. "But I can't see what value it's going to give us if we speculate."

"But it's stunning," Hardcastle argued.

"No more stunning than what we already knew," Lock said. He stooped over a huge clip with rusty, crocodilian teeth. It connected the 1940s cable to a node in the cannon support column. He prodded the clip with his gloved hand then looked up at Hardcastle. "Are you going to help me get this off?"

Some distance away, Gwenda Evans lifted one of the blankets. This merely revealed more of what she and Norton had seen as they approached. Skulls, bones, helmets and pieces of armour looked as though they had been swept here. There was a thick line of calciferous dust forming a defined edge to the pile. It was shaped by brush marks.

"Hundreds of them here," Norton observed.

"Yes," Gwenda agreed. "Looks like the guys in the forties were clearing the floor before they gave up or were interrupted." She looked around, eyes following the contours of the blankets.

Norton grimaced disapprovingly. "They just brushed them into heaps like they were rubbish."

"I suppose they were busy with other stuff," Gwenda said. She pointed. "Those skeletons there though, they haven't been moved." She looked at the entrance, then returned her attention to the line of blankets and scattered remains.

Jones was seated facing a laptop on the table when Lock and Hardcastle arrived back from the central area. A few yards away, the returning Norton and Evans spoke quietly to each other.

"We disconnected the cable," Lock told Jones. "God knows what the wartime guys thought they were doing running high voltage into that cannon thing."

Jones looked at the laptop, lifted a flash drive and held it up so the others could see it as he spoke. "Our orders are to connect this to the technology down here. This chip contains a message, which we are to find a way of sending." He turned in his chair to look at Norton and Gwenda. They came to a halt.

"Is that message intended for those who built this place?" Norton asked.

"That's the idea," Jones answered. "Trouble is, Circus never told me how I was supposed to connect the laptop." He waved a hand over a litter of cables on the floor. "There's nothing physical here to connect any of this stuff to, but—"

"*Our* laptop is talking to it back there," Hardcastle interjected.

"That's what I was about to get to," Jones said. "This one is doing the same." He pointed at the laptop screen. "Firewall is trying to block an intrusion."

"You could disable the firewall and see what happens," Hardcastle suggested.

Jones nodded. "Precisely what I intend. But before I do that, it might be a good idea for the rest of you to get out of here."

"Why?" Lock asked.

"A load of people got killed in this chamber," Jones answered.

"I don't think it was the chamber that killed those people over there," Gwenda told him.

"I don't think so either," Lock said.

Gwenda pointed at the blankets and bones. "I think they might have been deliberately killed in some sort of one-sided battle or retreat."

"I can concur with that," Lock said. "The positions of the skeletons… It looks to me like they were pursued down here and this was their final redoubt."

"So, judging by what they were wearing, there was an advanced human civilisation able to access this place thousands of years ago?" Norton asked.

"Maybe the last remains of one," Jones answered before taking a deep breath. "But at this moment in time, it's rather academic. Stay here or go back to join Banes. But I have to go ahead with this right now."

"Well I'm staying," Lock announced.

Norton hesitated, looking at Jones. "I'm also staying," she said. "If this place kills you, then we fail and we'll all be tortured and killed anyway."

"That much is true, unfortunately," Jones agreed.

"And I am not going to miss all the fun," Hardcastle said. He took hold of one of the chairs. He was about to seat himself close to the table when he looked at the two women. "Sorry. Would either of you ladies like to sit down?"

Gwenda merely smiled and sat on the floor. Norton sat next to her. She reached for a bottle of water from her rucksack.

Hardcastle leaned over at the table.

"You know," Jones said, "maybe you had better tell Banes what we are doing."

Hardcastle sighed but moved to get up.

"It's okay, I'll go," Lock told him. Hardcastle seemed delighted. He fixed his eyes on the laptop.

Lock was nearing the entrance when the dome-shaped ceiling changed colour. It faded rapidly from white before turning completely black. The floor and circular wall glowed more intensely as though to compensate. The blackness above was then swiftly populated by brightly glowing stars. The Milky Way was clearly visible. Lock stared with astonishment.

Gazing at the ceiling from the laptop some distance behind him, Jones said, "My my, that is so clear."

Hardcastle switched his attention between the laptop and the field of stars. "It might look like a planetarium, but I think it's much more than that." He leaned closer to the laptop. Its screen was displaying two columns of new windows.

New Hardware Detected each window announced in one column. The other column stated *Installing Software*.

Norton and Gwenda leaned back against their supporting arms on the floor and stared up at the huge panorama above them. Norton pointed. "Orion... It's so clear."

Some distance away, Lock approached Banes, who had reappeared and was gazing up at the ceiling from the chamber entrance.

"Remember that you need to stay that side of the door," Lock warned him.

"I am, definitely," Banes insisted.

"Because if that suddenly closes with you on its threshold..."

"I'm well behind it," Banes said. The younger man's eyes were animated as he stared upwards.

Lock sighed and went through. He threaded past the diving suit man and the other skeleton, and through into the next chamber. He studied the laptop in there before turning to the German naval officer's skeleton. It was still seated, eye sockets staring, teeth grinning. Its hat was tilted at an angle.

Lock straightened this, aligning its peak neatly above the eye sockets. "I bet you didn't see anything like *this*, did you, Herr Kapitan?" he asked it drily before stepping around its chair and heading along the passage.

Standing near the bikes, Lock looked along the main tunnel in the direction of the unseen stairway. Now that this area was brightly lit, it was like being on the floor of an immense trench. The silvery coils running along the walls glinted like precious metal. Lock listened. The silence was absolute.

Something caught Lock's attention. He looked down, eyes widening. A circle of yellow had appeared. It surrounded his boots in the otherwise blue-lit floor. He moved a few paces. Like a shadow, the yellow glow moved with him.

Back in the circular chamber, Emily Norton and Gwenda Evans had also noticed their own yellow shadows. Norton pointed at one below the still seated Jones at the trellis table.

Jones was more interested in a huge rectangle mimicking the laptop screen that had appeared in the ceiling. It contrasted high up in the dome against the star field displayed there.

This was directly opposite where Jones was seated and at a thirty-degree height in the curvature. On it, windows continued to display messages that multiple programs were installing on the laptop.

Norton and Evans walked back and to with a curious fascination for the yellow shadows following their feet.

"At least they're not red," Gwenda observed.

"But maybe yellow was the equivalent danger colour for whoever built this place," Norton said. "We have no idea what it might mean."

Jones looked at them, glanced at his own yellow circle and kneaded at the small of his back with his hand. There was a puzzled expression on his face.

"You okay?" Gwenda asked him.

"Pain's gone," he answered. "All of a sudden."

"That's good," she responded.

"Good but unusual," Jones said. "I've put up with back pain for years. If I pull it, it usually takes weeks for the pain to die down. Now it's gone completely."

"Maybe it's a coincidence," Norton suggested.

Jones pointed at his laptop and then at the ceiling. "I don't think so. Whatever it is, it's abundantly obvious that something here is interacting with our computers." Turning to face the two women again, he said, "I think it's now also monitoring us as well. Whatever it is, it's aware of us."

-o-

Wyn Ellis reached out to silence the alarm clock in the bedroom gloom. Mair instantly got out of bed from beside him. Her eyes were narrow slits. She staggered as though sleepwalking to the bedroom door, lifting her dressing gown automatically from the back of a chair.

Downstairs in the kitchen, as they ate breakfast together, a now alert Mair Ellis picked disconsolately at her food with a fork. "Do you really have to go?"

"Mair, we've gone over this. Think of the potential consequences if I don't."

"Like what? What's the worst they could do?"

Wyn placed his knife and fork on his plate and finished chewing. One of the kitchen spotlights reflected from his spectacles. "The Russians could blackmail us," he said. "It would be easy enough to leak information about our recruitment in college to Special Branch."

"But it was years ago. We haven't done anything, except wait and wait for a call that never came until now."

"That wouldn't matter to Special Branch."

Mair Ellis held back and conquered oncoming tears when she heard this. "I don't want to go to prison."

"Then let me meet whoever it is they're sending," Wyn Ellis said. "The Russians wouldn't want us to go spying on military installations or anything dangerous like that at our age. It's probably

101

just belated housekeeping. Maybe it's to say hello as they tell us goodbye."

"What about next door? It was the reason the KGB told us to buy this house."

"There's only one way to find out," Wyn Ellis said.

Mair nodded sadly then got up from the table. "That's settled then. But don't let them bully you into doing anything ridiculous."

"Of course."

"And if they ask about next door," Mair Ellis said grimly, "tell them there's nothing going on there."

"That would be the truth, as far as I can tell at any rate."

"No UFOs, no lights above that mountain, not a word about anything like that either."

"Absolutely," Wyn agreed. "There hasn't been anything like that for years."

"And be careful where you park the car in Bangor," Mair warned.

"It'll be safe at the station."

A few minutes later, Wyn Ellis pulled out onto the road in the car. Mair Ellis waved to him from the front door then closed it.

To the east, clouds glowed purple and red as the sun began to rise.

-o-

Lock, Hardcastle and Norton reached the top of the gigantic stairway underground. Rucksacks were light and empty on their backs. The two men were each also carrying an empty equipment case.

Lock paused to catch his breath, looking back from this height along the brightly illuminated tunnel. Its sides receded into the distance, foreshortened almost to a dot.

He then looked down as something caught his eye. "My shadow is back," he told the others. A yellow glow surrounded his feet.

"Not mine," Norton observed. The floor around hers was blue like the rest of it.

"Mine neither," Hardcastle said. "Whatever I had wrong with me is cured, if that's what this place was doing to us."

"How are your knees?" Norton asked Lock. "You said you had problems going down the stairs."

Lock moved on towards the tubular tunnel. "I must admit the pain went away very quickly when the yellow shadow appeared. Got a bit of a twinge now though."

All three removed their EMF suits when they reached the work tunnel. They seemed more at ease here in an underground environment created by a mix of 1940s and modern human activity.

Lock produced a mobile phone. He checked his watch. "Is seven-thirty a civilised time to be sending an e-mail?" he asked the others.

"Sure," Hardcastle answered. "Why?"

"This is our American friend's phone," Lock explained. "The e-mail is to the Ellis couple next door. He told them he was visiting friends in Bala and will be back today. The e-mail is to update them he'll be late."

When the other two shrugged, Lock touched the phone screen and waited a few seconds for the e-mail to send before switching it off. He then placed the phone on the workbench under the poster proclaiming *Walls Have Ears*.

-o-

The centre of Liverpool was noisy with morning traffic when Wyn Ellis crossed the road outside Lime Street Station.

He carried a rolled-up black umbrella. It was something he did awkwardly, unable to decide whether to use it as a walking stick or just hold it. After a few changes of position, he balanced the umbrella like a rifle in the crook of his arm, pointed end aimed at the ground ahead of him. It swayed gently as he walked.

Moving through the public gardens near the station, he checked the statues and monuments until he found a giant William Gladstone towering in a frozen pose on its masonry plinth.

Wearing a German coal scuttle helmet, an angel caressed a sword below it. Glancing curiously at this, Ellis seated himself on a curving bench that ran along the bottom of a high wall at Gladstone's monumental rear.

It was relatively peaceful in the gardens. A man and woman walked along the main path, headed for work. A trio of starlings argued over something on the ground between Ellis and the statue. Wyn sighed and waited, eyes turning to the overcast sky.

An innocuous-looking man came around the monument. He was mid-thirties and wore baggy faded denims, a sports jacket and an open collar shirt. The man walked purposefully up to Wyn Ellis and sat next to him, placing a brown leather briefcase on the bench between them. He too carried a black umbrella.

"Good morning," the man greeted in a strange accent. "It is quite peaceful here, no?" There was a mix of eastern European and Liverpool in there.

Wyn glanced at the man and said, "Yes, and not raining either." He then fixed his gaze on the back of Gladstone's mostly hairless bronze head.

"No buskers playing Yellow Submarine today," the man prompted.

"Or dolphins chasing tangerines," Wyn responded.

The man extended a hand. "You can call me Dimitri, Mister Ellis. I am very pleased to meet you."

Wyn Ellis shook his hand in silence. The Russian smiled with an expectant lift of his eyebrows, as though encouraging Wyn to speak. Now Wyn did so, reluctantly it seemed. "Have you had to travel far?" It was awkward, nervous.

"Not at all," the Russian answered casually and at ease. "I have lived here with my family for some time now, in an official capacity of course. Do you like Liverpool?"

"It's okay," Ellis answered. "How about you?"

The Russian shrugged. "It is a city of contradictions. Here, for example, we see monuments to imperialism. Elsewhere in the city, a rather theatrical apology for the slave trade. Yet one of those immortalised in this park was in the business of blockade running to help the Confederacy during the American Civil War." His face grew serious. "But I suspect you would prefer to know why we are here after all this time, yes?"

Wyn Ellis was clearly nervous as he spoke. "We felt, my wife

104

and I, that the cause we joined died after the ninety-one coup and Yeltsin took power. The collapse of the Soviet Union seemed catastrophic."

"Nevertheless, you continued sending to the magazines, mostly to report in code that you had nothing to report. Your UFO sightings were most entertaining. We appreciated that."

"I didn't think anyone was interested, after Yeltsin."

Now the Russian leaned closer. There was intensity in his eyes. "The cause is not dead, because the cause never died. Do you remember Nikita Sergeyevich?"

"Khrushchev, of course, but I was only a child."

"He and President Kennedy had a good relationship. Both men knew what was truly going on in the world. They knew precisely that Nazism, and the power that hid behind it, was not defeated in nineteen forty-five."

"This I knew about the Nazis," Wyn Ellis said. "Germany was defeated, but the Nazi corporations simply moved house. It had become very evident by the time we joined the cause, Vietnam, Iran, Indonesia and Chile for example. Chile was the final straw for Mair and I when we were in college."

Dimitri pursed his lips. "And Kennedy was killed because he tried to interrupt their consolidation of power."

Wyn nodded gravely at this. "His assassination is one of the clearest memories of my childhood. My mother cried. It was a sad day."

"Yes, very sad," the Russian agreed. "But did you know that Nikita Sergeyevich advised Kennedy of the precise year the Berlin Wall would come down?"

"No, I didn't."

"He revealed a small part of the strategic plan," Dimitri expanded, "that all countries, including Russia, must go through a capitalist phase if the enemies of humanity are to be defeated."

"Are you saying that what happened in the nineties was all planned?" Wyn Ellis asked incredulously.

Now the man calling himself Dimitri spoke with intensity. "Western capitalism is already defeated because it is always self-

105

defeating. It is just taking a long time to die on this occasion. Cyclical death and reincarnation of capital always occurs, but this time the cause will have the upper hand. Of this I am certain."

"This is all very interesting and I am sure truthful," Wyn Ellis said, "but where do my wife and I fit into this at our age?"

"There was an incident two nights ago. You did not report it." The Russian's eyes, piercing, fixed interrogatively on Wyn's.

"Incident? What incident?"

"A peculiar and very intense storm."

"We get storms quite often. We must have slept through it."

"Not like this one," the Russian said, then relaxed his face. "But I accept you might have slept through it. What about activity at the neighbouring house since then?"

"Just normal," Wyn answered, "apart from having a thing about bikes all of a sudden."

"Bicycles?"

"Yes, they all got bikes, and in a hurry it seemed to me."

"Now that is very interesting," Dimitri said. "And has there been any increased interest in your bed and breakfast offer since two nights ago?"

A pigeon waddled past the memorial to Gladstone, turned and cocked its head to point one eye at the two men talking quietly on the bench. It continued, now heading towards them.

"This man Caycey Jones is almost certainly CIA," the Russian told Wyn Ellis. "The Japanese ladies arriving with you today are probably also connected."

"But Jones has a genuine link to an ancestor from Amharfarn," Wyn protested. "I checked his story on an ancestry website."

"And did you check who submitted the documents to that site and when they did so?"

"No."

"Because you can't, of course. Such documents can be faked and the CIA has a track record of doing so to protect their cover stories. After the war, they laundered the ancestry of thousands of Nazis of so-called pure Aryan stock into having Jewish heritage in order to place them where they could continue their dirty work. They ran

106

schools to teach them how to be Jewish. Giving a black man Welsh heritage in your village would be simple for them."

"What do you want us to do?" Wyn asked.

"A more intensive surveillance," the Russian told him.

Wyn Ellis fiddled nervously with his umbrella handle, his face drained of colour. "This is starting to sound dangerous. Why is Amharfarn so important?"

Dimitri reached into a pocket with one hand and pointed with the other at the pigeon now halted, staring expectantly at them near their feet. "You see this bird? It has a ring, a racing pigeon. She probably landed here to rest and search for food."

The Russian undid the wrapper on a small pack of biscuits, crushed one, then reached down with the crumbs in his palm. The pigeon pecked gently at it. Dimitri made a peculiar cooing sound through puckered lips.

Wyn Ellis watched this with some apprehension.

When he straightened up again, Dimitri turned to Wyn and said, "I mentioned slavery earlier. Those who were enslaved on the plantations, at least they knew they were slaves. Knowing created the desire for freedom, the key precondition for achieving it." He pointed at the pigeon. "She ate from what I offered only to her, but if I scattered the crumbs, the feral pigeons would come. She is useful, a slave, but the others are useless so we do not feed them. Today, the slaves, most of us, have no awareness of being a slave. Useless eaters are equally oblivious to *their* status. The essential precondition of *knowing* what they truly are is absent in both cases."

"And Amharfarn?" Ellis reminded him.

"Could be the key to overthrowing the hidden slave masters, who also now intend a new *final solution*." The Russian said this with all seriousness.

Wyn Ellis briefly had the expression of a man who finds himself confronted by a lunatic. But he managed to calm his face. "I have known Andy Lock and Gwenda for years. I have watched them and seen them nearly every day. They can't possibly be involved in something so important, not in Amharfarn."

The Russian leaned closer, face patient. "I want you to think," he

107

said. "You have had the bed and breakfast sign in your window ever since you bought the house all those years ago, yes?"

"Well yes," Ellis answered. "Those were our instructions. We also advertised in the tourist brochures every year, as instructed."

"And how many bookings did you get in all those years until a few days ago?"

Wyn Ellis thought carefully. He seemed to be conducting some mental arithmetic. "Five," he answered eventually.

"Five *independent* bookings?" the Russian asked, tilting his face forward as though cross-examining a child.

"No," Ellis admitted. "They were a family we met on holiday in Majorca. They came five years in a row. We had a disagreement over money when their son became a teenager. His behaviour... He got drunk and messed up his bedroom. We never spoke to them after that."

Dimitri smiled. "And now, all of a sudden, you have an African American tracing his *Welsh* roots on a ruined farm, only a stone's throw from Andy Lock's compound on the mountain. He arrives in his Jaguar very soon after the incident, and two Japanese ladies are expected by you today." Dimitri watched Ellis absorb this. "And do you really think Russian Intelligence Service would be wasting our time talking to you here, now, if it wasn't a serious matter?"

"But the internet," Wyn said feebly.

The Russian shook his head, reached inside his jacket and produced an envelope. "Mister Ellis, I am GRU. I am not a madman, I am a professional and so are the people I take orders from. Your guest house has always been promoted. The KGB made sure it was. GRU continued to do so." He handed over a photograph. "Do you recognise this?"

Wyn looked at it. "I'm not sure. It looks like a compound."

"The same compound in the charge of *Commander* Andrew Morris Lock, your neighbour. It was taken by a Kosmos satellite now monitoring what goes on there above ground."

"Above ground?"

Dimitri positioned another photograph in front of Wyn and pointed. "Do you see that?"

"Yes."

"It is a steel door in the rock face at Lock's compound. It was renewed two years ago. The tunnels beyond it go deep underground and out below the sea. It contains highly exotic technology."

"Good God."

"Indeed," the Russian agreed, now returning the photographs to his pocket. "If Commander Lock and his team are doing what I think, then they must succeed. This is essential. We must detect both those who would interfere and those who might be sent to help."

"And what if Caycey Jones *is* here to interfere, not help?"

"Either way we need to know. Same goes for the Japanese ladies, though they may be of less concern."

"And then?"

The Russian smiled. "You are worried we might kill Jones, yes?"

"Yes, exactly."

"We would do no such thing. Such an act would be pointless and barbaric. Killing him would have the same outcome as his discovery of what is going on there, if Jones is an *enemy* that is."

"And how exactly can I help?"

Dimitri patted his briefcase. "This is for you," he said. "And this is what you are going to do. Listen carefully."

-o-

Kyle crossed the bridge near his gran's and headed in the direction of the safe house.

There, the mud-spattered 4x4 was parked where it had been reversed to the garage door. Kyle passed it and hesitated on the lawn. He looked at the shed at the bottom of the garden, then seemed to make up his mind. He went to the kitchen door at the rear of the house. After taking a deep breath, Kyle knocked.

It was Emily Norton who opened the door. She was wearing a dressing gown and had a towel wrapped around her hair. "Good morning, Kyle," she greeted. "Is there something you need?" It was polite, friendly.

"I was wondering if Mister Lock was here."

109

Norton smiled and turned towards the kitchen.

Lock appeared. Compared to Norton, who moved out of sight, Lock looked tired and grubby in his work clothes at the doorframe. His chin was covered in thick stubble. He greeted the young man with a simple nod and a smile. "Kyle, you okay?"

"I've got some news, sort of," Kyle told him nervously. "It might be important."

Lock considered this and studied the young man's face. "You'd better come in then." He stepped aside at the door to allow Kyle to pass, which Kyle did with some trepidation.

Inside the kitchen, Kyle saw that Norton was now seated at the table with Hardcastle. They were eating. Hardcastle raised a hand as he chewed. "Yo, Kyle."

"Yo," Kyle answered feebly.

"Have a seat," Lock said in a familiar tone as he closed the back door. "Do you want some breakfast? We've got scrambled eggs, toast. How about some bacon?"

"No thanks," Kyle answered.

"Tea? Coffee?"

"Very kind of you, Mister Lock, but I'm okay, really, thanks." Kyle sat down uneasily opposite Norton and Hardcastle. He glanced at the closed French doors behind them.

Lock slid onto a chair at the head of the table and leaned forward on his elbows. "Tell me about this *news* of yours," he prompted, alert eyes looking directly into Kyle's.

The young man glanced at Norton and Hardcastle, before turning to Lock with an alarmed, questioning expression.

"It's fine," Lock said. "Anything you want to tell me, you can say in front of these people."

Still nervous, Kyle shrugged and accepted it. "It's the Scousers," he said. "They've been nosing around."

"Where exactly?" Lock asked, remaining casual.

"Around the village, knocking on doors, asking questions. They came to my gran's last night. They're looking for one of their mates, a guy called Jampox. He's gone missing."

Lock sipped from a mug. "Why would this be important to us here?"

"I never told them," Kyle answered, "but I saw him a couple of days ago. He was after me in a black car. Sharon told them I had their money, but..."

"Go on," Lock coaxed. Norton stopped eating. She and Hardcastle, who continued chewing, were listening with noticeable interest.

"Well, here's the thing," Kyle continued. "I doubled back on him and came through your garden, Mister Lock. I went over the back fence then down the Bonks to the beach path. I lost him easily."

"Well done," Lock said. "Is that it?"

"Bonks?" Norton queried.

"Local word for the sand dunes," Lock told her before returning his attention to Kyle. "Is that it?" he repeated softly.

"No," Kyle said. "There was a lot of chatter last night on party."

Lock frowned. "Party?"

"Xbox social," Kyle told him.

"And?"

"Someone thinks they saw Jampox's car parked outside here about the same time I got away from him. He must have seen me cut through here."

Lock shrugged. "And apart from us now, you haven't told anyone you saw him, not even your friends?"

"No, they all gab too much. They'd grass me out without thinking."

"So, what's the problem?" Lock asked. "What if he did park by here for a short while? He certainly didn't come to the house. Maybe he decided you weren't that important to him and just went away."

Kyle nodded, showing some relief, but retained some concern as he looked at Lock. "Thing is," he said, "one of my mates told me Bibby Libby was talking to Crazy Box when she went for a walk to the Magraps."

"Excuse me," Norton interrupted, leaning forward. "This is so interesting but I'm lost on Crazy Box and Magraps. Could you decode, please? *Bibby Libby*, I assume, is just a nickname?"

111

"No, that's her real name, I think," Kyle told her.

Lock said, "Real name is Elin Lewis. She's a teenager. Crazy Box, as the kids call him, lives along the lane to the forestry. Real name is Hefin Gwynedd and he has a thing about old television sets, but I don't know Magraps." He turned to Kyle.

"You cut to the left a few yards the other side of the forestry gate," Kyle explained. "Magraps is a place with a load of dead trees. Tons of mushrooms grow there. Some of my mates eat them to get high and chill. Bibby Libby says she can see angels when she eats them."

"What did Hefin tell Bibby that's so important?" Lock asked patiently.

"He said he saw a black car going to the forest on the mountain. He said the windows were really tinted." Now Kyle appeared increasingly nervous.

"And?" Lock prompted, still patient.

"He said a few minutes later you went past in a truck, with a big clock on the back. Then your car with you people in it."

"Did he see Jampox?" Lock asked.

"I don't think so," Kyle answered. "The windows were so tinted I don't think they're legal. I only just recognised Jampox inside the car. But that's the same car, Mister Lock."

"I can understand your concern," Lock said, before turning to a wide-eyed Hardcastle who had a forkful of bacon hovering in a frozen position between his plate and mouth. "Get the photographs, please," Lock instructed.

Norton's hands were on the table, palms down. She had a fixed smile on her face.

Hardcastle looked baffled. "Photographs?"

"Of the clock," Lock said patiently. "I think Kyle would be interested to see them."

"Oh, the clock, of course," Hardcastle said. He put the fork down, spilling its contents onto the table by his plate, then quickly got up and hurried through the French doors, leaving them open behind him.

112

Kyle was now able to see into the next room. Multiple laptops glowed with flashing indicators and brightly coloured bar charts on the tables in there.

"You monitoring telecoms stuff here, Mister Lock?" Kyle asked.

"Yes, telecoms," Lock answered. "That's what we do here."

"And antiques," Kyle said helpfully.

"That's a sort of hobby of mine," Lock told him. "It's not just work-work here. We have to live as well. And us older people have fun and hobbies too."

Hardcastle hurried back into the kitchen, closing the French doors behind him. He slid a sheaf of glossy A4 prints in front of Lock before returning to his seat. Lock's face displayed brief irritation towards the man before the prints were slid over to Kyle.

"These are Mister Hardcastle's photographs. It's his hobby." Lock gave a prompting look to Hardcastle.

"Uh, yes, photography," Hardcastle said. "F-stops, depth of field, composition, that's me, I love it."

Kyle looked at the colourful prints. A grandfather clock stood like a dwarfed monolith surrounded by pine trees. The photos showed a variety of angles of this. "Wow, these are really good," he told Hardcastle. "Never seen anything like that before."

Hardcastle perked up at this. "Well, that was the point. I wanted to do something different and, you know, convey that, uh, clocks are different to trees."

Norton briefly looked sideways at the man but managed to keep a calm face. "*Different* to trees?"

Hardcastle seemed hurt by this.

"Juxtaposition," Kyle announced, looking at the photographs. "They're good, really good."

"Yeh, that's it, juxtaposition," Hardcastle agreed, grinning with enthusiasm. "Great word, Kyle. Thank you."

"Great word indeed," Lock said. "Don't let this young man fool you. He is extremely intelligent. How many A levels, Kyle?"

Kyle's face turned a bright red. "No, Mister Lock, please."

"Well he has seven," Lock said. "Four of them A stars. He could get a scholarship to Oxford or Cambridge just like that," he added, snapping his fingers.

"I prefer working for you," Kyle said.

"Next year, you go to university," Lock told him in a fatherly tone. "Anyway, we were going up there to move a few pieces of telecoms equipment around with the truck. Mister Hardcastle thought it was a great opportunity for him to turn an idea into reality with the clock and the trees, so we were happy to help him, weren't we, Miss Norton?"

"Absolutely," she agreed.

"I didn't see any other cars up there though, never mind a black compact with tinted windows," Lock said. "Did either of you?"

"No," Norton answered.

"Me neither," Hardcastle added.

"So," Lock continued to Kyle, "maybe this Jampox individual went that way hoping it was a shortcut to the other side of the mountain. Maybe his satnav fooled him, as they frequently do."

"Must have done," Kyle agreed, half nodding as though this hadn't really solved the puzzle for him.

"And the important thing is you don't tell anyone you saw him," Lock emphasised. "Not ever. We can't have the Scousers nosing around here."

"Absolutely never," Kyle confirmed. "Not a word from me, Mister Lock, you know that."

Lock smiled. "You going to do some gardening and keep an eye out for us today?"

Kyle smiled happily. "Absolutely, Mister Lock."

-o-

Gwenda Evans sat back in her chair as she began reading the next file from a stack of them on the trellis tables.

Most of the wartime equipment had now been removed from the tables, but the laptop remained. Its display still echoed in the glassy wall behind it.

"This one's all about you," Gwenda said to the German naval officer's remains. The skeleton was still seated on a chair. Its empty eye sockets seemed to be staring at her.

Two of those who had died with him, the civilian and British navy officer, now reclined neatly against the chamber side wall. Equally dead radio transmitters were lined up close to them.

Dwarfed by his surroundings in the circular chamber, Caycey Jones had his eyes fixed on the laptop screen. He looked like the proverbial man meditating a kettle that never boils. High above, the giant echo in the ceiling repeated the same parade of *Installing software* messages. Jones sighed, rubbed his eyes, then adjusted his position on the fold-out chair, which creaked.

Behind him, Banes slept on a bivouac mat on the floor. The scientist emitted a feeble snore, chewed at air, then turned onto his side. As he did so, the laptop beeped.

A dialogue box flashed: *Ready to Send*. The ceiling echo announced the same thing.

Jones shook Banes, who sat up with a startled expression.

"We're good to go," Jones said. "You'd better tell Missus Evans. She can stand at the entrance and watch if she wants. Best if you stay there as well."

"Understood," Banes acknowledged. Now alert, he commenced an easy jog towards the entrance.

Jones observed him for a little while before turning his attention back to the laptop. He shifted the mouse until the cursor hovered over a button.

The American then stood up and watched Banes. The man was now going through the opening in the chamber wall. Jones checked his watch.

Banes reappeared. Then Gwenda joined him to stand at the threshold. Both raised a hand in the air.

"Here goes then," Jones said. He turned back to the table, reached for the mouse button and clicked.

The dialogue box stayed as it was for a couple of seconds. Then the *Ready to Send* changed to *Sending* and the box vanished from the screen. Jones sat down again and waited, but only briefly this time.

With a quiet hum, the three cannon-shaped objects moved into life in the chamber centre. In unison, like giant robots on a production line, their barrels rapidly tilted and aimed towards a point in the domed ceiling.

A circular area in the field of stars then became fluid as though zooming into some distant zone, stars flashing past and out of the circle. When it stopped, a single star shone in the centre of that area.

Overlaid graphics appeared: strange, rune-like symbols in green, violet and blue. Yellow dotted lines marched around the star. One of the violet symbols rotated, moved to a point in the orbit and started flashing repeatedly. The image zoomed in on this.

The cannons adjusted. Tangible beams of light stretched from each of them to touch the violet symbol.

A new message appeared on the laptop screen: *Message sent... Listening for response.* The strange beams from the cannons vanished.

"That's it, I think," Banes said at the entrance. He and Gwenda watched the cannons return to their original position.

"Now what do we do?" Gwenda asked.

"We wait for a response," Banes answered.

In the distance, Jones stood up, faced them, and raised both arms in the air.

-o-

The late afternoon sun was beginning to dip behind low cloud when a yellow Toyota compact came purring along smooth tarmac. It was following a small cargo truck on the Llŷn Peninsula spine road.

The satnav in the Toyota's dashboard announced something in Japanese, but the young woman driving it kept her eyes focussed on the cargo truck ahead.

A black Audi overtook her, darting into the space behind the truck to avoid an oncoming car. Once this had passed, the Audi pulled out again and raced past the truck at speed.

The Toyota driver checked her mirror. She sighed when she saw an impatient queue of cars behind hers.

The cargo truck now signalled it was turning left. At the same time, the satnav female voice announced: *anata no mokutekichi ni tōtatsu shimashita*. The Japanese woman tapped the signal lever, changed gear and slowed down.

Faded *Closed* signs flanked the ramp to the disused service station. The truck turned onto a lane at the top of this and drove around the back of the largest building.

Wearing a blue boiler suit, Lock was waiting by the open roller door. He waved the cargo truck in. He did the same for the yellow Toyota. Lock darted swiftly inside. The roller door came down.

Both vehicle engines shut off inside the derelict service building. A young woman climbed out of the truck. The other one got out of the Toyota.

"*Hajimemashite*," Lock greeted them.

Both women bowed. Lock bowed back, rather awkwardly, eyes glancing at each of their faces as he straightened up.

The one from the truck smiled. "Good afternoon, Mister Lock. I am Miiko and this is Kikuko."

The second woman said something in Japanese. Miiko laughed, nodded, and said something in the same language in response.

Lock raised his eyebrows, puzzled.

Miiko laughed again. "We think you look very distinguished."

"Very kind," Lock said, but his expression remained serious. "First you must check in at the bed and breakfast house. Do you need directions?"

"No, we are fine," Miiko answered.

"Tell them you are going out sightseeing, or something, and will be late back. Make sure they give you a key to the house, then return here. Do you need to eat?"

"We have food in the truck for later," Miiko answered.

Lock checked his watch. "Try to be back within an hour. We're running late."

Both women bowed. "*Hai.*"

-o-

Wyn Ellis had returned from Liverpool. He was at his binoculars, peering in the direction of the mountain. Mair stood at the bay window.

"The Japanese ladies are nearly an hour late," Mair announced as she checked her watch.

Wyn lifted his head, then moved closer to his window to look along the driveway next door.

"That English lady and the Hardcastle man have come out the back," he said. "They're getting into a white van." He shifted his head to look at the front lawn next door. "Kyle is still gardening. God knows what he's doing. Seems to be sifting stones out of the borders. He's very alert. It's like he's on lookout duty."

Mair Ellis sighed. "Is this our life now? Spying on our neighbours?"

Wyn frowned. "We've been doing that for years."

"Not like this, like it's real. I don't like it."

"Me neither," Wyn agreed. "Oh, here they go."

Mair adjusted her position. She saw the white van pull out onto the road. Kyle waved at it; he spotted Mair in the window and waved at her as well.

"Oh," Mair said, stepping back a pace. "The cheeky thing."

"He's just being friendly," Wyn warned. "Wave back."

Mair did so, but Kyle had returned his attention to the border out there.

Kyle smiled to himself as he adjusted his knees on the lawn. He continued poking soil meaninglessly with a hand fork. He noticed that the light was beginning to dim in the sky, then heard an approaching car. He stood up, maintaining his gardener act by studying the flower border.

The yellow Toyota pulled to a halt at the kerb next door. Kyle glanced at it before returning his gaze downwards, twiddling the fork in his gloved hands.

Two young Japanese women got out of the car. They were talking to each other in their own language. Kyle raised his eyebrows at this but could not prevent himself from looking in their direction.

They towed their suitcases up the B&B driveway, still chatting but now looking directly at Kyle, and exchanging glances with each other.

Miiko smiled. "Hi," she called over the wall to Kyle.

Kyle blushed, but he managed to open his lips. "Hi," he responded, embarrassed.

Kikuko scolded Miiko, but the woman laughed before turning to wave at Kyle, who feebly waved back.

Averting his gaze, Kyle walked up the side of the safe house. Moving faster when he got to the rear, he crossed the lawn, went inside the shed, and lifted his mobile.

"Mister Lock," he said excitedly. "Two women just arrived next door. They're Chinese, I think, or Korean. Uh, no, correction, Japanese… definitely… I think."

Miiko and Kikuko halted with their suitcases in the B&B hallway. Mair Ellis closed the front door. Wyn Ellis appeared from the adjoining lounge.

"This is Miiko and Kikuko," Mair announced. She had a fixed smile. "This is Mister Ellis, my husband."

They bowed politely to him.

Wyn Ellis began to do the same, then hesitated and halted himself. "Pleased to meet you," he said.

"Now then," Mair Ellis announced. She spoke in that slow, accentuated and raised voice indicative of communication with foreigners. "You are a long way from home. Do your mothers and fathers know where you are?"

Miiko translated this for Kikuko, who responded with one word in Japanese.

"I am twenty-four years old," Miiko said, smiling at Mair. "So is Kikuko. We are postgraduate art students, but our parents do know where we are."

"But you look so young," Mair Ellis responded.

"Thank you," Miiko said, lifting her suitcase. "May we see our room? We need to go out immediately."

Wyn Ellis was putting on a black coat in the hallway when Mair returned from upstairs. "They are so polite," she told him, "but they look like schoolgirls."

"All young people look younger than they really are at our age," Wyn said.

Now Mair noticed his coat. "Where are you going?"

Wyn Ellis winked at her. "I'm popping to see Frank, but I won't be long."

Mair was puzzled by this and was about to say something when Wyn put a finger to his lips. Mair nodded with silent understanding and some obvious alarm. "*Be careful*," she whispered.

Mair stared at the door, as though stunned after he had gone out. Pulling herself together, she returned to the lounge and hurried to the bay window. Outside, the car pulled out onto the road. Mair clasped her hands together, thumbs twiddling nervously as she watched the car go out of sight.

She was then startled by the reappearance of the two young women at the door to the hallway. They were now wearing identical green parkas. Both had cameras hanging from their necks.

"We are going out now," Miiko announced.

Mair composed herself. "I hope you have a nice time. Are you going anywhere interesting?"

"To the Students' Union in Bangor," Miiko answered. "We could be very late coming back. Is that okay?"

"That's fine dear," Mair said. "Just make sure you have your key."

Miiko patted her pocket. "I have it. We will try to be quiet."

Mair Ellis followed them to the front door and watched as they walked down the driveway and got into the yellow Toyota. She waved. They waved back.

She started looking fretful again.

-o-

The Ellis car was parked behind some bushes in a lay-by on the main road. Wyn Ellis leaned over the steering wheel, watching the turn-off to Amharfarn.

A few cars passed in both directions, then the yellow Toyota appeared. It pulled out onto the main road, headed east. An express bus came along from the west.

Chippings popping from its tyres, the Ellis car pulled out of the lay-by and followed the bus.

At the wheel, Wyn Ellis tried to shrink into his seat as he passed the disused service station on the other side of the road. The yellow Toyota was making its way up the access ramp.

Eyebrows raised, he checked his rear-view mirror as he continued following the bus.

Inside the disused service station, the yellow Toyota stood in one of the old MOT bays next to the Jaguar, the Toyota engine ticking as it cooled. The sound of a vehicle door closing echoed from the other side of the garage.

Emily Norton moved to the roller door and waited by the chains. Lock positioned himself by the 4x4. He watched Miiko and Kikuko put their parkas into the cargo truck cabin. In unison, they donned black baseball caps and slid equally black sunglasses onto their faces.

The sunglasses were huge, making their faces seem almost featureless. They nodded at Lock before climbing into the truck.

Outside, the roller door ascended, Norton dimly visible in the dying light as she hauled down on the chains.

The 4x4 pulled out and halted a short distance along the access lane, engine idling. The cargo truck then reversed out with a muffled *beep, beep, beep* of its caution alarm. Gears crunched. It then moved forward to the 4x4 and halted behind it. Hardcastle pulled out of the garage in a white van.

All three vehicles put on their running lights when they joined the main road.

In a field a couple of hundred yards to the east, where he was hidden by the hedge next to a farmer's gate, Wyn Ellis lowered his pocket binoculars.

FOUR

Hefin Gwynedd leaned over his gate along the narrow lane leading to the forestry track. He sighed, glared into the bowl of the pipe he was smoking, then tested it with his thumb before reaching down to tap the ash out against his boot heel.

Dusk turned towards darkness. A blackbird sang its lullaby from a nearby tree.

Pero cocked an ear. Chin resting on his outstretched paws, the dog was lying under the television set display table. He watched his master carefully for any sign the man might be about to move from the gate.

Hefin opened a tobacco pouch but returned it to his pocket as lights appeared along the lane.

Andy Lock's 4x4 drove past, its headlights dazzling him.

The cargo truck was next, but this slowed down for the uneven surface near the gate. The old man's eyes widened when he saw two small figures illuminated by dashboard lights in its cab. They wore baseball hats and had what appeared to him to be huge black eyes.

He shook his head in disbelief, tracking the vehicle as it pulled away. The white van passed next, its driver waving cheekily at him. Hefin raised a hand in a dismissive response.

"Did you see that?" Hefin asked Pero, who had moved from under the table to sit beside him. But the dog seemed more concerned about whether at last his master was going to retire for the evening. Pero glanced at the table, pricked his ears towards Hefin and issued a soft whine.

Hefin shrugged at this and turned to the old television sets. Lifting one of them with a groan, he carried it towards the farmhouse. Pero ran ahead to the open door where he turned and waited.

"Men in black," the old man said. He teetered with the television towards Pero. "Small ones driving a truck."

Pero uttered a friendly bark then wisely got out of the way.

"Well maybe not," his master admitted, puffing with the weight on the doorstep. "But they were strangers for sure."

He put the TV down on the stone floor in a wide passage leading directly to the back of the farmhouse.

The television joined a congregation of others along the wall, some stacked on top of each other: *Rediffusion, Telefusion, Pye* and several other ancient models. One had a dark-pink frame around its almost circular screen.

"Getting too old for this," he told the dog. "I'll have to hollow out a couple of duff ones for display."

Pero wagged his tail and followed Hefin to the back door. This opened onto an outhouse. It was lit by naked light bulbs. The connecting cables were strung across exposed roof timbers.

On one side of this former dairy, stone troughs and drainers were cluttered with dust-covered television parts, tubes and valves. A coiled aerial cable was looped over a rusted water pump.

As the man and dog entered, two hens fluttered across the interior and landed on the closed lower half of a stable door. They clucked their alarm at a disinterested Pero, before escaping outside.

"Go round them up into the henhouse," the old man ordered as he opened the lower half of the door. The dog flattened its ears and darted out.

Hefin went to a corner, where he tilted a sack of dog biscuits to pour some into an upturned milk-pail lid. He then went outside.

It was getting darker fast as he approached the henhouse. Pero guarded its open door. Hens clucked inside.

The man counted with a finger as he squinted at the gloom inside. "Is this all of them?" he asked Pero, who wagged his tail. "Could have sworn I had more yesterday."

Hefin closed the door on his hens, then jumped, startled, whites of his eyes gleaming when a voice rang out behind him.

"*Hox hot iar hensh?*"

Ventriloquist Jack was standing there in the twilight, hands stuffed into his boiler suit pockets, glowing cigarette end sticking out of the corner of his closed lips.

"Jesus Christ," Hefin complained. "Why do you keep doing that?"

Jack grinned thinly, eyes narrowed to impart an air of unapologetic enigma. "Fine guard dog you are," he said to Pero. "Go get your food."

Pero ran off to the house.

"Where did you park?" Hefin asked.

"Inside the gate. I moved the table but don't worry, I'll put it back when I leave. I brought the other televisions inside as well."

"Did you bring it?"

Jack pointed down to a sack at his feet. "It's heavy."

"Well you can carry it then," Hefin Gwynedd said. He marched off up the sloping cobbled yard towards a barn.

A generator ticking over became audible as they approached. The old man went to a waist-height timber lean-to attached to the barn and hunched over to open its double doors.

The generator inside was a strange affair. The engine and dynamo occupied one end. An exhaust pipe connected the engine to a tank at the other end. Clear tubes fed liquid from the tank to the engine.

Hefin lifted out a bucket and handed it to Ventriloquist Jack, who had to put down whatever he was carrying in the sack to accept it.

"Put some water in that," Hefin said.

Jack hunted with his eyes, then spotted a leaking tap along the side of the barn.

The old man had a funnel ready when Jack returned with the bucket. He poured some water into the generator tank then replaced the cap.

"How much water does it go through for you?" Jack asked him.

"Couple of pints a day," the old man answered. "What vexes me is having to use the metered 'lectric for the lights in the house to avoid suspicion. Pension is getting stretched these days."

"What about your heating?"

"Separate circuit, wired to the jenny," he said proudly as he opened the barn door.

Jack picked up the sack and went inside the barn. He smiled as the lights came on. "Copper, copper everywhere, not a bloody ounce to spare."

The interior looked like a cross between a steampunk museum and a mad scientist's lab in a 1950s B-movie.

Overhead, white loop insulators fastened to the timber beams connected a lattice of thick, naked copper wire to a suspended pattern of toroidal coils intricately wound from thinner copper.

An industrial gantry stood at the far end of the barn. It supported a huge, similarly doughnut-shaped coil facing the centre.

A workbench along one side housed a range of old and new television sets, the newest of which, with a flat screen, was wired up to four computer cases and a keyboard and mouse workstation.

The other side housed a cage constructed of timbers and fence mesh in an old calf pen. A green-and-yellow earth cable was clipped to the fencing, the other end sunk into the dirt floor outside it.

But it was the object illuminated by spotlights in the centre of the barn that dominated. A roughly stippled, circular fibreglass bowl sat on a timber supporting frame on the ground. It looked like some lunatic's home-made communal bath, and big enough to seat half a dozen men. Shiny copper toroidal coils were fixed around the underside at even distances, like portholes in a ship.

Ventriloquist Jack swung the sack into the bowl, resting it on a mess of cables and boxes containing printed circuits in there. He climbed in after it.

"You'll never guess what I saw ten minutes ago," the old man said.

"What?"

"Andy Lock went up the forestry with a small convoy."

"And?"

126

"There was a cargo truck. It was being driven by small men wearing black hats and sunglasses."

"Two Japanese women arrived in the village," Jack said as he removed yet another copper coil from his sack. "They're staying at Mair and Wyn's."

"How do you know?"

"Kyle saw them, told his grandmother. She told Tom Grockle when she bought milk. Tom told me."

"Ah, so it was them in disguise, probably. Probably working undercover for Andy Lock up the mountain."

"Maybe," Ventriloquist Jack said. He attached the coil to something inside the fibreglass bath.

"They were definitely in a convoy," the old man said as his companion climbed out of the contraption. "Are we ready?"

"Yes."

"I wonder why it seems to work better here than your place?"

Jack shrugged. "Maybe it's the mountain. Maybe it's just the way we set it up here, or fairies in the woods. I *don't know*. How many times you going to ask me? Next, you'll be asking me yet again how we know what to do."

Hefin Gwynedd grinned and tapped the side of his head. "Well, sure I know that. The mountain's been talking to me all my life."

"You and me and half the village," Jack confirmed. "Nice English lady called Emily Norton working with Andy Lock. Only been here a couple of days, but I'm pretty sure she's tuned in already."

"Gifted like us then."

"Nah," Jack retorted gently. "I'm the one who's gifted, you're just touched."

Pero returned and sat near the men, eyeing the fibreglass bath with suspicion.

"We going to give it a try then?" the old man asked Jack.

"Five seconds only," he answered, then headed for the fence mesh cage. Hefin Gwynedd snapped his fingers for Pero to follow him.

Two insulated circuit breakers were fixed to a short wooden plank bolted to the inside. Jack pondered them briefly with a stopwatch in

127

his hand. He looked out through the mesh and pointed at the strange bath. "You clear on what we're doing?" he asked the old man.

"Five seconds."

"On both. And remember to observe."

"Of course."

"No, not just watching," Jack said patiently. "Active observation. Remember Heisenberg and Tesla. *Think* it up, and both circuits."

Hefin adjusted his position next to the circuit breakers in the cage. "Think it up, sure, but why do we need both circuits?"

On the ground between them, Pero cocked an ear and looked up at Ventriloquist Jack as though also interested in an answer.

Jack sighed. "Because we are inducing the primer tonight, the coil I just fitted inside the test bed."

"Primer?"

"It's a bit like the special coal oil I gave you for the generator. The oil doesn't burn but it tells the water vapour how to behave. It's like a memory. The coil here is a bit like that. It will get quantum packets and remember them if it works. But we need the bigger ones around the barn to get the packets in there."

"Way over my head," the old man said.

"Remember what I told you," Jack coaxed. "The universe and how it behaves is like an information system. Just like the water in my generators, we are telling the coils *how* to behave in the universe and then they will remember."

"Okay," the old man said, raising his eyebrows with irritation, "so let's do it then."

Ventriloquist Jack lifted his stopwatch. "On my mark... Go."

Hefin Gwynedd closed both circuit breakers.

The coils arranged around the barn each emitted a faint blue glow. They beamed towards the bath-like contraption, which abruptly rose, trailing cables a few feet into the air. It remained there briefly until Ventriloquist Jack said "Off" and the blue glow vanished. Then the bath slowly descended back onto its timber supports.

In the cage with the men, Pero uttered a short bark, as though in amazement.

Outside, in the dark on the farmland lane, a Range Rover

approached Hefin's farm gate. It slowed almost to a halt before accelerating towards the forestry track. The glare of its headlights lit up the trees ahead.

-o-

Wyn Ellis moved his face away from the binoculars and turned to Mair, who was peering out through a crack between the drawn curtains in the bay window. The lounge was dimly illuminated by a table lamp.

"Why don't you go to bed," Wyn suggested.

"It's only half ten," Mair said. "I want to see what happens, especially with Caycey Jones."

"His e-mail said he would be late, but not how late."

Mair Ellis shrugged. "Have you seen anything else up there?"

Wyn peered through the binoculars again. "Nothing moving for over an hour now."

"Well," Mair said from the bay window, "I definitely saw Andy Lock's car, that cargo truck you saw, and the white van from next door going past outside. Then I saw their headlights turning towards the compound a bit later. But I never saw a fourth vehicle."

"You might have been looking through the binoculars when it came along the road. I only just got back when I saw one on its own up there."

"That one might have been somebody from the village," Mair suggested.

"Not this time of night," Wyn disagreed. "And anyway, it's for sure that our Japanese ladies are working with Andy Lock. You should have seen it at the old service station. It was a well-oiled operation to move people and equipment around in secret."

"Not so well oiled for it to be kept a secret from us though," Mair said. "But Caycey Jones is still a mystery. Why don't *you* go to bed, you must be tired?"

Wyn adjusted the focus on the binoculars. "No way I could sleep right now. And anyway, as soon as I see them heading back, I'll jump in the car and go to my observation point."

..*ion point*? Now you're even talking like a spy."

..y yn Ellis sighed. "I'd like to say this is the most fun I've had in a long time. But it isn't fun. It's serious, and we haven't been trained for this sort of thing."

Mair Ellis glanced uneasily at him before returning her face to the crack in the curtains. She squinted through it, her face marked with determination.

-o-

The Japanese ladies' cargo truck was parked in the compound, tail end a few feet from the closed steel door. The halogen lamp was off. The compound was dark, quiet, apart from a faint rustle from the surrounding trees.

In stark contrast, the work tunnel inside the mountain was brightly lit and noisy. A high-pitched machine noise flooded the enclosed spaces. It sounded like a giant dentist's drill: a whirring of steel against stone or something equally hard.

All tensed up, Lock was seated at the workbench. Studying one of the laptops, he gritted his teeth when the noise pitched higher and louder. *Walls Have Ears*, the mildewed poster facing him warned. The noise got worse. Lock clamped hands over his own ears as though heeding this advice.

A little further along the tunnel, a sheet of polythene was draped across the entrance to the electrical chamber. It was lit up like a blurred cinema screen, billowing shadows instead of images, and that nerve-shredding noise from behind it as a soundtrack.

On the other side, the air swirled with red dust. Kikuko was engulfed in a violent cloud of it. Wearing protective clothing, the small woman was hunched over some sort of workbench in there. This had bricks lined up on its top, with a steel bar clamping them into position. Kikuko advanced a disc cutter along a guide track. Spewing dust and noise, it shaved long tiles off the brick faces.

130

Miiko was similarly attired with goggles, face mask and a hard hat. Crouched over a pile of bricks, she was using a small hammer to chip mortar off a single brick. When this was clean, she placed it on a second pile.

More plastic sheets shielded the banks of electrical equipment here. But the half-demolished brickwork and the resultant gap leading to the deeper tunnels remained exposed. Floodlights illuminated the chamber, but not the old miners' tunnel to the deep underground.

Now three faint lights swayed unevenly side to side as someone approached from the darkness down there.

Kikuko completed cutting the final brick in the row then switched off the machine.

Banes, Gwenda Evans and Caycey Jones arrived in their silvery suits and miners' helmets. Miiko and Kikuko bowed. Banes bowed back. Gwenda Evans placed a cloth over her mouth and nose in the airborne dust as she also returned the courtesy.

"Getting ready for our photograph, I see," Caycey Jones said to the Japanese women. "*Hajimemashite*," he greeted formally as he bowed. "I am so pleased you could get here. We are honoured to have your skills at our service."

Miiko's voice was muffled by her face mask. "Thank you," she said, before indicating with her outstretched arm for the three of them to go through. Her mannerisms suggested she wanted them out of the way quickly.

Andy Lock was peering from the work tunnel. He held the plastic sheet aside ready for the returning trio.

The Japanese women stood back as the group passed. They trod carefully to avoid machinery and steel components that were new to the electrical chamber.

Lock and the others moved with some haste when they got out into the compound. Now normally attired, Gwenda Evans held open the white van's rear door. Caycey Jones climbed in.

"There's a blanket in there if you need to hide yourself," Gwenda said.

Jones sat on the floor of the van and drew the blanket over his shoulders. "Do you think Norton will be okay alone down there with Hardcastle?"

"She'll have to be," Gwenda answered. "But I think she's professional enough to keep it together."

"Norton seems the sensitive type," Jones said.

Gwenda shrugged. "Let's get you back to civilisation." She closed the door.

Lock and Banes were already in the 4x4 nearby. Lock checked his mirror, turned the starter and switched on the headlights. The 4x4 pulled forward onto the tree-flanked lane. The white van followed it downhill.

The security gate opened to allow the vehicles through, closing immediately behind them. Headlights illuminated the curving lane descending ahead.

Lock frowned behind the wheel and applied the brake. The 4x4 ground to a halt. His headlights illuminated a silver Range Rover blocking the exit onto the main forestry track. Lock waited, observing, eyes alert.

The Range Rover sat there lifelessly for a moment, its lights and engine off. A gust of wind blew pine needles from nearby trees as the mysterious car's front doors opened. Two young men got out. They were the same individuals who had paid an unwelcome night visit to Kyle at his gran's. They paired up alongside the Range Rover, faced the 4x4 and just stood there.

Lock cursed under his breath. "Stay here," he told Banes then got out, leaving the 4x4 engine running. Lock walked into the headlights' glare and approached to within ten feet of the two men. He held up an identity card. "This is government property. Authorised vehicles only up here, so you'll need to go back that way." He pointed in the general direction of the village.

"We're looking for a black Corsa," the first Scouser said in his heavy Liverpool accent. "Have you seen it up here?"

"No," Lock answered. "Now if you don't mind, you need to move your car and go back that way. You're blocking us in."

In the back of the white van, Caycey Jones peeked over as

Gwenda Evans did something with a bag from the passenger seat. Craning his neck, he could barely make out the 4x4 and the steam rising from its exhaust up ahead. He then saw that Gwenda was screwing a silencer onto a pistol. "Put that damn thing away," Jones said in a low growl.

"Sorry, sir," she whispered. "Looks like a couple of druggies could be out for trouble up ahead. They've blocked our way."

"You are *not* to shoot them," Jones warned.

"It's just a precaution. Wait here and keep out of sight."

Gwenda switched off the headlights and got out of the van. Holding the silenced pistol behind her back, she moved behind the 4x4, adjusting slightly to keep out of its exhaust fumes. Concealed by darkness, she then edged sideways, halted, and watched ahead.

One of the Range Rover's rear passenger doors opened. A tall, mature man got out. He wore a tailored navy-blue coat with a burgundy scarf draped over his shoulders. "Get back in the car," he ordered the two Scousers. They obeyed immediately.

The man in the coat then walked towards Lock, who was still holding up his identity card. Unsighted by the headlights, the man moved along the side of the track to get closer. Lock turned to face him. Now both could see each other in the 4x4 headlights.

The man leaned his head forward to study Lock's identity card. His greying hair was neatly cropped, his face perfectly groomed to match his haughty air. "Security Service," he said, raising his eyebrows at the card. His accent was of a highly affected English upper-class sort. "Can I show you mine?" He reached slowly inside his coat.

Lock looked back towards the white van and raised his hand in that direction. Gwenda could not be seen over there.

The man feigned an expression of surprise. "No guns here, I promise," he called out towards the van in his heavy accent, the word *promise* sounding more like *pwomise*. "We're all on the same side here."

Lock kept his hand up. The man pulled out two cards and held them for Lock to see.

"Not my real name, of course, but you can call me Burke," the

133

man said. "Real name has a title and a seat in the Lords, which I've never bothered with. But you can see the seniority here, old boy. SIS and Special Branch. Kind of trumps yours, don't you think?"

"So, you're a member of that so-exclusive club in Section D," Lock said, lowering his hand. "Big deal, what do you want?"

"Not much," Burke answered. "Two things, really simple things, but reassurance basically."

"And how can I provide you with that?"

"By telling me where the black Corsa and my man went to, for a start. And your absolute guarantee you are not muscling in on my business along the coast here."

"I have no idea what you are talking about."

Burke smiled, tilted his head back and stared as though looking down his nose. "Much as I hate to disturb your job as a security guard, but your department does have a service level agreement to fulfil for mine. The car was seen parked outside your house."

Lock stared back with neither a smile nor a sneer, blue eyes glinting in the headlights from the 4x4. "I can assure you," he said in a low, calm, resonating voice, "I have not seen your man or his car. He *might* have parked, who knows, but we never saw him and he didn't come to the house. And as for muscling in, I want nothing to do with your drugs trade. I go out in the boat once a month for you gangsters and I hand every ounce of it to your people."

Lock's eyes were angry as he continued. "You can keep it, finance terrorists, overthrow governments and do whatever the hell you and your corporate masters like with it but I never will and never have touched a filthy ounce of it. Is that reassurance enough for you?"

"No need to be impertinent, old boy," Burke said. "You need to know your place."

"Oh, I do," Lock answered. "And I know yours, with your airs and graces, Savile Row clothes and titles. You might walk the red carpets and hi de hi with the City toffs at their mayoral banquets, but you're nothing more than gangsters, all of you."

"You really don't want me as an enemy," Burke told him. "But I'll put it down this once to you being tired, it's late. And anyway, sticks and stones as they say."

"Why are *you* here?" Lock asked. "Seems to me you have plenty of minions, so isn't this man and his car a bit beneath you? And another thing, the guys in your trade never operate alone. But here *you* are looking, apparently, for *one* man. Why is that?"

"Well, that's simple, old boy. For precisely the reason you just touched upon. He set off into Wales *alone*, against the rules, delivered to all the distributors up to here, where *you* are and where, coincidentally, the trail vanishes. The car, *my* car actually, is spotted parked outside your place, and then coming up here where you do most of your security work. You can't blame a man for adding two and two together and wondering if he was maybe defecting to you, or something like that. I couldn't send my minions to talk to you about *that*, could I?"

"I'm sorry I can't help you," Lock said. "I don't know where your man went to. He has not defected to me. It's a ridiculous proposition. None of us saw him. And anyway, what's one man? You'll have dozens ready to take his place in Liverpool."

"But it's not that simple," Burke answered. "For one thing, he was carrying a lot of money in that car, some of it mine, by the time he got here. But more importantly, I want to be certain my future business in these parts is secure. So, here's the thing, Mister Lock. If you have any thought of creating your own sideline, think again. Am I making myself clear?"

Lock shook his head in exasperation. "Absolutely clear. Now I want *you* to be absolutely clear that I have no interest in any sort of sideline involving your shitty business. Get your car out of my way and *keep* out of my way, or your next shipment of heroin, cocaine or whatever it is will go to the bottom of the Irish Sea."

Burke glared at him for a moment then turned and headed for the Range Rover. "This isn't over," he called back. "I'll be keeping an eye on you." He opened the car door and then hesitated. "Oh, I almost forgot. There's just one more thing, the big elephant in the room so to speak. Seems you have a CIA chappie in the area." Burke smiled as he pointed beyond Lock. "I'm to accompany him when he inspects your little compound up there. So, I'll be seeing you tomorrow, old boy." He got into the car and slammed its door shut.

Lock clenched his fists behind his back as he watched them drive away. Gwenda Evans joined him, concern etched into her face.

"Unforgivable," Lock said. "I lost my temper."

-o-

Wyn Ellis hurried to his car on the driveway by the side of the house. He glanced up at the binoculars window to wave at Mair. Her silhouetted head was dimly visible there, moving side to side, agitated. Now she tapped at the glass. Wyn moved close enough to see that she was holding up three fingers.

He got into the car.

Nearer the mountain, Burke's silver Range Rover purred along the farmland lane, slowing by Hefin Gwynedd's gate, before accelerating towards the village. It slowed again as it passed the safe house beyond the village centre.

Crossing the bridge by Kyle's gran's a little later, Lock's 4x4 was immediately followed by the white van. They kept a constant speed as they too passed the safe house and B&B further on, headlights bobbing from bumps in the road.

The wind picked up, rustling the hazel trees along the hedgerows. A flash of lightning illuminated the mountainous horizon south of the coast.

Without warning, rain hammered at the main road. The Ellis car came to a halt and switched off its headlights. It reversed off the road, manoeuvred along a muddy track, and halted by an agricultural gate flanked by oak trees.

Wyn Ellis got out, stepping into mud. He approached the gate, which was padlocked, and started to climb. The downpour blasted him; his foot slipped, forehead bumping the top of the gate. With a quiet groan, and a better foothold this time, he managed to hoist himself over. There was a streak of dirt across his forehead when he hurried across the top of the field.

The Range Rover pulled out from the Amharfarn turn-off, windscreen wipers working at double speed.

A thoroughly drenched Wyn Ellis was fumbling with his pocket binoculars when he saw the car passing the disused service station. He ducked behind the hedge. Illuminating roadside trees, the headlights passed and sped away, heading east.

Still crouched in the rain, Wyn now turned to face the north-west. Two sets of lights were coming along the Amharfarn road. They were visible to him from their glow in the rain. He squinted through his binoculars, hissed, then tried to clear water from the lenses. Lightning flashed. Drenched and miserable, Wyn wiped his eyes. The dirt on his forehead streaked into them. He blinked, fumbled with the binoculars again, then cursed and gave up, stuck them in his pocket and peered over the hedge.

Lock's 4x4 pulled out onto the main road, closely followed by the white van. They turned off onto the ramp at the disused service station.

The roller door opened. Lightning flashed. Thunder accompanied the white van as it rolled inside.

Back at the B&B, Mair Ellis was nearly in tears. The table lamp was off, the lounge subsequently in darkness. Lightning flashed through a gap in the front window curtains. Rain hammered at the glass and thunder rumbled. Mair clutched a mobile phone to her breast as though hugging a loved one.

Out in spy territory, from his observation point, Wyn Ellis saw the Jaguar clearly lit up from an electrical flash in the sky. His guest's car was leaving the disused service station. Wyn gasped at this. Rain assaulted him. Thunder rumbled. Without further thought, he turned and hurried in the direction of his own car, water-logged shoes farting with every step he took.

Andy Lock put down *his* binoculars after he had watched the Ellis car turn onto the minor road to Amharfarn. He started the 4x4 engine and drove the vehicle to a position at the top of the ramp.

There was now enough of a gap for the white van to drive past. Its headlights went on as it joined the main road in pursuit of the Ellis car.

Lock reversed the 4x4 back to its hidden vantage point. He picked up his mobile phone and dialled. It connected immediately. "Yes, it's me... It was your male host. You were right."

Lightning forks streaked across the sky to the west, turning the rain hitting the windscreen into daggers and splashes of light.

Lock watched the road. Thunder exploded, now much closer than before. There was a mixture of worry and sadness in his eyes when he put the car in gear.

-o-

Emily Norton removed her gloves and put them on the table, where laptops and scientific instruments had replaced the wartime radio transmitters.

She glanced at the German naval officer's skeletal corpse. Its eye sockets seemed to be watching her as she lifted something from a plastic case next to the gloves.

"This isn't going to hurt me, I promise," Norton told the skeleton, then unwrapped a blood test lancet. Squeezing the side of her thumb against the forefinger of one hand, she used the lancet to prick flesh near the thumbnail. A drop of blood appeared.

Norton looked down at her booted feet. A yellow glow had appeared in the floor around them. She lifted an instrument, pointed it at the yellow glow and watched a laptop screen. Complex charts measured in MHz fluctuated there.

Norton moved the instrument up her body, then along her arm until it reached the thumb, where she held it for a few seconds. She frowned, adjusted her helmet and pressed against the two electrical pickups taped either side of her forehead.

The laptop now displayed a three-dimensional human body in various lattice colours, together with numerical read-outs.

"All in the Schumann range," Norton told the skeleton. "Seems healing is just a matter of complex frequencies." She frowned as Hardcastle's faint and distant voice interrupted her thoughts. "Excuse me a moment," Norton apologised to the dead German naval officer.

Hardcastle was standing a dozen yards from the entrance in the circular chamber, his helmet slanted untidily on his head under the EMF suit hood. He also had pickups taped to his forehead.

"You're supposed to be monitoring for a reply," Norton called out from her side of the threshold.

Hardcastle pointed up at the echo screen in the domed ceiling. "There's that, and there's this," he responded, holding up a smartphone. Hardcastle then shrugged, walked towards the entrance and halted a few feet away. "You and I could sit here and play chess, have a chat and still do our jobs. Bit of company while we're down here wouldn't go amiss, don't you think?"

Norton maintained a patient expression. "What do you want?"

"Standing wave's been getting a few bumps," he answered.

"It's just weather, purely thermal. There's been a thunderstorm above ground, but only a normal one."

"I just wanted to be sure," Hardcastle said. "You did the test then?" He pointed at the circular field of yellow at Norton's feet. This was now shrinking.

"I did," Norton said, then made a play of noticing the man did not have a yellow shadow himself. "How about you?"

"Not yet."

"Squeamish?"

"Of course not. I know it doesn't hurt."

"Well then," Norton said, eyebrows raised.

Hardcastle looked at the table nearer the centre of the chamber. "I left the pricker things over there."

"Then you had better get back there and do the test," Norton told him. "And continue monitoring."

Hardcastle looked awkward and embarrassed. He was about to turn around but hesitated. "I was wondering if you could supervise my test."

"Ah," Norton said, "bit of a phobia about blood?"

"It's stupid," Hardcastle answered. "No big problem with blood. I didn't faint when El Capitano took the druggie out with a head shot."

"El Capitano?"

"Missus Evans… Seems pretty lethal, don't you think?"

"It's part of her job," Norton said. "Is it just a combined needles and blood thing then?"

"Don't even say the words," Hardcastle warned, closing his eyes briefly.

"Okay," Norton told him in a calm tone. "I'm getting the picture. No need to be ashamed. We all have hang-ups, including me. Mine's guns. I hate them."

"Really?"

Norton smiled. "Why don't you fetch a chair, your medical laptop and a lancet. You can do the test here by the entry where I can keep an eye on you."

"That would be great," the man answered. "And believe me, I can monitor for a reply from the Clangers, or whatever they are out there, just as effectively from here. Get a chair yourself. We can play chess or something."

Norton rolled her eyes, took a deep breath, and watched him hurrying back towards the table in the giant chamber.

-o-

Wyn's face was wet, dirt-streaked and pensive in the glow from the dashboard. He glanced in the mirror at the headlights following him. Up ahead, the American's Jaguar was parked on the road outside the B&B, which was now all lit up inside behind closed curtains.

The windscreen wipers squeaked across drying glass as the rain reduced to a drizzle. Wyn turned up the drive and halted.

He got out of the car and saw it was the white van that had followed him. It was now stopped a short distance up the driveway next door, engine running, headlights on full beam, as though its occupants were watching him.

His mud-splashed trousers and the back of his soaked jacket were clearly lit as he approached the B&B front door. It opened before he reached it.

Mair Ellis faced him. She looked terrified. Caycey Jones was waiting behind her in the hallway.

140

As he went in and turned to close the front door, Wyn noticed the white van pulling further up the neighbouring drive. Then he saw the 4x4 arriving behind it.

"We'd better have a chat, Mister Ellis," Caycey Jones said in a quiet voice. "Mister Lock will be joining us shortly."

The drizzle had ceased when Andy Lock came out of the safe house. He had a large brown envelope tucked under his arm.

Caycey Jones opened the B&B front door for him.

Mair and Wyn were seated together on a sofa. There was a trail of wet footprints across the carpet. Mair was in silent tears, face half hidden by her hands. Wyn Ellis had an arm over her shoulders.

"Now now," Lock said to Mair, "there's no need to cry."

"I have tried to explain," Jones said. "All we want is for them to tell us who they are working for."

Lock and Jones eased themselves onto the opposite sofa. Lock placed his brown envelope on a coffee table in the centre. His eyes then fixed on Wyn Ellis with an expression that was neither a smile nor a sneer.

"We haven't done anything wrong," Wyn Ellis protested.

Lock tilted his head a fraction and leaned forward. "Quite evidently Mair seems to think you have. And the law, quite rightly, allows me to question and detain you both for spying on government employees."

Now Mair Ellis sobbed openly.

"I was only curious," Wyn Ellis said as he tried to comfort Mair. "You know about my interest in UFOs. I know I shouldn't have, but I was curious about you. That's all it is. Mair had nothing to do with it and didn't know where I was going."

"Missus Ellis told me you would co-operate," Caycey Jones said.

"I said no such thing," Mair blurted through her tears. "I said he would answer your questions. I didn't know you were going to follow him."

Jones tried hard but could not prevent a slight smile at this.

Wyn Ellis glared at Jones. "Did you threaten my wife?" He removed his arm from Mair's shoulders and made as though to stand up.

Mair grabbed him. "No, he didn't. He just said they knew everything and wanted to ask you some questions."

"About UFOs?" Lock asked.

"Yes," Mair answered, now wiping her tear-stained face. "I have warned him that it's all nonsense, but you know how it is."

"The public has a right to know," Wyn Ellis added.

Lock shrugged. "Actually, the public has no right to know anything that's classified secret. UFOs are classified *above* top secret, and it's an offence to even attempt to discover classified information."

"Well I didn't get any," Wyn Ellis countered.

"But you've just admitted attempting to do so," Lock told him. "Anyway, it's a flimsy story." Lock then turned to Jones. "Could I hand them over to you? How long to get them to Guantanamo Bay?"

Jones looked shocked. "Twenty-four hours, but this is purely a British matter. And anyway, they've been wonderful hosts. I couldn't possibly do that to them."

"But you could if you wanted," Lock said as the horrified man and wife listened across the gap between the sofas. "If they don't co-operate…"

Jones adopted a casual, relaxed manner as he looked at Wyn Ellis and said, "CIA can pretty much do anything if we decide to, but I'm sure that won't be necessary."

"We don't want to go to prison," Mair blurted. She was crying again. "We were blackmailed."

Wyn Ellis reacted with dismay and horror to this, but was speechless, mouth opening and closing like a fish as he tried to say something in response to her outburst, then thought better of it.

In contrast, both Lock and Jones went into heightened alert. Lock's already serious face grew more intense. "Who blackmailed you?" Lock demanded.

"Tell him," Mair whispered, loud enough for the two others to hear.

Wyn Ellis sighed and his body seemed to deflate into the sofa. His hands then shook as he clasped Mair to hold her closer to him.

"They didn't blackmail us," he said, "but we thought they might if we didn't do what they wanted."

"Who?" Lock asked quietly. "Who are *they*?"

"The Russians," Wyn admitted.

-o-

Kyle was propped up fully clothed on his bed. He was shooting at Ottoman Turks in a desert ruin on his console game. The doorbell rang downstairs.

He hissed at the TV screen, put the controller down and vaulted off his bed to the bedroom door. Gran's door opened when he was midway to the bottom of the stairs.

Gran rubbed her eyes and pulled her pink dressing gown tighter around her waist. "It's two o'clock in the morning." Her voice was puzzled, sleepy.

"I'll get it, don't worry, go back to bed," Kyle told her, but she was already making her slow descent behind him.

Kyle peeked through the front window then jerked his head back in dismay. "It's Sharon," he told Gran, who now balanced herself dopily on the bottom stair.

"Then tell her to go away. What does she think she's doing, this time of night? Is she on drugs?"

"Please go back to bed."

"She's not to come inside," Gran told him.

"Absolutely," Kyle agreed. "I'll tell her to go home, promise."

Kyle opened the front door. Gran watched with suspicious eyes.

The young woman standing outside in a dirty tracksuit looked like something out of The Walking Dead. Dark shadows ringed her eyes. Her nose was red, nostrils caked with scabs. She swayed drunkenly.

Kyle glared at her. His voice was hushed to a whispered demand. "What are you doing here?"

"I'm in trouble," she said loudly.

Kyle put a finger to his lips. "Shush... Keep it down."

"Don't you shush me. You left me on my own."

143

"And you know why."

"And you know I can't help it," Sharon whined. "But, Kyle, the bailiffs are coming to kick me out tomorrow."

"It's not my problem," Kyle said. "I gave you more than enough money for rent, but you put it up your nose. Go home to your mother in Birmingham."

"She won't even talk to me. And I can't go back there anyway because of that fucking perv she's living with."

"Then get help. Go to the council or your doctor and get into rehab."

"I tried," Sharon said, now tearful. "Believe me, I tried. But there's nothing around here. The nearest one is Flintshire and there's a waiting list, like two years, to get in there."

"But I can't help you," Kyle said. "This isn't my house."

"I can go to my cousin's in Wolverhampton. My real dad's still there as well."

"Katie?"

"Yeh, Katie. She says I can doss down there for a while."

"So, what's your problem? Go back to Wolverhampton."

"I haven't got the fare," Sharon told him.

"How much?" Kyle asked.

"It's like a hundred pounds and I haven't even got ten," Sharon pleaded.

"Well I haven't got any cash here," Kyle told her. "I'd have to go to the bank in the morning."

"Too late. I have to go now."

"But there's no buses," Kyle said exasperatedly. "It's the middle of the night."

"I can get a taxi to Bangor and there's a train at four o'clock."

"But I haven't got any cash."

"I've got it," Gran called out from where she had been listening. She started up the stairs.

"No, Gran," Kyle protested, but she ignored him.

A bedroom curtain was moved at the terraced house next door as Sharon waited, glaring at Kyle in the doorway. "You said you loved me," she accused.

144

"Yeh," Kyle admitted. "But that was the old Sharon. The drugs turned you into something else. You're not her any more."

"And you're a fucking bastard," Sharon said, almost toppling over.

"Shush," Kyle warned. Gran reappeared breathlessly beside him. She held out some folded banknotes to the young woman, who grabbed them immediately.

Without a word, Sharon then turned and headed for the road.

Kyle went after her. He caught up at the centre of the bridge and grabbed her arm.

"Get off me," she shouted.

"Be quiet," Kyle warned in a clipped tone. "I want to make sure you get your taxi."

"Get the fuck off me," Sharon yelled louder. "I'll scream."

Kyle let go and watched her. Sharon crossed the bridge and staggered past the Jones Bros yard.

As he turned to go back, he noticed something beyond the far side of the other bridge. Kyle moved closer.

The lights were all on at Lock's house along the road. The B&B next door to it as well. Both front doors were wide open.

Kyle frowned. He saw Gwenda Evans going into the B&B. Then he spotted Lock waiting at the end of the drive as the American came out of the B&B.

He continued watching as these two joined up before turning along the other drive to Lock's house. They passed the 4x4 then both went inside.

Eyebrows raised, Kyle returned to his gran's.

-o-

"That's it, dear," Gwenda Evans encouraged as Mair's trembling hand hovered a ballpoint pen over the papers on the coffee table. "Just sign the bottom of the form."

Wyn Ellis was slumped back on the sofa, watching with a stunned expression.

"Now I'll just witness your signatures," Gwenda said. She leaned

145

over from the other sofa and spun the papers around, "and you'll both be signed up to the Official Secrets Act. There, that's done."

Gwenda stacked the papers and slid them into the brown envelope, which she then clasped loosely to her chest.

"Now we're working for British Intelligence," Wyn said, face still stunned.

"Sort of," Gwenda told him. "More like on probation really, if I can put it that way to you." She patted the brown envelope. "This is your stay out of jail card. But only if you do exactly what we tell you."

"But you'll protect us from the Russians, won't you?" Mair Ellis asked, her eyes pleading in a tear-stained face.

"Of course," Gwenda answered cheerfully. "Doing exactly what I tell you will protect you."

"So, what do we do?" Wyn asked.

"We're going to put you under surveillance at all times of course, but first thing, now, I want all your notebooks, cameras and mobile phones. Everything and anything on which you have kept records of what you've seen us doing."

"We've only got a small notebook," Mair Ellis said. "And we only started it today, after Wyn got back from Liverpool."

"Amazing, isn't it," Gwenda said, "how things can change so quickly? One minute you're retired teachers and nosy neighbours doing bed and breakfast, next you are Russian spies because of wobbly stuff you did years ago. Now you're distressed double agents with us in counter-intelligence. And here in little Amharfarn of all places, all in the blink of an eye. Who would believe it?"

"I had no idea you were MI5," Mair Ellis said. "What must you think of us?"

Now Gwenda leaned forward seriously. "I think you are innocents who acted from a moral conviction when you were younger. There are some evil people in this world, but neither of you is one of them. You're still our friends and neighbours, and I will not allow any harm to come to you. Do you understand?"

Mair Ellis burst into tears. Wyn Ellis hugged her. "Thank you," he whispered across to Gwenda.

Next door in the safe house kitchen, Caycey Jones took a gulp from a mug, put it down on the table, then eased back in his chair. "They're amateurs," he said, voice almost growling. "What in the hell are the Russians up to activating them after all these years? I don't know how to even begin to assess this situation."

Lock sat down. Banes leaned himself up against the worktop next to the sink, listening and alert.

"There's tomorrow as well," Lock told Jones. "London confirmed what Burke said. We are to afford you hospitality at the compound and get a photograph of you and the brickwork. Burke is going to pick you up at eleven o'clock and take you up there, where I will show you both a *bricked-up* entrance to the big thing. He's your official stamp for this diplomatic backchannel."

"I haven't looked at my e-mails yet," Jones said. "But that is my CIA mission, verify that the electromagnetic incident wasn't deliberate. But eleven o'clock is real tight. Does Miiko know?"

Andy Lock shrugged. "When I told her, she said it wasn't a problem. They're going to work all night. She reckons they can finish it and get a forensic clean done before then."

"Their vehicle is still up there," Jones said.

"Banes and I can handle the small cargo truck," Lock responded. "The Japanese girls should be hidden the other side of the wall by the time you and Burke arrive up there."

"And if they don't finish on time?"

"Well that's the big risk, I think," Banes chipped in, tapping his mug with his fingernails. "Simple construction work looks easy before you start, but it never is. And what they're attempting to do isn't even remotely simple."

"They'll text me if they over-run," Lock said.

Jones shifted on his chair. "What's your contingency plan if they do?"

"I think it has to be dovetailed into managing Mair and Wyn Ellis next door."

"And how are you going to do that?"

147

Lock shook his head. "I won't know properly until Gwenda completes their first debrief. It will take her most of what's left of the night, but we'll have a better idea of what this Russian Dimitri character in Liverpool is up to by then."

"And that's the curveball, isn't it?" Caycey Jones muttered as he leaned over the table towards Lock. "Do you think he could be in with Burke?"

Lock shook his head. "A double agent? I have no idea, but *Liverpool*... Burke's import/export business and his food wholesale subsidiary are both there. He runs his section from there, all off the books. I suppose it's possible Dimitri could be in with him."

Jones pursed his lips into a thin smile. "Burke's setup sounds just like the private sector side of CIA."

"Yes," Lock agreed. "Except Burke has a title as well."

"And this Dimitri's activation of them next door?"

"He might well have pushed Mair and Wyn to see how we would react if we caught them, the likelihood of which was high, obviously, given their total lack of training."

"Jesus Christ," Banes complained. "We're dead. If Dimitri *is* a double agent and if you *don't* tell London you caught sleepers, but *he* does, they'll be all over us."

"Then we will have to find a way of giving the appearance of *not* catching them," Lock said.

"Or *turning* them," Jones added. "You can't even do that, officially, without involving South Bank in London. Turn them wrong and Dimitri will detect it. They're amateurs."

"Maybe you should have thought of all this before barging in next door," Banes said, voice revealing some anger.

Jones gestured with his hand. "Keep cool. We don't know if Dimitri is a double yet. And no, we did the right thing. We had to confront them. If they had reported seeing the Japanese ladies, never mind *me*, at that service station, and it got to the wrong people, we'd all be cooked."

"UFOs," Lock declared. "I think that's how we handle Bonnie and Clyde next door. It's also how we cover our interaction with them tonight."

Kyle's arm reached out and silenced his alarm clock. He lifted his head, blinked, rubbed his eyes and then slid out of bed.

Outside, a cloud shifted to reveal the sun, signalling that a heavy shower was dying. The road surface glistened as rainwater ran along the gullies.

Kyle jogged over the bridge, hand shading his face from the remaining drizzle. A rainbow shimmered to the east.

He was halfway across the back lawn at the safe house when Lock opened the kitchen door. Lock whistled, beckoning to Kyle with a sharp, conspiratorial tilt of his head.

"Everything okay, Mister Lock?" Kyle asked in the kitchen.

"Yes, fine. Take a seat. Want some breakfast?"

"No thanks," Kyle responded.

Gwenda Evans and Banes were seated at the table. Kyle greeted them with an awkward uncertainty as he joined them.

Gwenda smiled. "Good morning, Kyle." She was cheerful and welcoming in her demeanour. Banes seemed worried, serious.

Lock sat down opposite Kyle, rested his elbows on the table, smiled at the young man and leaned forward. "Did you see the light in the sky last night?"

"What light? No, I was in all night."

"But you were out at about two in the morning, weren't you? I wondered if you saw it?"

"Ah," Kyle said. "It was Sharon. She was scrounging for money so she could go to Wolverhampton. I did go out for a bit."

"Did you give her the money?"

"Gran did, to get rid of her, she was disturbing the neighbours."

"And *did* she go to Wolverhampton?"

"No way," Kyle said, shrinking a little into his chair from shame. "She just wanted money for a fix."

"I think you're right," Lock agreed. "We were up and about here then as well. Missus Evans saw your little consternation with Sharon across the bridge."

Kyle looked at Gwenda, who was slicing an apple on a small

149

plate. "Don't worry about it, dear," she said. "Sharon's problems are not your fault."

"Does she have relatives in Wolverhampton?" Lock asked.

Kyle was about to answer, but Gwenda did it for him. "Her father lives there, her aunt and uncle, and a cousin the same age as her as well. They've been trying to persuade her to go there so they can get her into rehab."

Kyle looked at Gwenda with a stunned expression. She grinned at him. "You know what we women are like. We know everything that's going on in the village. Nobody blames you for the mess she's got herself into."

"Anyway," Lock continued to Kyle. "Mister Ellis and I saw a light in the sky."

Kyle's eyes widened with interest. "A UFO? Really?"

"Mister Ellis thinks it was. But you know, back end of a thunderstorm passing over, it was just ball lightning. I was coming back from Caernarfon and Wyn Ellis was out of his car in the middle of the road, watching it in the rain."

"Wow," Kyle said. "I saw ball lightning once, up in the woods, in broad daylight."

"It's the high iron content in the geology here," Lock said. "And the fact we are close to a geological fault line. Mister Ellis is adamant it was a UFO, but you didn't see a light in the sky last night?"

"No, I didn't see anything like that."

"That's a shame," Lock said, "because if you *had* seen it, you would know it was only ball lightning, and *that* would save me a whole load of hassle. Any chance you could back me up this once?"

"Lie, you mean?" Kyle said, mildly alarmed. "To who?"

Gwenda Evans leaned over as she took a bite from a slice of apple. "You know, dear, I could get Sharon on a train to Wolverhampton today. There's one goes directly there from Bangor at lunchtime. We can't have you getting more hassle from her."

As Kyle tried to digest this, Lock reached along the table and slid a brown envelope from under a newspaper. "Kyle, you're more important to what we do here than just as a gardener and odd-job man. It's time we employed you at a proper level."

150

Kyle nearly said something, but inclined his head, listening, waiting for more.

Lock pulled some neatly stapled papers from the envelope. "This is an Official Secrets Act declaration. I'd like you to sign it so you can be a full member of my crew." He smiled and gestured as though offering a gift.

"Wow," Kyle said in a low voice, but with some obvious excitement in his eyes.

"But before you do," Lock continued, "you asked me who I want you to lie to. And it is a lie."

Kyle sat up, alert. "Is it because of the American next door? Is he CIA?"

"Not at all. We spoke to him about the ball lightning. He was just interested. Nice man, used to work for NASA, so he knows a thing or two about weather and stuff."

"Yeh, I saw you with him last night," Kyle admitted, a new understanding in his eyes. "What do you want me to do?"

"Just tell all your mates you saw a strange light over the Bonks," Lock explained. "And do it now, straight away. BBC will be here about eleven o'clock. Tell your mates about that as well."

Kyle frowned. "They'll still be in bed."

"Their girlfriends won't though," Lock said. "The ones with babies."

Kyle smiled and issued half a chuckle. "Maybe I really did see something up there last night. I don't mind telling my mates that."

"That's the way," Lock soothed, sliding the papers and a pen across the table.

Kyle scrawled his signature without hesitation.

-o-

Burke was alone driving the silver Range Rover when he passed the rusty *Amharfarn* sign. He frowned when he saw a small crowd outside the B&B and Lock's safe house. The Range Rover pulled up and mounted a grass verge a short distance away.

Eyes alert, Burke adjusted his striped tie, buttoned up his navy-blue overcoat and walked towards the scene.

Two young women with babies in buggies spoke to a reporter with a microphone held by his side. He was not recording them, but one of the girls was pointing at the sky above the B&B, her finger describing an arc.

A man wearing an anorak and carrying a TV camera glanced at Burke then returned his bored attention to the reporter and his admirers.

Burke halted behind the Jaguar. He stared at a Land Rover that had RAF markings on it, parked along the B&B driveway, then returned his attention to the scene on the roadside. Two scruffy young men wearing tracksuits approached from the other direction on the pavement. They hovered a few feet away, listening to the young women with the reporter.

Across the road, Ventriloquist Jack stood watching, hands in his boiler suit pockets, cigarette stuck in the corner of his mouth. Without shifting his head, Jack's eyes tracked Burke moving around the back of the Jaguar and into the road to avoid a group of teenagers.

The reporter was now talking to the cameraman. The two girls wheeled their babies to the pavement, obviously disappointed with his lack of interest. Three others immediately approached to take their place. They were younger and none of these had babies. The reporter seemed more interested in them.

Jack's forehead creased in his otherwise immobile face when he saw Lock coming out of his house.

The immaculately dressed Burke headed for Lock, avoiding a grinning youth, who was wearing a hoodie to shield an obvious hangover. The youth burped as Burke passed him.

"What the hell's going on?" Burke demanded when he got closer to Lock.

Managing to appear apologetic, Lock said, "Seems half the village think they saw a UFO last night. Someone phoned RAF Valley and the BBC somehow got hold of it as well."

Burke puffed himself up, expression irritated. "You can't have *that* sort of stuff going on here, you know that."

"Don't worry," Lock told him. "It was ball lightning, saw it myself. I'll talk to the BBC, tell them it was just ball lightning *and* I'll kill the story."

"Can you do that?"

"Oh yes, I'll just remind them of the standing D Notice here. The reporter won't even be able to blog or tweet about it. I'll tell him in a minute."

"How long will it take to wrap this up?" Burke demanded. "I've got other things to do."

"Maybe you should come back in two hours," Lock answered. "This will have evaporated by then."

Burke studied Lock's eyes with some suspicion. "This is very inconvenient. I hope you haven't engineered all this just to annoy me."

"Why would I do that?" Lock said innocently. "Last thing any of us wants is attention to this place. We need to go really low profile here and *you* standing on my driveway is… you know…"

"What do you mean?"

"The way you're dressed, all official looking. You're just adding to the speculation."

Burke grunted at this and was about to say something but then thought better of it. "Two hours then," he said grudgingly. He retreated along the driveway, glaring at the youth who had burped at him.

Across the road, Ventriloquist Jack watched Burke return to the Range Rover. The man got in quickly and slammed the door shut. The car turned around, then accelerated away from the village with an angry splash of chippings.

Jack's eyes swivelled in the other direction. He grinned, cigarette stump twirling in the corner of his mouth. He had spotted Kyle approaching from the bridge.

The reporter looked harassed. A very thin teenage girl, who was wearing a combination of cowboy boots, blue polka-dot skirt, pink top and white gloves, was in amongst the group of three young women pressing in on him.

"We going to be on the telly?" one of them demanded.

The cameraman now had his camera set up on a tripod. He tapped the reporter on his shoulder and pointed at the thin girl in the polka-dot skirt. "Why don't you talk to Minnie Mouse there," he suggested in a whisper.

The reporter nodded knowingly at the cameraman and turned to the girl. "Good morning," he said. "I'm with the BBC. What's your name?"

Kyle arrived and stood near the group, listening.

"Bibby Libby," the thin girl told the reporter, who wrote in his notebook with a slight frown on his face.

"Did you see anything in the sky last night?"

"Yeh," she said, pointing, "up there. It was like a flying saucer. Definitely extraterrestrials."

"Would you mind recording an interview with me about it on camera?"

"Sure," Bibby Libby said, smiling with pride. She gestured to her two friends to make space. Bibby had perfect white teeth and her blue eyes sparkled.

Across the road, Ventriloquist Jack openly grinned towards Kyle as the reporter and cameraman prepared to interview the girl.

The TV camera light flared into life, illuminating Bibby's enthralled face.

The reporter held up his microphone. "We're in Amharfarn on the Llŷn Peninsula in North Wales, and it seems a lot of people saw something in the sky here last night. Can you tell us what you saw?" The microphone arrived near Bibby Libby's face.

"Yeh, it was fantastic, brighter than the sun. It flew from over there…" She pointed, then swung her finger in an arc. "To over there."

The reporter smiled at her. "Some local people have been telling me that Amharfarn is a really quiet place and nothing like this has ever happened here before—"

"Oh no," Bibby Libby said. "There's always something happening here. The sea caught fire and the mountain blew smoke rings, coz it's really a volcano, and there's angels singing in the woods every night. I reckon they brought the flying saucer here."

She flashed her eyes seriously at the reporter.

The reporter glanced with disbelief and a wry grin at his cameraman. The camera light went out.

Kyle stepped forward. "I saw it. It was ball lightning. There was a thunderstorm. It happens quite often here because of the iron content in the mountain."

"Hi, Kyle," Bibby Libby said with a shy smile.

Now Lock appeared by the side of the cameraman.

"Mind if I have a word," Lock said to the reporter. "In private." He pointed up the driveway. At the same time, two young women in RAF uniform came out of the B&B.

The reporter followed Lock, who leaned over the wall halfway to catch the attention of the RAF women. One of them was a sergeant. They approached the wall on its other side.

"This gentleman is from the BBC," Lock told them, holding up an identity card. He then showed it to the reporter.

"Is there a problem?" the reporter asked.

"It was only ball lightning," Lock answered, then glanced at the airwomen.

"We think so as well," the sergeant agreed. "We detected a thunderstorm in the early hours this morning, and this sort of lightning phenomenon is relatively common around here."

"Unfortunately," Lock told the reporter, "you can't even report that."

The RAF women did not seem surprised by this.

"Why?" the reporter asked.

Lock leaned forward and spoke in a hushed voice. "Because we are on a defence systems communications corridor here, and it's got blanket cover from a D Notice."

"The office never told me that," the reporter said.

Lock reached into his pocket, pulled out a sheet of paper and handed it over. "I made a copy for you."

The man studied it with disbelief. "But this is dated nineteen forty-one."

"And it's until further notice."

The BBC man conducted more study. Disbelief turned to surprise. "So it is. Original must be buried in the filing system somewhere, probably in London."

Lock pointed at the paper. "Keep it, consider yourself gagged. But it's likely your people haven't been referred to it since the war. Nothing ever happens here, except ball lightning every few years or so."

"That's a shame," the reporter said, "because that young woman's piece would have made a great novelty story at the end of the evening news."

"Shame on you," Lock said. "Bibby is a bit of a flake, but she's a nice girl. Her real name is Elin, by the way."

The reporter's expression transformed into haughty and officious. "You could have phoned the office about the D Notice."

"We weren't expecting the BBC," Lock responded, "but by all accounts, it was a pretty good display of an unusual natural phenomenon. I imagine a few people could have phoned it in."

"I was to interview a Mister Ellis."

"We spoke to him, sir," the RAF sergeant interrupted. "He's satisfied now it was just ball lightning, and I can confirm what this gentleman just told you. Localised weather phenomena in this area *are* classified. You can't report it and you can't interview anyone about it."

"Is that clear?" Lock asked the now deflated BBC man.

Inside the B&B, Mair Ellis was standing near the bay window looking out at the crowd at the end of the driveway. Wyn was on the sofa, fiddling with a camera. Caycey Jones came in, yawning, hand covering his mouth. "Pardon me," Jones said. He looked at Wyn Ellis. "Did you get it?"

"Mair got five shots," Wyn answered. He handed the camera to Jones, who looked at the viewing screen. It displayed a clear image of Lock talking to Burke on the driveway next door.

Jones smiled. "Excellent. When the reporter has gone, I'll go out there and talk to Mister Lock over the wall. Get a few shots of that as well. But the important thing is to get some shots when that man comes back, and when I get into the car with him and Mister Lock.

156

Stay out of sight when you do it. Keep at least two feet back from the window."

"Will do," Wyn Ellis said. He had a resigned tone to his voice.

"Who *was* that smartly dressed man?" Mair Ellis asked.

"I don't know his real name," Jones said, "but he works for a rival agency that would like nothing better than to get their hands on you, if they found out you were sleeper agents. But if you do exactly as we say, we'll be able to protect you from him and the Russians. They'll never know, and after today most of this should blow over."

-o-

Banes was waiting near the steel door when the silver Range Rover drove up from the compound gate.

Lock got out of the front passenger side. Jones emerged from the rear, carrying a briefcase. Burke descended from the driver's seat with an envelope in his hand.

"This is Doctor Banes," Lock told Jones. "He's one of three scientists monitoring the stabilisation of the geomagnetic activity."

Jones greeted Banes, shaking his hand convivially as though he had never seen the man before. "Caycey Jones," he introduced himself, "NASA and CIA."

Burke seemed to be ignoring them. He was eyeing up the compound. "Where does that track go?" he asked.

"Up to the comms mast," Lock answered. "Shall we go inside?"

Burke shrugged, becoming more alert. "Uh, sure, forgive me. I was miles away." He looked at Banes but did not offer a handshake. "I'm Burke, Section D. Where are the others?"

Banes kept his face in a neutral expression. "Day off. We work in shifts."

"I love it," Jones said to Burke. "This is so British. Back in the States, something this important, we'd have a hundred-mile perimeter and a small army guarding it."

"We prefer the 'nothing going on here' approach," Lock said. "It's also less expensive."

Jones grinned at Burke, who shrugged.

157

"You don't seem to approve?" Jones suggested to him.

Burke was immediately defensive. "It's not my department's call, but it's worked just fine like this for over sixty years now. Not one security alert. You have my assurance of that."

Jones looked at Lock, who said, "It's true. Aside from the recent electromagnetic event, we've never had a problem."

"And the locals," Jones said. "I've spoken to a few of them in my tourist cover and casually mentioned the mountain here. But you know, not one of them said anything about this compound. If anything, I found them tight-lipped about the mountain. My hosts, for example, when I asked them about their neighbours, they just said you are telecommunications contractors."

"I have a good relationship with all the locals," Lock said. "I *am* a local."

"You certainly are," Burke said. He issued a mock smile. "Shall we go inside?"

Lock gave a nod to Banes, who tapped digits on the keypad next to the steel door.

They walked silently through the work tunnel, Jones making a play of being fascinated by the posters. He crouched to open his briefcase on the floor in the electrical chamber and rose with a photograph in his hand. Beside him, Burke slid out another photograph from the envelope he was carrying. They compared these and nodded to each other.

Jones then approached the brickwork blocking the way to the deeper underground. It looked complete, as though its partial demolition had never happened. He tapped one side with his knuckles then drew a finger across its width. A faint mark appeared in a thin sheen of white dust.

Burke watched with boredom and disdain as Lock positioned himself with a camera.

"Would you like to be in the photograph?" Jones asked Burke.

"I generally avoid having my picture taken," Burke responded. He checked his watch. "Are you satisfied with what you've seen so far?"

"I sure am," Jones said, "but I would like to spend some time here with Commander Lock, to observe the monitoring operation. Maybe a week, if that's okay?"

Burke looked at Lock, who said, "That's no problem. You can stay as long as you like." Lock aimed the camera at Jones. The flash popped three times. He shifted slightly. It popped again.

"Then if you don't mind," Burke said as he again looked at his watch, "I need to go. Can I leave Mister Jones in your care, old boy?"

"Certainly," Lock told him.

"Well, it was nice meeting you," Burke said to Jones. "Enjoy your stay in Britain."

Outside in the compound, Banes held up a remote controller. The gate rattled open, electric motors whining.

Burke's silver Range Rover drove off at speed, spraying wet gravel towards Banes. He cursed, waited for the car to make its exit, then signalled the gate to close again. He ran back to the door in the rock face.

When Banes arrived in the electrical chamber, Lock was busy tapping one side of the brickwork as though trying to detect something. Jones seemed more concerned with studying the display screen on the back of the camera Lock had used.

"This is amazing," Lock said. "I can't find a loose brick anywhere. How the hell do we open it?"

"They wouldn't let me in here until they finished clearing up the dust," Banes said as he approached. "What they did here is bloody miraculous."

Banes pointed a finger and counted along a row of bricks from the side grouted to solid rock. Using a penknife, he eased out a brick tile from near the centre of the wall, then slid his hand into a small hole its removal exposed.

There was a dull click. He pushed. Half the wall pivoted away from him, revealing the toothy edge of the part that had not been demolished.

In the gloom the other side, the two Japanese women looked up from where they were seated on the miners' tunnel floor. It was cluttered with plastic sheeting, piles of bricks, electronic tools,

159

cables, and the workbench. The women were covered in red dust and looked exhausted.

"Well done," Jones told them. "Fantastic job. You deserve to get some sleep."

As they rose stiffly, Miiko said, "We'll clean this side first, then wash and get changed."

"There's a shower by the entrance," Lock said.

"But then we would like to see," Miiko said, pointing in the direction of the deeper underground.

Jones smiled. "Absolutely, you deserve it."

"Don't they just," Lock agreed.

"Amazing work," Banes added.

Miiko and Kikuko smiled. They looked as though they were wearing red masks, white teeth glinting in stark contrast to the brick dust pattern on their faces.

-o-

The sun had established itself with some permanence in the sky when Ventriloquist Jack saw a car approach. It was coming fast from the direction of the mountain on the farmland lane.

Still dressed in his boiler suit, he hopped across a gurgling drainage ditch and grabbed a branch of a hazel tree in the hedgerow to maintain his balance. Burke's silver Range Rover did not slow as it sped past, dangerously close.

Jack shouted "Idiot!" and raised his free hand in a middle-finger curse to its driver. Water shaken from the tree rained down on him as the car raced away.

Up ahead, Hefin Gwynedd was leaning over his gate, smoking a pipe.

"Did you see that nutter?" Jack demanded as he approached.

The old man tapped ash from his pipe. "Not from around here, that's for sure. Want to come in?"

"No, it's okay."

"What happened in the village then?"

160

"It was nothing to do with our stuff," Jack said. "The man driving that Range Rover was there though. He spoke to Andy Lock."

"Yeh, well, Andy Lock was in the car with him, and the American, when they went up the forestry about half an hour ago."

"But they weren't with him now," Jack pointed out.

"So they're still up there in that compound."

Pero raised his ears under the trellis table behind Hefin. The televisions had plastic sheets over the tops, held down in place with bricks.

"They're up to something," Jack said. "BBC were in the village as well, but Andy warned them off, showed them something official like. Two RAF girls backed him up."

Hefin frowned with alarm. "RAF?"

"Don't worry. Some of the youngsters reckoned they saw a light in the sky last night, but it was half one in the morning, nothing to do with us."

"UFO?"

"Lock told everyone it was ball lightning. It was just after the thunderstorm passed over, but I never saw it, and I was having a smoke in the yard about that time."

"You couldn't sleep then?"

"No."

Hefin had begun refilling his pipe from a tobacco pouch. "Me neither, it *actually works*. We conquered *gravity*."

Ventriloquist Jack raised a finger to his lips. "Keep it down. The bloody establishment would kill us if they found out what we've been up to."

"Wasn't talking loud, was I?" Hefin asked Pero. The dog barked his disagreement from under the table then pricked his ears towards Jack.

"I've been studying the data from CERN and the MMS satellites as well," Jack said.

Hefin grinned at this. "And of course I have no idea what you are talking about."

"I already told you. What CERN is doing when they run their accelerator interferes with the Earth's magnetic field, which protects us from solar radiation."

"Yeh," Hefin said. "I remember you telling me now. What of it?"

Ventriloquist Jack leaned closer. "I found the data from a few nights ago. That weird thunderstorm. There was a magnetic peak, much more powerful than what comes out of CERN. It came from our mountain."

"So? We've always known there's something in the mountain."

Glancing around before continuing in a low voice, Ventriloquist Jack said, "CERN's electromagnetic field is a thousand times more powerful than the Earth's. It disrupts the pattern. But the one that briefly appeared here was even more powerful. *And* it didn't disrupt it, made it more coherent, *better* protection from cosmic rays… but only briefly."

Hefin Gwynedd relit his pipe, eyes glinting. "And since then, people have been coming here. The American, and those Japanese women you said were here."

"We've got to lie low," Jack said. "No more tests for a while until we find out what's going on."

"And how do we find out?" the old man asked.

Pero got up from under the trellis table, trotted to the gate and looked up at the two men. Ventriloquist Jack whispered something to Hefin.

"Kyle?" Hefin said. "Really?"

-o-

Amharfarn was back to normal. A solitary white van passed the safe house as Kyle worked in the front garden. He swept a hover mower over the lawn with practised ease, keeping a watchful eye on the departing van and the now otherwise empty road.

Some of the young people, who had earlier gathered outside the safe house, were now sitting, bored, on the benches overlooking the tiny harbour. A few smoked; others ate, sharing potato crisps between themselves. A seagull eyed them craftily from the ground near their feet.

Up on the forested part of the mountain, the 4x4 roared along, spraying chippings as it headed downhill towards Amharfarn.

Further up, a young owl dozed on one of the tree branches overlooking the compound. It opened its eyes intermittently as the sun progressed on its afternoon journey across the sky.

Later, the owl glared with surprise when the 4x4 came back to the compound. It then preened itself with relief. Nearby, a crow screamed like a small child as a buzzard carried it away.

In the B&B kitchen, Wyn Ellis watched the end of the Welsh TV news on the BBC.

"Nothing," Wyn announced.

"Good," Mair said. She carried on scouring a frying pan under a running tap at the sink.

In the lounge, Caycey Jones watched CNN. They were reporting the commencement of a closed session of the United Nations General Assembly. Jones leaned forward, face intense, eyes fixed on the TV.

Upstairs, Miiko and Kikuko slept in their shared bedroom.

-o-

It was getting near dusk, and Kyle was finishing an evening meal at his gran's when the doorbell rang.

Gran issued a puzzled glare from the other side of the table. Kyle went to the door.

"You got a minute?" Ventriloquist Jack asked. He was standing outside in his usual pose, hands deep in his boiler suit pockets, cigarette end rotating in the corner of his mouth.

"Sure," Kyle answered from the doorway. "What's up?"

"You know your way around computers," Jack said. "I've got a problem with one of mine. Wondered if you could have a look."

Kyle glanced back at his gran before responding. "What sort of problem?"

163

"Blank screen. I'll pay you, don't worry about that."

Kyle reached for his jacket. "I'm going to have a look at Mister Thomas's computer," he called to Gran. "I don't want paying just to have a look," he told Ventriloquist Jack.

They walked together towards the road.

-o-

Lock glanced up as Caycey Jones entered the safe house kitchen. Emily Norton closed the door behind him before returning to the table.

Jones sat down next to Hardcastle, who yawned noisily.

"Did you two manage to get some sleep?" Jones asked.

"Couple of hours," Norton said. She lifted a teapot, poured some of the contents into a mug, and handed it to Jones.

"About the same," Hardcastle said.

"We're all tired," Lock reminded them from the other end of the table. He looked at Jones. "Who's looking after Mair and Wyn next door?" The question was asked casually.

Jones pursed his lips. "Miiko and Kikuko are keeping an eye on them for now. But we don't have the manpower to watch them all the time."

"But they do think they're under surveillance," Lock said.

"That much is clear," Jones agreed. "Gwenda went all around the house, made a big show of it. They think it's bugged better than Nixon's Oval Office. I had to reassure Missus Ellis their bedrooms and bathrooms are audio only."

"Could the Japanese ladies do some shifts underground?" Norton asked Jones.

"No way. Sooner they go home the better."

Hardcastle issued a tired sigh. "We were down there fourteen hours."

"I know, couldn't be helped with Burke and the photo and all that," Jones said.

"Gwenda had to make a trip to Bangor as well," Lock added. "That didn't help."

164

"Ah, Sharon," Emily Norton said. "Poor Kyle. Can he drive?"

"Yes," Lock answered.

Norton leaned forward. "And are you going to let him in on the big secret?"

"Absolutely not," Lock answered. "No way am I going to put his life in danger."

"Good," Norton said, "but he could run errands, do the shopping, including for next door. As long as he doesn't go near the compound."

"My thinking exactly," Lock told her.

Jones put his mug down and leaned forward. "Have you heard anything from London?"

"No," Lock answered. "Should we have?"

Jones looked at Norton, who shook her head.

"I don't know, it might be nothing," Jones said, easing back in his chair. "But I saw a CNN report that the UN General Assembly has gone into closed session."

"Is that unusual?" Hardcastle asked.

"Yes," Jones confirmed. "Also, the report disappeared from their next bulletin, and there's nothing about it on the web."

"How about Circus?" Norton asked.

Jones looked at her. "They're not sure, but they think something is going on, because the UN is all locked down over there in New York. Nobody's allowed into the building."

"Do you think this could be it?" Lock asked in a low voice.

"I have no idea," Jones told him. "It might be the Cuckoos making their expected move. Or it could be foreign powers not convinced by the British explanation of the event the other night. Who knows, they could all be looking at the photograph you took this afternoon."

"And if it *is* the Cuckoos," Norton said, "what then?"

Jones lifted his mug again, tilted it slightly as he contemplated its contents. "Some sort of outrage on a similar scale, or worse, than the nine-eleven attack."

Hardcastle took a deep breath and exhaled noisily. "What about the Clangers out there? They're taking a long time to respond... if they are *ever* going to respond."

Jones frowned. "Clangers?"

"His nickname for our supposed saviours," Norton explained. "But what I still don't understand is how our message can get across the galaxy instantly, light speed and all that."

"The message itself doesn't travel," Hardcastle told her. "It's encoding aimed at a scalar field resonance. Provided the other side is looking for that coding, they'll have got it instantly. It's not exactly a gravity wave, but a manipulation on a very small scale of the underlying force holding the universe together."

"You've lost me," Norton said.

"Don't worry," Hardcastle said. "It's what nearly got me kicked out of the postgraduate programme but also into the welcoming arms of Circus."

Norton pursed her lips. "Problem for me is that *if* it is so simple, for the Clangers as you call them, couldn't the Cuckoos pick it up as well?"

Jones held up his hands. "That's enough Clangers and Cuckoos, but yes, theoretically the enemy could have picked it up, though they could never locate its source. And decoding it without the precise quantum key is *supposed* to be impossible. But *if* Circus intelligence is all wrong on that and the enemy *were* able to decode it, then yes, they would likely react."

"And do what they intended to do soon anyway," Lock added.

"So, we just carry on with our mission and wait," Norton said.

"And hope," Jones agreed calmly.

-o-

Kyle followed Ventriloquist Jack along the main hall in the bungalow. The boiler-suited man unlocked a door towards the rear.

"Wow," Kyle said. A workstation occupied the centre of the room. It faced multiple wide screens mounted on a metal framework. "It's like something out of NASA."

166

Jack pointed. "This one here." One of the screens displayed a garbled blue mess with yellow lines. "It's been doing this off and on for a while, but usually corrects itself. Not this time though."

Kyle moved around the other side of the workstation and reached under the offending monitor. It switched off. He prodded a finger. It switched on again, this time with a coherent desktop image with multiple icons. "It's your express gate," Kyle said. "Next time you boot up, press any key and it should install the monitor properly."

Ventriloquist Jack sighed with a thin grin. "That simple. I never thought to switch it off and on again."

"You could try a reboot now," Kyle suggested.

"No, it's okay," Jack said. He waved a hand as though presenting the array of screens. "What do you think?"

Kyle looked. Some of the screens depicted real-time graphs with what looked like seismic readings. One showed a depiction of the Earth with a bow wave of green and blue tapering to a tail. This was fluctuating slowly. Another had multiple windows.

"Amazing," Kyle said. "What's it all about, Mister Thomas?"

Jack sat down in a black swivel office chair and rotated to face the young man. "Why haven't you gone to university?"

"Oh, I will do, probably next year," Kyle answered. He slid onto a stool near the workstation to gaze up at the screens.

"You don't want to leave the village, do you?" Jack asked, as though stating a fact.

"True," Kyle said absently, still focussed on the array of puzzling information.

"You feel connected here, don't you? As though you are part of the land here, and *it* is a part of you."

"Never thought of it like that," Kyle said, looking at the man. "But yes, that's sort of how I feel."

"See that," Jack said, pointing at one of the screens; the chart on this one was static. "It's data from four Earth science satellites. That there was an extremely unusual geomagnetic wave. It lasted only about half an hour, then suddenly declined. See the date and time?"

"Oh yeh... only a few nights ago."

"And see those co-ordinates?"

The young man looked puzzled at this.

"Those are the co-ordinates for here, this village, our mountain," Jack told him. "I only found the data today on my own storage devices. It's like nothing ever recorded or published in scientific history."

"What are you saying, Mister Thomas?"

"Don't tell anyone, but something big is going on in that mountain."

Kyle's expression took on a mix of curiosity and fleeting alarm. "Like volcanic or something?"

Ventriloquist Jack almost laughed but quickly reverted to serious. "Nothing natural, young friend," he said in a low voice. "Something like this could only come from a machine, and one that is far more powerful than the one at CERN that cost hundreds of billions of dollars to build."

Kyle's face was fixed with disbelief. "Here in Amharfarn? Maybe your data got corrupted."

"I don't think so, but anyway, thank you for fixing my monitor. And don't forget, don't tell anyone about this…" He pointed at the screen. "Except Andy Lock. You can tell him if you want, but only him."

"But, Mister Thomas, surely it's impossible to build something that big underground without anyone knowing?"

"Not if it was built hundreds of thousands of years ago," the man said.

"Historians might have a bit of a problem with that idea," Kyle said, but he kept his voice low and respectful.

Jack reached for a computer mouse on the workstation. "Have a look at this," he prompted. The screen Kyle had brought to life by switching it off and on went black. A digital time display ticked above a date in its upper right corner.

"That's recorded video from a webcam on Anglesey," Jack explained. "It's pointed across the sea in our direction. Takes a frame every two seconds. Keep watching."

Kyle's eyes widened as a flash appeared on the screen. Frozen images of what looked like a white sheet stepped across it, until the whole screen lit up with a black-and-white landscape illuminated by a wall of lightning.

"Recognise that on the left?" Jack asked, then answered the question himself. "That's our mountain."

Kyle looked at the man. "The date and time match that other one, the Earth science stuff."

"That's what the magnetic wave looked like in the atmosphere," Jack said. "And what created it goes about ten miles out to sea. Nature can't do that, not with that sort of precision."

"But if it's a machine, who built it?"

Ventriloquist Jack leaned back in his chair and rotated it. "My family has lived here for generations," he said quietly. "They were here during Queen Victoria's time when dozens of miners were killed underground and the army closed the mines. My grandfather was here during the Second World War when the navy came in force. Some of them were killed in that mountain in nineteen forty-five. He was friendly with one of the survivors, asked him what was in there underground."

Kyle leaned forward, eyes serious. "What did he say?"

Jack smiled. "They made everyone in the village, including my grandfather, sign the Official Secrets Act. My grandfather was told that what is in that mountain, the technology and concepts it represents, the sheer consequences of it for humanity, is too big to fit inside our puny brains. His words, not mine."

Kyle relaxed slightly. "I don't know. It's kind of hearsay, don't you think?"

Ventriloquist Jack laughed and waved a hand towards his screens. "I don't go on hearsay. I'm a scientist and what that data tells me is that, yes, there is something under our mountain, and it's bigger, better and more powerful than the best of our scientists, with all that money, have been able to build at CERN." He stared at Kyle.

Kyle remained uncomfortably silent for a moment as the stare continued. He glanced at the door. "I think I'd better go home now. Hope your monitor is okay when you boot it up next time."

"Sure, you go home, kid, and thank you," Jack said, rising a little stiffly. "And don't worry, I won't tell anyone that you are working for them or connected in any way to that." He pointed at the screen. "You've signed it, haven't you?"

Kyle now looked distinctly worried. "Signed what?"

"The Official Secrets Act."

"I have to go," Kyle said, turning for the door.

FIVE

Deep underground, Emily Norton and Hardcastle rode their bicycles along the giant tunnel. It was as bright as daylight in there, and as unnatural in appearance as two people pedalling along it in silvery white suits. Tyres squeaked against the blue floor.

The pair dismounted when they reached the now dead lighting unit. Leaving the bikes on the floor, they entered the passageway.

"Yoo-hoo," Hardcastle called out in a cheerful falsetto voice.

Hearing this in the first chamber, Gwenda Evans gathered up folders, sliding yellowed papers into one of them. She was seated a few feet from the German naval officer's skeleton. It was still on its chair, eye sockets watching her.

"Greetings," Emily Norton said when she and Hardcastle entered. "Any sign of a reply?"

Gwenda dumped the folders onto a pile on the table. "Afraid not. It's been very quiet here."

"You could have kept each other company either side of the entrance," Hardcastle said.

Gwenda glanced at him. "We did for a while, but we ran out of things to say." She turned her attention to Norton. "Anything going on above ground?"

Norton set down her backpack and began briefing Gwenda, who took on the expression of a woman listening to juicy gossip. "The UN has been in secret session," Norton said. "Jones thinks the Cuckoos might be about to act."

Hardcastle seemed to decide he was being excluded from this female chat, so left them to it and moved through to the next chamber. He glanced at the diving suit skeleton on the floor before approaching the final doorway.

Midway to the centre of the circular chamber, Banes sat at the trellis table with its laptops. Head tilted forward, he was reading a paperback in his gloved hands. Now he dog-eared the page and put the book down as Hardcastle walked from the distant entrance towards him.

"Hola, amigo," Hardcastle called out. "How's it cooking? Any reply from the Clangers?"

"I do wish you wouldn't call them that," Banes answered. "But no, nothing."

Hardcastle dumped his backpack on the floor. He adjusted the EMF suit hood over his helmet. "Then how do you think we should imagine and name them? Would you prefer a Darth Vader type, all hissy with a gurgling breath? Or maybe Dalek-oriented life of the party blobs encased in machines that glide along the floor? Floors here are good for Daleks, don't you think?"

"But not the stairway," Banes argued. "The facilities aren't exactly great for us hominids either."

Hardcastle grinned. "On the subject of facilities, what's the urine score for today then?"

Banes groaned as he stood up. "Knock off the schoolboy humour please. It's unbefitting, even for a scientist of your low calibre."

Hardcastle maintained a cheerful grin as he gazed around the chamber. "It's what keeps me feeling undaunted, and my way of trying to keep morale above certain death and about to be exterminated levels. But okay, you're suggesting we forget our British traditions and proceed without any comic relief."

"It's your twelve-hour shift that's about to start," Banes said as he prepared his backpack for departure. "You can do it with whatever humour you like. Maybe all those apparently human remains over there will grant you inspiration." He pointed at the skeletons littering the floor of the chamber towards and beyond its centre, where the cannon-like structures remained bowed and inactive.

Hardcastle instead looked up at the domed ceiling, the expanse of stars and nebulae artificially depicted there and surrounding the giant echo of the laptop screen. "It's awesome, though, isn't it?"

"Am I relieved?" Banes asked as he fastened his pack.

"But aren't you curious about how intelligent this place actually is, and whether its builders have achieved a truly socially advanced level of civilisation?"

"Define truly, socially advanced," Banes challenged.

"Application of the right to life, dignity and respect for all sentient living beings of course."

Banes hiked the pack onto his shoulders. "And its enforcement against those who violate such rights? Intelligent predators for example?"

"Like humans," Hardcastle agreed. "Killing systematically without remorse, and axiomatic of our systems of government for millennia."

That moment, a high-pitched voice echoed in the chamber. "What are you boys doing that's taking so long?" It was Gwenda Evans. Looking like some diminutive winter warfare soldier in her hooded suit, she was striding towards them from the entrance.

Hardcastle pointed at Banes. "It's his fault, Miss," he called out. "Getting all philosophical on me." He then turned and whispered to Banes. "Better be careful El Capitano doesn't enforce you with her pop-gun."

It was pre-midnight dark when Banes and Gwenda finally made it to the open air of the compound.

-o-

Early morning in the centre of Amharfarn brought the arrival on foot, by car, and just one on a bicycle of the handful of blue-collar workers, bus drivers and a couple of female office types.

These converged on the Jones Bros bus depot, plant and vehicle hire compound and scrap yard.

In the middle of the derelict cars in the yard, a yellow JCB roared into life and raised its clawed grabber to the heavens.

Not that far from this activity, Kyle hurried in the other direction towards Lock's safe house. The young man looked worried. He kept glancing over his shoulders, eyes scanning as though for enemies in a war zone.

And along the farmland road away on the opposite side of the village, a relaxed Hefin Gwynedd opened his front door and sniffed the country air as Pero darted out from beside his feet.

The dog disappeared around the side of the house to the yard at the back. He pounced up at the hen hut door, front paws scratching at its paint-flaked timber, gripped the bolt with his teeth and, growling quietly, wrestled the bolt, head and body jerking methodically. He got it halfway before dropping to the ground, where he panted, head turned expectantly towards the farmhouse.

Pero emitted a small whine when his master did not appear. He jumped up again, this time succeeding in getting the bolt fully disengaged. Pero then butted the bottom corner of the door with the side of his head and snout, before clawing at it with a paw.

When it swung outwards a few inches, he retreated towards the farmhouse, halting halfway to turn and issue an encouraging bark.

The first couple of hens emerged, clucking as though disgruntled with the arrival of yet another day of their routine existence.

Still clinging to the world of sleep at the B&B, Caycey Jones stirred under his duvet as a digital alarm clock display changed to 08:00. Resting next to it on the bedside table, a mobile phone vibrated and beeped.

Jones was immediately alert and sat upright, reaching for the phone.

Miiko and Kikuko were halfway down the stairs with their suitcases when Mair Ellis came out from the lounge. "You'd better come and see this on television," Mair told them. "There's problems at the airports."

A hurriedly dressed Jones appeared on the landing above the Japanese ladies.

At the same time in the safe house next door, Lock's, Banes's and Gwenda's mobile phones variously beeped, clanged and vibrated in unison. They were seated at the kitchen table with a very serious-looking Kyle. All three glanced at each other and reached for their phones.

"I'll go and talk to Mister Thomas," Lock told Kyle, before looking at his mobile.

Banes got up after reading the message on his and went into the office, where he switched on a small TV.

"I thought it best to tell you about Ventriloquist Jack," Kyle said to Lock in the kitchen.

Lock frowned at his mobile and then glanced up, distracted. "You were absolutely right to do so. I'll handle him, so don't worry about it, but don't mention it to anyone else."

"Sure," Kyle said. "But I mean, is he right about there being something in the mountain?"

"You must forget everything that crazy man told you," Lock answered.

"It's the airports," Banes called from the other room. "They've cancelled all flights."

"From which airports?" Gwenda Evans called back.

"All of them," Banes answered.

Someone knocked at the back door. Lock opened it. The hurriedly dressed and unshaved Caycey Jones came in. "Have you heard?" He then saw Kyle. "Good morning, young man. I've been hearing good things about you. I'm Jones by the way. I have a Welsh ancestor."

Gwenda Evans held up her phone. "Prime Minister is making a national announcement at two o'clock."

Jones nodded. "President is doing one at the same time. UN Secretary-General as well. Co-ordinated announcements by all world leaders from what I can gather."

"There's obviously a big problem then," Kyle said.

"You'd better go home to your gran and keep her company for today," Lock told Kyle as mobile phones blew their individual fanfares yet again. "Tell her not to worry. I'll come around later if you want."

"Whoa whoa whoa," Banes called from the other room. "You'd better come and see this."

Instead of leaving, Kyle followed Lock and the others into the

175

office. Banes was hunched forward on an armchair facing the television.

On the screen, a garish green-and-blue footer bar, with TBLTV in yellow letters, bottomed a sequence of what looked like CCTV footage. A marina was illuminated by moonlight, only to be interrupted by a bright flash. A BBC voice covered it:

"If you've just joined us, we are getting a flood of reports of a massive explosion off the coast of Florida, and we're speculating whether it might have something to do with the global cancellation of all commercial airline flights this morning.

"We have just received this footage from a local TV station near Tampa Bay."

On the screen, palm trees suddenly bent over, boats tilted and capsized in the marina, then the screen went blank.

"Try CNN," Jones suggested. Banes prodded the remote controller. Kyle leaned forward to watch.

"...believe the explosion occurred half an hour after all international and domestic flights were cancelled, worldwide," an American female news anchor voice was saying.

On the screen, a police pursuit camera showed headlights shining along a dirt road. It was picking up speed when a bright flash lit up the sea to the side of it beyond some palm trees. The car halted, then began to perform a U-turn before it stopped again.

Now a rising column of fire occupied the centre of the screen out to sea. A mushroom cloud was forming as it billowed upwards. The screen abruptly turned black.

The sequence then clipped back to the beginning of the loop and a small multiscreen rectangle appeared. "We're now linking to the White House," the news anchor said, "where we are told an official statement is imminent."

The rest of the screen showed the post-explosion activity and growing mushroom cloud once again.

Jones spoke quietly. "That looks an awful lot like a nuclear explosion."

"Oh shit," Kyle muttered.

"Shush, listen," Lock cautioned.

A flustered spokeswoman appeared on the TV at a podium bearing the Seal of the President of the United States.

"I am going to make a brief statement," she announced. "There will be no questions." She looked down at the podium. "Following recent threats and demands from a new and previously unknown terrorist organisation, the United States government, together with some other national governments across the globe, received a one-hour warning at approximately one thirty EST this morning that a nuclear device was going to be detonated at sea near an unspecified coastline.

"All branches of the United States military were put on immediate high alert. And as a precaution, at one forty-five EST, all international civilian airline flights were grounded until further notice. Warnings were also issued to maritime vessels.

"The United States is able to confirm that at two thirty-one EST this morning a nuclear explosion of approximately twelve kilotons yield was detected eight miles off the Florida gulf coast. There are no reported casualties at this time.

"Telephone hotlines to all nuclear powers were active from the moment the threat was received, and the United States is able to assure the world that no nuclear retaliation by the United States is intended at this time. That is the end of the statement."

There was an immediate chorus of reporters' petulant voices.

"I will not be answering any questions," the spokeswoman told them. "But I can confirm that the President will address the nation this morning." She then walked away from the podium.

"It's the bloody Cuckoos," Banes said angrily. Lock glared at him.

Kyle stared at the TV for a moment then glanced around at the others.

"You'd better go home," Lock told him in a sombre voice.

"Is there going to be a war?" Kyle asked.

"I don't think so," Lock said. "But go look after your gran. She'll be worried."

Kyle's mobile issued a *yak yak yak, yak yak yak* as he contemplated this. "Hi, Gran," he answered as he headed for the kitchen. "Yeh, I heard... I'm coming home right now. Don't worry... No, it isn't a war."

-o-

Miiko and Kikuko were seated in the B&B lounge with Mair and Wyn Ellis. They were watching the same repeating news on TV when Caycey Jones returned from next door.

"There's a change of plan," Jones announced. "Switch off the TV, please."

Wyn Ellis used the remote to comply. Jones sat next to him and faced the Japanese ladies.

"Are we at war?" Mair Ellis asked.

"Not exactly," Jones answered. "But events are going to move rapidly over the next few days." He looked at Miiko. "Quite clearly, you can't get home, but it's not safe for any of us, especially for Mister and Missus Ellis, for you two to stay here."

"We will find somewhere else to stay, perhaps Betsy why Cod?" Miiko responded, looking at Mair.

"Betws y Coed," Wyn corrected. Miiko smiled.

"There's another option," Jones said to Miiko. "It's not a very comfortable one for you, but it would help us a great deal."

"We will do anything you wish, if it helps you," Miiko responded, then spoke rapidly in Japanese to Kikuko.

"Ah so," Kikuko said, nodding her agreement. "You want... us go to mountain?" she asked Jones. "This great honour. Ancient technology very interesting."

Miiko scolded her in Japanese, with Kikuko evidently protesting innocent ignorance back at her in similar Japanese.

"Ancient technology?" Wyn Ellis queried.

Jones sighed. "That sort of information could get you and all of us killed," he told Mair and Wyn. "But you might as well know now since you are part of the team. Your interest in UFOs isn't exactly nonsense, Mister Ellis. That mountain is extremely important to our survival."

"Whose survival exactly?" Mair Ellis demanded.

178

"The entire human race," Jones told her. Miiko nodded from the other sofa.

Mair brushed a trembling finger under her eye. "Nonsense. This is Amharfarn for goodness' sake. Nothing ever happens here." A couple of tears leaked past the finger.

Wyn Ellis put his arm around her. "It's okay, really it's okay, calm down," he said. "But the last few days have been rather strong evidence to the contrary. We must play our part. These are good people... Andy, Gwenda, we've known them for years. And Mister Jones here, these ladies, they're good people. You know that. We have to trust them, Mair, and we have to help them."

"Life to you," Miiko cheered quietly from the other sofa, raising both hands in the air. Kikuko started to raise her arms to do the same.

Jones held up his hand, fingers stretched out to caution the two young women not to do this.

"My God," a wide-eyed Mair Ellis whispered in disbelief. "All I wanted was a quiet retirement running bed and breakfast."

-o-

Ventriloquist Jack headed for the door in the high wall as a rattling buzzer sounded repeatedly on the side of the bungalow. He was wearing a boiler suit, a glowing cigarette stuck in the corner of his mouth. There were no signs of coal dust either on his face or clothes this morning.

Jack grunted as he opened the door. Andy Lock was standing there holding a large brown envelope.

"I was half expecting you last night," Jack said. "Come in." He pointed at the envelope. "What's that? And have you heard the news from Florida?"

"In good time," Lock answered. He stepped across the threshold into the yard. "Is there somewhere we can talk?"

Jack closed the door in the wall, then indicated a direction with a sweep of his arm. "This way."

His lips chewed and rotated the cigarette end as he led Lock along the weed-bounded path. It took them down past the junk, heaps of coal and the strange-looking crucible.

"Still at it with your illegal generator, I see," Lock said.

The boiler-suited man halted, turned, and shook his head in disapproval. He spoke calmly as though to a child. "Well, that's just another indicator, isn't it, Andy? That a non-polluting, virtually free energy system is illegal across the entire planet, and that humanity is being held back. I would like to know by whom?"

"Not here," Lock warned.

Ventriloquist Jack bowed slightly and indicated towards the house. He flicked his cigarette end into the weeds.

Lock was shown into a long, almost normal-looking lounge with a huge window facing the sea. Spotlessly clean, and otherwise classically furnished, it was *almost* normal due to the half-dozen tropical fish aquaria arranged along two of its walls. Potted palm trees, some reaching the ceiling, densely occupied the corner between them, giving it a jungle-like appearance. The aquaria bubbled away either side with bright displays of multicoloured fish.

Lock flinched when a white parrot fluttered out from the jungle corner and landed on Ventriloquist Jack's shoulder. It nibbled fondly at the man's ear.

"Cuh o' tea. How now hown cow," the parrot said to Lock in a remarkable imitation of its owner's ventriloquist diction. Eyeing him curiously, it commenced a yo-yo motion with its head.

"Go to your perch," Jack told the parrot.

It fluttered instead to land on the cover of an aquarium.

"So," Lock said, "you've been talking to Kyle."

Jack pointed to an armchair. "Have a seat. Can I get you some tea?"

"Thank you, no," Lock declined as he sat down.

Jack pulled up a dining chair and perched himself sideways on it, facing Lock. "You *have* seen the news this morning?"

"Of course, but that's not why I am here," Lock answered. He placed the brown envelope on his lap. "Why did you have to frighten Kyle with all that nonsense about the mountain?"

Jack raised his eyebrows and smiled. "Can you look me in the eye and tell me that it *is* nonsense, Andy? My family's been here for years. My ancestors were here when the Victorians sent the army to close the mine."

"Even so…"

"And how about the Royal Navy during the war with Nazi Germany, when the whole village had to sign the Official Secrets Act? Is *that* what you've got for me in that envelope?"

"Actually, it is," Lock said. He slid out A4 sheets from the envelope and produced a pen. "You need to sign."

"And what if I refuse?"

"That could make things difficult and dangerous for all of us, including you," Lock told him.

"Fishy, fishy, fishy," the parrot called from the top of the aquarium. Its head was tilted precariously, eyeing a small shoal of golden fish through the glass.

Jack issued a wry but pragmatic smile. "I saw that little show you staged yesterday. How you got Kyle to spread the story of a light in the sky that never happened. And who was that stuck-up ponce in the fancy coat? The one you took up the mountain with your new American friend? You did it to fool the ponce, didn't you?"

"You are meddling in things you couldn't possibly understand," Lock warned. "And you'll be endangering yourself and everyone else in the village if you don't co-operate with me on this." He held out the papers.

"Oh, I'll sign the bloody thing," Jack said, accepting them. "But I want to make it clear that if I do this, I want to be part of the team. With what's happened off the coast of Florida, especially, you're going to need all the help you can get."

Lock's stern expression turned to mild surprise. "I'm glad you're being sensible, but there is no team, as you put it."

Now Ventriloquist Jack became frustrated. "You know full well that there is something bordering on sentience in that mountain. It has been trying to communicate with a few of us in this village for years. And you know full well there is a global order that is the enemy of humanity, and against which, I believe, you are trying to protect whatever it is that's in that mountain. You need my help, Andy. More than that, you're going to need near enough everyone in this village behind you if we are going to have any chance of surviving what's coming. You know that. I know that. So, when are we going to put an end to this pretence of business as usual?"

Lock glanced up at the ceiling. He issued a deep sigh. "Okay, okay. Now sign those forms. You'll be *in* when the time is right, which will be very soon, I promise you. But for now it is absolutely vital that you keep up the appearance of business as usual. Is that understood?"

Jack bowed his head in acknowledgement. He then leafed through the papers. "There's two forms here," he observed. "This other one is a contract for me to be your confidential informant."

"That's right," Lock said.

"You fully intended to bring me on board when you came here, didn't you?"

"I did," Lock said with a pained expression. "But you must do what I tell you, or you will endanger everything. No more chatter, especially about the stuff you told Kyle. Do you understand?"

"Absolutely," Jack agreed. "But you'll have to sign up Hefin as well."

"Crazy Box? For goodness' sake, why would I need to sign him up? He thinks he's the King of Wales."

Ventriloquist Jack glared with a touch of anger in his eyes. "Nonsense. It was his dad who painted that on the house. But the important thing is because he's been helping me with my gravity tests up at his place. He also knows what I told Kyle about CERN, and the anomalous standing wave going out to sea from the mountain. Also, Andy, *our* UFO is not far off from being ready to fly."

The parrot fluttered back to the man's shoulder. "Good boy sweetie," it said, nibbling his ear. "Want a piece of apple?"

Andy Lock just looked stunned as he tried to absorb what the man had told him. "*Gravity* tests?"

-o-

The sun had risen closer to its midday height by the time Miiko and Kikuko towed their wheeled suitcases to the end of the B&B driveway. They loaded them into their car on the street.

The engine coughed into life.

Wyn Ellis waved as they drove off, with Mair Ellis doing so tearfully in the front doorway by his side. Wyn then glanced along the road in both directions before inclining his head towards the interior of the B&B. "All clear," he called.

Caycey Jones came out carrying a backpack in response. He walked casually down the drive and just as casually headed up the drive to the safe house next door.

Mair and Wyn watched Andy Lock answer the front door there, letting Jones in. Gwenda Evans then immediately came out, waving over the wall at Mair and Wyn, before getting into the white van. She drove it out, turning in the same direction taken by the Japanese ladies.

The Ellis couple then returned to the lounge. Wyn went to the bay window and looked out.

"Alone at last," Mair said.

"Apart from the listening devices they planted all over the house," Wyn reminded her.

Mair put a hand over her mouth. "I didn't mean anything by it."

"I know." He inclined his head at the window. "Here they go."

Mair joined him in time to see Andy Lock and Caycey Jones getting into the 4x4 next door. It drove out and went towards the village.

As it did so, Banes stepped out into view and looked towards them from the adjacent driveway. He waved.

Wyn Ellis waved back. "They are smooth though, aren't they?" Wyn said to Mair.

"Do you think so? They're not exactly like the spies in the films."

"Well, this isn't a film. This is Amharfarn and it's real. If it was a film, everything would be dramatic."

"Terrorists detonating an atomic bomb off the coast of Florida isn't dramatic then?" Mair Ellis countered. "You heard Jones.

There's clearly a connection between that bomb in Florida and what's going on here, or what's about to happen here. Isn't that something *seriously* dramatic?"

Wyn Ellis approached his binoculars by the side window and tapped his fingers against them. "Terrorists is what the establishment is saying, obviously. But then they told us some guy in a cave in Afghanistan directed an attack which brought down three steel-framed buildings in New York due to fires, one of which wasn't even hit by a plane. That was dramatic enough, wasn't it? And no modern steel-framed buildings have ever been brought down by fire before, or since."

"So you say." Mair's tone suggested she had heard it all before.

"If the official story was true," Wyn said, "then all the architectural and structural engineering standards for such buildings would have been changed the world over in response to the September eleven attacks. But they haven't."

"Not that *you* know of," Mair retorted.

Outside, next door, Banes stubbed out his cigarette then went back inside. Wyn Ellis noticed this and returned to the bay window. He stared at the road. "I've kept up with all the professional journals. They were controlled demolitions. And now the same elitist gangsters are probably behind what happened in Florida. It's their endgame, or part of it."

"And your UFOs?" Mair asked. "What have they got to do with all of this and our mountain?"

"Just look at history," Wyn said, turning to face her. "Wars, genocide... They are a constantly repeating pattern that's still happening even as we speak. It's impossible to believe that such a precise continuity of brutal inhumanity in our organised behaviour can be maintained generation after generation. Surely people aren't such sheep? Something inhuman that lives much longer than us behind it all would explain a hell of a lot, wouldn't you agree?"

"I always thought it was caused by corporations, capitalism, greed and elite families," Mair said. "Fascist oligarchy disguised as democracy. It's why we joined the socialist cause."

Wyn Ellis shook his head. "I thought the same, but no. It's not

184

about wealth. It's not about power. The dynastic families already have more of both than they or their descendants could ever possibly need. It's something else, something utterly inhuman."

"If that is true," Mair Ellis said, "then I was a lot happier living under an illusion."

"That might have worked if we had been living somewhere else," Wyn sympathised. "But this is Amharfarn. Whatever faint grip we still had on that comfort zone is disappearing fast."

-o-

Hefin Gwynedd and Ventriloquist Jack were leaning over the farm gate in front of the TV display table. Lock's 4x4 came along the narrow lane from the village. Both men waved at the car as it sped past without slowing.

Andy Lock sighed behind the wheel. He glanced at Jones beside him. "Well, there they were. Perhaps the Circus acronym is proving to be an unfortunate choice."

"On that, I've always had my doubts," Caycey Jones agreed, "but especially since I arrived in this village."

The car pulled up around a bend a little along the road. A black-and-white barrier was now in its closed position, blocking vehicle access to the forestry track.

Jones got out. He slipped a key into the padlock then walked across to lean on the counterweight to lift the barrier for Lock to drive through. The 4x4 parked on a flat area of grass between some trees on the edge of the forest.

Jones approached from the barrier after locking it closed again.

The exhaust sputtered once when the 4x4 engine was killed. The car door opened and was slammed shut.

"This way," Lock said. He was carrying another brown envelope in his hand.

He led the way along a barely visible path into the trees. This headed downhill in the general direction of the distant village.

185

"He actually used the word *sentience*?" Jones asked. "I've seen that guy in the boiler suit before, by the way. I didn't talk to him, but he did some strange trick with his voice."

"That's Ventriloquist Jack alright. Tries it on everyone, but yes, *sentience*. It sort of tallies with the nineteen forty-five incident reports. But they used the term *impaired judgement* back then. After the incident, apparently, a percentage of navy personnel and villagers acted a bit odd. Thought they were getting messages in their heads."

"I've actually spoken to that old guy at the farm," Jones said. "Second day I was here. Tried to sell me an old TV set when I was on my way to see if you were at the compound. He said stuff about the mountain, and when you think about it, it does have a sideband output in the megahertz range that can induce entrainment in human brain frequencies."

"That's covered in later technical reports and is one of the things I'm supposed to keep an eye out for," Lock said. He came to a halt between the trees. It was quite dark here now under the thick pines. He peered through the gloom as though unsure of the direction to take. "I think we've come too far. It's got to be back that way."

Jones followed him as they doubled back, booted feet sinking into the thick carpet of pine needles on the ground.

Lock stepped over a partly obscured drainage channel then waited for his companion, holding out a hand to help him across. "This way," Lock announced. It looked brighter ahead.

The pine trees gave way to a downward-sloping fire-barrier space, across which stood rough hedgerow and a cluster of deciduous oaks, sycamores and chestnut trees. Hefin Gwynedd was standing at a gap in the hedge, waving to them.

"This guy said the mountain talks to him," Jones said quietly. "And that he watches Gilligan's Island on his old televisions."

Pero gave a welcoming bark from beside Hefin's feet. Ventriloquist Jack's face poked out from the edge of the gap.

"Here we go then," Lock said, sighing as he and Jones headed down there.

-o-

Miiko and Kikuko easily followed Gwenda Evans as she pedalled a mountain bike with some difficulty along the tunnel. Gwenda seemed to be having problems keeping her feet on the pedals. All three were wearing EMF suits.

"Would you like to swap?" Miiko called.

"No, it's alright, dear," Gwenda answered. "Neither of you is much taller than me. But I probably should have left this monster for Andy."

Miiko translated into Japanese for Kikuko, who responded with laughter and something else in that language. Kikuko was riding Gwenda's pink chopper.

"Kikuko says her legs are longer than yours," Miiko told Gwenda as the two younger women now drew alongside, freewheeling to keep their pace down.

Gwenda rotated her head to try to face Kikuko but managed to get only one eye looking beyond her EMF suit hood. The bike wobbled; she returned her attention to the handlebars and front wheel. "I know," she said, voice rising in pitch. "She's got longer legs than me but I'm not getting off this one, because if I do I won't be getting on a bike again for at least half an hour, if ever."

"You are determined lady," Kikuko said.

"Your English is coming along," Gwenda responded. She lifted her head, eyes suddenly alert. "Hey, what's that?" In the distance, a white dot was coming towards them along the tunnel floor.

Within a few seconds, they could see it was someone in an EMF suit riding a bike. Gwenda groaned and pedalled faster. "Something must have happened."

Emily Norton applied her brakes as she approached, steering away from Gwenda's bike as its brakes failed to bring the machine to a timely halt. Norton was out of breath. "Something's happened back there," she said between gasps.

"Have we had a reply?" Gwenda demanded.

"I don't think so. It's a person, or looks like one... A man, I think. It appeared out of thin air. One minute we were playing chess at the

187

doorway, next thing I knew when I looked up he was just standing there way over on the other side of the chamber."

Gwenda took this in with a serious expression. "Where's Hardcastle?"

Norton waved an arm. "Still down there, staying close to the chamber entrance. He suggested I get to the surface and phone Commander Lock."

"Did it look like a threat?"

"I didn't stay long enough to find out."

Gwenda struggled to get ready to re-launch her bike. "Get to the surface and phone Andy," she told Norton, then pointed at Kikuko. "You go with her please, quick as you can."

Miiko started translating but her partner was already turning her bike around.

Gwenda took a deep breath and started her bike moving again, pushing hard on the pedal to get the first wobbling revolution of its wheels.

Norton and Kikuko pedalled easily at speed in the opposite direction.

-o-

Hardcastle stood pensively at the chamber entrance. His eyes were fixed on a distant, humanlike figure. It wasn't moving over there beyond the towering, cannon-shaped devices.

"If you think I'm coming over there to say hello alone, you're mistaken," Hardcastle whispered between clenched teeth. He narrowed his eyes, tilted his head, squinting as he tried to make out details of the thing standing there.

Taking a deep breath, Hardcastle unzipped the top of his EMF suit jacket. He reached inside, gingerly produced a pair of pocket binoculars and put them to his eyes.

Magnified through the lenses, the figure took on a more distinct though wobbly form. Even magnified, the facial area was too small to make out any features, but it did resemble a man. He, or it, was wearing a white shirt and black trousers. It was also directly facing

188

Hardcastle and seemed completely motionless. The head was topped with startlingly white hair.

Hardcastle's gloved finger adjusted focus. "Are you alive, or some sort of statue?"

As though in response, the man-thing moved its arms and clasped its hands together in front at waist height.

Hardcastle immediately lowered the binoculars and turned to face the entrance. "You guys better hurry up," he prayed quietly to himself.

-o-

Lock and Jones followed Hefin Gwynedd and Ventriloquist Jack across a small paddock surrounded by oak trees and an age-rotted fence.

The old man opened a metal gate covered in chicken wire to let them all through. The yard was a little way down a slope beyond this. Pero ran ahead and went into the back of the farmhouse.

"It's in here," Ventriloquist Jack said, pointing at the barn. Hefin unlocked its doors.

"Oh my God," Caycey Jones said. He had seen the copper coils and lattices fixed to the roof beams. "It's a wonder you haven't fried your brains in here."

Jack pointed. "Faraday cage."

Jones peered at the enclosure, eyes taking in the chain-link fencing nailed to a timber frame in one of the disused calf pens. He then approached the fibreglass, bath-like contraption in the centre of the barn and looked inside it.

Ventriloquist Jack and Hefin Gwynedd waited proudly to one side as Lock joined Jones at the object.

"I've never seen anything like this," Jones said in a low voice, "even at NASA. And I saw some freaky contraptions there, I can tell you." He turned to Jack. "You say this actually works?"

"I can show you," the man answered, starting forward.

"No," Jones warned. "This thing could microwave us to ashes."

Jack approached and patted the fibreglass rim. "It won't. I don't

189

need to use the primer circuits. The testbed gives off ten watts at the most, but it's also way above the one-metre range, so no microwaves at all."

"But it couldn't possibly work," Jones argued. "Where's your field-spin coming from?"

Jack pointed at the mess of electronics inside the bath. "The driver coils are primed. They create a cognitive AC-generated negative mass field."

"Impossible," Jones argued, almost laughing. "That would be a singularity in theoretical terms. You could never reconcile the math, let alone define *cognitive*."

"Only if you're stuck with Einstein," Jack countered.

Jones grinned with disbelief. "So you wrecked E equals MC squared, did you? I'd certainly like to see that."

"Doubting Einstein is what got me thrown out of theoretical science," Jack said. "I went over to experimental and got my PhD anyway."

"Okay, so show me," Jones prompted.

Lock seemed surprised at this. "Do you really think that's a good idea? One-metre stuff around here isn't exactly without risk."

"Ten watts," Ventriloquist Jack said. "Sure, it could be detected, but the only person I worried about detecting it was you, Andy. And now you're here."

Pero came running in through the barn door. He sat in front of Hefin Gwynedd and barked.

"Dog says we are good to go," the old man announced.

Caycey Jones, Andy Lock and Hefin, together with Pero, were watching when the circular fibreglass bath lifted off. It rose higher than their heads before settling slowly back to the ground.

Ventriloquist Jack smiled. He was positioned by the circuit breakers inside the Faraday cage. He lit a cigarette as he came out of there.

Caycey Jones stared at the man. "You do know that this is forbidden?"

Jack grinned. "Did you ever hear what Hitler said?"

Jones pointed at the fibreglass bath. "About this sort of technology?"

"No, Hitler talked about a future with all humanity governed by a new and glorious elite, about whom he was not permitted to speak."

"I never heard that one," Jones said.

"The Nazis wrote down everything uttered by that man during his table talks," Ventriloquist Jack continued. "I always wondered who was able to withhold their permission, from Adolf Hitler of all people."

-o-

Wyn Ellis continued to keep watch from the bay window. Mair noisily heaved a vacuum cleaner back and forth on the carpets behind him.

The phone rang. Mair switched the cleaner off and stared at the flashing instrument.

Wyn Ellis stared at it as well, even though he was standing closer. "Are you going to answer it?" he asked Mair.

"What if it's about bed and breakfast?"

"Gwenda said we should behave normally," Wyn reminded her.

Mair Ellis hesitated as though hoping it would stop. She then stepped forward and answered it with a syrupy voice. "Ellis residence, who's calling please?"

Wyn glanced back at her from the window as she listened to the caller.

"Please hold the line while I check," Mair said, then put her hand over the mouthpiece. "It's an agency. They want to book a room for a couple and their eight-year-old daughter."

"Well, wouldn't that be a nice bit of normalcy?" Wyn suggested.

Mair put the receiver back to her ear. "Yes, we do have a vacancy. The room has a double and single bed... Would that be... Wonderful, do you have a name?"

Wyn Ellis became alert at the window. A vehicle was approaching Amharfarn along the road outside.

"Today?" Mair said with surprise into the phone as Wyn watched a silver Range Rover drive past and continue in the direction of the village. "My, that *is* an urgent booking. Mister and Missus Peter Smith then... I'll have the room ready for them... Thank you."

Mair put the phone down. Wyn lifted his mobile.

"They're coming this afternoon," Mair told him. "I hope they're nice people."

"Andy," Wyn said into his mobile. "I think Mister Burke is back. Silver Range Rover headed your way... Yes, definitely... Two druggies in the front of it."

-o-

Caycey Jones was about to get back into the 4x4.

"Burke's headed here," Lock said, lowering his phone.

Jones pointed at the pole barrier a little further down the track. "Do you think that will stop him?"

"He could always walk," Lock answered. "Anyway, let's get out of here before he sees us."

They got into the 4x4. The car accelerated up the steep track, spraying chippings as it turned the first bend. The car sped out of sight beyond the trees.

Burke's silver Range Rover pulled to a halt. The young Scouser from the passenger side got out and went to the barrier. He examined the padlock holding its end in the closed position.

"Fookit," he cursed, then faced the car. "High-security padlock, sir."

Wearing his posh coat, Burke got out of the back of the car. He went around the rear and opened the tail door. The man reappeared holding a pair of heavy-duty bolt cutters, which he handed over. "Try that."

Cursing and groaning, the Scouser strained against the bolt cutter handles. His face went red; the blades gripped the padlock loop, but to no avail.

"Bloody useless," Burke scolded. "Give it here." He then tried to defeat the padlock himself, his face also going red. Eventually, he relented, leaning over for a closer look. "What the hell is this thing made out of? Can it be picked?"

"No way," the Scouser answered.

The driver, the other Scouser, had got out of the car and was standing by it, watching. "What now, boss?"

"Well, I'm not walking all the way up there," Burke said. "We'll go to their house. One of the bastards can unlock it for us."

"We could try the disc cutter," the first Scouser suggested.

"It's back in Liverpool," the driver told him.

Burke rounded on them. "You should have packed it, shouldn't you?" He prodded the driver in the chest. "What are you both? Come on, tell me, what are you?"

"Morons, sir," the young man answered, fear in his eyes.

"Morons, both of you," Burke agreed, raising his arm as though to slap the driver, who darted out of the way and back to the car. The other one avoided a wild kick from Burke.

Burke's mouth and exposed teeth made him look as though he was snarling. He threw the bolt cutters into the back of the car and slammed the tail door shut.

-o-

Gwenda Evans pulled on the brakes to bring her bike to a halt. She and Miiko hurried along the smaller passage and through the first chamber. Hardcastle was waiting a few feet beyond the dome entrance.

"Where's Lock?" Hardcastle whispered.

"Complications," Gwenda told him. She stepped through, immediately peering towards the distant figure on the other side of the huge chamber.

Hardcastle handed her his pocket binoculars.

She looked through them. "Has it done anything?"

"Moved its hands but be careful what you say. I think it can hear us."

"It… him… what are you?" Gwenda muttered. It remained motionless in the binoculars' field of view, hands still clasped in front of it.

"Wow," Miiko said from the threshold to the smaller chamber. She also had a small pair of binoculars at her eyes. "Is it a hologram maybe?"

"I'm going to find out," Gwenda said, turning to Hardcastle. "You're coming with me."

"What about this door?" Hardcastle asked.

"Miiko can stay here," Gwenda said, then pointed at the woman. "Stay that side. If this door closes, there's an icon on the laptop in there. It says *door*. Click on it if you need to."

Miiko nodded her understanding.

"Though fat lot of good that might be if this place decides to shut us in," Hardcastle said.

"It hasn't harmed us yet," Gwenda told him. "And don't forget, according to Circus, it was constructed by the good guys."

Hardcastle pointed up at the ceiling and its glowing planetarium of stars. "Who are supposedly way out there somewhere."

"Well this one, whatever it is, is a bit closer," Gwenda said. "So let's go and say a proper hello to it." She commenced walking towards the centre of the chamber.

Hardcastle looked at Miiko. "It's the red-and-green icon, near the bottom left on the laptop screen."

Miiko bowed slightly. "Good luck."

Hardcastle jogged to catch up with the diminutive Gwenda Evans, whose shorter legs were progressing her at a hurried pace.

The pair passed the trellis table without paying it a glance, eyes fixed on that unmoving figure beyond the cannon-like devices. They halted near these to stare at it.

Now slightly clearer at this distance, its face continued to reveal few features. The white-haired man, if it was a man, seemed to have eyes, a nose and a mouth, but it was eerily static, as though frozen like a mannequin in a department store window.

"You definitely saw it move?" Gwenda asked Hardcastle.

"Just its hands."

As though in response to this, the figure slowly lowered its arms to its sides.

"It does seem to be able to hear and understand us," Gwenda said. She moved forward again. Hardcastle followed.

Its unmoving eyes seemed to stare beyond them. They were blue. The skin was a tanned white; it had a normally proportioned nose and barely defined lips, which were closed. The clothes were clearly not real, but rather a patterned, coloured continuation of the whole. It was as though the figure was moulded like a child's plastic toy.

Gwenda walked up and faced it from a few feet away. Her face underwent the expression of someone arriving at a decision. She inhaled slowly. "Who are you?"

The thing remained motionless as a low-key sound came from it. It began with a hum that was like a constant deep note from an electronic instrument. This gradually bent upwards in pitch until it reached a note about an octave below middle C. The timbre and tenor then fluctuated, moving through what vaguely began to resemble vowel sounds.

Now the mouth opened into a slit. "Ku tu pah kah keh, rha rhe rhu, sah seh soh, fah feh fi foh."

Hardcastle raised his eyebrows. "If it says 'I smell the blood of an Englishman,' I'm leaving."

Gwenda glared angrily at him. "Enough!"

"Sorry."

"Engalisssh-muuuum, if it, if it, sezesezesez," the figure proclaimed in an electronic voice. Its unmoving lip skills were better than those of Ventriloquist Jack's.

Gwenda waited, calm, patient. Hardcastle's eyes remained wide.

"Weeer, weeer, we are," the figure continued, "weer, conta, tay, tay men tee."

"You are containment?" Gwenda asked. "Is that what you are trying to say, that you are containment?"

The thing's eyes moved a fraction. "Containment," it announced. "Net... netwa... wok... wark... wark..."

"Containment network," Hardcastle said. "I think it understands our language fine. Maybe learned it from TV signals or radio, but it's having to learn how to execute phonetics and pronunciation as though it's a child."

Now the figure turned its head and fixed its eyes on Hardcastle. "Failure," it said. "Containment failure."

Hardcastle was about to say something, but Gwenda put a gloved finger to her lips before turning to the figure again.

"We are humans," she said slowly. "We… our species… we are humans."

"Primitive language," it answered. "We are no longer functioning as intended. Higher functions are isolated."

"What is it that you are supposed to contain?" Gwenda asked.

The man-thing did not move. "We are containment to prevent the hostiles from leaving this planet. We are no longer functioning as intended." Now its face seemed to shimmer. One of its arms moved then froze. "Pah, peh, pih, poh, puh… bata beeta biber… bick… bock… abeet…"

"There it goes again," Hardcastle said. "Like it's practising phonetics. But I don't think it's firing on all cylinders."

"It's actually said that much," Gwenda agreed.

The man-thing fell silent. Hardcastle took a breath to speak to it again, but Gwenda nudged him with her elbow. "I think we'd better wait until Jones gets here," she warned.

-o-

From the office window in the safe house, Banes saw the silver Range Rover pull onto the driveway and halt. He had a mobile to his ear. "Their car just arrived. What do I do?" He listened. "Okay, understood."

The Scouser from the passenger side got out of the car and walked up to the house. He rang the bell, keeping his finger on the button for a few seconds before knocking loudly at the door.

Banes eyed him cautiously when he opened it.

"Gentleman in the car wants to talk to you," the Scouser announced in his heavily Liverpool accent.

Banes followed the young man to the Range Rover, where a rear window hummed as it wound down.

Up at the compound, Lock was standing outside the open steel door. His mobile rang. "Yes…" Lock listened and frowned.

Caycey Jones poked his head out from the steel doorway. Lifting a hand to caution Jones, Lock pressed the phone closer to his ear. "Oh he does, does he? But no, don't get in the car with him. Tell him I'll drive down and meet him at the barrier."

Lock listened. "Absolutely not… put the bastard on the phone." He paced away from the steel door, then back again. "Burke," he then said angrily into his mobile. "What the hell do you think you are doing? This is my station, my command. My people have a job to do. If you want to come up here, fine, I'll meet you at the barrier, but leave my people alone. Do you understand?"

Wyn Ellis watched from the B&B lounge window. He saw Banes go back into the safe house and the silver Range Rover reversing out of the driveway.

Mair Ellis was sitting on one of the sofas writing a list. "Smith sounds English," she said. "So presumably they'll eat normal food like us."

"They're headed back for the mountain," Wyn said. "That Burke man looked angry. I don't like the look of him at all."

"We need to do some shopping," Mair Ellis told him from the sofa.

"You know what they said," Wyn reminded her. "We don't go out of the village without one of them, or we send Kyle."

"We could order it to be delivered on the dot-com," Mair said, raising her eyebrows as though surprised at her own suggestion.

"At last," Wyn said, sighing. "I'll help you set up our account, but we'd better put the television on first. Prime Minister is due to speak in five minutes."

"I'm trying to be normal here," Mair protested. "Mister and Missus Peter Smith and their daughter, planning their food. It would be so nice to be normal."

-o-

Kyle leaned forward in the armchair closest to the TV at his gran's. "It's on," he announced, beginning to stand up.

"No, you sit there," Gran said as she came away from the kitchen area. "I'll be fine on the settee."

On the screen, a middle-aged woman wearing a pearl necklace below her sagging jowls looked earnestly into the camera. *Prime Minister's Announcement*, the text banner proclaimed. She looked serious but was trying to put on a reassuring tone. Her eyes were clearly watching a teleprompter.

"I am speaking to you today in co-ordination with other world leaders, to tell you about a grave situation threatening the security of all civilised nations, including the United Kingdom.

"We have all been aware of the terrorist threats around the world, and the difficult, often unpopular steps world leaders have taken to combat them. But in the early hours of this morning, as many of you will be aware, a new and faceless terrorist organisation carried out their threat to explode a nuclear device. This occurred off the coast of Florida in the United States.

"So far, there have been no reported fatalities, though many have been injured, some seriously, and a number of people are missing.

"Clearly, this new capability in the hands of criminals presents the risk of accidental and unintended nuclear retaliation in a complex world, where tensions between some nations have been at a heightened level.

"As a consequence, and in order to prevent such an escalation, the United Kingdom, together with all other nuclear powers, including Russia, France, China and the United States, have agreed to delegate command of our armed forces to the United Nations.

"The list of other nations taking this unprecedented step includes North Korea, India, Israel and Pakistan, but is not limited to nuclear powers. Indeed, the international community is almost entirely unanimous that blind military responses to this new terrorist threat must be avoided.

"The world of civilised nations cannot take action until such time the perpetrators can be definitively identified. Our actions then must be collective, calculated and proportionate.

"United Nations command of all military forces around the world, including all British armed forces, will commence immediately.

"In addition, in line with other nations with similar legislation, and with the authority of Parliament, I am today also activating the Civil Contingencies Act granting government emergency powers to strengthen internal security.

"United Nations command of British armed forces will ensure that we play our part within the international community. This will make certain that terrorists cannot trigger wars between nations, and that we engage effectively against this new threat.

"Further information and guidance will be issued by individual government departments via the press and media today as matters progress, but I can reassure all citizens and all visitors to the United Kingdom that your safety is of the highest priority to the British Government."

Gran switched off the TV. "You know what this is, don't you?"

Kyle looked a bit baffled. "Very serious?"

"One-world government," Gran told him. "It's what they've been after all along. I wouldn't mind betting they exploded that bomb themselves."

Kyle frowned. "But, Gran—"

"No good will come of it, you'll see," Gran insisted. "Emergency powers, that's how Hitler got his dictatorship started in Germany. They're going to do it to the whole world this time."

"Never heard you talk like this before," Kyle said with quiet approval. "Cool."

-o-

Lock was alone driving downhill in the 4x4. He pulled to a halt on the patch of grass above the pole barrier near the bottom of the forestry track. The silver Range Rover was waiting, engine idling, the other side.

Burke climbed out of the back of the car in his fancy coat and approached the barrier where he stared, frowning, at the 4x4.

Lock observed this from behind the wheel. He reached inside the top of his jacket, where something issued a metallic click. He then got out of the car and walked to the barrier, eyes fixed on Burke's.

Burke tapped the barrier with his knuckles. "Are you deliberately trying to annoy me?"

"I had no idea you would need access," Lock responded, "or why you might need it. What do you want?"

"To find that car. It's up there somewhere. I can feel it in my bones."

Lock glared at Burke, went to the end of the pole and unlocked the padlock there. He then doubled back to the counterweight, raised the barrier, and attached the padlock to secure the contraption in its open position. "Be my guest," he said to Burke, who had been watching him suspiciously, "but I would have thought you have more serious things to do right now with everything that's going on."

"Oh I do, old boy," Burke agreed. "But this trade will still continue. You will still go out in your boat and bring the goods in. The money and that car are mine and I want them back."

"You have got to be kidding me," Lock said. "We've got martial law, a world government in the making, and you still want money for black ops?"

Burke laughed disdainfully. "Well, that *is* the black op, you idiot. Do you really think we can rely on the army to do what's needed? Auxiliaries, old boy. We've already recruited and trained them. We feed them with drugs and money, don't you see? No other way we can achieve the desired statistics."

"I don't like the sound of that," Lock said.

"Of course you don't," Burke dismissed, "but it's going to happen whether we like it or not." He pointed up the track. "So, any idea where that bastard Jampox could have hidden my car up there?"

"It's a big forest," Lock answered. "If it was up there and I knew about it, I would tell you."

Burke got back in his car.

Lock's forehead creased slightly as he watched the silver Range

200

Rover speed away up the forestry road. It disappeared behind the trees at the first bend.

He was about to return to the 4x4 when the sound of young voices reached him. A group of teenagers dressed in school uniform came around the bend from the farmland lane. Bibby Libby was with them. "Hi, Mister Lock," she called.

Lock glanced up the track, then hesitated near the open barrier. "Hello, Elin. Why aren't you all in school?"

"Hardly any teachers turned up," Bibby Libby answered. The others cut across the forestry track behind her. They were following a path along the pine forest edge towards some deciduous trees. Bibby watched them. "School sent us home. What do you reckon to the atomic bomb going off? Is there going to be a war?"

Lock looked into her worried, innocent eyes. "I don't think so, but this isn't the time to go eating magic mushrooms. You should all be at home with your families."

Bibby Libby laughed. "Oh no, Mister Lock, they're not *magic* mushrooms, just ordinary ones and I don't eat them anyway. Some of the others think they are, but they smoke, you know... and well..."

"You told that BBC reporter you see angels," Lock said, smiling. "Did you make that up?"

The thin teenager frowned and thought deeply. "There's something about this place. Doesn't happen as much anywhere else, but every now and then some of us see, like small orbs of light. They are so bright, brighter than the sun, but they don't dazzle you. It's hard to explain. And they sing, like angels."

Lock thought about this for a moment, then smiled at her again, as though trying to be reassuring. "And what you told him about the UFO and smoke from the mountain?"

"Kyle asked me to say about the UFO to help protect the village," she answered, eyes wide. "But the smoke from the mountain was the truth. We all saw it after the sea caught fire. I didn't mean to tell him. It sort of slipped out when the reporter said nothing ever happens here."

"Well, I appreciate your honesty," Lock said, "but you shouldn't talk about smoke from the mountain or orbs of light to any strangers from now on."

"I know," Bibby Libby acknowledged. "We must all protect the angels and the village." The girl issued a cheerful smile. "Bye, Mister Lock." She then abruptly jogged away to catch up with her friends.

Wearing an expression of sadness and puzzled concern, Lock watched her thin, diminishing figure disappear beyond the trees before he returned to the 4x4.

Caycey Jones was waiting in the work tunnel when Lock arrived. Norton and Kikuko were with him, faces serious. Jones wore an expression of optimistic urgency.

-o-

The silver Range Rover halted alongside the ruined farmhouse Jones had photographed days earlier.

Burke slid across the passenger seat in the back and peered out. The shell of the building was surrounded in undergrowth and a pine tree poked upwards from its roofless interior.

"Good place for a stash," Burke observed, "but there's no way anyone could get a car in there." He studied a half-folded map in his hands. "Drive on."

"Yes, sir," the driver responded.

The car progressed down the dip. The track levelled out and ran through the forest towards another rising bank of trees in the distance.

"There should be a turn-off on the left along here," Burke said, sliding with his map to the other side of the car.

"You don't think Jampox might have pushed it into that pool under the waterfall back there?" the other Scouser asked him.

"Fucking idiot," Burke scolded. "There were no tyre tracks, and you saw all those saplings on the bank down to the pool, didn't you?"

"Yes, sir."

"And none of them were broken, were they?"

"No, sir."

Burke leaned his head against the window, looking out, eyes keenly alert.

The car slowed as a gap appeared between the trees up ahead on the left. The track was narrow, with grass in its centre. "Turn down here," Burke ordered.

This track pitched downhill until it reached a junction splitting right and left at a vegetated rock outcrop the size of a house. Beyond this, either side, the pine trees were taller, their trunks thicker. The car came to an undecided halt.

Burke leaned forward. "It's like a bloody maze up here. Take the right and drive slowly. Watch out for ditches."

The driver obeyed, hauling hard on the wheel as the car progressed into the dark area of older forest.

Further on, the gap between the trees widened and it became difficult to define the track in the undergrowth. Burke's eyes were wide as he watched ahead. The grass grew thick and brush vegetation scraped the sides of the car as it progressed.

The Range Rover came to a halt on the edge of a rough clearing. An old security fence and gate stood in the centre. It was the same place where Lock and Gwenda had pushed a car with a corpse inside it down a mineshaft.

Burke got out first. He took off his coat and threw it into the back of his car. The two Scousers got out and watched him with unease. Burke walked forward and gazed around. In his smart suit, he had the appearance of a man about to enter a boardroom meeting.

The faded sign on the gate stated, *Disused Mineshaft. Danger, Keep Out*. But Burke seemed more interested in the undergrowth and saplings in the clearing around the gated area. "Well well," he said quietly. "Look at that." He pointed at a baby tree that was snapped over, and to signs of damage to other vegetation.

"Looks like a vehicle turned around here," the driver observed.

"It does indeed," Burke agreed conspiratorially. "And recent maybe." He approached the gate and peered through. The Scousers joined him, the driver examining the relatively new padlock.

"What do you reckon to that fence in there?" Burke asked them.

"Woolly-back fencing, sir," the passenger answered. "Looks like it's been cut and repaired with wire."

"So it does," Burke agreed. "What about the padlock? Would Jampox have been able to pick it?"

"Easy, sir," the other Scouser answered. "Two-lever job. My little sister could open this."

"Then show me," Burke said. He stepped away from the gate and stared at the Scouser.

"Don't have my kit on me, sir," the young man said fearfully.

"Hmm," Burke responded but maintained his temper this time. He reached inside his jacket and handed over a leather wallet. "Try this, but don't break any of them."

Grubby fingers prodded and twisted thin steel instruments into the padlock until it clicked. The Scousers then lifted and opened the gate for Burke to step through. He approached the fence inside.

"This is it," he said, looking down into the old mineshaft.

"You reckon he shoved the car down here, sir?" the driver asked.

"That's one scenario," Burke answered. "Came up here with an accomplice in another car, pushed mine down there and made off with the money."

"Ireland on the ferry," the other Scouser agreed.

Burke contemplated this. "There are many eyes looking out for him in Ireland. If he is there, he must be lying really low because he's kind of hard to miss, wouldn't you agree?"

Both young men nodded at this. One of them pointed at the edge of the mineshaft. "Paint scrape there, sir."

"I've seen it," Burke said patiently. "And the scrape on the rock there from the sump when it went over. But there are other scenarios."

"What do you mean, sir?" the driver asked.

"Don't be impertinent," Burke scolded. He then sighed. "What I mean is that we can't be sure until we go down there and have a look."

Both young men looked horrified at this.

"Oh, don't shit yourselves just yet," Burke taunted them. "I don't mean now. Close this up again and lock it. We'll come back in a few days with the proper gear to get one of you down there."

The two Scousers hurried, hissing and whispering to each other as Burke headed for the car and they struggled to close the gate again.

"No way I'm going down there," the driver said.

"Me neither," the other one agreed. "He's going to get us fucking killed."

"Move it, morons," Burke shouted from beside the Range Rover. "I need to get back to Liverpool."

-o-

Bibby Libby sighed. She sat on a toppled, rotting oak. It was in a glade formed by a mix of dead and living trees. She seemed unconcerned by the green algae that immediately stained her school trousers.

Three of the boys were picking mushrooms from a ground littered with hundreds of the white domes. One boy peeled the skin from an individual mushroom cap and began eating the flesh with relish.

Bibby watched them with a smile then looked over at the two girls leaning up against the trunk of a healthy oak. Both had their smartphones in their hands, thumbs tapping away. "Are you getting a signal?" she asked.

"Yeh," one answered, "but no internet."

Bibby checked her own mobile. "I'm not even getting a signal." She got up and walked towards the girls.

A teenage boy with a mouth crammed with half-chewed mushrooms leered at her.

"They're not magic mushrooms, you know," she told him.

The boy laughed, spilling out some of the white flesh from his mouth. One of the others jabbed a fist at his arm. Another one grabbed his head in an arm-lock. They all broke away and started spitting and throwing mushrooms at each other.

Bibby Libby joined the girls, held up her phone and checked it.

"Getting a signal here, but no internet." She put the phone back in her bag, then turned, startled.

Several small glowing orbs of light flitted at speed into the glade. They swarmed above the boys, who obliviously continued their mushroom fight.

"There," Bibby shouted. "Do you see them?"

The fight ceased immediately. One of the boys ducked an orb then skittered to Bibby's side. He turned to watch the lights still circling the other two teenagers' heads.

"Where?" one of them demanded.

"Right above your heads," Bibby said, pointing.

"There's nothing there," the boy responded, even though an orb was now hovering in front of his face.

The youth standing near Bibby said, "There's at least ten of them. Can't you see them?"

"I don't see anything," one of the girls remarked in a bored voice.

"Me neither," the other girl agreed, returning her attention to her mobile as though accustomed to this sort of event. "Still no Facebook."

"I thought you were just nuts," the boy who could see them told Bibby.

"Huh, thanks…" She then flinched when one of the orbs flew towards her. It hovered a few inches from her nose. Bibby smiled. "Now they're singing. Can you hear them?"

-o-

Clad in their EMF suits, Caycey Jones and Andy Lock arrived at the first chamber. The German naval officer's skeleton continued to occupy its seat of honour by the trellis table. Emily Norton and Kikuko came in next.

Miiko bowed at the dome entrance. Lock acknowledged this with a nod of his head, before going through.

"The rest of you had better stay here," Jones said, then hurried after Lock.

The white-haired figure remained frozen immobile on the far side of the giant chamber. Its eyes were fixed like glass in a mannequin's head. One of them moved. The iris adjusted. Lock and Jones were white dots, growing bigger as they crossed the floor from the distant entrance.

At the table, Hardcastle and Gwenda gazed at the ceiling. New imagery had appeared alongside the echo of the laptop screen up there.

Lock's face was craned upwards, eyes staring as he walked. It was an image of a young woman. Lock halted and looked back. Jones lagged a few yards behind him. "That's Elin Lewis," Lock said, pointing at the image.

Jones was slightly out of breath. "What?"

"I know that girl. Nickname is Bibby Libby. She lives in the village. I spoke to her a few minutes after letting Burke through the barrier."

The two men now approached Hardcastle and Gwenda at the table.

"Report, please," Jones said.

On the far side of the chamber, one of the blue eyes moved again. This time the pupil was a constant, unchanging dot. From this position, the people at the table were blurred white shapes huddled together in the middle distance. One poked a hand into the air, pointing at the ceiling. Another leaned in closer over the table.

The blue iris changed shape, pupil diminishing to an even smaller dot. The eye moved again, then the other one. Now the white-haired thing's head rotated.

At the table itself, Jones frowned as he leaned over to look closer at the laptop. "And what is that?" he demanded.

"It was sitting there behind the environment, lighting and door routine recipient," Hardcastle answered. "I opened it to see what was going on."

The American's eyes widened but he managed to keep his voice calm. "You hacked this place?"

Gwenda looked up with some alarm. "I had no idea what he was doing."

Hardcastle puffed himself up defensively. "I haven't hacked

207

anything. It's a port that's absolutely open to this laptop. I just spotted it and had a look. We need to find out what it's doing, and it *is* doing something."

"So, can you now tell me what it's doing?" Jones asked Hardcastle.

"I don't know for sure, but it seems to be downloading huge quantities of data and it's writing some sort of code. I didn't start it off doing that. I just opened the port to listen to it."

"Hardcastle…" Lock groaned.

"Don't blame me," Hardcastle rebuked. "*It* was already doing that. I only detected it."

Jones patted the younger man on his shoulder. "And you're sure that thing, whatever it is over there, said something about higher functions not working?"

"Yeh," Hardcastle responded. "I got the impression we were talking to a visual interface of some sort of backup system, some sort of basic AI that's trying to recover the higher functions of this place."

"True artificial intelligence," Jones murmured. "I'm not sure…"

"Not yet," Hardcastle answered. "I suspect the higher functions will possess true intelligence, maybe even sentience given how advanced this technology is… Oh shit!"

The others flinched, startled. Miraculously, the white-haired figure was now standing a few yards from them on the other side of the table. It lifted an arm, which seemed like fluid as it shimmered upwards. A finger pointed to something behind them.

They all turned, slowly, reluctantly. An exact and full-size replica of the safe house in Amharfarn was now standing there. The front door was open. A glowing figure walked out, coalescing into distinctiveness. It looked like a young woman, apparently oblivious to her surroundings, her face bright, cheerful. She was dressed in a school uniform over her obviously thin body. Her lips moved as though she was singing, her body swaying in a dance. It was all soundless.

"Elin Lewis," Gwenda Evans said.

"Bibby Libby," Lock agreed.

"This one," the white-haired figure said in a voice like a synthesiser. "This one must be brought here to repair our higher functions."

The glowing Bibby Libby figure then simply vanished, leaving the house replica still standing there with its door open.

-o-

Mair Ellis was happily polishing brass ornaments on a newspaper-protected coffee table when the doorbell rang. "Ah," she said, holding up yellow-gloved hands stained with Brasso fluid. "That'll be the Smiths. You can let them in while I tidy this away."

Wyn Ellis withdrew his head from the binoculars at the side window.

A strikingly blonde woman stood at the door with an equally blonde young girl, about eight years old, by her side. Both had pale-blue eyes.

"I am Lara Smith," the woman said. Her accent was faintly Liverpool, but with something else in there as well. She held out her hand.

Wyn Ellis shook the hand, but he already had something of a frown of worry and suspicion above his eyes. "You booked a room, yes?"

"This is Marina," Lara said, patting the young girl on the shoulder. "Say hello to the gentleman." The child merely glared at Wyn Ellis.

Flustered, Wyn glanced at a white camper now parked on the road behind the American's Jaguar. He then quickly gathered himself to pay attention to the child.

"Well hello, Marina," he said to her. "Welcome to Wales. I hope you're going to have a nice holiday here."

"We're not on holiday," the girl told him in a pure Liverpool accent. "We're hiding from the goons."

"Marina!" Lara scolded her daughter.

Wyn's expression of slight worry converted to something more serious. The girl stared at him, ignoring her mother.

209

Now Mair appeared in a hurry at the door, smiling broadly. "Oh hello." Her head busily rotated attention from the woman to the camper on the road, to the small girl on her doorstep. "I'm Mair Ellis. Welcome, please come in. Where's Mister Smith? What a lovely little girl. What's your name, dear?"

"Marina."

"And what do you like to eat?"

"Fish and chips from the chippie."

"We don't have a chippie here, but I can cook anything they can for you," Mair told her.

"Aw, I loved that chippie back home," the child complained to her mother as they stepped into the hall together.

"Marina!" the mother again scolded as Mair showed the woman and the girl into the lounge.

Still stunned, Wyn Ellis stayed at the doorway, eyes fixed on the camper. A man wearing baggy faded denims and a smart sports jacket got out backwards from its side, hauling on suitcases. He turned around, revealing his face. "*Zdrastvooyte*, comrade," He called loudly to Wyn. "Help me with these cases, please."

"Oh Jesus," Wyn Ellis muttered as he hurried down the drive. "What are you doing here?"

Dimitri, the Russian spy from Liverpool, just smiled in response, grabbed Wyn Ellis in a violent hug and kissed his cheeks. "You will have to call me Peter Smith from now on," he said when he finally let go. "But I apologise of course for the short notice."

"Short notice? You gave me *no* notice. What are you doing here? The risks…"

"No time," Dimitri responded. "Grab a case." The Russian picked up two of them and marched up the drive.

Wyn Ellis grabbed the remaining suitcase and hurried after the Russian. He saw Banes peering out with wide eyes from the safe house window.

"One of Commander Lock's men, I assume," the Russian said loudly. He halted when he got to the B&B front door. "There was no time for coded messages or niceties. No time for a plan. The enemy made their move without warning. Had I left it till tomorrow, I would never have got here. Even now, I barely got beyond Bangor before they set up their roadblocks there."

Wyn's expression remained stunned, horrified, but he managed to croak out a puzzled question. "Roadblocks?"

"The British are slow, but they will block all the roads, just as other countries are doing today worldwide. We are all in danger… every human being. It has begun."

-o-

Lock held out his gloved hand and touched the grandfather clock. He and Gwenda were inside the duplicate safe house that had appeared from nowhere in the domed chamber. His fingers followed the clock's winding door edge. He tapped it with his knuckles. "It's solid," he told Gwenda, who opened the functioning French doors to the kitchen in response.

"Look at that," Gwenda said in a low voice.

Lock went through. The kitchen seemed normal at first, but on closer scrutiny, the table and chairs were all constructed from the same mass, all connected to each other by brown twines. This plastic material seemed to be still growing the pieces of furniture.

Lock approached the sink. Gwenda joined him. Looking out through the window, they could see the chamber outside, and Norton's and the two Japanese ladies' forms waiting at its entrance.

Lock turned one of the taps in the sink. Clear water flowed out of it. Gwenda closed it hurriedly. "It works," Lock said.

EMF suits rustling, they went back through the duplicate office to the hallway. Here Gwenda opened one of the doors under the stairs. There was a toilet inside. Gwenda pumped the lever repeatedly until it flushed.

"That's as cranky as the one back home," Gwenda said. "It's even got the same cracks in the enamel. But running water… That could make things a heck of a lot better for us down here."

"It'll have to be tested first," Lock said. "Let's go back outside."

Outside the copy of the house, Jones was facing the white-haired figure.

211

"Primitive language," the figure said with unmoving lips in its synthesised voice. "Ambiguity... imperfection of concept articulation... repair of higher functions critical."

"Why do you want us to bring the girl here?" Jones asked it.

"Ambiguity in phrasing... specific syntax functions absent..."

Lock and Gwenda approached, listening.

"This is impossible," Jones said to Hardcastle.

Hardcastle was seated at the table, staring into the laptop screen as it scrolled through windows of zeros and ones, all parading and changing at a speed the eye could barely follow. "It's like it's got dementia, or is only semi-conscious." He pointed at the laptop. "This, though, seems automated. This place is learning, downloading information, but God knows from where or how."

"The house is accurate inside," Lock said. "Taps work, even has a functioning toilet, all complete with running water, which we'll need to test before we even think of drinking it. It's obviously able to gather extremely accurate information from above ground somehow."

"How is it doing this?" Hardcastle mused aloud.

"Bibby Libby said something about seeing orbs of light," Lock said.

"Are you sure that's her image up there?" Jones asked.

"Absolutely certain," Lock answered. "Same girl whose image came out of the house. Why would it want her brought down here?"

"I keep asking it that," Jones said, "but it doesn't seem to understand the question, no matter how I rephrase it."

Hardcastle's eyes lit up with an idea. "We could try phrasing it as an instruction."

Jones held out an inviting hand. "Be my guest."

Hardcastle stood up, moved around the table and closer to the figure. It remained frozen, its face and eyes apparently lifeless. He addressed it with a strict and demanding tone. "Explain *why* it is necessary for the person in the image to be brought to this place."

"In order for containment to access higher functions," the figure responded.

"That's basically what it told us in the first place," Lock said quietly. "She's just a kid. How could it possibly need her?"

Jones tilted his head slightly. "I don't know... A kid who sees orbs of light and whose image was projected here." He then faced the thing. "What will happen when this person is brought to this place?"

"We will join with this person," it answered. "We will access higher functions and repair."

With an expression of alarm, Lock now spoke directly to it. "Will that cause any harm to this person?"

"Define harm," the thing responded in its dull electronic voice.

SIX

Dawn broke red in a grey sky. Fingers of light stretched from between the clouds, generating reflections from the wave-splashed masonry of the Amharfarn sea wall.

A seagull took to the air from the derelict timber pier and was soon joined by others as brighter hues broke above the eastern horizon.

The village itself seemed devoid of human life. There were no early arrivals at the Jones Bros yard.

Here, the scrap-grabber JCB rested motionless and alone. Its rusty double bucket was inclined against the ground, as though in a solitary funeral for the dead cars and absent workers.

Yet life continued to awaken. Birds flitted along hedgerows. Sparrows squabbled near Gran's cottage, and a blackbird hopped across the lawn at the safe house.

Lights went on behind some closed curtains in the village. Other curtains were opened.

Very much alive, Ventriloquist Jack pedalled through the village on a bike, front wheel wobbling slightly. He was wearing a boiler suit as usual, a cigarette pinched into the corner of his mouth.

Jack's eyes narrowed as he passed the safe house. He noticed the camper parked outside the B&B next door. And as he continued pedalling, his forehead creased, storing the camper in his mind with a question alongside it.

Inland from the village, a convoy of military vehicles passed the disused service station. Lead vehicles, with yellow UNSC stickers on their sides, continued beyond the turn-off to Amharfarn. They

215

headed instead along the Llŷn Peninsula's main road, as though intending an invasion of its furthest extremities.

Two civilian cars stood halted at the junction, their path to the village blocked by a series of spiked, portable barriers. People from the cars, a young man and two women, were talking animatedly to a soldier wearing combat fatigues and a pale-blue beret at the outermost barrier. Behind them, the military convoy continued to pass along the main road.

A soldier stepped out, hand raised when Ventriloquist Jack approached along the narrow lane from the village.

Jack applied his brakes. *"Whass goin' on then?"* he asked, lips barely moving.

A puzzled expression was followed by a smile from the young soldier. "Temporary restricted civilian movement order, sir."

Jack dismounted his bike, held its seat and puffed at his still glowing cigarette stump. "Why's that then?"

"Don't know, sir. We're advising people to check the news and the internet. We can't allow you through unless you have a pass."

"Internet's been down since yesterday," Jack told the soldier. He then pointed at the people who were still talking to soldiers on the main road beyond the barriers. "I know those people. They work in the village." A military truck roared past behind the civilians as he spoke.

The soldier glanced in that direction. "You know what the government is like. They're probably sorting out passes so people can get to work." He grinned. "Probably in the post."

Ventriloquist Jack peered over the hedge. A military truck stood idle in the adjacent field. A couple of soldiers seated in the back of it were cleaning their weapons. He also noticed where the hedge had been torn down, and a gate put up, along the blocked stretch between him and the junction with the main road.

The civilians were now returning to their cars over there. A tank carrier passed them, the huge tank and its main gun covered over with a camouflage tarpaulin on a long trailer.

Jack looked at the soldier's blue beret. "United Nations then?"

"Big emergency."

216

"Well okay, you're just doing your job," Jack conceded. "I'll go home. God knows what I'll do for food."

"Food trucks are being organised," the soldier said.

Jack turned his bike around. "I'll believe that when I see it." He waved at the soldier and rode off.

-o-

There was a short queue of villagers on the safe house driveway when Ventriloquist Jack arrived. He wheeled his bike past the people to the front door, where Emily Norton and Hardcastle were behind a table that was heaped with papers and white cards.

Jack smiled at Norton, then looked at Hardcastle. "Where's Andy Lock?"

"In the kitchen, around the back," Hardcastle answered. "Just knock on the door."

Jack wheeled his bike along the side of the house, squeezing it past the 4x4 and a white van parked close to the garage at the rear. He leaned the bike against the garage, before taking the path to the kitchen door where he knocked.

Lock opened it to allow him in.

Gwenda Evans was seated at the table, alongside a rather stunned-looking Kyle.

Jack greeted them before turning to address Lock. "Soldiers are blocking the junction with the main road. And there was a whole bloody convoy of them headed west."

"They're dividing the country into military zones," Lock told him.

"But they're not allowing anyone in or out of the village."

"And they won't until you have an identity card and a pass. I'm issuing essential worker cards to people here."

"Will that allow us to leave the village?"

"No," Lock said in a resigned tone.

Jack frowned. "So what's the use of the cards you are handing out?"

Lock sat down, facing Kyle at the table, then looked up at the

217

man. "Hopefully it will provide some protection, for a little while at least."

"Protection from what?"

"From being carted away to so-called registration centres. They're calling it population dispersal. Have a seat."

Jack looked baffled for a second, then his expression darkened. "Population dispersal? Jesus, that sounds like something out of Nazi Germany." He slid a chair out and sat sideways on it.

Gwenda Evans poured a mug of tea. "We need to look on the bright side," she said. "At least we have the mountain and a plan of sorts." She handed the mug to Jack.

"What plan?" he asked.

"We've just been briefing Kyle about it," Gwenda told him.

Kyle nodded seriously at Ventriloquist Jack. "It's way out, Mister Thomas, like nothing you ever imagined."

"You need to listen to me," Lock told the man. "And then you must follow my orders with absolute secrecy. Because if you don't, and if anyone in government finds out what we are really doing here, we are all dead... everyone... every last person in this village."

-o-

Caycey Jones dabbed his lips with a napkin. He looked into the eyes of a worried Wyn Ellis seated opposite in the B&B dining room. Jones removed tiny plugs from his ears and coiled the connecting wires on the table next to his smartphone. "Okay, I've listened to the surveillance recordings."

Wyn leaned forward. "He brought his family with him, so he must be a friend, surely?"

"I can't be sure of that just yet," Jones answered. He then smiled as though from an afterthought. "But he detected the bug in his room and actually spoke into it. If he's a shill, I like his style."

Wyn Ellis seemed to accept this. "Have you listened to the radio this morning?"

"What are they saying?"

Wyn frowned. "Government information broadcasts, every ten

minutes. They've declared neighbourhood curfews in some places and a complete travel ban for the rest of us, all of it supposed to be temporary, and a warning of harsh consequences for any refusal to obey official instructions."

"That's just what they're telling the public," Jones said. "Public internet is shut down but I'm still able to access government networks. There's been civil unrest, riots and even armed insurrection in some places, especially America. Thousands have been shot dead already, but so far it's been contained. And with the internet and phone networks closed off, there's not much chance any organised rebellion could succeed."

Mair Ellis stuck her head out from the kitchen doorway at the far end of the dining room. "I can hear the Russians moving upstairs," she whispered. Her voice came out like a hiss but was loud enough to be understood.

Caycey Jones waved her to come in. She approached with wide eyes.

"Just usher them to that table over there and offer them breakfast as though everything is normal," Jones said.

Mair issued a nervous frown. "Well of course." She went to the hallway door and opened it.

Jones heard a child's voice, followed by Mair's greetings in her overacted version of normal. The stairway creaked from descending feet. More greetings followed in unidentifiable accents. The Russian family entered the dining room.

Mair Ellis gestured to a table on the other side of the room, but Dimitri's alert eyes were fixed on Caycey Jones. He approached that table as Lara and Marina followed Mair to the other one.

"Mister Jones, I presume," Dimitri greeted in his accent mix of Liverpool and Russian. He held out his hand.

Jones half rose and shook it. "I'm surprised you know my name."

The Russian grinned and sat down next to Wyn's visibly tense form opposite. "Well, it's not the first time I have spoken to you. The bug in our room... Did you listen yet?"

Jones shrugged enigmatically.

Dimitri issued a wry smile. "Why don't we put our cards out. I

219

know you know. I know Mister Ellis here knows. I know you probably turned him."

Caycey Jones lifted a cup from the table, took a sip and put it down, eyes remaining fixed on the Russian. "Why now?" Jones asked. "Why come here with your family? Why not get on one of the diplomatic flights back to the motherland?"

Dimitri's eyes narrowed, but a glint of his smile remained. "Vacations on the Caspian Sea are not exactly fashionable."

Jones was clearly taken aback by this. Noticing the American's reaction, Wyn's expression grew even more tense and bewildered.

Standing over at the other dining table, a similarly anxious Mair Ellis waited with a notepad in her hand, eyes fixed on the child. "You are such a pretty girl," she said, her amiable tone slightly forced. "What would you like for breakfast?"

Marina opened her mouth to speak, but her mother intervened with a raised finger. "Don't you dare say fish and chips."

This appeared to relax Mair slightly. Marina went into silent thought about her breakfast needs. Mair smiled with genuine compassion for the child.

At the other table, still in deep thought about what the Russian had said, Caycey Jones appeared to arrive at a decision. He placed the palms of his hands on the table. "I hear Alexander the Great thought otherwise."

Dimitri's face hardened. He looked like a man gauging an opponent at chess. "But Alexander was a man before his time and sought the secrets of India."

Wyn Ellis shot glances at the men as though he considered them both insane.

Ignoring Wyn, Jones held out the palm of his hand towards Dimitri. "You will forgive me for being cautious, but what does this sign represent on a Sunday?"

"Only the trapeze of the waxing moon," the Russian answered, now holding up his own palm towards Jones. "And what about this on Mondays?"

"The clown of the hellion's breath," Jones completed.

Dimitri then turned to Wyn Ellis and slapped him enthusiastically on the back. "So, you can see, all is well, my friend, we are all Circus."

Wyn Ellis issued a cautious, bewildered smile to each of the men, though his eyes remained angled as though he still considered them insane.

"He doesn't know about Circus yet," Jones told the Russian. "And you and your family cannot stay here." His voice was slightly louder this time.

Dimitri's wife glanced over her shoulder with a worried expression.

"I hate circuses," Marina announced loudly in a Liverpool accent, "especially clowns." The girl seemed angry and on the brink of tears.

"How about bacon and egg and a nice cup of tea?" Mair suggested in a forced cheerful voice.

Lara put an arm around her daughter, then gazed pleadingly up at Mair.

-o-

Miiko came out of the duplicate safe house in the domed chamber. Here, Banes was seated with his back to her at the table, the strange mannequin-like figure still fixed and frozen a few yards from him.

Adjusting her EMF suit, Miiko approached Banes. She pointed at the white-haired thing. "Have you been talking to it?"

"Absolutely not. Did you manage to get some sleep?"

"Yes, thank you. The rooms upstairs have beds and even quilts. It is amazing."

"Indeed," Banes agreed. "This place is well beyond our scientific theories, never mind our abilities. I don't know if it's some sort of mechanically induced nanotechnology, or whether matter is being manipulated on a sub-atomic scale. Either way, it's beyond human capability."

"It is not my field," Miiko said. "But how did it get the information to be able to recreate the house?"

"No idea. And it's not just any house. It's specific to us. How did it know enough about us to duplicate that building, never mind the clock and other furniture? It's impossible, but there it is, standing there like it's always been there."

"That grandfather clock inside is now ticking," Miiko said. "It was solid and inanimate before I went upstairs and slept. Now it is hollow and the mechanisms inside seem genuine, even aged." She studied the white-haired figure and moved a few paces to look beyond it, before gazing up at the domed ceiling.

The stars and cloudlike structure of the Milky Way looked so real up there, their artificiality betrayed only by the giant version of the laptop screen occupying part of it. Windows of binary code zeros and ones continued parading speedily within that part of the image.

"Do you need to sleep?" she asked Banes.

"Thank you, but no. You two ladies need it more than me. The others should be relieving me soon."

Miiko bowed. "Then I will tell Kikuko to get some sleep." She glanced once more at the inanimate approximation of a human, before heading towards the doorway to the passages. The figure seemed to be staring at the floor, its mannequin eyes glassy and lifeless.

-o-

The queue had grown when Caycey Jones came out of the B&B. He walked swiftly around the boundary wall, then up past the side of the safe house and around the back.

In the kitchen, he saw Gwenda, Kyle and Ventriloquist Jack still seated at the table.

"The Russian?" Lock prompted as he closed the door behind the American.

"Is one of us," Caycey Jones answered. "His mission was to come here and help us if the shit hit the fan."

"So why didn't we know about him?"

"Circus is deliberately compartmentalised. Trouble is that it seems to have become fragmented since yesterday."

Ventriloquist Jack looked at Jones with what seemed a hefty amount of respect.

222

"Have you been fully briefed?" Jones asked him.

Jack's face was grim. "Yes I have, it's…"

But Jones had shifted his attention. "The queue outside is getting longer," he said to Lock. "How many people are you giving essential worker papers to?"

"All of them, if I can," Lock answered.

"Extremely risky."

"I know, but Five has given me blanket authority to sign up as many as I need to keep the station secure. They didn't specify a maximum number."

"How many people are there in this village?" Jones asked.

"Maybe eighty," Lock guessed.

"More like a hundred when you include the farms," Gwenda said.

"Okay," Jones conceded. "I'll leave all that to your judgement, but we have to get the Russians out of here."

"That much is obvious," Lock said. "But to where? They can't camp in the woods."

"What about that Lewis girl, Bibby Libby?" Jones asked.

Gwenda shifted in her chair. "Kyle and I are going to talk to her parents shortly."

Jones gave this some thought, then held up a finger. "Okay… We kill two birds with one stone. Take the Russians down there as well. That's where this Dimitri says he wants to go anyway."

Lock seemed stunned. "Really? Keep them down there? The logistics are going to be horrendous."

Jones issued an ironic chuckle. "I suspect logistics are going to be the least of our worries in the coming days."

-o-

Outside, Emily Norton handed over some cards to a woman at the table. "Now don't forget," Norton said, "pass the word around. We need everyone to sign up. Tell them it's very important for their own safety."

Hardcastle was saying the same thing to a man. The queue now extended to the road.

The front door opened. Lock came out, looked at the queue and spoke to Hardcastle. "What are the numbers like?"

Some of the people called out greetings to Lock, who waved and smiled in response.

"We've signed fifteen so far," Hardcastle said.

Lock studied the queue. "Maybe another fifteen here," he observed, then watched as Ventriloquist Jack wheeled his bike past the waiting people to the road. The man was followed a few seconds later by Kyle and Gwenda coming from the back of the house.

Gwenda's short legs were moving swiftly. It was Kyle who had to keep up with her as they headed down the drive.

"We need more bikes," Lock told Norton and Hardcastle at the table. "Start asking them if they can spare any, on loan."

Ventriloquist Jack finished lighting a cigarette, then mounted his bike and pedalled away towards the bridge. Kyle and Gwenda were walking briskly in the same direction. At the same time, the sound of heavy vehicles approaching the village came from behind them.

Kyle glanced back to see an army Land Rover coming around the bend towards the safe house. It was followed by an armoured personnel carrier, the loudest source of noise.

"Keep walking," Gwenda told Kyle.

Most of the people in the queue had turned to watch the military vehicles approach. Lock walked past these worried individuals and waited at the end of the drive.

The Land Rover halted directly across from the safe house. The APC stopped twenty yards behind it. An army officer, wearing a pale-blue beret, climbed out of the first vehicle as its engine was shut down. He issued hand signals to the APC. Its engine ceased with the whining after-sound of a decelerating turbine. Lock approached him.

"Are you Commander Lock?" the officer asked.

Lock produced an identity card. "How can I help you?"

"It's the other way around," the officer answered. "I'm Captain Hoyland. I'm here to see if you need a hand with security."

Lock was surprised. "Actually, I think we've got everything under control." He glanced back at the queue. "The people here have been integral to our security measures for many years."

"You have a compound on the mountain though," Hoyland said, "hush-hush and all that. I have an APC and six soldiers I can post there if you need them."

"I appreciate the offer, but it would be a waste of manpower," Lock told him.

"Well that's a relief," Hoyland admitted. "I'm short of men as it is. But are you sure? Things are going to get a bit iffy here, don't you think, when the list for this village gets implemented?"

"I haven't seen the list," Lock answered.

"I have it here." Hoyland opened the Land Rover door and reached inside. He turned around with a sheet of paper, which he handed to Lock.

"This is half the village," Lock said, frowning as he studied it.

"I guessed it would be about half," Hoyland agreed. "All destined for the local registration centre, which is *really* iffy if you ask me. It's next to a council waste and recycling depot outside Caernarfon. Word is they had some rather heavy and strange plant and machinery arriving at these centres all over the country for months before this scare."

"Who's in charge of them?" Lock asked.

"Not us… Auxiliaries… They're not under normal military command, but they're in uniform and carrying guns. I can tell you, I don't like the idea of those people rounding up civilians."

"All the people on this list are essential workers." Lock handed the paper back.

"Well good for you," Hoyland acknowledged with a smile. "I wish we had more like you in other places. It's going to get unpleasant I think before all this is over."

"What's it like in other places?" Lock asked.

"Not too bad here for now in North Wales," Hoyland said. "But it's bloody chaos in parts of England. There are riots in areas of Liverpool and Manchester where they've already started rounding people up. Population dispersal… what do you think of it?"

"I don't know what to think, Captain, believe me."

"Ah well," Hoyland said. "Bus will be here at about sixteen hundred hours today. Anyone on this list who isn't an essential worker will be hauled off by auxiliaries. I *really* don't like the sound of them. Do you understand?"

"Of course."

Hoyland smiled conspiratorially. "Well then, you know what to do, nudge-nudge, wink-wink and all of that. I won't tell if you don't."

"I appreciate it," Lock said. "But really, everyone here is essential. Having a cohesive village is our best security. It would collapse if anyone was carted off."

"Well done, Commander, you are a good man," Hoyland said. He saluted Lock, then pointed at the APC with a series of hand signals, culminating with him spinning a finger in the air. "Be seeing you," he called cheerfully before getting back into the Land Rover.

Some of the people in the queue flinched when the APC roared into life.

The vehicle swiftly reversed to the bus-turning triangle at the bend. It manoeuvred there until it was pointing back towards the main road. The Land Rover passed and the APC then followed it, noisily belching exhaust fumes.

-o-

Burke's silver Range Rover came out of the Kingsway Tunnel under the River Mersey from Liverpool. It drove at high speed onto the express road.

On the other carriageway, headed in the opposite direction, a fire tender swished towards Liverpool with its blue lights flashing. The road was otherwise deserted.

Behind the Range Rover on the horizon to the east, the city looked as though it had suffered an air raid. Black smoke rose from multiple fires across a hazy built landscape.

Now decorated with blue transfers on its sides, with the bold letters UNSC/APTF in contrasting yellow, Burke's car took the first exit from the expressway. Here an army roadblock straddled the slip road heading south. Soldiers wearing blue berets pulled back the barriers to let the car through.

The road going south here was equally devoid of normal human activity. It was also littered, as though a passing refuse truck had spilled some of its cargo. Newspaper sheets, black bin bags and empty cans blew aside in the car's slipstream as it passed the docks.

Tethered there, merchant ships, and the antenna-bristling vessels of war alongside them, seemed completely lifeless.

To the south ahead of the car was more smoke from distant fires.

Burke's Range Rover continued to speed along the road on an expanse of flat, mostly derelict, post-industrial terrain. Grass on rough ground was a dirty, dusty green; stunted trees were muted in colour by ghost pollution and a caked dust from the demolitions of an industrial history.

Some turn-offs were blocked by soldiers, others entirely devoid of life. The scattered new office blocks and distribution centres were fronted by empty car parks.

In the back of the Range Rover, Burke leaned forward to bark an order at the young Scouser driving it. "Turn into that depot up ahead."

The driver said, "Yes, sir." He then glanced nervously at his friend in the passenger seat by his side.

"This is the first stop on your new round on Tuesdays," Burke told them in his gruff, uncaring tone.

The entrance to the depot was guarded by men in black uniforms. They had submachine guns cradled in their arms.

The passenger pointed, alarmed. "Jesus, they've got guns."

"So have you, you fucking idiot," Burke snarled. "Show your ID cards... those things you've got hanging around your stupid necks."

The car came to a halt. A young male security guard approached it. The eyes above the submachine gun hanging by straps from his neck were bloodshot, pupils visibly dilated. His speech was slurred when he leaned towards the driver's window. "Ya got ID?"

The driver showed his card, but the guard barely looked at it, staggered back a couple of paces as though drunk, and waved for them to go through.

A frown appeared on Burke's face as the car moved on. He turned his head and glared through the rear window.

Further in, after they had passed over a railway crossing, the car halted by a tilt barrier. Here the guards were older, very much alert.

One of them trotted over. He was in his late twenties, with a skinhead haircut, and tattoos on his bulging neck. This time Burke stuck his head out through his opened window.

The tattooed man gave a clumsy salute when he saw Burke's identity card. "Raise the barrier," he called to his companions.

"Are you the captain of the guard?" Burke demanded.

"Yes, sir."

"One of your men is stoned out of his head at the first checkpoint," Burke told him.

"Sorry, sir."

"Have him disarmed and put on the next bus that arrives."

"But, sir—"

"No buts," Burke insisted. "You all know the drug rules. Chilled is okay, but not stoned."

"But he might panic the passengers."

"Ah," Burke admitted grudgingly. "I suppose you're right. Disarm him and have him brought to the reception building. He's going in with this batch. Do it now." Burke then tapped his driver on the shoulder. "Drive on."

The silver Range Rover purred past the lifted barrier and drove along a straight road lined with young trees, tall lighting columns and some radio masts.

Refuse trucks were parked and lifeless in long rows between anonymous-looking buildings. There were no people in those areas.

Three buses were halted up ahead. They were parked on the approach to a low, squat building that looked as though it had been constructed out of shipping container panels.

The buses were all painted pale blue, with yellow UNSC labels on their sides. Even the side windows were painted, obscuring any passengers inside.

"Park over there," Burke ordered.

The car swung to the left over rough gravel and came to a halt

228

near a tall builders' hoarding. This formed one of two extending wings, positioned either side of the steel building, as though to conceal whatever resided behind it.

The building itself had three double doors in its yellow painted front. They were separated by frosted windows, and a long sign above them stated:

EMERGENCY POPULATION DISPERSAL
REGISTRATION CENTRE

Two groups of black-uniformed guards were gathered on a tarmac apron between the building and the access road. Submachine guns held flat against their chests, they loitered, smoking, talking casually.

Burke and his younger companions got out of the car. "You two wait here and watch," Burke ordered. "See that guy over there, with the gold bars on his shoulders?"

"Yes, sir," the Scousers answered in unison.

"He's the superintendent here. You'll find one just like him at every centre on the new round. Have you got that?"

"Yes, sir."

"The superintendents are also our wholesale distributors on the new round. You got that?"

"Yes, sir."

"You deliver to them and to them alone, same price per kilo as before. Got it? Now wait here and watch."

The two Scousers stayed by the car. Burke marched over to talk to the man he had described as the superintendent. That individual clumsily saluted Burke, listened to him, then waved to the three buses, which started their engines. One by one, the blue-painted vehicles moved forward onto the apron in front of the building.

The people getting off the first bus looked dazed and confused. They were a mixture: men and women of varying ages, a minority were children. One elderly woman was especially frail and had to be helped off the bus.

Burke returned to his car and the two Scousers. "I want you to watch what happens here," he told them as the guards guided, coaxed and pointed the passengers from the first bus into the squat building.

Some of the people asked questions, others protested. Guards shouted responses:

"It's only registration…"

"Form orderly queues inside…"

"You'll be back on the bus in a few minutes…"

"You will all be taken to your designated safe zone after registration…"

"You'll be home in a few days…"

And to the few who protested, guards approached them and said something which seemed to evaporate any sort of resistance.

The second and third buses started offloading their passengers.

Burke's Scousers glanced worriedly at each other as they watched.

A pale-blue minibus came up the road and halted close to the Range Rover. The guard captain got out and opened the door in its side, before dragging out the stoned and scruffy guard who had annoyed Burke at the first checkpoint.

The young man seemed even worse from the influence of drugs and could barely stay on his feet. The burly, tattooed older man supported him, coaxing him step by step towards the building as the last of the bus passengers entered it.

Burke nodded with satisfaction when he saw the stoned guard pushed inside. Other guards then pulled levers over on the double doors to lock them.

"Come over here," Burke ordered the Scousers. He led them around the back of the tall builders' hoarding.

Two heavy road trailers were parked on sloping ground, each with mounted stainless-steel cylinders and pumping machinery.

From here it could be seen that the building itself was sticking out over a slope. It was supported by a framework of girders and hydraulic jacks. None of this had been visible from the front.

Steps and a gantry went up to the side of it. Two thick hoses snaked along this, one of which was connected to a valve in the building's side wall.

"See that trailer," Burke said to the Scousers. "It's a high-pressure, high-volume membrane filtration system. It pumps out almost pure nitrogen."

The Scousers exchanged more glances with each other. The driver especially looked worried, a frown creasing his forehead.

A shrill siren rang out. The guard on the gantry turned and gave a thumbs-up signal. Another guard at the trailer pulled a series of levers. The pump revved up; the thick hose stiffened.

Burke checked his watch and led the way further down the slope. At the bottom was a long railway hopper, with a diesel locomotive attached. It stood on a track immediately under the rear of the strange building.

Slightly beyond this, a JCB stood idle, clawed bucket raised. Its operator was a silhouette behind cabin glass.

"What's going on here, sir?" Burke's driver asked.

"You'll see," Burke answered. "And you need to know, so you don't get freaked out visiting these places during your delivery rounds."

The other Scouser exchanged another worried glance with the driver.

"One hundred and twenty men, women and children went into that contraption up there," Burke continued, checking his watch again. "Correction... one hundred and twenty-one with that stoner. There are hundreds of similar installations large and small around the country. And just one of them can easily handle two hundred and forty people an hour, twenty-four hours a day."

Another siren rang out, this time with three short blasts.

The guard at the trailer switched off the pump. The other guard on the gantry disconnected the hose from the valve in the building. He then signalled to someone up the slope near the hoarding.

Motors whined noisily as the building began to tilt upwards at the front, gradually pivoting its rear over the railway hopper. As it did so, the rear wall of the building began to swing outwards.

Once the contraption had been raised to a steep angle, the rear wall finally pivoted over its hinges with a sharp metal clang.

Limp bodies tumbled into the railway hopper, filling it almost instantly.

Burke's driver flinched, as though he had been punched in the stomach, and slapped his hands to his head in disbelief. The other young man turned his horrified face away from the sight.

Below them, a man's body had missed the hopper and was sprawled out on the rough ground.

In response, and as though well rehearsed, the JCB revved up and moved, its clawed grabber swinging over and downwards. This gripped the body and lifted it, arms and legs hanging limply, to dump it on top of the others in the hopper.

Now the diesel locomotive roared black exhaust fumes into the air. It pushed against the hopper. There was a jetting sound of compressed air being released before the locomotive began moving forward, propelling the hopper in front, brake systems hissing, wheel flanges squealing against the rails as the short train accelerated. The first clickety-clack noises from rail joints reached the two horrified Scousers as it rolled smoothly away.

For a moment, they watched it heading along the track towards a building with tall chimneys.

Behind the Scousers, the tilted gas chamber began lowering itself back to its original position.

"They've got quarter of an hour to clean up any piss or puke inside before the next three buses arrive," Burke told the Scousers. "But there shouldn't be any problems like that really. Nitrogen is odourless, painless and euphoric, much like some of the drugs your types like to imbue. They all died happy, you'll be glad to know."

"But why, sir?" the driver asked. His face was ashen white.

"Because we have to," Burke told him. "And if *we* don't do it, then it is simple. *We* get put on the buses."

"This is *so* wrong," the other Scouser whispered, turning his face away from Burke, who somehow heard him.

"Of course it's *wrong*, you idiot," Burke said, snarling. "But do *you* want to volunteer for happy gas, or do you want to be a survivor?"

They followed Burke up the slope and headed for the car. "Well

232

done," Burke called out to the superintendent. "Keep it as smooth as that every time and we'll have no problems."

The two Scousers shook their heads at each other behind Burke's back, then turned to look at the distant building where the train had gone.

Yellowish smoke was starting to billow from the chimneys over there. A flock of seagulls circled it, adding to a panorama of diminishing plumes of black smoke from scattered fires in the nearby world.

-o-

Bibby Libby's eyes were wide as she sat listening on the settee between her mother and father.

Gwenda Evans sat opposite. She was doing the talking. Kyle was seated on an armchair beside her in an open-plan lounge. Bibby's mother was about to respond.

At that moment, however, there was a clattering noise. A skateboard sped down the polished timber stairs and into the lounge. It was followed by a gangly youth, who managed to halt a sliding descent on his rear before he was halfway down.

"He was listening at the top of the stairs again," Bibby Libby protested. The skateboard rolled across the floor and bumped into a wall with a dull thud.

"Bibby-ibby-libby," the youth complained. He stood up, groaning, and nursed his rear. He was older than his sister and possessed a fluffy goatee beard.

"That's what he used to call Elin when she was a toddler," the mother explained to Gwenda.

"And he spread it around the entire village," Bibby Libby told Kyle. "I don't mind it though."

The father glared with a long-suffering expression at his son. "I don't see why you can't sit down here and listen," he said. "This affects us all."

"Do I have to sign the Official Secrets Act as well?" The youth grabbed a dining chair and scraped it noisily across the polished floor. "Yo, Kyle," he greeted.

"Yo, bro," Kyle responded, grinning.

Bibby Libby's smile grew as she gazed at Kyle.

"I don't know," the mother said, leaning forward as she addressed Gwenda Evans. "Why would you need Elin, of all people, to go with you?"

"Because I've seen the angels," Bibby Libby interrupted.

The father shook his head and groaned. "You do know she had problems when she was younger?" he said to Gwenda.

"Autistic," the brother teased. "That's why she sees things."

"Shut up," Bibby Libby scolded. "I don't *see things* at all, only the balls of light. And I'm not the only one."

"You *did* have problems, dear," the mother told the girl, before turning to Gwenda again. "She just doesn't remember it."

"But I do," Bibby Libby protested. "I want to go with them. I want to help them protect the village."

Gwenda had her face fixed in an image of patience. "I understand your concerns, but—"

"No you don't," the mother said. "She started getting better" – the woman pointed accusingly at her son – "around about the time you took her for a walk with your mates to the Magraps. She was eight years old, could barely speak. After that, she started talking and doing all sorts of other stuff."

"Like vortex mathematics," the father said.

"I was muddled," Bibby Libby said. "Then the angels talked to me and helped me."

"So you can see why we need to be careful," the mother warned.

"Really, I understand," Gwenda said, still patient. "The thing is, these orbs of light are actually *real*, not imagined. They are connected to the work we do. And that is why you must sign the Official Secrets Act, and why we need Elin's help, just for a few hours." She turned to Kyle. "Isn't that right, dear?"

Kyle sat up to attention. "Absolutely… I've signed. I know what's really going on, sort of, and I promise I'll keep Elin safe."

Now the father leaned forward. "That's all very well, and yes, fine, Elin can help you, but I'm coming along as well. I'll sign... we'll all sign."

"If she goes with you, we all go," the mother insisted. "Nobody's being left behind while you go gallivanting up that mountain. Not with atomic bombs and the army coming here, and all that stuff going on. We are not going to be separated as a family."

Gwenda considered this, took a deep breath and let it out slowly. "Agreed. Complicates things, but yes okay, you can all come along. But you must all sign now." She chuckled. "Otherwise I'll have to shoot you."

The family immediately laughed at this, but not Kyle. He had to force a laugh when the father noticed his serious face.

Bibby Libby glanced at Kyle with a teenager's crush-smitten eyes, before turning her attention to Gwenda, who was holding out some papers and a pen.

-o-

An APC, followed by two military trucks, all painted blue, came roaring towards Amharfarn. They passed the bus stop, came around the bend towards the safe house, then slowed to a halt.

Andy Lock stood in the middle of the road, his hand held up in a stop signal. He was wearing the full uniform of a Royal Navy officer, white hat, gold braid and buttons glinting.

A soldier climbed out of the APC. Wearing a black uniform and blue beret, the man stared at Lock as though undecided about what to do.

At the same time, a blue bus arrived and halted behind the trucks. All its windows, apart from the windscreen, were painted over in the same pale blue as the bodywork.

Lock kept his feet planted and gritted his teeth. "Can I see your list, please?"

"Pardon?" the soldier shouted back; the APC engine was idling noisily behind him.

"I want to see your list," Lock answered, louder.

The soldier faced the APC and issued hand signals. The engine died with a diminishing whirring sound.

Lock moved closer. Behind him, Wyn and Mair Ellis were watching from their lounge bay window at the B&B. There were also faces in windows at some of the bungalows edging the road to the first bridge.

"Don't you salute officers?" Lock demanded.

The soldier saluted, arm moving to a clumsy right angle from his body; the hand snapped to the side of his head, palm outwards but crooked. "Sergeant Connelly, Auxiliary Task Force North West. I didn't know the Royal Navy was here, sir."

Lock returned the salute with the straight up, tilted hand version employed by the navy. "I'm Lock," he told Connelly. "I'm in command of this security zone."

"Nobody told me."

Lock glared at the man. "Can I see your list, please?"

The sergeant hurried to the back of the APC and returned with a clipboard. Four auxiliary soldiers appeared from behind the vehicle and took up positions either side of the road, all facing Andy Lock. They were all carrying bull-pup rifles.

Lock ignored this, accepted the clipboard, briefly studied the printed sheet, then handed it back. "I'm sorry, Sergeant, you've wasted a trip. These people are all essential workers."

The sergeant looked him up and down with suspicion, then turned around. He signalled to the trucks. More armed auxiliaries dropped from the backs of the vehicles. They hurried to take up positions, some along the sides of the road; a few went back towards the blue bus; others crouched in positions of cover by walls and hedges. Some lifted their weapons, conducting scans of the surrounding area through the sights. The four men from the APC remained facing Lock in more casual positions behind the sergeant, weapons pointed at the ground.

"And who did you say you were again?" the sergeant asked Lock, this time with more confidence.

Lock held out his identity card. "I am Andrew Morris Lock, Royal Naval Reserve and Her Majesty's Security Service. My department here is excluded from United Nations command."

"Well, we've got a bit of a balls-up then, haven't we, sir?" the sergeant responded. "My orders come from Division and Division takes its orders from the new government."

Lock's facial expression was neither a smile nor a sneer. "I understand that, but your authority does not extend to security-sensitive zones. There's obviously been a communications failure somewhere."

The sergeant pondered this uncomfortably, but still suspicious, still studying Lock's uniform and the three gold rings and loops on the ends of his sleeves. "Do you have anything in writing to confirm your authority?"

Lock reached inside his jacket then handed over some thickly folded papers. "Came through same time they announced the emergency," he said casually. "Look at bullet points four and five, below my enhanced powers of arrest and detention without trial. Gives me authority to designate essential workers and expand my security zone, at my discretion."

The sergeant looked deflated. "Can I have a copy of this?"

"What does it say at the top of each sheet?" Lock asked him.

"Top secret, sir," the man responded; he returned the papers to Lock's outstretched hand.

Lock stared into the man's eyes. "My security zone extends to the junction with the main road and all land north of the main road, including the mountain behind me and entire foreshore. I'm certain you will report that back to your command, but no photocopies I'm afraid. Strictly hush-hush, firing squad stuff. Do you understand, Sergeant?"

The man saluted, this time with some respect in his eyes. Lock returned the salute, then simply turned around and headed for the safe house.

The bus, APC and trucks had reversed to the turning area by the time Lock halted by the wall on the driveway. He stared at the blue vehicles revving their engines over there.

Caycey Jones came out of the B&B and stood on the other side of the wall, near Lock, to watch the manoeuvres.

The bus was the first to leave, headed back towards the main road and away from the village.

"It worked then," Jones said.

"But I don't know for how long."

Jones grinned, looking him up and down. "You look quite good in that get-up."

"I'm surprised he didn't smell the mothballs," Lock said. "As soon as they've gone, I'll get changed. We need to get moving."

Over at the turning area, the trucks and APC were conducting a series of choreographed moves to get them pointed in the correct direction to leave Amharfarn.

-o-

The village began returning to some semblance of normality after the auxiliary soldiers' departure. A few people came out of their houses.

Young mothers, some accompanied by husbands or boyfriends, appeared on the beach road, conversing seriously with each other as they headed down towards the harbour.

Back in the village centre, two men fiddled with the locks on the door to the *For Sale* chapel. Ventriloquist Jack sat watching them from his pickup truck. The vehicle was a dazzle of paintwork and chrome trim.

Now a vehicle approached from the bridges. Jack reversed to allow Lock to pass in the mud-spattered 4x4. This had bikes wobbling on its roof rack, and was followed by Caycey Jones in his posh Jaguar. And that was immediately followed by the camper driven by a stranger with a strikingly blonde woman and young girl seated by his side.

All three vehicles took the turn onto the lane; they were headed for the farmland and forestry beyond the village.

The chapel door was opened at last. One of the men there cheered in victory. Seeing this, Ventriloquist Jack got out of the pickup and handed a bracket and padlock to one of the men, before going inside the shuttered chapel.

He flicked a switch on the wall; the lights came on. All the pews had been removed, but the raised area with its *Big Seats* for deacons, and a preacher's pulpit, remained in place at the far end.

"Plenty of floor space in here," Jack told the two men. "Best fix the padlock and lock it up again until we need it."

When he went back outside, two women and a man were waiting with bikes, one of which was small enough for a child.

"Well done," Jack said, then climbed onto the pickup to lift the bikes one by one into its cargo deck. He then dropped down and got into the truck cabin.

The man and woman stepped back as something clicked under the vehicle; a starter motor *yah yahed* a few times, then a low turbine sound accompanied a hiss of steam from the chrome exhaust sticking up behind the cab.

Jack saluted the man and woman, then put his foot down. The truck moved away silently. It turned onto the farmland lane.

-o-

A white minibus pulled up to the start of the forestry track. It halted at the closed barrier, beyond which Ventriloquist Jack's pickup truck was now parked.

Hefin Gwynedd approached from the barrier. He had a shotgun crooked over his right forearm. Pero followed at his heels, dutifully scrutinising the minibus with intelligent eyes.

It was Gwenda Evans who rolled down the driver's window and leaned out.

Hefin peered into the vehicle as though conducting an inspection. He saw that Kyle was seated by Gwenda's side. Bibby Libby sat behind them with her mother and father. The brother was grinning widely with disbelief at the old man from one of the rear seats.

"I'll open the barrier then," Hefin told Gwenda.

"Lock it behind us," Gwenda ordered. "And that shotgun isn't a good idea. Best put it away."

"It isn't loaded," Hefin said, "but okay, if you insist." He moved to the barrier and tilted it open.

The minibus pulled through and halted alongside the pickup truck, where Ventriloquist Jack grinned at them from its open window, cigarette end pinched into the corner of his mouth.

Seeing him, Bibby Libby's brother groaned from the back of the minibus. "All the fucking nutters," he whispered.

His father turned and issued a curt warning. "That's enough."

Outside, Hefin Gwynedd locked the barrier then hurried to Jack's truck, where he allowed Pero to jump in first.

Up at the compound, Lock directed the Russian family's camper as it reversed towards him between some pine trees.

Jones stood a little away from him, gazing up at the sky. "At least the cloud cover is holding."

Dimitri and his family got out of the camper. They followed Lock to the rock face, where he ushered them in through the open steel door.

Jones peered up at the sky again, before walking alongside Lock towards the 4x4 and its roof-mounted bikes.

In the work tunnel, Hardcastle was studying one of the laptops. He looked up as the Russians came in.

"I am Dimitri," the man announced.

Hardcastle stood up, then noticed the little girl holding tight to her mother's hand. The child was gazing at the Second World War posters on the wall. She then took in the bleak interior with its naked light bulbs, mouldy concrete walls and intermittent tumours of bare rock. "What is this place?" she demanded.

Dimitri lifted the child and hugged her. "There's nothing to be afraid of." The man then hinted to Hardcastle. "It's quite safe here, isn't it?"

"Actually, yes, very safe," Hardcastle agreed, totally missing the concept of child reassurance. "Standing wave is now in low yellow territory."

"That's good then, isn't it?" Dimitri encouraged.

"Makes things a lot easier," Hardcastle said. "Chances of being zapped are slim, so we won't need EMF suits." He chuckled. "Don't have enough to go around anyway."

"It's a cave... I want to go home," Marina scolded her father. She clasped his face with her small hands, as though trying to point him back towards the entrance. "I don't want to be in this place."

"We have important work to do," Dimitri said. "And we are much safer here than anywhere in the world right now."

The girl's chin wobbled, bottom lip trembling as tears appeared in the corners of her eyes. She issued a shuddering low sob, then heard the noise of people talking and moving.

Lock and Jones came in wheeling bicycles. They were followed by Bibby Libby and her family, together with Gwenda Evans and Kyle. The newcomers were busily taking in their surroundings.

Bibby Libby immediately focussed on the tearful little girl. "Who are you then?"

"This is Marina," Dimitri answered. "She's homesick."

Marina now pushed against her father's chest. "Put me down."

Dimitri obeyed, then studied the newcomers. His wife, Lara, gripped his hand, watching their daughter.

Bibby Libby went down on her haunches, head tilted to one side to face the little girl. Bibby's expression radiated smiling warmth and kindness. "Marina is a lovely name," she said in her sing-song accent. "I'm Bibby Libby."

The child's face brightened a bit. "Really?"

"It's my nickname," Bibby Libby confirmed with a huge smile. "We're all going on an adventure. Don't you think that's ace?"

"I suppose," Marina answered, but she took the hand offered by Bibby Libby, gripping it as the teenager led her towards the workbench to look at the posters and the laptops.

Jones and Lock wheeled bikes through to the electrical chamber. Jones glanced back with some concern for the child. Lock kept his face fixed ahead, as though trying to ignore the fact his tunnel was now full of civilians, one of whom was a small child.

Gwenda Evans approached one of the laptops on the bench, glanced at it, then patted Marina on the head. "You're very pretty, but you're going to need a special helmet."

"Why?"

Gwenda chuckled. "We all have to wear them here, it's the rules."

Now Pero came running in, tail wagging, sniffing eagerly at the tunnel floor. He then made a beeline for Marina and Bibby Libby, sat down and lifted his paw.

Ventriloquist Jack and Hefin Gwynedd entered, both wheeling two bikes apiece, one of which was a child's.

"*Whass all this then?*" Ventriloquist Jack called in a high-pitched voice through unmoving lips. "*Hicycle har the critty little girl.*" He then tilted his head, eyes startled, as though hunting for the source of the sound he himself had made.

Marina laughed at this. With one hand, Ventriloquist Jack presented a small bike as though it was some sort of prize. Marina's laughter grew when Pero competed for her attention, nuzzling his head between the front wheel of the bike and her knee. She stroked him. Bibby Libby did the same.

"Dog likes you both," Hefin told them, his eyes taking in the posters and the rest of the work tunnel in general. "Where do these bikes go?"

"Through here I think," Kyle answered. The young man was standing near the electrical chamber entrance. He had been quietly observing Jones and Lock preparing backpacks in there, but with most of his attention focussed on the strange, toothy opening in the bricked-up archway at the far end.

-o-

Emily Norton stood in an upstairs bedroom at the safe house. Using binoculars, she scanned the countryside inland towards the mountains. The magnified view revealed a convoy of three blue buses, and escorting vehicles, headed east on the distant main road. They passed out of sight behind higher ground and trees.

Norton moved closer to the window. She was about to scan to the east but was distracted by movement in her peripheral vision: Ventriloquist Jack's strange pickup truck had rolled to a halt on the road outside. Norton glanced at a plume of thick, yellowish smoke rising in the distance before heading downstairs.

242

Gwenda and Jack were approaching the front door when it opened.

"That smoke to the east hasn't stopped since around the time those auxiliaries left," Norton told them in the hallway. "Three buses on the main road every half-hour in both directions."

"There's an incinerator on the go in Anglesey as well," Gwenda said. "Saw it when we were coming down the forestry road." She looked deep in thought for a moment, then snapped out of it. "Anyway, nothing we can do about that. We need to check the cellar."

Norton acknowledged Ventriloquist Jack's polite greeting, locked the front door, then accompanied Gwenda to the cellar door at the back of the hallway. Jack followed them.

The cellar was crammed with storage racks. Crates and sacks were arranged untidily on the floor. Gwenda led them past some long cardboard boxes, labelled *Body Bags*, to a corner where loaded shelves hugged the wall.

She started counting flat plastic packs on the shelves, but quickly gave up, irritation in her eyes. "I'd guess there's about one hundred and fifty," she said, lifting one to study its label. "Contains four days' dehydrated field rations. Expires in fifteen years. Must have enough preservatives to mummify old King Tut." She threw the item back onto the shelf.

"Why have you got all this stuff?" Ventriloquist Jack asked.

Gwenda tapped her foot against a carton on the ground. "Civil contingencies... emergency planning." She glanced at Jack, then moved to another corner. "There's enough food and medicines here to keep our team alive for several months if things get really bad. But now Andy has decided to look after the whole village, maybe a couple of weeks."

"Don't you agree with him?" Norton asked.

"It's not that," Gwenda answered. "But there are potential scenarios ahead that could make saving the village incompatible with our mission."

"That's true," Norton said quietly. "But I also agree with Commander Lock that we should do our best for the village."

243

Jack followed behind them, watching and listening.

"Then I hope that our best is going to be enough," Gwenda said. She approached a steel cupboard and unlocked it. It was crammed with firearms.

Jack exhaled with a hiss between his teeth.

"These look well preserved if we need them," Gwenda said, before locking it up again and pointing at some crates. "These are full of ammunition."

"Are you an expert with guns?" Jack asked her.

"I suppose I am, but it doesn't mean I like using them."

"I'm a pacifist," Jack said. "I couldn't shoot an animal, never mind a human being."

Norton looked at the man. Her eyes seemed faintly moist. "If things go really bad, human beings might be the least of our problems."

Ventriloquist Jack's eyes widened with puzzled alarm when he heard this.

"Listen, Jack," Gwenda said, "I'm showing you this so you understand we can't have just anyone coming down here."

"I agree," the man said.

Gwenda smiled. "For now, your job is to get all the food rations upstairs into the hallway. You need to organise a few men to help move most of it in your truck to the chapel. Can you do that?"

"Not a problem."

"Once that's done," Gwenda continued, "we'll be loading a supply of food onto your truck and taking it up to the compound."

"Is that when I get to see the technology underground?" Jack asked.

"You'll see plenty when you and the rest of us are hauling food down there like pack horses on bikes."

"Sounds fun," Jack said.

"I hate bikes," Gwenda said, but her eyes looked as though they were being haunted by something unseen and distant as she stared at the locked gun cupboard.

Norton noticed this and turned to Ventriloquist Jack. "We'd better get moving then. I'll give you a hand."

Lights on helmets swayed, illuminating the descending miners' tunnel with moving, uncoordinated patterns. Water dripped from the ceiling here and there. Some of the drops glinted in the beams of light.

Lock led the way, carrying a child's bike with one hand. Apart from his miner's helmet, he wore normal clothes. He had a rucksack on his back.

Hardcastle wheeled a larger bike behind him. Bibby Libby followed, holding hands with the Russian girl.

Marina's helmet almost obscured her face. The little girl constantly tilted her head up, down and sideways to allow intense eyes to see her surroundings. She looked tiny under the adult-sized miner's hat with its glowing lamp.

The girls' mothers were immediately behind them, wheeling bikes but watching for any trips or stumbles from their offspring on the wet and uneven rock floor.

Laden with rucksacks behind them, Bibby's brother was closely followed by their father and Dimitri, each wheeling a bicycle.

Kyle came along with a bike, and Caycey Jones brought up the rear, with neither a bike nor rucksack to impede his bulky form. He was keeping a watchful eye on those ahead of him.

None of them wore EMF suits.

Up ahead, that strange, almost neon glow illuminated the rockfall.

"Halt here," Lock ordered. They had reached the place where miners in the past had broken through into something strange and unworldly.

"Wow," Bibby Libby said. She gripped Marina's hand as they walked onto the concrete floor with its rusted steel plate and bolts. Both stared through the breach. The tubular tunnel inside was all smooth and glowing.

Bibby's mother and the Russian woman looked around with wide eyes, at the rockfall blocking the old tunnel, then with even more concern at the breach, the shards of glassy material on its edge, and

245

the glowing technology of the smooth tunnel beyond it. It was something that clearly did not belong here.

"Wow indeed," Dimitri agreed.

Bibby's brother looked as though he had been stunned out of his usual bored disdain. "Jeez, who built this place?"

"Your attention, please," Lock demanded. "No questions... We can't answer them." He waited for silence. They shuffled to face him. Jones watched from behind.

Lock pointed at the breach. "Those with bikes will need to carry them over the edge here to avoid puncturing the tyres. It still slopes quite severely in there, so no riding. Keep a firm hold of the bikes. We don't want them rolling down this thing on their own." He studied their faces as he switched off his helmet lamp. The others began doing the same. "Does anyone need a rest?"

Still holding Marina's hand, Bibby Libby said, "I told you it would be an adventure."

The little girl, face lit by the strange glow from beyond the breach, now seemed fascinated. Lara's expression was more serious when she took hold of Marina's other hand.

-o-

Four men from the village were hauling cartons and sacks to the high-tech pickup truck reverse-parked on the safe house drive. Ventriloquist Jack was at the front door, handing the stuff out to them. Wyn Ellis supervised loading onto the truck. Mair Ellis marched down the B&B driveway, next door, carrying a tray of steaming mugs. She had a determined-importance expression on her face.

Inside the safe house, at the back of the hallway, Gwenda Evans spoke in a hushed voice to Emily Norton. Gwenda held out a smartphone so Norton could read its screen.

"For goodness' sake, why now with all this going on?" Norton asked, keeping her voice down.

Gwenda put the phone away and glanced at the open front door. Jack grunted as he handed over a heavy bag. Gwenda's expression was one of resigned pragmatism. "Burke did say the shipments would keep coming," she said to Norton. "The drugs keep their murdering goons happy and compliant. But this shipment is extremely short notice, out of the blue. And if we don't meet it, the goons will be all over us. There's no alternative. We have to comply, simple as that."

"So, you and Commander Lock will be going out on a boat tomorrow?"

"If you can call it a boat," Gwenda said. "It's a bit bigger than that. But it means Lock and I will be away for at least eight hours."

Norton frowned. "Where is it berthed?"

"Ah, I forgot they didn't tell you about that aspect of things here. It's on the other side of the mountain. And the road down to it, I can tell you..." Gwenda shuddered. "I hate heights."

"Who'll be in charge while you two are gone?"

"Mister Jones and yourself of course."

-o-

Hardcastle and Lock walked out onto the landing in the main tunnel. Both looked surprised. "It's been busy," Hardcastle said.

"And considerate," Lock agreed.

Their attention was fixed on solid balustrades that had appeared since their last visit to this strange underground world. The landing and stairway's previously sheer edges were now protected by chest-height barriers, glowing with the same green luminosity as the tunnel walls.

Hardcastle approached a balustrade, still wheeling a bike. He tapped the new structure with the back of his hand. Knuckles produced a dull sound of bone rapping against something as solid as rock. "I wonder where it gets the mass from."

But Lock's attention had switched to the tubular tunnel behind them. He could see the others coming down it, about 20 yards away. "Wait there, please," he shouted.

Hardcastle glanced at him. "Why are you holding them up?"

Lock headed for the stairway, child's bike slung from his right hand. "We need to cover up that skeleton on the stairs."

Hardcastle moved in the same direction. "I don't see the point of covering it up. There's plenty more skeletons down there, and we can't cover them all up."

Lock halted at the top step. "It's gone."

Hardcastle joined him. "So it has. Why did you want to cover it up?"

"That little girl."

"We could just brief them about the skeletons," Hardcastle suggested. "Children are likely to be more curious than scared if they know we're not trying to conceal things from them."

"I'm not very good with children," Lock said. "It disturbs me when they cry. Could *you* handle it perhaps?"

Hardcastle leaned his bike against the balustrade then went back to the tubular tunnel. He called out to the others, watched them emerge, heard their hushed exclamations of astonishment about the size of the place, then gestured to them to gather near him. "Can I have your attention, please?" His voice echoed in the massive underground space.

Jones joined Lock, who was still looking downwards from the top step. "It's made some alterations," Jones observed. "That skeleton's gone as well."

Lock was about to say something, but then heard Hardcastle's voice. Lock and Jones turned to listen.

"Have you ever been to a museum and seen Egyptian mummies?" Hardcastle began, eyes fixed on the Russian girl.

Marina shook her head. Slightly flummoxed by this, Hardcastle then asked, "Well, have you seen Pirates of the Caribbean then?"

"What the hell's he saying," Jones said to Lock, then hurried towards Hardcastle.

But Hardcastle got his next words out before the American could intervene. "There are a lot of skeletons down here," Hardcastle said. "But they've been dead for thousands of years, like the mummies in Egypt."

Marina's eyes widened. She gripped Bibby Libby's hand tighter.

"Really?"

"There's nothing to be frightened of," Jones announced in his deep voice. "It's a bit like a museum, this place. A few bones here and there, but no danger."

"We're going to see skeletons," Marina said to Bibby Libby. "Cool."

"You can all put your bikes down for a bit," Jones said. "We'll rest here for five minutes." He then gestured to the parents to follow him to one side.

Dimitri gazed up at the immense silvery coils on the walls and ceiling. He and his wife then followed Jones.

"This is awesome," Bibby Libby's brother said. His mother and father looked stunned, speechless. Their eyes were fixed on Jones, who was now leaning against one of the balustrades. Lock approached and stood near him.

Kyle had stayed where he was with his bike. He glanced over at Bibby Libby, who was talking to the Russian girl, then stared up at the silvery coil running along the ceiling. He approached Hardcastle and grinned at him. "Pirates of the Caribbean, Mister Hardcastle?"

Hardcastle issued a sheepish smile. "Slip of the tongue."

"How old are these skeletons you talked about?"

"Some are very old," the scientist said. "Older than history."

"Then our history must be very incomplete," Kyle suggested, looking down the stairway and out into the brightly lit tunnel.

Hardcastle kept his voice low. "If you mean the history that puts us alone in the centre of the universe... then yes."

"Another civilisation must have existed before ours," Kyle said. "Judging by this, I think it could make ours look primitive."

"You haven't seen anything yet," Hardcastle said. "Prepare to be dazzled when we reach our destination."

It was Hardcastle who was the first to arrive at the connecting passage, well ahead of the others. His bike skidded to a halt, left foot scraping along the smooth floor. He lowered the machine to the ground and hurried into the smaller tunnel.

Miiko looked up from her seat in the first small chamber. Hardcastle arrived, his attention immediately fixed on the German officer's skeleton.

"We've got civilians on the way," Hardcastle warned.

"Ah," Miiko responded, slightly puzzled.

Hardcastle lowered his rucksack and gazed at the skeleton. "We need to move Herr Kapitan out of sight." His hands moved hesitantly, as though to get hold of it.

"We can carry him in his chair," Miiko prompted. She leaned over, ready to lift from her side.

"Very carefully," Hardcastle cautioned.

"And with dignity," Miiko agreed. "He was an honourable man, I think."

Hardcastle chuckled. "And good company." They carried the chair and skeleton into the side chamber containing the rotted camp beds and blankets.

The skeleton's head seemed to nod when they set it down, as though grateful for getting it here in one piece. Miiko straightened its hat.

Hardcastle draped an old blanket over it. "There's the other four as well." He grabbed some more blankets from the pile on the floor. "We'll wrap them up in these."

"Things have been happening here," Miiko told Hardcastle as they headed for their next task.

"What things?"

"More changes… This place has been active."

Lock arrived at the side passage on his bike. The rest of the group were close behind him. The two girls, flanked by their parents and Kyle, were riding in line abreast. Bibby Libby's brother weaved along on his bike. Caycey Jones freewheeled sedately a safe distance from the youth.

Lock approached Hardcastle, who was waiting at the passage entrance. "You and Mister Jones need to see something before any of the civilians go in there," Hardcastle said quietly. "I'll wait here and keep an eye on them." He smiled and waved at Marina.

"Where are the skeletons?" Marina called out. Bibby Libby laughed gently beside her.

"What's going on?" Lock asked Hardcastle. Now Jones approached, wearing a frown.

"Banes is waiting to brief you inside," Hardcastle told them both.

"What's up?" Jones asked.

"You need to go through," Hardcastle warned in a hushed voice, face fixed in a smile for the benefit of the others now watching them.

"Okay," Jones called out to the civilians. "Wait here, please."

Lock and Jones passed through the first chamber. Miiko bowed and returned their brief greetings. Banes and Kikuko were waiting by the far doorway in the second small chamber.

"You're supposed to be monitoring that laptop for a response," Lock told Banes.

"Take a look," Banes responded.

Jones and Lock approached the dome entrance. Jones gasped when he got there. Although a wide gap permitted them to see towards the centre and beyond, some of the floor's outer orbit now seemed to be populated with houses. It was as though the village of Amharfarn was being reconstructed here.

The houses nearest looked complete. Those further away appeared to be rising like glutinous fluid from the floor, slowly shaping into walls, roofs and chimneys. A satellite dish popped suddenly and noiselessly into shape on the wall of one of the closer bungalows.

On the furthest side, beyond the cannon-like devices, farm buildings were taking form. A bridge crossed what looked like a fully functioning river, flanked by still rapidly developing oak and pine trees. Some of the chamber floor over there appeared to be covered in lush grass, speckled with buttercups and daisies. It was visibly growing, spreading.

"We thought it safer to wait here until the activity stops," Banes told Lock.

"Quite right," Lock conceded as he stared wide-eyed at what was going on in there. "Sorry I was a bit short with you..."

Beside him, Jones was taking it all in with a dropped jaw.

In the main tunnel, the bikes lay on the floor in a tidy space away from the passageway to the chambers. Some of the group here sat down while others remained standing. Hardcastle guarded the passage entrance, keeping a discreet eye on them.

The Russian couple were cross-legged on the floor, talking quietly in Russian to their daughter. Marina seemed fairly at ease, though she kept glancing across at Hardcastle's position.

A short distance away, Bibby Libby was with her parents and brother. The brother still looked stunned by his surroundings. They spoke to each other in Welsh. Bibby kept pointing at her own feet.

Kyle waited awkwardly alone for a while before approaching Hardcastle. "What's going on in there?" Kyle whispered.

Hardcastle put a finger to his lips and kept his voice low. "I shouldn't really talk about it, but this place is really advanced technology."

"I think I already gathered that," Kyle said.

"You haven't seen anything yet," Hardcastle warned. "It's able to form things from the outside world in very accurate detail. It seems to be building the village in there, growing it out of the ground like magic."

Kyle's forehead creased. "Wow. Is it using nanotechnology, do you think?"

"Keep your voice down. We don't know. It's beyond us, but it looks like it's anticipating something."

"Intelligent then," Kyle concluded, nodding.

"Evidently so."

Kyle's face seemed relaxed, but his voice was serious. "I've read stuff by that scientist in the wheelchair. He reckoned artificial intelligence could destroy us all if it ever happened."

"There's a few who favoured that theory," Hardcastle agreed. "But they all made the same assumption."

"What assumption is that, Mister Hardcastle?"

"It's been taken for granted that AI doesn't already exist, either out there in the universe somewhere or even here on Earth."

"Do you think it does already exist?"

Hardcastle smiled thinly. "I'm starting to think it might."

Kyle nodded in a matter-of-fact way. "I've always thought it was arrogant to assume we are alone in the universe. But it still comes as a bit of a shock to see all this."

Lock and Jones walked through the space between the precise replica of the safe house and a row of newly arrived semi-detached bungalows. All were duplicates of those over five miles away on land, and above ground, in the real village.

The duplicate safe house now had a front lawn and garden. The B&B next door to it did not. The chamber floor in front of that one seemed to be simmering like liquid toffee.

Houses, trees, hedgerows, streams and bridges had taken full form on one side. Even the chapel was along there, complete with its *For Sale* signs, the post office convenience store next door to it.

The furthest side conveyed green open spaces – hedgerows, trees, farm gates – and the occasional farmhouses, complete with yards, barns and sheds. All of this looked like some sort of gigantic stadium museum, all growing miraculously under the ceiling, with its stars, nebulae, and the laptop screen depiction up there in huge curving Cinerama.

Jones and Lock arrived at the table; the figure was standing motionless beside it. Lock studied the laptop, checking that it was showing the same information as that depicted above them in the ceiling.

Zeros and ones continued parading across multiple stacked windows on part of its screen. The window awaiting a response to the message they had sent, days earlier, continued to flash the words: *Message sent… Listening for response.*

Caycey Jones stared at the inanimate figure. He glanced at Lock, whose eyes now met his. Lock gestured towards the figure. Jones took the cue. "We wish to have dialogue with you."

Immediately there was movement across the surface of its mannequin-like face. A plastic skin became more realistic, its textures more lifelike. The eyes turned into white fluid, before reforming to become eyes with colour, complete with eyelids and lashes.

The clothes clarified from something imprecise, into the fabric and textures of something that appeared very real, on a man who actually looked alive.

Yet there remained something odd, something partly indiscernible, partly obvious about this man to confirm he was not human. He was too perfect, his features too symmetric, his skin completely free of any ticks or blemishes; the whites of his eyes were too perfect a white, blue irises too blue, too thin, too perfectly circular. Its hair was white and styled; it fitted the scalp closely, edges delineated precisely around its ears.

But it was impossible to assess the age it was supposed to represent. It could have been 30 or 90 years old, or anything between. Its visual appearance, the hundreds of small visual cues, added up to something approximating a human but remained clearly artificial to a real human's perception.

Jones glanced at Lock, whose eyes were wide yet fascinated.

The thing spoke: "We now... now... now... aby... aby... able... dialogue with greater precision and understanding, to conduct... to conduct..." Its lips were unmoving as it enunciated those words with an electronic twang.

Now Caycey Jones spoke again. "We have brought the individual you requested."

"The young woman," it responded, speech now clarifying. "We acknowledge this." It then merely stared at Jones.

Puzzled, the American looked at Andy Lock, who shrugged, baffled.

Jones faced the strange figure again. "You stated her presence was needed in order to conduct repairs to your higher functions. What do you now require her to do?"

"Repaar... reeper... repairs of higher fung... fung... functions... have... have... have... commenced," it responded. "No further action is required."

"Do you need the young woman to remain here?"

"Nono... nono... nono... not required."

Out in the big tunnel, the others turned expectantly when Lock reappeared. Banes came with him.

Bibby Libby stepped forward closer to them, an eager expression on her face. Marina followed her.

Lock faced them, arms raised to attract attention. "Please listen, all of you, Mister and Missus Lewis especially." He then nodded towards Bibby Libby. "There's been a change of plan. It seems you have already provided us with the help we needed just by coming this far."

"I think I already knew that," Bibby Libby told him. She tapped the glassy floor with her foot. A faint yellow tinge briefly appeared there. "I've been seeing the lights and hearing whispers in my head ever since we arrived. It's amazing."

Lock smiled. "We are very grateful to you and your family."

"Are you saying we're done here and can go home?" Bibby Libby's mother demanded.

"I am," Lock answered.

"Aww," Marina said disappointedly.

"It's okay," Bibby told her. "You'll be safe here." She then turned to Lock. "But I would have liked to actually see what's in there."

"I know," Lock said. "But Mister Jones and I have concluded that it would be better for your security, and ours, if Doctor Banes here gets you home immediately." He looked at the Russians. "Dimitri, you and your family will be coming in with us and staying for a little while, for the same security reasons."

-o-

At the real safe house, on land and above ground, Gwenda Evans lowered her binoculars at the upstairs bay window. The evening sky was beginning to dim, and Burke's silver Range Rover was approaching along the lane from the main road.

When the car pulled to a halt outside, Gwenda was already marching down the driveway towards it.

Burke got out of the back. He was wearing his fancy coat, white shirt and striped tie neatly framed by its collar. He glared at Gwenda. "Where's Commander Lock?"

255

"Carrying out security checks in the countryside somewhere. What do you want?"

"Access to the mountain."

"Which part?"

"Just the forestry."

Gwenda frowned. "It's a bit inconvenient, but I'll unlock the barrier for you. I'll just get my keys." She began to turn to go back into the house, but Burke spoke again, the driver listening from his open window in the car.

"Do you know where I could find some winding gear around here?"

Gwenda looked puzzled. "Winding gear? What do you mean?"

"Portable mining equipment," Burke answered. "The sort of stuff that mine rescue teams use to lower people and equipment into deep shafts."

"Why on Earth would you need something like that?"

Burke smiled broadly. "I think my missing man might have dumped the car down one of the old mineshafts on your mountain."

"I'll get my keys," Gwenda told him with a dead-pan expression.

She closed the door behind her inside the safe house hallway and immediately lifted her mobile.

Up on the mountain, behind the steel door in the rock face at the compound, a similar mobile phone rested beside one of the laptops on the bench in the deserted work tunnel.

It rang four times then stopped. A red light began flashing in a corner of its screen. There was nobody here to notice it.

SEVEN

"How did it go when half the villagers were carted off to registration?" Burke asked Gwenda Evans in the back of his Range Rover. They were being driven along the farmland lane.

The passenger Scouser tilted his head in the front of the car, listening for her response as though particularly interested.

"I don't know," Gwenda said. "I was busy with an inventory check." Her eyes were fixed, looking out through the side window.

"Your colleagues though," Burke persisted. "Didn't they say anything? And the other villagers must be talking by now?"

"Nobody's mentioned it to me," Gwenda answered.

"You seem reluctant to talk."

Irritated, she turned to face him. "It's a habit..." The car lurched over a pothole in the lane as she spoke. "Goes with the job... security... tight lips."

Burke's face flushed with disdain. He then seemed to decide not to press her on that subject. "Are you ready for the shipment tomorrow?" he asked instead.

"Of course."

"It's very important."

"It's also very inconvenient. With all this emergency stuff going on, we've got a pile of bureaucratic rubbish on top of our normal duties."

"Couldn't be helped. Our Gibraltar op had to take a surplus from Spain. Last-minute storage problems, hence an early arrival here."

"I'm not the slightest bit interested in why," Gwenda said sharply. "I just do my job, distasteful as that part of it is. Smuggling narcotics for the likes of you wasn't why I joined the service."

Burke's eyes fixed on hers. She returned the stare. He leaned his head closer, voice oozing malevolence. "That night up by your compound, when I was talking to Lock about my missing car, it was you pointing a gun at me from the dark, wasn't it?"

Gwenda remained silent.

"If you ever do anything like that again," Burke said, then paused. His mouth broadened, white teeth bared. "I'll rip that stupid Welsh face off your fucking skull."

The passenger Scouser in front seemed to flinch at this. At the same time, the driver said, "Up ahead."

Gwenda shifted her gaze. The country lane was blocked by Ventriloquist Jack's pickup truck. It was parked at an angle outside Hefin's farm gate.

The Range Rover came to a halt.

Gwenda smiled at Burke, her hostility revealed rather than hidden behind this mask. "Well, it's been an interesting chat." She leaned forward and tapped the driver's shoulder. "I'll be going to the barrier in that pickup truck, so you follow behind it, young man... okay?"

"Okay, Miss," the driver agreed as Gwenda opened her door.

Up ahead, Jack came out from behind the farm hedgerow and the rear of his truck. His hands were stuffed into boiler suit pockets, a lit cigarette rotating in the corner of his mouth. He stared at the Range Rover.

Concealed a few feet away, Hefin Gwynedd kept his head low and out of sight behind the hedge in the farmyard. There were no televisions on show today. Pero lay quietly on the ground beside the old man's feet, ears cocked to the sounds from the lane.

Gwenda held the Range Rover door open and looked in at Burke. "Be careful you don't fall down any mineshafts up there."

Burke's expression reverted to its usual sneer. He patted an instrument case by his feet. "We are only going to measure the depth this time, but I'll be back with gear soon..." He chuckled. "Besides, I won't be going down myself, old girl. One of my boys will be doing

258

that. And anyway, I have to pay a visit to someone important along this hick coast of yours tonight."

Gwenda slammed the door shut. She looked in at the driver as she passed. The young man was staring ahead over the steering wheel, but he glanced at her with sideways eyes and a worried expression.

Ventriloquist Jack opened the truck passenger door for Gwenda to get in. He then faced the silver Range Rover, brought his heels together and raised his arm in a mock Nazi salute. He spat out his cigarette end before climbing into his vehicle.

Burke gritted his teeth in the back of the Range Rover. "Cheeky Welsh bastard," he said to the Scousers. "Remind me to arrange a trip to the local registration centre for him."

Steam hissed from the vertical exhaust behind the cab as the pickup reversed a few feet. It then turned and headed for the forestry road.

The Range Rover followed it. Both vehicles pulled away out of sight around a bend.

"Bad shenanigans for sure," Hefin told Pero as he moved from behind the hedge.

Pero issued a whine of agreement.

"Let's hope our mountain can stop the bastards," the old man concluded as he closed his gate.

Pero cocked his ears and stared at his master. Another low whine followed from the dog.

On higher terrain, the silver Range Rover roared uphill along the dirt forestry road.

Behind it, Jack's truck was now parked on a grassy area just above the open barrier. Gwenda leaned forward in the passenger seat. "Wait for it," she cautioned.

Jack stared over the steering wheel, watching as Burke's car sped away, a cloud of dust billowing behind it. The vehicle finally disappeared around a bend up there.

"Now get me back to the safe house as quick as you can," Gwenda ordered. "I need to get something."

Jack grunted as he turned the wheel.

-o-

Emily Norton became alert at the safe house office window. She saw Ventriloquist Jack's high-tech pickup speed to a halt on the road outside. Gwenda Evans got out.

"Did you get it?" Gwenda demanded when Norton opened the front door.

Norton pointed into the hallway. "In that bag there." She looked out and saw that the pickup truck was reversing onto the drive, getting ready to turn around. "Is that Mister Thomas driving?"

"Certainly is," Gwenda answered. She opened the duffle bag on the floor and pulled out a short assault rifle. "Refuses point blank to let me drive it myself." The small woman cocked the weapon then pulled its trigger with practised ease. The firing mechanism gave off a dull metallic click.

"What if things get violent?" Norton asked.

Gwenda slotted a magazine into the weapon. "I did warn him, but he's very precious about that truck." She then lifted and tapped more magazines with her knuckles before putting them, and the now loaded gun, back in the bag.

"I wouldn't want anything to happen to him," Norton said.

"Try not to worry, dear," Gwenda soothed. "It does no good and I'll do my best to look after Jack Thomas if things go hot. Anyway, Burke says he's only checking the shaft depth tonight. He's got a radar gun or something. Shouldn't have any trouble."

"Let's hope you're right."

Gwenda hoisted the duffle bag over her shoulder and moved to the front door. "Burke *is* a wildcard and deceptive. If he goes nosing around near the compound, he might see things he shouldn't see. Then we'd have trouble for sure."

"What exactly are you going to do?" Norton asked.

"I'm going to monitor Burke until he leaves the mountain. But don't worry. I won't shoot him unless I have to."

-o-

Up in the electrical chamber, almost half of the solid-looking brickwork in the arch pivoted into darkness. Someone was opening it, pulling the toothy mechanism from behind. Helmet lights moved in the gap beyond.

Banes stepped through into the glow from naked light bulbs in the electrical chamber. Kyle came next. Banes hurried through to the work tunnel, where he saw the mobile phone flashing red on the bench.

Kyle stayed and watched Bibby Libby and her family. One by one, they came through from the dark, eyes curiously examining the solid half of the brickwork. Bibby's young face looked pale under her miner's helmet.

Banes had the mobile phone at his ear when the others arrived in the work tunnel. He held up a hand, signalling to the group to keep quiet. "Yeh, I got that. Stay inside till we get your go ahead."

The scientist disconnected the call and put the phone back on the bench. "We have to wait here a little while," he told the family. "That was Missus Evans. She left a voicemail to call her before we open the outer door."

"Problems?" Kyle asked him.

"That guy Burke is up on the mountain somewhere. But he's not coming here apparently."

"Is this dangerous?" Bibby Libby's father demanded.

"No," Banes answered. "Just security. We don't want this man to see any of you up here, that's all."

"So it is dangerous," the mother argued. Her voice was petulant and louder than her husband's.

Kyle's normally passive face became animated. "Yes it is dangerous," he told the parents. "Everything that's happening is dangerous, which is why we need to keep calm, do as we are told, and wait here until we get further orders."

Banes looked at Kyle with some surprise. Bibby Libby gazed admiringly at him. Her brother sniggered behind his parents' backs.

The parents themselves were about to say something in response, but then, after glancing at each other, appeared to think better of it.

Ventriloquist Jack's truck climbed the forestry road easily at speed. With little noise other than its tyres against packed dirt and chippings, it passed the turn-off to the compound, then clipped over the hump to the first dip along the side of the upper forestry. The banks of trees here were in dark shadow cast by the mountain slopes.

"I want you to halt short of the next brow," Gwenda said when they passed the ruined farmhouse. The small truck came to a stop at a tight passing point halfway up the next rise.

"Can you turn it around here?" Gwenda asked.

Jack peered at the track's outer edge. "I think so." The forestry sloped downwards here. It was a precipitous drop.

"You do that while I go up there and take a look," Gwenda said. "Once you've got it turned, you need to reverse it halfway, then you can walk to my position."

"Will do," Jack said.

Gwenda got out and stood with the passenger door still open, duffle bag over her shoulder. "Keep watching me. If you see me doing this" – Gwenda lifted her hand and mimicked pulling down on something – "you get back in the truck and drive like hell to the village. You got that?"

"Got it," Jack answered.

Gwenda slammed the door shut and hurried away.

The gearbox clunked and the truck reversed, steering at full lock. The next move took the front wheels to the outer edge. Stones, chippings and dust spilled down the slope.

Gwenda was short of breath when she reached the brow. Keeping her head down, she skirted the upward side of the track and crouched under some overhanging pine branches.

Using her binoculars, she was able to see over the brow into the next dip. The forestry road meandered downwards to a level stretch, then rose again towards more rising banks of trees in the distance.

Her binoculars focussed on a turn-off halfway along the level stretch, then panned downwards to the left: more trees. It was getting darker down there as dusk arrived prematurely this side of the mountain.

Ventriloquist Jack arrived.

"Keep down," Gwenda warned.

The man crouched and lowered his head. "Have you spotted them?"

"Not yet."

Jack studied her, then peered down the slope himself.

"Got him," Gwenda said, pointing with a finger. "They just put their headlights on."

Jack saw a glow down there in the otherwise dark trees.

"It's not moving," Gwenda observed. She put her mobile phone to her ear and got an immediate response. "You can leave now, but move fast," she instructed. "Call me if you hit any snags." She listened briefly then put the phone away, lifting the binoculars to her eyes again.

"What's that man Burke looking for down there?" Jack asked Gwenda.

"Remember what I told you?" she shot back.

"Not to ask."

"Well then…"

"*Heter hiher hicked a hiece of hickled heher*," Jack said. His lips barely moved.

"You're improving," Gwenda said, without taking her eyes from the binoculars. "But you've still got some work to do on your lip consonants." Her mobile buzzed and she lifted it to her ear. "Still clear to go," she responded into it. "That was Banes again," she told Jack, "now leaving the compound. The Lewis family and Kyle are with him in the minibus."

Jack glanced at the diminutive woman with her gun and binoculars. "I'm looking forward to seeing what's down there under the mountain," he told her.

Gwenda shifted her feet below her crouched form. "You'll get your chance, but the real business is way out under the Irish Sea." The binoculars became fixed to her eyes again. "Shit, that was quick. Too quick."

"What?"

Gwenda moved. "They're coming back. Come on, we've got a four-minute start on them at the most." She scurried away from the brow.

Jack groaned. He heaved himself upright and followed behind her, jogging awkwardly in an ape-like gait.

The minibus carrying Kyle and the Lewis family swerved downhill around the first bend on the eastern slopes. It passed the low cliff and turn-off to the hidden waterfall. Its headlights were off, and it was getting darker.

Some distance behind it, Jack's pickup truck came over the brow above the branch track leading to the compound. Its headlights were also off.

At the other end of the dip beyond the ruined farmhouse, almost at the same time, Burke's Range Rover came over that brow at speed, kicking up dust, headlights glaring. It raced downhill and then along the level part of the dip.

Jack's truck completed the turn at the mud-rock cliff a fraction of a second before the Range Rover topped its next brow. Burke's car was faster.

"This is a longer stretch," Jack warned Gwenda. "If I go any faster, we'll make too much dust. They'll see it."

"Put your foot down," Gwenda ordered. Assault rifle ready in her arms, she was twisted around in her seat, her attention fixed through the rear window. "All we need to do is make sure Burke doesn't see the minibus. Any sign of it ahead?"

"No."

The Range Rover came down a slope at speed, front end bouncing its headlight beams up and down over the uneven surface.

Leaning forward in the back of it, Burke tapped the driver's shoulder. "Slow down here and stop at the next turn on the left."

"Yes, sir," the driver responded. The young man peered over the steering wheel as though he had seen something at the next bend below, but he said nothing.

The Range Rover came to a halt. Burke looked out of his side window at the compound turn-off. "Pull forward a bit more," he ordered. "Then reverse up there towards the gate. Can you do that?"

"Yes, sir," the driver responded.

Below on the farmland lane, Hefin Gwynedd ducked behind his hedge as he heard a vehicle race towards him. He lifted his head in time to see the rear of the minibus bouncing along the potholed tarmac towards the village.

Well behind and above the farmyard beyond the trees, the pickup truck whirred almost silently down the final slope to the barrier, leaving a cloud of dust behind it.

Still looking through the back window in the cab, Gwenda Evans said, "Turn it around here quickly."

"Can you see them?" Jack asked.

"Not yet."

The pickup swerved to a halt on the wider area above the barrier. It reversed a bit, then made a tight turnaround to pull onto the grassy side facing up the slope once more.

Gwenda peered through the windscreen. There was no sign of the Range Rover. She wound down her window and looked out at the ground. "Move it back a couple of feet."

"Why?"

"So we are near as possible in the same position he last saw us."

"Okay."

"Where is he?" Gwenda whispered. She leaned towards the windscreen and stared up the forestry track. It was nearly dark.

Up there, well beyond her sight, Burke stood in his smart coat facing the compound security gate. He leaned forward, nose almost touching the heavy-duty mesh. The man stared through, eyes searching.

A halogen light somewhere up there cast a glow through the trees, throwing eerie shadows onto the limited part of the internal track that Burke could see.

The Range Rover purred behind him, its engine ticking over.

Down at the entrance to the forestry road, Ventriloquist Jack lowered the barrier. He went back to the pickup truck where Gwenda's head was visible in the open side window.

"What now?" Jack asked.

Gwenda looked mystified. "He must have stopped for some reason. Stay down there by the barrier on this side of the road. Let him through when he comes. But if there's trouble, if there's any shooting and I fail to put them down, leg it through those trees on the left, and keep running until you get to Hefin's farm. The pair of you will need to find somewhere to hide if things come to that."

Headlights appeared through the trees up the slope ahead. Jack retreated to get into position.

Gwenda gripped her weapon and cocked its arming mechanism. She thumbed the safety catch, then held it ready and out of sight below the open side window.

"Well well," Burke said in the back of the Range Rover. He had spotted the pickup truck. "Pull up alongside their vehicle."

Ventriloquist Jack watched from his position by the barrier as the headlights approached. The Range Rover slowed and came to a halt directly alongside the pickup. He craned his neck to try to see what was going on, before lifting the barrier.

Burke wound down his window and leaned out. He grinned at Gwenda. Her face was framed in the open window in the pickup.

"You waited," Burke said, issuing a short laugh. "So thoughtful…"

Gwenda's face maintained a neutral expression. "Did you find what you were looking for?"

Burke's face retained a bored sneer. "I won't know for sure until I return with winding gear. Is Commander Lock back yet?"

"No. I think he's checking the boat ready for tomorrow. When will *you* be back?"

Burke managed to shrug. "Maybe a couple of days."

"We'll keep an eye out for you."

"I'm sure you will," Burke said. "Where are the others?"

"Why?"

"Just interested, old girl."

Gwenda stared at Burke. "If you must know, Miss Norton and Doctor Banes are keeping watch at the house. Doctor Hardcastle is monitoring things up at the compound with Mister Jones."

Burke smiled thinly. He then stuck his hand out through the car window and pointed towards Ventriloquist Jack. "And your new man down there… Has he signed a declaration form?"

"Of course," Gwenda answered.

"Pity," Burke said. "I had something else in mind for him. Ah well, be seeing you soon, old girl." He leaned forward inside the car. "Drive on."

Gwenda watched the Range Rover pull away. Ventriloquist Jack spat on the ground as it passed through the open barrier.

-o-

Gran was watching TV in her cottage when a key turned in the front door. She turned the volume down when Kyle came in.

"Where have you been?" she demanded. "I've been worried about you."

"Sorry, Nain, been helping Mister Lock's people."

Gran switched off the TV. "Nothing dangerous I hope?"

"Of course not," Kyle said. "I've just popped in to see if you're okay. Any news?"

"Nothing new. All the news channels are the same. They're just endlessly repeating themselves about that atomic bomb going off in Florida, saying life will be back to normal soon. And that we all have to obey the military. All the other channels are showing old films and soap operas."

"Nothing about people being hauled off in blue buses?" Kyle asked.

"Population dispersal, they're calling it. It's supposed to prevent whole communities from being wiped out if there was a terrorist attack." Gran shook her head disdainfully. "Or so they say. The news channels have always been propaganda machines for the establishment. But what have you been doing all this time?"

"I can't talk about it, Nain, you know that."

"But I've signed that official secrets thing as well. You can tell me."

Kyle sat in an armchair facing her. "Doesn't work like that and I can't stay long. We're supposed to be getting a food truck tonight, and I've got to supervise offloading it into the chapel."

"It's dark, and supervise who? And why isn't Andy Lock or one of his people doing that?"

"They're really busy. Mister Lewis, Huw Stamps, Dai Twice and some others are supposed to help me."

Gran issued a hiss of disdain between her teeth. "Good luck with that. Never seen any of them lift a finger for the village before."

"Well, they're all willing now," Kyle said, "after hearing about those auxiliary soldiers and Mister Lock turning them away."

"He did, fair play," Gran admitted. "Brave man, but there's an army of them out there. How long do you think he can keep it up? We've got tyranny now, a form of government that's murdering people."

"We don't know they're doing that," Kyle argued.

"Of course they are," Gran insisted. "Dilys called with some eggs. Her husband can see the main road from somewhere on their farm. Those buses have been up and down that road all day. And there's some sort of crematorium on the go towards Caernarfon, belching out horrible smoke. Doesn't matter what rubbish the BBC is putting out. *Population dispersal* my foot."

"Mister Lock is going to keep the village safe," Kyle said, but his eyes lacked conviction.

-o-

Burke's Range Rover came to a halt at the junction in the village centre.

Up ahead in the streetlights, three men were loitering outside the chapel. The car moved on, passing them. Like a predator, it purred along slowly to a junction with two turn-offs. Small groups of modern houses stood either side in their own circular cul-de-sacs.

"Turn around here," Burke ordered. He peered out. Decorative street lamps lit the faux-brick street and pavement surfaces. House front windows were lit behind closed curtains.

The Range Rover then headed back into the village, passed the chapel and the post office, and turned towards the first bridge. The Jones Bros yard was lit by security lights, one of which was flickering.

Burke shifted in the back of the car, looking out as it went over the next bridge. Lights reflected on the narrow river, warm glows from the windows of the tidy row of cottages alongside it.

A delivery van came the other way as they passed the bungalows. Burke glanced at it with annoyed surprise.

Emily Norton watched the Range Rover from an upstairs window at the safe house. Both Wyn and Mair Ellis watched from their bay window.

"Notice anything, boys?" Burke asked as the car picked up speed. They were now headed towards the main road.

"No, sir," the driver answered.

"Not sure what you mean, sir," the other one added.

"Didn't you notice anything at all about the village?" Burke persisted.

"No, sir."

Burke laughed. "Idiots. Nearly all the houses back there had lights on. Half the hicks living there are supposed to have gone to happy-gas land. They clearly haven't."

-o-

The moon peeked through clouds, its glow no competition for the amber street lights in the village. To the east along the coast, thick smoke billowed in a distant, rising column.

Emily Norton stood in the office bay window. She was keeping watch on the road outside. Behind her, Gwenda Evans slept curled up on an armchair, head on the frayed upholstery of one of its arms. She, like the office, was lit by only what reached her from a street lamp outside.

Something caught Norton's attention. She turned in the window

269

as headlights briefly sent beams flashing above village roofs to the west. She continued watching in that direction.

A moment later the 4x4 pulled onto the driveway outside, its lights dazzling Norton. She closed the curtains, switched on a table lamp then went over and shook the sleeping woman's form.

Gwenda Evans groaned as she awoke.

A little later in the kitchen, a toaster popped eight slices of tanned bread. One of them spilled out and landed on the worktop.

Banes lifted his head from the table, startled, his eyes suddenly open. He blinked.

"You need to go to bed," Lock told him. He was seated the other side, drinking from a mug.

"I need to hear what you're planning," Banes said. The man's eyelids looked heavy.

"But you keep nodding off," Caycey Jones warned from along the table. "Go to bed. You're going back to relieve Hardcastle in four hours."

"Only four hours," Banes muttered. He rose to his feet and, staggering a bit, went through the French doorway.

Lock studied Gwenda's tired face. "You and I going out on the boat tomorrow is a problem."

"Maybe," she said. "Maybe not."

"What if Burke actually finds some winding gear?" Lock pondered aloud. "What if he discovers the car, and our friend with a bullet in his head, while we are out at sea?"

"Where would Burke get equipment like that?" Jones asked.

"I have no idea," Lock told him.

"Think," Jones demanded of all of them. "Is it possible he could locate some gear and return tomorrow? And what do we do if he does?"

Norton perked up and put her mug down. "Why don't we analyse the problem in reverse."

"What do you mean?" Jones asked.

"Well," Norton said, leaning on her elbows. Her thumbs rotated as she creased her forehead behind them in thought. "Our problem is the car and the body down that mineshaft. We need a solution to that, not a reactive plan to Burke finding it."

"Go on," Lock encouraged.

"It's simple," Norton continued. "We take measures to prevent him from finding it."

"We can't kill him," Gwenda Evans said. "Though I wouldn't hesitate if I had to."

"Killing him would truly send the balloon up," Lock agreed.

"I don't mean that," Norton said. "We have to do something at the mineshaft so nobody can get down to that car."

Jones was sceptical. "Like dynamite?"

"I'm not talking about blowing it up," Norton told him. "Think of it this way..."

Upstairs, Banes flopped onto a single bed without taking off his clothes or shoes. His eyes closed immediately. An alarm clock ticked on his bedside table.

In the kitchen, Jones stared at Norton. "Are you serious? It sounds almost as crazy as an illegal funeral involving a grandfather clock."

"But it could actually work," Lock said.

Jones now stared at Lock before reluctantly easing his expression of doubt. "What the hell," the American conceded. "I must be acclimatising to this place. Let's think it through. How wide is that shaft?"

-o-

Burke's car pulled up to a floodlit military checkpoint. Rain hit the windscreen as a regular army soldier approached. He was carrying a rifle.

High stone walls flanked a wide and ornate gateway beyond the barrier. A National Trust information board was barely visible.

Burke opened his window and offered an identity card. The soldier studied it with a handlamp.

"I need to see the commanding officer," Burke said.

271

"Wait here." The soldier took the card to a camouflaged tent on the other side of the barrier.

Four others kept watch on the car, weapons held flat against their chests, muzzles pointed at the ground, fingers extended over trigger guards.

The rain was heavier when the soldier returned. "The colonel will see you, sir," he told Burke, before tapping the driver's window. "I'll need to see your identification as well if you're all going through."

The soldier studied the Scousers' cards before handing them back. He pointed beyond the barrier. "Go through the gate. Turn left when you pass the old smithy and a stable block. The driveway will take you to the manor house after that."

Other soldiers opened the barrier and the car passed through.

The lane beyond the gate took it through the centre of a visitor parking area. It was crammed with army trucks on one side, APCs and a light tank in the coach park on the other.

Another high stone wall and gate was illuminated beyond it through the rain. This was flanked by alert soldiers wearing capes, hoods large over their helmets. They stared at the car as it passed through.

Military floodlights were positioned in front of the manor house, dazzling the car's occupants. Burke was barely able to see the mansion. But he could see the tank that was dug in, hull down, and ruining the stately lawn. Its turret rotated, gun barrel tracking his car as it drove.

The Range Rover swept to a halt under a covered porch. Burke got out.

A junior officer waited at the entrance door. "This way, sir."

Burke followed along a corridor lined with paintings and wall hangings.

The baronial hall was crammed with portable desks. Soldiers leaned over laptops. A quiet chatter in here suddenly hushed when Burke entered with his escort. Most avoided looking at him, but a few turned to watch Burke as he was taken to another door.

He was greeted in a library by two officers wearing combat uniforms and khaki berets. They stood in front of a desk that had part

272

of a visitor rope barrier coiled on top of it. Both men had holsters strapped to their legs.

A bulky soldier holding a submachine gun watched Burke carefully from one end of the library, feet planted next to a toppled brass post. He also wore a khaki beret. A thin microphone hovered below his tightly pursed lips.

"I'm Lieutenant Colonel Morris," one of the commissioned officers said. He did not offer a handshake or a salute. "Please take a seat." A solitary chair stood in the centre of a red carpet.

Burke began unbuttoning his fancy coat. "Thank you, Colonel."

The colonel stared at him. "No need to take your coat off. I don't have much time."

Burke eyed the chair. "Ah, I see. I won't sit down then." His eyes quickly examined the men facing him. "By the way, where are your blue berets? You're out of uniform surely?"

The colonel smiled. "We wore those for a little while before deciding the old ones are more comfortable..." He glanced at the other officer standing beside him. "Didn't we, Jenks?"

"We did indeed, sir," the man answered, then stared coolly at Burke.

"I'll get to the point then," Burke said. "My people are concerned about an apparent diminishment in co-operation from the army. I'd like you to correct that perception. For example, there's a problem at one of the villages... Amhar... farm... can't pronounce the bloody thing."

"We know it," the colonel answered. "It's under Commander Lock's Security Service jurisdiction. What's the problem?"

"Quite simple really," Burke told him. "The auxiliaries haven't been able to take the quota of people from there."

"My men are not involved with that sort of thing."

"They are supposed to be if needed," Burke shot back. "Lock is flagrantly disobeying the new government. I want you to assist the auxiliaries to do a proper roundup there, as soon as possible, please. And not just there, other places as well."

"My soldiers will do no such thing," the colonel said. "Moreover, and henceforth, they will not permit any auxiliaries to enter that particular village."

Burke narrowed his eyes. "Don't you think the government might take a dim view of that?" He then focussed on the man's cap and its badge. "So why are you really wearing that unofficial beret?"

"I already told you, Mister Burke, this one is more comfortable." The colonel turned to the other officer. "Wouldn't you agree, Jenks?"

"Absolutely, sir. Those blue ones seemed to dig into one's scalp."

"And how about you, Staff Sergeant?" the colonel now asked the bulky soldier guarding the library. "What do you think we should do with all those blue berets?"

The soldier snapped to attention and pursed his lips in surprise. "Wouldn't like to say, sir. Not in front of a gentleman."

The colonel laughed. "Are you saying that Captain Jenks and I are not gentlemen?"

"Yes, sir," the man answered seriously.

"You're right of course," the colonel admitted with a smile. "But anyway, you can tell this *gentleman* exactly what you suggested we should do with the blue ones."

The soldier puffed his chest to full attention. "Cremate the fuckers with napalm, sir."

"So there you have it," the colonel said to Burke. "Jenks, please show the *gentleman* back to his car."

Burke glared at each of them in turn. "You need to be very careful," he warned. "The consequences, if we fail, could be more horrendous than you can imagine."

"And you need to understand something about the army," the colonel responded. "We obey *lawful* orders. Do you understand? Lawful orders only, and our standing orders are to protect the citizens of this country."

"Which is precisely what all this is about," Burke shot back. "You must understand that, surely?"

"That's what we were told," the colonel said. "But now you must go, I'm busy. Escort him to his car, Jenks. Make sure it leaves my headquarters promptly."

The Range Rover drove out through the entrance and joined the main road, leaving the sentries watching its departing tail lights in the rain.

"Fuck it," Burke cursed in the back of the car.

The driver Scouser glanced at his friend in the front.

"I knew we couldn't trust the army," Burke added angrily. "What do you think, boys?"

"Don't know what you mean, sir," the passenger answered.

"Course you don't," Burke said, now quietly. "But if we don't get the numbers, somebody else will come along and do something much worse."

The two Scousers again exchanged glances with each other.

-o-

Dawn broke, bringing an early feeble light to the mountain forestry.

Lit purple by the rising sun, a bloated cloud was mirrored in the side window of a JCB from the Jones Bros yard. The machine was lodged on its hydraulic jacks near the edge of the old mineshaft.

The engine roared. The grabber arm swung over the rear of a long Hiab truck parked at the small compound entrance. With open jaws, the grabber rammed down into the roof of a rusty car perched across the tops of two others on the truck's cargo deck.

Lock stood on the other side of the mineshaft inside the compound. He issued hand signals to the JCB operator; the car was swung, creaking noisily, in a half circle over the fence. It continued until it reached a position directly over the shaft. Lock held up both hands.

Pieces of metal and plastic fell from the suspended car. Lock moved around, checking its alignment, then gave a thumbs-up signal to the operator.

The grabber jaws opened. Crunching and careening, the car bounced from side to side against the shaft wall as it plunged into darkness.

The JCB engine revved again. The grabber rotated back for the second car on the truck's deck.

Gwenda Evans stood beyond the parked 4x4. She was guarding the approach track, a short assault rifle cradled in her arms.

Emily Norton hovered between the 4x4 and the truck, watching the manoeuvres at a barely safe distance, and with a worried expression. Norton was wearing a shoulder holster, the pistol grip sticking out from under her left arm. The woman groaned with dismay; a number plate, shards of plastic, and a metal panel fell off the next car as it was swung over the security fence. More crunching sounds came from the mineshaft.

Lock squeezed out from the entrance. He watched as the jacks were raised. Then he guided the JCB to inch closer to the truck.

The jacks were lowered again. The grabber swung over to the third car, this one positioned at the front of the deck. It lifted the car, then the arm tightened to draw it closer before putting it down again. Rust and pieces of metal spilled to the ground.

The operator was a round-faced man wearing a flat hat. He waved at Norton to move further away. She stepped back a couple of paces.

The JCB then moved back towards the edge of the mineshaft.

Lock guided the next manoeuvres until the final car was positioned over the void. The car dropped just as noisily and easily as the others.

Gwenda Evans approached Norton. The two women watched Lock climb into the Hiab truck. Its engine started.

"Seems to have gone well," Gwenda said.

Norton's fretful eyes scanned the ground. "Quite a bit of junk fell off those cars. It has to be cleared away."

The truck moved forward a few yards, then halted. Lock dropped out of the cab and approached the JCB, beckoning the machine with his hands.

Gwenda assessed the debris then checked her watch. "It's only a bit of rubbish. Andy and I will see to it…" She faced Norton. "Now, are you comfortable with what you have to do?"

"Escort the JCB back to the village, then fetch Hardcastle."

"Hardcastle should be back at the surface by the time you get to the compound," Gwenda said, looking at her watch again. "Banes should have reached the big chamber by now."

Norton seemed sceptical. "What if Burke comes back before I get this machine to the village?"

"He'll have to get past our American friend first. Did you see the way he handled that rifle I gave him?"

"Not really."

"You're not on your own, dear," Gwenda said. "Don't forget that. Remember your training. If things turn bad and you get into a tight spot, shoot to kill and keep shooting until you've put them down."

"I'll try to remember," Norton said, but her eyes lacked conviction.

Lock finished talking to the JCB operator, who looked over at Norton. The engine revved, as though impatient. Norton hurried to the 4x4 and got into it alone.

Gwenda and Lock were already picking up car-wreck debris when both vehicles moved away.

-o-

Kyle stood in the open chapel entrance. Six people were inside. They were eyeing stacked cartons of tinned food and bags of vegetables arranged across half the floor. Fold-out chairs formed a barrier in front of emergency ration packs piled at the back.

"Can I take some of these baked beans?" a woman asked.

"Choice is yours and you can take enough food for two days," Kyle told her. "Those are Mister Lock's instructions." He then heard something and turned around at the doorway.

Ventriloquist Jack was approaching on foot from along the beach road. "*Whass hor wreckhast?*" he called out.

277

Kyle feigned surprise and bewilderment, eyes hunting for the source of the sound. Jack laughed appreciatively at this.

"Good morning, Mister Thomas," Kyle greeted.

Jack squinted into the chapel interior. "Vultures arrived already I see." The man was carrying a canvas shopping bag himself. "Any bacon left?"

"They didn't bring any," Kyle answered. "Just tins and a few fresh vegetables. Plenty of tins though."

"I'll have a look for some canned peaches." Jack winked as he went inside. "And maybe some evaporated milk. Haven't had that since I was a kid."

"Cool," Kyle responded. "Hope you find some."

More people began zeroing in on the chapel from along the winding streets.

Further out, beyond the two bridges, Wyn and Mair Ellis were in an upstairs window at the B&B.

Wyn's eyes were fixed to his tripod-mounted binoculars. Mair was looking through a smaller pair, fiddling with the focusing ring.

"Over there," Wyn Ellis said, pointing. "In the lay-by to the east of the main road junction. Do you see it?"

"I can't even see the lay-by," Mair responded irritably. She switched her binoculars in another direction. "I can see the army trucks in the field over there, but I can't see any soldiers."

"They're probably in cover along the hedges," Wyn told her, now looking out with naked eyes before putting them back to his binoculars.

"What exactly do you think you've seen in that lay-by?" Mair asked.

"It's well camouflaged, but I'm pretty sure it's a light tank. It definitely wasn't there yesterday."

-o-

Just above the barrier to the forestry road, Caycey Jones rested up against the front of his Jaguar, booted feet apart on the ground. There was an automatic rifle and four magazines of ammunition on the car's hood beside him. He was eating a sandwich.

Across the track and standing slightly to the side of the barrier itself, Hefin Gwynedd was gazing at the curve in the farmland lane below. Pero sat beside him.

"Don't know why Gwenda wouldn't let me carry a gun," the old man called out.

The American finished chewing. "Maybe it's because you haven't been trained."

"It's not that," Hefin said. "She knows I was with the paras in the Falklands. She must reckon I'm too old."

"Wow, but that was a long time ago," Jones said. "Was it bad?"

"Worse than bad," the old man admitted, lowering his eyes. "After the fighting, I got a message that my dad was seriously ill. I didn't get home until four weeks after his funeral. He'd gone bonkers a few months before he died. Painted King of Wales on the side of the house."

"I'm sorry to hear that," Jones said. "It must have been hard." The American turned when he heard a noise behind him.

Coming around the first bend in the distance, the 4x4 was crawling down the slope, the JCB grumbling noisily behind it.

"Here they come," Jones told the old man. "You should go home now."

"Are you sure?"

Pero issued a single bark of encouragement, as though fully in agreement.

Jones smiled. "I'll be going myself in a minute, to catch up on some sleep. You go home."

The 4x4 and the JCB behind it drew closer.

-o-

The track winding its way past the turn-off to the waterfall was silent and deserted, so too the dip higher up beyond the compound.

279

Further on and down the sloping forest, the shaft compound gate was closed and padlocked once more, the ground outside now cleared of the plastic and metal litter that might have spoken of activity here.

And on a steep hairpin road, cut into sheer cliffs on the far side of the mountain, the Hiab truck was making a cautious descent towards a cove. The road was narrow; it had no barriers, the drop precipitous.

In the cab, Gwenda Evans gripped a handle above the door with one hand, the edge of her passenger seat with the other. Her eyes were tightly closed. "How much further?" she demanded.

Lock kept a tight hold on the steering wheel. "Two more turns. I'll tell you when you can open your eyes."

The road was formed by concrete slabs that were cracked and uneven; there were voids under the edges in places. Tyres bumped over gaping potholes. Below the truck, a cliff dropped to the next descending arm of the hairpin. Waves crashed further below, throwing white spray onto rocks on the other side of the cove.

There was no forestry on this side of the mountain. Dirty yellow, flinty-clay spoke of erosion and instability above the cliffs.

And the dark slates of a ruined village in the enclosed cove spoke of the Victorian age.

The truck took the last bend of the descent. Lock steered between two drystone walls alongside the ghost village. Gwenda's eyes were now open. Up ahead, a security gate blocked the approach to a crumbling concrete dock that clearly belonged to an age of war.

Steel-framed firing slits were bloated with rust in a pillbox overlooking the dock. The concrete steps up to it were half absent, signs of their disintegration and collapse evident from the twisted rust of reinforcing rods and cables. These hung out into the air like frozen red tentacles. Waves lapped into the rock face beneath them.

Bigger waves crashed over seaweed-covered boulders on the outside of the dock as Gwenda Evans opened the security gate. The Hiab truck drove through and waited for her.

In the dock itself, a launch belonging to this era floated berthed low to the side near a fixed crane. The truck turned onto the landward end of cracked and weathered concrete, then reversed to park near it.

The pair got out. Lock put on a rucksack then grabbed the rails of a steel ladder going down to a floating platform, onto which the launch was tied. Lock's head was below Gwenda's feet when he got down there.

Gwenda stared at the radar dome on the vessel. "I hate this tub," she announced, swinging her assault rifle over a shoulder.

It looked rather like a drably coloured fishing boat. A flat deck incorporated cargo hatches behind a raised wheelhouse.

Lock watched Gwenda descend the ladder before he stepped onto the vessel. He helped her aboard.

"Tide's coming in," Lock said. "High tide by the time we get back. Do you want to start her up?"

"If you insist." Gwenda climbed steps to the wheelhouse. When she reached the door, waves crashed into the end of the dock, sending ripples that rocked the boat. "My God," Gwenda called to Lock. "I can feel it already."

Lock contemplated the forward berthing rope. "Well, you wanted to be in the navy."

"You say that every time. And every time I have to remind you, I was a teenager back then. I've got more sense now."

The engine started. Seagulls took to the air from the dominating cliffs. They swooped down towards the boat in increasing numbers, getting ready to escort it out to sea. Two of them landed on the wheelhouse roof.

Lock cast off the stern rope; he threw it onto the boat then stepped back aboard. He gave Gwenda a thumbs-up signal and headed up the gangway to join her.

Propellers generated white foam as the vessel eased away from the side. A distinctive wake trailed behind as it finally pulled out onto the sea beyond, cutting easily through the incoming waves.

-o-

Hardcastle put down his mug at the safe house kitchen. "I think I'll

281

go for a walk," he told Norton. "Thanks for picking me up by the way, very prompt."

"Don't you need some sleep?" Norton asked.

"I need fresh air," he answered. "Did our seniors say anything else about our white-haired friend down there, and what *it* might have said to them?"

"Not really," Norton told him. "They're applying caution. Very wise in my view."

"They ordered me not to talk to it."

"But did you talk to it anyway?"

"Not at all. I just watched that damned laptop for hours, waiting for an answer that never comes."

"Well, that is our mission, after all," Norton said, "sending the message and awaiting a response."

Hardcastle's face was sceptical. "But what if it's the wrong mission? What if our mission would be better accomplished by harnessing that technology down there?"

"Dangerous."

"How so?"

Norton shrugged. "I can imagine dozens of scenarios, but the one that sticks out, which Mister Jones and Commander Lock totally agree about, is the one where our hidden masters find out we triggered its revival."

"In which case, it must present a threat to them," Hardcastle argued. "*Containment* is the word White Hair used, remember."

"But we don't know precisely what that means," Norton said. "We've been all around that word dozens of times, you know that. And Circus hasn't got a clue what it means in a technological sense, otherwise they would have told us, surely."

"Group think," Hardcastle muttered, "isn't always correct think."

"I can agree with that," Norton said. "Analysis and extrapolation wins easy. But that's what we are doing as we learn more about it."

Hardcastle shook his head as though no longer interested. "Anyway, I'm going for a walk."

"Be careful out there," Norton said as the scientist went through to the office. She stood contemplatively by the sink for a moment

282

then hurried to the front window. She heard Hardcastle's departure as he slammed the front door shut behind him.

Norton pressed against the window and glanced upward to the left. She saw Mair Ellis dutifully keeping watch from upstairs at the B&B. Norton then switched her gaze to observe Hardcastle heading towards the bridges.

In the village centre, Kyle spotted Hardcastle approaching. The man lit a cigarette as he got closer to the chapel.

"Yo, Kyle," Hardcastle greeted cheerfully.

"Good morning," Kyle responded.

"Polite as ever," Hardcastle said. He walked up the steps holding out his cigarette pack. "Want one?"

"No thanks, very kind all the same," Kyle answered. "Any news?"

"Nothing… How's the food distribution business going? Are you making a profit yet?" Hardcastle grinned.

Kyle's eyes widened with alarm. "I would never—"

"Just kidding," Hardcastle said. He looked through the chapel doorway. It was deserted inside. "Nobody here?"

"Bit of a lull before lunchtime," Kyle told him. "Reckon it'll get busy again about half eleven."

"You seen that ventriloquist guy?"

"Mister Thomas, yeh. He was here earlier, went that way. I think he goes to see Hefin in the mornings."

"The guy with the useless television sets?"

"That's him, but don't ever say those tellies are useless to him. He'll go bonkers."

"I'll mind I don't," Hardcastle said. He pointed into the chapel. "Keep up the good work. You got the phone Commander Lock gave you?"

"Yes, sir."

"Well done. Keep an eye out on things from here. Use the phone if you see any strangers. One of us will answer, but not Lock. He's gone out on a boat with Missus Evans."

"Wow," Kyle said incredulously, "an antiques shipment with all this stuff going on?"

Hardcastle winked at him. "Hush-hush stuff, but yeh, antiques... I'm going for a walk but I won't be far. Use the phone if you need to."

"Will do," the young man answered as Hardcastle walked away. He now noticed a pistol clipped into a holster on the rear of the man's belt.

-o-

"You want more eggs?" Hefin Gwynedd asked from the stove in his farmhouse kitchen.

"No thanks," Ventriloquist Jack answered. He was seated at an oak table big enough to seat ten or more people. He stuck a forkful of fried bread and bacon into his mouth. His plate was streaked with spicy brown sauce. A canvas shopping bag slouched half-full on the table next to it. "Your bacon is the best," he added as he chewed.

"Home cured," the old man said. "I get it from Dylis Farmyard, cures it herself. I think I'll have another egg. You sure you don't want one?"

"Positive. I'm stuffed."

Just then Pero barked twice outside.

"Visitor," Hefin announced, putting down the egg he had been about to crack. He turned the stove off.

"How do you know?" Jack asked; he got up and followed his friend to the central passageway of the house.

"He barks in code. Definitely a visitor and friendly."

Outside on the slate doorstep, Hardcastle was bent over stroking Pero's head with one hand and about to knock on the farmhouse door with the other when it opened.

The old man and Ventriloquist Jack both peered curiously down at him.

"Really friendly dog," Hardcastle said as he straightened up.

"Only because he knows you," Hefin told him. "What do you want? Would you like some bacon and eggs?"

"That sounds wonderful," Hardcastle said, "but I was actually hoping to have a look at this test device you two have built."

284

"Not me," Hefin answered, pointing at Jack beside him. "He built it."

Pero issued a gentle bark of agreement before running inside between the men's feet. The old man pursued the dog, shouting, "Dammit, you stay off that table, Pero."

"Did Andy Lock tell you about my test bed?" Ventriloquist Jack asked Hardcastle.

"Certainly did."

"This way then." Jack led the way through the farmhouse passage lined with old TV sets. Hardcastle glanced curiously at these as he was taken to the dairy and rear door at the back. Hens fluttered and squawked in there.

"I'll be with you in a minute," Hefin shouted from somewhere behind them in the house. "Don't start without me."

-o-

Out at sea, the village and some of its adjacent coastline was now beyond the horizon, but the mountain remained visible like a stray jagged tooth. Higher peaks towered behind it inland.

In the wheelhouse, Lock throttled back as he studied the navigation screen. He glanced at Gwenda. She was seated on the floor close behind him, an aluminium bowl clutched in her hands. Both were now wearing life jackets.

"We're at the rendezvous point," Lock announced. "You feeling any better?"

"I haven't thrown up so far," she answered, groaning. "Maybe I'm starting to get the hang of it."

"The swell isn't too bad today," Lock said; he watched her getting to her feet.

"Don't talk about it."

"Okay." Lock returned his gaze to the open sea and throttled the engines down to an idle. "Three pings on the sonar, please."

285

A green-looking Gwenda Evans approached the instrument panel and pressed a button. The ghostly sonar sound matched a growing circle on a coloured screen. She pressed it again, waited a few seconds, then sent the final ping.

Both lifted binoculars to their eyes. There were no other vessels to be seen.

"You'd think they'd put a halt to this with everything that's going on," Gwenda said.

"Well, they haven't. It's a valuable commodity."

"It can't be just about money, not now."

"The money was to help finance their preparations," Lock told her. "But now the stuff itself is fuel for their auxiliaries."

Gwenda pointed. "It's bloody close this time. Over there."

A periscope drew a wake across the swell off the starboard side. It rapidly grew in height as it cut across their bow only a short distance ahead. A conning tower then broke the surface causing a wave to arch, foaming, towards their boat. Gwenda gripped a fixed chair. The bow lurched upward before crashing down.

The deck of a huge submarine then appeared, white foam spilling from it. The vessel was a hulk, speckled with more rust than paint. Its conning tower was built onto a structure near its front, a crane arm stretching out flat over its rear deck. Tons of water ran off it.

Lock and Gwenda's boat rocked violently.

"Idiots," Gwenda complained. "They nearly capsized us."

Lock throttled up the engine. He steered to keep pace with the submarine and pulled alongside. Heads appeared on its superstructure.

-o-

Hardcastle gazed at the lattices of copper wire and the suspended coils above the bath-like device in Hefin's barn. He then spotted the fence mesh construction in an old calf pen. "Faraday cage," he said, "very wise. So how did you prime the coils?"

"You seem to know about this sort of thing," Ventriloquist Jack observed.

Hardcastle gestured at the suspended coils. "The theoretical side of this sort of thing, as you put it, nearly got me kicked out of college. They were going to do it, or get me killed, never figured out which option they might have chosen. Then I was recruited by the Security Service instead."

"I nearly got into big trouble myself," Jack told him.

"Too bloody clever for his own good," Hefin said. Pero woofed in agreement.

"So how did you avoid that?" Hardcastle asked.

Jack issued a wry grin. "Dropped out of my masters at Oxford, switched to experimental and finally got accepted in Bangor. I went through their entire postgraduate programme."

"But your doctorate couldn't have included any of this stuff?"

"It didn't."

Hardcastle ran his fingers over the edge of the fibreglass bath and studied the seemingly junk gear inside it. "So why did you carry on with it? You must have known you were risking your life, everything?"

Ventriloquist Jack shrugged. "I figured if I could convince industry we could do away with fossil fuel for power and if we didn't need rocketry for space exploration, I could make the world a better place."

"But then you didn't know about the hidden masters... The Cuckoos as we tend to refer to them."

"I always suspected," Jack said, "but reason gave me the ridiculous hope we were being suppressed by the stupidity and corruption of governments. Vested interests clinging to oil as the currency of empire and global power."

Hardcastle nodded. "I thought that as well before I was properly briefed."

"Do you want to see it working?" Hefin Gwynedd asked.

"I would love to," Hardcastle said, checking his watch. "But I haven't got time. Would you mind giving Mister Thomas and me a moment to talk privately?"

Hefin grimaced. "Do you hear that, Pero?" he complained to the dog. "My farm, my barn and they want me out of the way."

"It's for your own protection," Hardcastle told him.

The old man smiled. "I know. I was just kidding." He snapped his fingers; Pero followed him.

"Do you have fully worked-up drawings for a prototype?" Hardcastle asked as soon as the old man had left the barn.

Jack tapped the fibreglass bath. "Yes, but I haven't figured out a solution to the inertia problem yet."

"That's okay," Hardcastle said. "I think I know someone who can solve that. Andy Lock is bringing you underground tomorrow?"

"That's his promise," Jack agreed.

Hardcastle glanced around and then tilted his head forward. "Now here's the thing... I'll already be down there. I want you to smuggle the drawings to me in your rucksack. And bring one of those primed smaller coils as well."

"Good God, why?"

"Because our masterplan isn't working. The Clangers haven't responded."

Jack looked mystified. "Clangers? They were cartoon alien characters or something on TV when I was a kid. What on Earth are you talking about?"

Quietly, Hardcastle began to explain.

-o-

Dimitri took a deep breath at the bay window, then let it out in a voiceless sigh. He turned to look at his daughter. Marina was on her knees by a coffee table. She was eyeing a chess board; its black and white pieces were a few moves beyond the opening of a game.

Lara sat opposite on a sofa in the duplicate B&B. Two rucksacks were leaned against the coffee table, one of them open. A bottle of cola stood on a coaster next to the chess board.

Now Dimitri returned his attention to what was outside the window. He could see Banes out there in the domed chamber. The scientist was seated at the table, facing away from the duplicate safe house next door. The rest of the duplicated village buildings stretched around the outer curve beyond him.

The Russian leaned over and tilted his head sideways to look up at the ceiling outside: the seemingly vast expanse of stars, with an incongruous, equally surreal repeat of the laptop screen depicted there.

"I think I'll go out," Dimitri said.

"I'm coming as well," Marina responded.

"We were told to stay inside," Lara warned.

"And so you must," Dimitri told the child. "Stay here with your mother."

"But it's boring," Marina protested.

"Finish your game."

"That's boring as well. She always lets me win."

"Why don't you explore the house," Dimitri suggested.

The child grinned. "Can I look inside the drawers and cupboards?"

"No," Lara warned. "That's private. The things inside them belong to Mister and Missus Ellis."

"But they don't," the girl protested. "This isn't their real house."

Dimitri glanced around the room, then approached the duplicate antique bureau near the window. He opened its sloping lid, which lowered to form a writing shelf.

The slots inside were crammed with papers. Bills and leaflets spilled out over a cloth bag containing electrical adapters and tangled wires.

Brief surprise crossed Dimitri's face. "It seems everything is duplicated here. So we must behave as guests. Their things are private. Is that understood?" He looked at Marina until she nodded.

"I'm sure they wouldn't mind us looking in the kitchen," Lara suggested.

"Good idea," Dimitri said, then a thought struck him. "Actually, I think I had better check it out myself."

Marina asked him something in Russian.

Dimitri wagged a finger. "English… We must speak only in English."

Lara frowned. "Why?"

"Because we must be trusted. This place could be wired like the

289

real house. Now both of you stay in this room until I have checked the kitchen."

Outside in the chamber, Banes stared blankly at the laptop screen. It was still repeating binary code in small windows. A larger window continued to announce its unchanging statement: *Message sent... Listening for response.* He turned his attention towards the chamber centre.

The figure representing something human was standing near the cannon-like devices. It was facing outwards and seemed to be staring towards the entrance. It then turned its head slightly as Banes heard footsteps behind him.

Dimitri was coming from the duplicate B&B, something clasped in his hand.

"It would be safer if you stayed indoors," Banes called out.

"How so?" the Russian demanded in a mock-cheerful voice. "How is it safer inside there?" He put the item he was carrying on the table beside the laptop. "Look at that."

It was an opened, half-empty tubular pack of biscuits, torn plastic wrapper coiled and twisted at the open end.

Banes seemed puzzled. "Chocolate biscuits. You should ration your food."

"We didn't bring it. I don't think anybody did, unless you and your colleagues carried a half ton of food down here?"

"We didn't," Banes said, now interested. "Where did you get this?"

"In the kitchen inside that house," Dimitri said. "Have you examined these buildings thoroughly? The Ellis couple must have enough food for an army in their real house. It's been duplicated here. It's remarkable, unbelievable."

"We haven't had time to look inside them properly," Banes answered, "though Missus Evans did say the toilet works in the copy of our house, so I've been using that."

"Did you test the water?"

"Not sure. We bring our own drinking water every time we come down." Banes lifted the biscuit pack, took one out and studied it. He then sniffed it. "Question is, are they safe to eat?"

"Precisely. I have a bored little girl in there. Do you think she would hesitate if we took our eyes off her and she found something like this?"

"What do you suggest we do?"

"I think we have two options," the Russian said. "Either laboratory test the food and water or ask that funny-looking man over there." He pointed towards the centre.

"I'm under strict orders not to talk to it," Banes said. "It certainly smells like a chocolate biscuit," he added, placing the item on the table.

Dimitri shrugged with frustration; he grabbed the biscuit, sniffed it and took a bite. His eyes lit up as he chewed. "Tastes good, tastes real."

"Not exactly a laboratory test," Banes said.

A voice called out from somewhere behind them: "Aloha." Both men turned to look. Hardcastle was walking towards them from the entrance, thumbs tucked into rucksack straps.

"About bloody time," Banes said. He switched his attention back to Dimitri, observing the man as though he might collapse at any minute.

"I'm fine," the Russian said, licking his lips. "No ill effects, not yet at least."

Behind them now, Kikuko came out of the duplicate safe house. "The kitchen in here is full of food," she called to them. "It wasn't there earlier."

Three people – one of them English, the Russian spy, and a young Japanese woman – were staring at a pack of biscuits when Hardcastle arrived at their position.

"So," Hardcastle announced as he noticed this odd behaviour and set down his rucksack. "What new miracles are you going to tell me about today?"

-o-

291

Caycey Jones was keeping watch from the real safe house office window when the 4x4 arrived on the driveway outside. Banes and Norton got out.

"Anything to report?" Jones asked Banes when they came in.

"Plenty," Banes answered. "But I need a cup of tea."

Banes opened his rucksack in the kitchen as Norton filled the kettle. Jones watched the scientist place a half-eaten packet of biscuits, a tub of vegetable spread and a sliced loaf in a plastic wrapper on the table. A vacuum pack of bacon was the final item he pulled from the rucksack.

Caycey Jones looked puzzled.

"This is what I have to report," Banes said.

The American's eyes widened. "You found this stuff down there?"

"Certainly did. It just appeared a couple of hours ago when nobody was watching. If it's edible, there's enough food down there to feed an army."

Jones looked at Norton. "Did you test the water from down there?"

Norton seemed defensive. "Sorry, I thought Commander Lock had told you... It's pure distilled water. But that molecule is easy to test. Food is way too complex. It would take months, possibly years of trials to prove it safe for human consumption."

"We don't have months or years," Jones said.

"The Russian tried one of the biscuits," Banes said. "Said it tasted good, just like the real thing, better even."

"Are there any tests you *could* carry out?" Jones asked Norton.

She lifted the bacon pack and looked closely at the labelling. "Just for basic chemistry, but it might be useful to compare it to the originals. Where exactly did you get these?"

"From the duplicate bed and breakfast down there," Banes answered.

"You'd better go next door and retrieve the real things then," Jones told the scientist.

"I'll go with him," Norton said.

-o-

Some of the street lights had started their pink warm-up glow when the Hiab truck pulled to a halt outside the safe house. Its cargo deck was stacked with wooden crates.

Gwenda got out and hurried to the front door. Lock followed her at a more sedate pace.

Wyn Ellis was alone upstairs at the B&B. He adjusted his tripod-mounted binoculars to aim them at the truck outside.

Mair came in. "What do you make of that truck?" she asked.

"First time I've seen it without a tarpaulin over the back," Wyn answered, eyes fixed to the binoculars. "Crates have got labels but I can't read them from here."

"Why don't you go out and have a look?"

"Don't be daft."

Mair frowned. "I've always wanted to know what's on that truck every month."

Lock found Jones, Norton and Banes in the safe house kitchen. The two men were watching Norton as she leaned over a microscope at the table.

"How did it go?" Jones asked Lock.

"Not bad for a change," he answered. "Sea was calm, so we're in good time. We've only stopped to touch base and for Gwenda to use the facilities." He noticed the twin packs of bacon, loaves and biscuit wrappers, each with adhesive labels on them near the microscope. "What's going on?"

"These are from next door," Norton said, pointing at three of the food items. "And these others are from the duplicate bed and breakfast underground."

"Really? Is it safe to eat?"

"That's what we are trying to make an educated guess about," Jones said.

Norton tapped her microscope. "The only difference I've found so far is on the bacon. The real bacon has traces of bacteria on it. The one from underground has none, but otherwise it seems identical to the real thing."

293

Gwenda Evans came into the kitchen. "I'm ready," she told Lock, then pointed at the food. "What's all that?"

Outside, Mair Ellis came out of the B&B. She glanced at the neighbouring house and began down her driveway, eyes fixed on the truck.

Wyn Ellis shook his head with a resigned disapproval in the upstairs window behind her.

She had made it halfway down the drive when the safe house door opened. Hearing it, Mair made a swift about-turn. Andy Lock and Gwenda Evans strode purposefully down their driveway.

Lock looked across the wall at Mair as they passed.

"Just getting some fresh air," Mair told him.

Lock shook his head with a knowing expression. Mair haughtily continued towards her front door.

Lock glanced over his shoulder. "It's replica antique porcelain."

"Really?" Mair responded, eyes wide. She planted her feet on the drive and watched Lock and Gwenda climb into the truck cab.

Gwenda smiled and waved from her passenger window as it drove away.

Wyn Ellis tracked the truck with his binoculars from upstairs. It went out of sight behind some trees, before reappearing in the distance closer to the main road.

Inside the truck, Gwenda flinched as the windscreen narrowly missed an owl flying across the road. Lock glanced at her. The military roadblock appeared up ahead. Gwenda sighed. "Here's the first one."

A soldier examined their identity cards before handing them back to Lock. Others dragged barriers aside at the junction. The Hiab truck pulled out onto the main road.

Two soldiers lay prone along the side of a hedgerow. Their weapons were aimed as they watched the tail lights disappearing into the distance. The other soldiers returned the barriers to block the junction again.

The truck sped along, ignoring the centre lines of the deserted main road as it took the bends, headlights now piercing actual darkness.

Gwenda checked her mobile phone as Lock drove. She scrolled across its screens. "Still no public internet or phone signal. But GSX is still up and running."

"Any new e-mails?" Lock asked.

"Nothing on mine."

Keeping his eyes on the road, Lock fished his phone from his jacket and handed it to her. "Here you are, check mine, please."

"Password?"

"Same as it always was."

The truck passed along an elevated road through a town. A castle glowed in street lighting below. Nothing moved down there.

Regular army roadblocks awaited them at a roundabout further on, but they were quickly through. The laden truck climbed a curving slip road to a dual carriageway.

Like the roads that had brought them this far, the trunk highway taking them east along the North Wales coast was completely devoid of civilian life. The Hiab truck progressed at speed.

Gwenda Evans dozed in the passenger seat, her head leaning up against the door pillar. Her mouth was open. A hint of dribble rested on her lower lip. Lock gently patted her arm.

Gwenda opened her eyes. "What?"

Lock pointed through the windscreen. Up ahead to the left was a flat peninsula, terminating with a headland sticking out to sea. Smoke rose from a fire-glow encompassing an entire town over there.

"That's terrible," Gwenda said. The view was suddenly obscured. They had entered a short tunnel. Beyond it, the carriageway meandered under a sheer cliff, then a second tunnel, before veering downwards.

A quarry town high above the coastal highway looked normal, just street lights and those from some of its buildings. But the peninsula sticking out to sea, now visible again, looked like a war zone. Fires raged from every building that could be seen.

"I went shopping there only a couple of weeks ago," Gwenda said. "What a shame."

The dual carriageway was still deserted when they passed

through another tunnel, then another winding section below a cliff. The road then dipped down towards a tunnel going under an estuary.

A solitary tank with blue flashing lights was parked at the slip road, another one stood on the other side of the carriageway. Both faced west in the direction from which the Hiab truck had come. Barriers with red lights straddled both sides.

Lock pulled to a halt. Armed soldiers in black fatigues appeared from behind the nearest tank, four of them sprinting towards the truck. Others aimed their rifles. And now the nearest tank rotated its turret to point its main gun at the truck as well.

"These are not regular army," Gwenda told Lock as she peered down at one of the soldiers. He was wearing a coal scuttle-shaped helmet. His rifle was aimed at her face. His companion hurried around the front of the truck and looked up at Lock, who wound down his window and showed his identity card.

"I'm Commander Lock."

The auxiliary soldier smiled at him. A front tooth was missing. "Mister Burke sent orders to expect you."

"Very kind of him," Lock said, raising his voice as the truck air brakes hissed.

The auxiliary soldier arced his arm, pointing beyond the barrier. "Stay on this road. Turn your headlights off when you approach the next roadblocks, then flash three times. They'll be expecting you. You got that?"

"Got it," Lock answered.

"One more thing," the auxiliary continued. "When you make your return journey, please use this side of the carriageway. The other one is reserved for our traffic only."

"Same headlights routine?"

"That's right," the man said. He slapped the side of the cab then rotated his hand in the air towards the other auxiliaries. They darted across the carriageway to the barriers and swiftly moved them aside.

The truck brakes hissed as it pulled away. It drove on and downwards into the estuarial tunnel. Fans rotated where they were suspended at intervals in its ceiling.

"He seemed quite civilised," Gwenda said. Lock remained silent.

296

The lighting grew brighter towards the tunnel mid-point, before dimming again as they neared the exit on the eastern side of the estuary.

Gwenda leaned forward in her seat and gawked at the other carriageway when the road levelled out the other side. Tanks stood at intervals. Other heavy-weapon vehicles were parked on slip roads on both sides.

And a long convoy of trucks and personnel carriers was parked spaced out, well apart, for the next couple of miles.

As they drove further east along the coast, more vehicles passed on the other carriageway. Headlights glared, blue lights flashed, all headed west.

"What the hell are they up to?" Gwenda asked. "It looks like the arrival of a full armoured division."

"Certainly does," Lock agreed. "All auxiliaries, and whatever they're up to, it's trouble for sure."

"I don't like it at all," Gwenda said. "They seem to be preparing for war."

Up ahead, a town by the side of the expressway was engulfed in flames.

"Bastards," Lock said. "They already had one around here by the look of it."

Gwenda stared at the scene of destruction as they passed. She then lowered her head, fingertips of both hands resting below her eyes.

Lock glanced at her. Both remained silent as he drove.

Later, the expressway was unlit where it rose between steep banks either side. Up ahead in the headlights, an exit ramp climbed to the same level as a bridge crossing both carriageways.

"So here we are," Lock announced.

"Indeed," Gwenda said. She reached behind her seat and lifted a short assault rifle from the storage shelf there. "I'll get yours ready as well."

Lock steered the truck onto the ramp, switched off the headlights and then flashed them. Auxiliary soldiers lifted and swung a barrier out of the way at the head of the ramp.

The truck circled a roundabout, passing military vehicles parked near barriers to the other turns, before pulling onto the deserted two-lane overbridge. It halted midway across this.

Car headlights approached from the other side. The truck air brakes hissed; Lock turned off the engine.

Gwenda had some alarm in her eyes. "Where's the other truck?"

"I have no idea," Lock answered. Gwenda handed him the second weapon.

The car halted a few yards short of them. Lock and Gwenda saw two men wearing civilian clothes get out. Neither of them seemed to be carrying a weapon.

"Cover me," Lock instructed as he opened his door. Gwenda opened hers and lifted her weapon. She dropped to the road and took up her position at a crouch.

"Where's the other truck?" Lock demanded as he approached the two men.

"What's with the artillery?" one of them asked, pointing at Lock's gun.

"Just a precaution. We live in interesting times. Where's our empty truck?"

The second man pointed back at the car. "You're taking a car back this time. Congratulations on delivering your final shipment. From now on they'll be handled at a port."

Lock beckoned to Gwenda to join him.

"Jesus Christ," the second man said as he saw that she too was carrying a weapon. "You people don't take half measures, do you?" He turned to Lock. "But anyway, I have a message for you from Mister Burke."

"Go on," Lock said as he raised his weapon.

The man flinched. "Cool it, mate. He only said to tell you to keep the barrier open tomorrow, whatever that means."

Lock lowered the weapon. "Anything else?"

"Nothing else," the man answered, offering up a key fob.

Lock took it and pointed it at the parked car. It beeped, its headlights flashing. He then handed over a bunch of keys. "Okay," he told the men. "Get in the truck and leave."

"Whatever you say," the first man said. Both hurried to the crate-laden vehicle. Gwenda tracked them with her weapon.

She kept tracking as the truck pulled away.

-o-

Back at the safe house, Norton was dozing in a chair when Caycey Jones came in. She sat up, instantly alert.

Jones showed her his phone before putting it down. "I finally heard from Circus Council."

"Bad news?"

"Doesn't look good," Jones answered, tightening his lips. "They want us to keep listening for a response, but to also think up a survival plan using the technology down there... If the world goes pear-shaped up here, that is."

"And is it going pear-shaped?"

Jones's expression turned grim. "Regular armed forces are in rebellion just about everywhere in the world. They haven't started a shooting war with the auxiliaries yet, but it isn't far off. UNSC are about to launch a last gasp attempt to get things back on track."

"And if that doesn't work?" Norton asked.

"The forty-seven treaty will be dead," Jones answered. "The Cuckoos will take over and do the killing themselves. But they'll wipe out everyone. Goodbye human race."

EIGHT

Ventriloquist Jack groaned in bed as a doorbell issued a defective, rattling burr somewhere in his bungalow.

Still drowsy, he walked in the near dark outside as it rang again, this time like a grinding motor sound from an outhouse.

Flip-flop sandals clapped against the path as he hurried past the coal heaps and other junk in his yard. Irritated nonsense spewed from his lips when he opened the wall door.

Lock and Jones were waiting outside.

"What do you want this time of the morning?" Jack demanded.

In contrast, Caycey Jones was calm, polite. "Sorry to disturb you, sir, but this is urgent."

Jack's demeanour relaxed slightly. "Why? What's happened?"

Jones glanced around. In the amber street lighting, the narrow lane passing the man's property was deserted. The American tapped an ear as if someone unseen might be listening. "We'd appreciate somewhere private to talk."

The conspiratorial manner and polite Texas accent seemed to impress Jack Thomas. He ushered them into his yard.

Streaks of pre-dawn twilight began to appear in the sky as he led the pair along the path. Jones stared at the crucible and coal heaps on the way.

"This will do," Lock said. They halted outside the bungalow.

"You can come in, you know," Jack offered.

"No time," Jones said in a hushed tone. "I want to talk to you about your device."

"What of it?" Jack's voice was now equally hushed.

"Do you have blueprints for an actual prototype?"

"Indeed I do."

Andy Lock leaned his head closer. "We want you to bring them, and one of your primed coils."

Jack raised his eyebrows. "You as well?"

Lock's expression was immediately suspicious. "What do you mean by that?"

"Nothing," Jack answered.

Jones stared at the man. "Has someone else spoken to you about blueprints and a coil?"

Ventriloquist Jack hesitated for a split second before recovering enough to evade the question. "You woke me up this early just to tell me to bring blueprints and a coil?"

"And to tell you we are going early," Jones said. "As soon as you are ready… like now. Did someone else mention blueprints to you?"

Jack again avoided the question. He glared at the American. "What about Hefin?"

Jones was puzzled by this.

Lock issued a low groan. "The man with the old televisions."

"We're not going without him," Jack insisted. "You promised we could both go down there together."

"Of course," Jones said. "We'll bring him along as well."

Jack's eyes glinted. "And his dog. He never goes anywhere without Pero."

Jones took a deep breath as he considered this. He then shrugged with an exasperated pragmatism. "What the hell, we've got a three-ring circus as it is. A dog won't make any difference."

Lock appeared surprised by this concession but said nothing.

Ventriloquist Jack cheered a fraction; he even cracked a faint smile. "Okay then. I'm looking forward to it."

"I'll pick you up in my car by the crossroads in ten minutes," Jones told him. "No need to bring any food or water. There's plenty down there."

Jack's smile broadened. "Sounds like home from home. I'll get ready."

Lock leaned closer to the man before he could turn away. "Did someone else ask you to bring a coil and the blueprints?"

Eyes avoiding theirs, Jack shook his head. "You're being a bit paranoid. I had the same idea, that's all." He turned towards his bungalow. "Make sure you close the door on your way out."

"Ten minutes," Jones reminded him.

"I'll be there."

Lock and Jones exchanged knowing glances with each other as the man went inside.

They walked back to the door in the wall. "Hardcastle," Lock said.

"I wouldn't be surprised," Jones agreed. "But what the hell... Turns out he was right. Unless there's a last-minute intervention from Hardcastle's so-called Clangers, we've got to try everything. That technology down there might be our only hope."

-o-

Hefin Gwynedd kneeled on a cushion in the central passage at his farmhouse. One of the ancient television sets stacked there was turned around on the stone floor, its interior exposed and glowing. An extension cable stretched from the TV to a battered socket in the wall.

"Bloody thing," Hefin cursed. He picked up a screwdriver from a scattering of tools and old TV parts.

Beside him, Pero raised his ears and barked softly twice, head pointing towards the front door.

Hefin checked his watch and put down the screwdriver, before struggling to his feet, issuing an old man's groan. "My knees are knackered, Pero. I'm getting too old for this. Who's out there then? Who've you heard?"

Pero barked again.

Hefin opened the front door. Pero's head pushed out between Hefin's legs and the doorframe. Ventriloquist Jack was approaching from the gate.

"You're early," Hefin said, then squinted beyond him. Jones was sitting in his Jaguar outside the gate.

"Get your boots on and some warm clothes," Jack said as he petted the dog.

"But I haven't fed the hens yet."

"I'll do that, get ready, we're in a hurry."

Alone behind the wheel in the Jaguar, Caycey Jones watched them through his side window. Hefin hurried back inside the house. Ventriloquist Jack broke into a curious ape-like canter to follow the dog around the back.

Jones groaned.

-o-

Lock, Gwenda Evans and Banes were gathered near the window in the unlit office at the safe house. A laptop displayed bar charts on a nearby table. An assault rifle rested alongside that.

Through the window, dawn was establishing itself with glowing streaks of purple.

Lock's mobile phone beeped. At the same time, Emily Norton's crackling voice spoke from another phone attached to a speaker on the table. "Still clear…"

Gwenda glanced at it, then fixed her attention through the window.

Lock fiddled with his phone, tapped its screen before it went to his ear. "Check… But you don't have to report unless you see something." He put the phone away and joined Gwenda by the window.

"They'll have reached the compound by now," Lock said.

Gwenda glanced at him. "I don't envy our American friend having to look after those two."

Lock sighed. "Those three… Hefin has his dog with him."

Gwenda smiled at this.

"So," Banes announced, a little impatiently. "What time do we start knocking on doors?"

Lock was about to say something when the phone speaker

crackled again. Norton's voice hissed from it. "APC approaching the crossroads from the west. Regular army… They're letting it through. It's coming our way."

"After we've handled whatever this is," Lock said to Banes.

The APC pulled up alongside the turning point at the outer edge of the village. Its engine revved with a turbine sound as Captain Hoyland got out. He headed towards the safe house.

Lock came down the drive to meet him.

"You're up early," Hoyland said.

"Always am. What can I do for you?"

Mair's face was at the downstairs window in the B&B next door. Wyn peered at them from upstairs. Emily Norton stared down from the safe house bedroom directly above.

Hoyland grinned at Lock. "Is there somewhere private we can talk?"

Upstairs, Emily Norton watched Lock and the officer go out of her view as the two men went indoors below her. She eyed a speaker emitting quiet static on a table, before returning her attention to the window.

Outside, the APC turned around on its tracks and reversed a short distance towards the B&B. With a mix of whining turbine and rumble of tracks, it halted before rotating. Then, with jerked moves, the machine positioned itself alongside a hedge on the opposite side of the road.

Norton switched her gaze in the other direction. Lights had come on in some of the bungalows towards the bridge. A man wearing a dressing gown stood in an open door, staring anxiously towards the military vehicle.

A single lamp illuminated a map in the safe house office.

Hoyland stepped away from the table in exasperation. "I don't know how much more I can say to get this through to you," he said to Lock. "Your village is likely to become a battleground. You are in *our* kill zone if the auxiliaries fan out into the village. And if we can't stop them, they will slaughter all the civilians here."

Gwenda straightened up from where she had been leaning over the map. Banes remained seated on the stuffed arm of a nearby chair, but his eyes were keenly alert. They both watched Lock, waiting for him to respond.

Lock shook his head. "The answer is still no. I can't evacuate today."

"For goodness' sake, why?" Hoyland demanded. "Explain to me why not? There are empty houses galore west of here. Just tell them to get in their cars and go. We'll do the rest."

Lock's expression remained firm. "Not today. We're expecting a certain gentleman by the name of Burke. He could create problems for *our* operation if he saw people leaving here in droves."

"Ah, *that* man," Hoyland said. "He visited our headquarters last night. Bastard is backwards and forwards across our lines and there's nothing we can do to stop him. Orders from above."

Lock seemed surprised. "Really?"

"Colonel wanted to have him shot, but the general staff wouldn't let him. The man is untouchable. Carries just about every credential imaginable, including UN diplomatic immunity."

"Could you maybe stop him from coming here today?" Gwenda asked. "At the roadblock?"

"No can do," Hoyland answered. "Our generals got their heads only partly screwed back the right way when they rebelled. Clearly, they're still conflicted about it. We are forbidden from interfering with him. And we fire on the auxiliaries only if and when they advance along the coast, which is imminent."

"Pity," Lock said. "It might have saved us from a bit of inconvenience. But we are ready for him anyway."

Hoyland pointed at the assault rifle on the table. "I can see that... Yours?"

"It is," Lock answered. "What of it?"

Hoyland shook his head in bewilderment then gestured towards Gwenda, who was nursing another assault rifle. Her hands had moved over its surfaces at the mention of Burke.

"You two both seem *very* ready for him," Hoyland observed as he folded his map. "Burke must represent a threat to something very big you've got going on here."

"Let me remind you that our operation is still top secret," Lock

306

warned in that relaxed, low tone of his. "And that this village remains under my command as a security zone. If either Burke, or the auxiliaries, or both violate that, we might have a surprise or two in store for them."

Hoyland seemed resigned. "Then I'll leave you to it. But remember this. If you see fireworks approaching along the coast from the east, you'll have very little time to get the people away from this village. Their safety was the only reason for my visit. From here on in, you're on your own."

"Accepted," Lock said. "I appreciate your concern and advice."

Hoyland was headed for the door when he hesitated. "Whatever you've got going on here must be really big. Even the mass murdering bastards in the new government ordered us not to interfere. Something described as forty-seven critical? We picked it up in their e-mail chatter."

"News to me," Lock said.

Hoyland shook his head with exasperation. His voice had an edge to it. "Let me paint this very clearly for you. The towns to the east of Conwy look like something from the dark ages. The auxiliaries are slaughtering people in their homes and burning everything. We evacuated Conwy and some of the coast west of it yesterday. Bangor and Caernarfon are evacuating today. I strongly suggest you immediately do the same, Burke or no Burke. Get the people out of this village, Commander Lock. When the fighting starts, we can't prevent them from coming here. Do you understand? They'll reach here within three hours from the moment they commence their advance."

"Duly noted," Lock said. "I will evacuate when operational priorities permit." He continued to gaze at Hoyland for a moment, then paced to the hallway, gesturing with a hand to usher the soldier out.

"Ah well, I tried," Hoyland said with a sigh as Lock opened the front door for him. "Good luck."

"And you, Captain."

Lock watched the officer go down the drive and turn towards his APC. He shut the door without returning the man's departing wave.

"They're going to choke them here," Gwenda told Lock when he re-entered the office.

"I figured that one out myself when I saw his map," Lock said.

"What do you mean?" Banes asked.

Lock shrugged but spoke seriously. "It means the regular army around here have chosen their ground on which to commence battle. It's *our* ground, the narrow coastal plain to this village. The auxiliaries will try to use our mountain as shelter."

"And the army will hit them with artillery from the other side of it," Gwenda added. "It's a choke point. Army will try to box them in."

"We need to get moving then," Banes said.

"The auxiliaries won't attack until Burke has concluded his business," Lock told him. "After that, we're banking on the technology down there being willing and able to protect us."

"And talking to that technology is in the hands of our American friend," Banes said.

"Our plan is a better option than evacuating the village to the care of the army," Lock said. "Forget the auxiliaries. When the Cuckoos begin their slaughter, nobody above ground will be safe."

"Are you absolutely certain the new government has failed?" Banes asked.

"It failed as soon as regular military forces around the world rebelled," Lock said. "An attack by the auxiliaries here will be just one of many acts of desperation. It won't change the global outcome."

Banes's face was tinged with disbelief. "Total genocide of the human race? Are you sure?"

"Well if you're not," Gwenda cut in, "why did you join Circus to try to prevent it?"

-o-

"Any bats down here?" Hefin Gwynedd called out, voice echoing. He was following Caycey Jones and Ventriloquist Jack along the descending miners' tunnel. Pero was close at his heels. Helmet lights swayed, beams mobile on the rock walls.

Jones led the way. "No bats," he called back.

Hefin tilted his head to look at the tunnel ceiling. "Shame... I like bats." His helmet beam jigged when he stumbled on the uneven floor. Pero yapped a sharp warning as the man barely managed to stay upright.

"Keep your eyes on the ground," Ventriloquist Jack warned, glancing back from slightly ahead. "Do you want a broken hip?"

"It's these boots," Hefin explained. "I'm not used to them." He then feigned another stumble.

This time Jack twisted around and almost fell over himself. "You're a bloody distraction. Go ahead of me so I can keep an eye on you. And what do you expect if you buy boots two sizes too big from a charity shop?"

Hefin's tone was one of defensive pride. "I only paid a pound for them."

"And what's that in your pocket?" Jack demanded.

"Tin of salmon." Both men faced each other. Hefin straightened his miner's helmet peak over defiant eyes. "And a tin opener. It's for Pero."

Jack became even more irritated. "For goodness' sake, it makes you both fart like sewers."

"He loves his salmon."

"Gentlemen," Caycey Jones warned. "We need to make progress, so less chatter and more focus on not falling over, please." The American waited for them, feet apart, hands on his bulky hips. His expression was one of forced patience.

"He started it," Hefin protested to Jones. "How far along this bloody tunnel do we have to go?"

"We're nearly at the breach. Couple of minutes, if we keep moving."

Pero kept his head low as he trotted, feet happily splashing through pools of water, nose sniffing at the dank air.

They arrived at the breach. Jones halted.

Ventriloquist Jack stared at it. "Now I wasn't expecting that." He adjusted his rucksack and followed Hefin onto the concrete surface by the rockfall.

"Neither was I," Jones answered in a low voice. He studied the breach as though he had never seen it before.

There were no jagged edges now where the miners' tunnel wall opened into illuminated, tubular smoothness. The glowing, glasslike material described a perfect square: a doorway with sides precisely curved and joined seamlessly to the tube.

"But you've been here before," Jack said.

Jones stepped through. "It's the technology down here. It keeps making changes." There was some concern in his voice.

The others followed him.

"Now what in the hell is *this*?" Jones muttered. He was now clearly worried.

The tubular tunnel was blocked. A coin-shaped bulkhead stood in the way. It had a closed door near its bottom edge.

Hefin and Jack exchanged glances as they followed Jones towards it. Pero pricked his ears on high alert.

Jones stepped up a ramp to the door, which slid open without a sound to reveal another layer, another opened door. Ahead of him inside, a carpeted aisle stretched down-slope between multiple rows of upholstered seats flanked by windows. It looked like the interior of a train carriage. Mystified, Jones went inside.

"There you are," Hardcastle's voice announced. His unshaven face appeared in a screen fixed to the ceiling above the aisle. He was clearly looking into the laptop camera in the distant chamber.

"Can you hear me?" Jones asked. Behind him, Jack and Hefin jostled noisily into the carriage-like space. Pero slipped inside between them.

"I hear you all loud and clear," Hardcastle responded with a smile from the monitor.

"What the hell have you been up to?" Jones demanded.

"Don't blame me," Hardcastle answered. "It did this off its own bat. White Hair just walked right up and told me it had installed a

310

transport system better suited to our imminent needs. Those were the words *it* used. And it spoke very clearly without stuttering this time."

"How do we control this transport system?" Jones asked.

"I have no idea," Hardcastle told him, face now coming very close to the screen until only one of his eyes remained visible. It bulged, rotating, magnified and distorted by the camera. "My orders are not to talk to it so I haven't asked. You could try taking a seat, or maybe issue a verbal instruction."

Jones walked closer to the overhead monitor and looked up at Hardcastle's image.

Face so close to the laptop camera, Hardcastle looked both insane and exasperated. "The window displaying you is tiny. I can only just make you out."

Jones and the others saw Hardcastle suddenly pull away as the man looked upwards at something. "Ah, there you are. There's another big screen in the ceiling. You brought the dog. How wonderful. Hello, Pero."

Pero issued a friendly bark at the monitor.

Ventriloquist Jack tapped the American's shoulder.

"What?"

Jack pointed at the door behind them. It was now closed. "I think we're moving."

All three men looked through the side windows. Jones leaned his knee on one of the seats for a closer view. There was only a glow from the featureless side of the tubular tunnel. It looked static. "I don't think so," Jones said, but then flinched reflexively and gripped the seat headrest.

The tube had vanished. The larger tunnel wall with its silvery coil streaked past instead. It looked as though the coil was rising. But this was an illusion brought about by the fact the vehicle was in a gradual descent. They were travelling at an insane speed.

"There's no inertia," Ventriloquist Jack observed.

It stopped abruptly. Jones saw a scattering of bikes on the tunnel floor outside. The side passageway was beyond them.

311

"Eighteen seconds," Hardcastle announced from the monitor. "It put up a map when you moved. Acceleration and deceleration were instantaneous. You should all be dead."

"Clearly, we are not," Jones said.

"No inertia," Ventriloquist Jack called towards the monitor. "And it flew. You don't need my blueprints or my coil."

"Didn't feel a thing, did we, boy?" Hefin said as he stroked Pero's head. He then pointed. "Another door."

Windowed panels slid open halfway along the carriage side.

-o-

Lock and Banes were having some sort of disagreement on the safe house driveway when Kyle arrived.

"I still don't think it's a good idea having me knocking on doors," Banes warned Lock. "The people here don't know me." He then glanced sideways and issued a half-hearted greeting to Kyle.

"Hope I'm not late, Mister Lock," Kyle said. "Forgot what time you wanted me here."

"Not a problem," Lock answered. "You're early if anything."

"Good morning, Doctor Banes," Kyle now responded to the dispirited scientist.

"Kyle will go with you," Lock told Banes. "Won't you, Kyle?"

"Sure," Kyle agreed. "What do you want us to do?"

"It's quite simple," Lock explained. "Talk to everyone in the village, knock on every door, ring every bell. I'll give you a list. You need to tick everyone on it. We've got an important message for them."

"Leaflets?" Kyle asked.

"No, it's got to be verbal, and they've got to keep their mouths shut about it. So warn them about that."

"You want us to tell them to keep their mouths shut," Kyle said, nodding innocently.

"About the message," Lock sighed.

"Which is?" Banes prompted.

312

"Do you know how much sleep I've had in the last forty-eight hours?" Lock responded in a low tone. "Let me finish, both of you."

"Sorry, Mister Lock," Kyle said.

"You've got to tell them to be prepared to move at a moment's notice," Lock continued. "When they hear the air raid siren, it's the signal we're evacuating the village. I want you to list how many cars are available, and make sure everyone is designated to a car."

"Where are they evacuating to?" Kyle asked.

"That's another thing," Lock expanded, lifting his hand and aiming a finger towards the mountain. "When the siren goes off, they need to get their cars pointed in that direction, ready to follow me in a convoy."

Kyle looked surprised. "You're taking them up the mountain?"

"Everyone," Lock confirmed. "Into the mountain to be more precise, including you and your gran. That's why they can't talk about it to anyone who might come to the village between now and then."

"And what if they don't want to go?" Banes demanded. "It would be far better if you told them."

"I can't," Lock said. "I'm going to be watching Burke, unless you want to rifle-up and get ready for that?"

"It won't come to violence, surely?" Banes argued.

"But it might," Lock told him. "And I'm not leaving Gwenda to handle that situation on her own."

"What do we do if some of the people don't want to go?" Banes asked.

Lock stared at the mountain. His expression contained no regret. "Then we'll just have to leave them behind."

-o-

Miiko rose from the table in the small chamber deep underground. She bowed when Caycey Jones came in, and bowed again to Ventriloquist Jack and Hefin Gwynedd.

The latter pair returned the greeting, Hefin Gwynedd doing so awkwardly. "*Hajimemashite*," Jack said.

313

Jones did not bow. "Any sort of pressure wave when that thing travelled?"

"Nothing," Miiko answered. "It was silent."

"It travelled faster than sound," Jones said. "Carried us five miles in eighteen seconds, and no inertia."

Pero trotted forward. He sat and lifted a paw to the young Japanese woman. She petted him. "Whose dog?" she asked in a fawning voice. "How cute you are."

"Mine," Hefin said. "Pero likes you."

Hardcastle and Dimitri were eating hamburgers at the trellis table in the huge chamber. Marina played catch with her mother outside the duplicate B&B.

Jones entered the dome. Jack and Hefin were wide-eyed behind him. They halted as Jones continued towards the table.

"I always knew there was something special about our mountain," Hefin said, his voice hushed. "But I never imagined anything like this. Just look at those houses."

Jack looked stunned. "And that ceiling..." He gazed at the expanse of stars and the incongruous image of a computer screen hanging there.

"Pero, dammit, come back," Hefin shouted. But the dog had already overtaken Jones and was sprinting towards the little girl playing ball with her mother.

"You should have put him on a lead," Jones called out loudly, now twenty yards away.

"And you should have told me to," Hefin called back. He looked at Jack. "Didn't tell us it would be like this."

"So how would you describe all this to someone?" Jack asked as they recommenced following Jones.

But Hefin Gwynedd pointed. "Over there, look. Right on the other side... That looks like my house."

Jones hunted around with his eyes as he approached the table; he managed to take in the fact that Hardcastle and the Russian were eating. They were holding plates under their chins.

"Where's the thing?" Jones demanded as he got closer.

"Do you mean White Hair?" Hardcastle mumbled. He had a mouthful of burger.

"Where is it?" Jones persisted.

Dimitri swallowed food as Hardcastle looked around. It was Dimitri who pointed. "Last time I saw it, over there, the other side of those cannons."

"They're not cannons," Jones said, getting his breath back as he came to a halt. He looked at the woman and girl in the front garden at the B&B. They were making a fuss of Pero, who rolled over on the perfect-looking lawn, legs in the air, while the girl tickled his stomach. "Report," Jones said to Hardcastle. "And what's that, a hamburger?"

The scientist lowered his plate. "It's like I told you when you were on that train thing. White Hair came over and told me it was improving transport. Those were *its* words. I didn't figure out what it meant until a window appeared on the laptop. It also told us the food here was safe to eat and that it will be replaced every day."

"It's a miracle," Dimitri told Jones. "Imagine what it could do. The Clangers, as my friend here refers to them, have not replied. This place, this technology, could be the means for our survival."

"I don't like the term Clangers," the American said. "And may I remind you that this place, this technology, was shut down by the Cuckoos thousands of years ago."

Dimitri issued a thin smile. "Cuckoos?"

The American sighed. "My term for the hostiles, hidden masters, the alien presence that has been on this planet since the beginning."

Dimitri shrugged. "I think Cuckoos is quite appropriate, but I also like Clangers." He took another bite at his hamburger. A piece of lettuce fell out.

Ventriloquist Jack and Hefin Gwynedd arrived, the latter heading directly to the B&B lawn and his dog.

"So," Jack said to Jones. "What's going on?"

Jones ignored him, continuing instead to address Hardcastle and the Russian. "Brief these two about this place. And make sure none of you talks to White Hair, even if it speaks. And if it does that, just listen to what it says and report it to me."

315

Jack narrowed his eyes. "White Hair?"

Dimitri grinned at the new arrival. "Here we have a world of wonder with strange nicknames galore. Cuckoos, Clangers and the mysterious White Hair. I am Dimitri. My wife and daughter are over there." He offered his hand. "Do *you* have a nickname by any chance?"

"They call me Ventriloquist Jack," Jack Thomas said as he accepted the handshake. "And my friend Crazy Box over there with your family is really called Hefin Gwynedd. His dog is called Pero. It means dog in Spanish. But nobody ever calls Hefin Crazy Box to his face."

Dimitri looked at Jones. But the serious-faced American turned towards the duplicate safe house.

"I need to pee," Jones muttered as he walked away. "Don't go wandering off, any of you." A tennis ball flew over the duplicate B&B garden wall, bouncing on the driveway just in front of him. Pero leaped over after it, chasing the ball across the lawn.

Jones groaned inwardly as he continued towards the perfectly copied safe house door.

"I have a PhD, you know," Jack told Dimitri as they watched the American go inside.

"You must tell me all about it," the Russian responded. "And why you are called Ventriloquist Jack."

-o-

Kyle led the way up the driveway to the final bungalow on the approach to the first bridge in the real village. Banes followed with a clipboard.

"So far so good," Banes said. "The people are really nice around here."

Kyle halted and spoke in a hushed voice. "The guy who lives in this one came to the village about a year ago. Nobody's seen much of him, but apparently he's a bit odd."

"Where's he from originally?" Banes asked.

"Don't know," Kyle answered. He knocked at the door.

316

Banes took more notice of the bungalow. All the curtains were closed. One of them twitched.

"Maybe he's gone away," Kyle suggested as he reached for the door again.

"No, there's definitely someone in," Banes warned.

"He didn't come to the chapel for food yesterday," Kyle said. "I would have remembered him for sure."

Banes looked at the printed list on his clipboard. "Mister Robert E Lee. According to this, Missus Evans signed him up and gave him an essential worker card."

Kyle leaned closer to the door, listening. "I can't hear anyone moving inside."

"Give him another knock."

Kyle did so. This time the lock mechanism turned. The door opened a few inches.

A tanned man with a trimmed white beard poked part of his head into the opening. He looked to be in his late sixties.

Banes adjusted his position to get a clearer view. Pale-blue eyes stared suspiciously back at him.

"Mister Lee?" Banes greeted.

"Who are you? North or South?"

"I beg your pardon?" Banes responded, puzzled. Kyle took a step back to let Banes get closer.

"Simple question, soldier," Lee said with an air of authority. "Are you with the North or South?"

"*South*," Kyle prompted Banes with a hissed whisper. Banes glanced back at him with bewilderment.

"I'm with Commander Lock," Banes instead told the man in the doorway.

Hearing this, the door opened wider. The man was wearing blue denim jeans with yellow stripes stitched untidily up the sides of the legs. A dirty pale-blue jacket was tied at the waist with an equally stained yellow sash. Rough embroidery spelled out *CSA* on his lapels. He had a bald head, marked with scabs and abrasions. "And what is your report?" he asked.

Banes seemed too stunned to respond.

Kyle spoke instead. "The village is to be evacuated, sir," he told the man. "Be ready to leave at a moment's notice. You'll hear an air raid siren sometime later today. That's the signal."

"Okay," the man agreed, then abruptly closed the door in their faces.

"Any more like that here?" Banes asked as he and Kyle left the driveway and headed for the bridge. "That guy was bonkers."

"Gran reckons the old lady a couple of doors from her has got signs of dementia," Kyle responded. "The neighbours keep an eye on her. She's okay some of the time but has spells when she does strange things."

"Any others like that in the village?"

"There's bound to be a few," Kyle said. "I mean, some people are a bit odd, but they're okay basically. But there are others who are, you know, maybe not quite right up there." He tapped a finger against the side of his head. "It's hard to tell sometimes."

Banes pursed his lips. "I think getting the people out of here and into that mountain is going to be a bit more complicated than Andy Lock imagines."

"I don't know," Kyle said. "I'm sure we'll make it work. I'll get Gran and her neighbours to round up the old lady and General Lee there when the siren goes off."

"Just like that?" Banes asked as they crossed the bridge.

"Everyone helps each other here," Kyle told him with a shrug.

Banes turned as something caught his eye. A trout leapt from the river below, splashing back with a glint of silver. The overlooking cottages with their hanging baskets of flowers looked peaceful and tidy.

-o-

Caycey Jones came out of the duplicate safe house. The Russian girl was now sitting on the lawn next door talking to her mother. Dimitri and Hardcastle were at the table. Jones could see no sign of the other two men or the dog.

"Where are they?" he asked as he approached the table.

318

"Gone to look at the old guy's duplicate farmhouse," Hardcastle said, pointing in that direction. "They also spotted what they think is Jack's yard."

Jones exhaled slowly. "I suppose it's time to get accustomed to people just wandering around down here. If everything goes to plan, the whole village will be here within the next twenty-four hours."

"It's reached that stage already then," Hardcastle said in a matter-of-fact tone.

"So, where's White Hair?" Jones asked, looking into the distance.

Dimitri responded, pointing. "Still over there beyond those cannons, whatever you call them."

"Cannons will do fine," Jones said. "I'm going to have a chat with it. Do you want to come along?"

Dimitri seemed surprised. "Me?"

"We're all in this together," Jones told the Russian, "so we need to build you into the team. At the moment I have no idea what this place is truly capable of, or how we are going to manage it. Talking to White Hair is complex to say the least."

"Count me in," Dimitri agreed.

Jones turned to Hardcastle. "If the other two and the dog come back, make sure they don't leave this chamber."

"I'll tell them to wait for you."

Jones nodded. "I'm going to order them to stay down here."

"This is it then," Hardcastle said. "No going back?"

"Highly probable," the American responded as he walked away.

The Russian ran off to tell his wife and child where he was going.

Hardcastle sighed.

-o-

Norton's voice hissed from the mobile on the office table in the real safe house. "Silver Range Rover approaching the roadblock. They're letting it through. It's towing something."

Lock lifted the device. "Copy," he answered.

Upstairs, Norton trained her binoculars on the car as it came along the road. She stepped back from the window when it drew closer.

Andy Lock and Gwenda Evans watched from the bay window downstairs. Burke's silver Range Rover passed at speed on the road outside. It was towing an aluminium-sided trailer.

Emily Norton came into the office in a hurry.

Lock raised his eyebrows at her. "You're supposed to be watching the main road from upstairs."

"An APC just headed east," Norton said, "followed by a light tank and two more troop carriers. Regular army... I didn't want to tell you that over the air."

"I don't think it matters," Lock said as he grabbed his assault rifle. "Keep watching the main road, please."

"The field of view isn't great from upstairs," Norton said.

Lock observed Gwenda lifting a duffle bag from the floor. "But keep watch all the same," he told Norton. "We're off to keep an eye on Burke."

Mair was upstairs with Wyn at the B&B next door. Wyn took a bite out of a sandwich, plate held under his chin. The pair gazed through the window. They saw Lock and Gwenda get into the 4x4 outside.

"They've got guns again," Mair commented as the vehicle pulled out onto the road. It headed in the same direction as the silver Range Rover. She then fixed her eyes to the tripod-mounted binoculars and adjusted the focus. "Lot of cars going along the main road now. Civilian cars."

"Let me look," Wyn said.

Mair moved aside. "I hope Gwenda and Andy don't have trouble with that nasty man." She saw the 4x4 disappear around the bend beyond the bridge at the village.

"*Loads* of cars," Wyn said from the binoculars. "They're going past the roadblock now, headed down the peninsula. And there's still more coming from the east."

"What's all that about then?"

"I have no idea. Why don't you go next door and ask Miss Norton?"

"I don't like to."

"She's in an upstairs window," Wyn persuaded. "She'll signal if she doesn't want to talk to you. Go on, go ask her. That army officer will have told them something for sure."

"Well okay then…" Mair Ellis put on her brave but important face and left the bedroom.

Outside, she walked swiftly down her driveway. Mair looked at the safe house upstairs window as she approached. Emily Norton smiled and beckoned before moving away from the window.

The front door opened when Mair reached it.

-o-

Up on the mountain, the 4x4 climbed the last part of the slope beyond the ruined farmhouse. Slowing to a crawl, Lock peered up at the brow from behind the steering wheel. Gwenda Evans propped herself forward over the dashboard on her side. She was cradling an assault rifle.

They both spotted the silver Range Rover in the distance. Lock hit the brake and allowed the 4x4 to roll back a couple of feet. He saw Burke's car turn off onto the side track below. Its trailer bounced over a hump, brake-lights flashing. It went out of sight behind banks of trees.

Lock gunned the engine. The 4x4 pulled over the brow and began its descent into the next dip.

Burke's Range Rover turned in an arc across the clearing, crushing shrubs and saplings as it came to a halt. Burke got out. The two Scousers followed him to the mineshaft compound gate.

Burke stared at the padlock. His face held an expression of disdain and impatience. The man's voice was a low growl, hidden below an illusion of calm. "Go on then, get it opened."

One of the Scousers produced a black wallet. His hands were shaking.

Burke strolled back to the trailer and looked in at a heap of aluminium beams and steel cables. A drum of wire was fixed to the trailer head alongside an electric motor. His eyes were cold, calculating. They relaxed a little when he heard the gate being dragged open.

"Get that sheep fence out of the way," Burke called out in his tone reserved for morons.

A little beyond, through banks of trees, engine off, the 4x4 rolled down a slope between rows of pine, branches scraping over its roof rack. Pine needles spilled down the windscreen as Lock brought the car to a halt. Very little light reached the forest floor here.

"Will this do?" Lock asked Gwenda in the gloomy interior of the car.

"This is the spot. They won't be able to see down here when they go back."

"How far on foot from here to the mineshaft?"

Gwenda tilted her head to peer through the side window. "About a hundred and fifty yards. But we'll still have to be careful they don't hear us closing the car doors. Just press them shut. Don't slam them."

Lock issued a grin of disbelief. "I still remember some of my fieldcraft, you know."

"And don't snap any dead branches on our approach," Gwenda warned.

"Are you being sarcastic?" Lock asked her.

"Just being careful," she answered, before opening her door. "It's a long time since either of us did anything like this."

Lock reached for his assault rifle on the back seat. "All we need to know is whether they find that car. We're not raiding Normandy Beach."

"Stealthy is all I'm saying," Gwenda whispered.

The pair headed up the slope between the trees in the gloom.

Up in the uninterrupted daylight of the clearing, Burke issued a satisfied grunt as the two Scousers finally pulled back a length of fence protecting the shaft. "Now you need to reverse the trailer through the gate," Burke told the driver.

"Don't know if I can do that, sir," the young man answered nervously. "It's like driving an artic."

"What do you mean?" Burke demanded, eyes narrowing.

"My dad borrowed a caravan once. When he tried to reverse it onto the drive, it went all over the place. Articulated truck driver next door had to reverse it for him."

Burke snarled at the driver. "Well, I've never driven a caravan or a truck. What about you?" he asked the other Scouser.

"No, sir, but you need to look at this."

Burke glared at him. "Look at what?"

The young man was standing at the edge of the mineshaft, finger pointing into it. "You really need to see it, sir."

"We're wasting time," Burke said. "Get that fucking trailer reversed into here. I don't care which one of you does it, just get it done."

He stared with disbelief at his driver, who had now edged closer to the mineshaft and was looking down at whatever his friend was pointing towards. "Sir," the driver urged. "You really do need to see this."

"For fuck's sake," Burke complained as he stepped forward. They moved aside to allow him to peer over the edge. "What have you seen then?" he demanded, but with a hint of curiosity.

With the briefest glance at each other, the young men pushed Burke from behind. With an expression of bewildered surprise and without a sound, the man sailed out over the shaft, arms flailing. He plummeted into the darkness.

Five seconds later, the sound of flesh colliding with soft metal reached the Scousers. They stared at each other with horrified disbelief.

The pair ran out of the shaft compound. "Do you think he's dead?" the driver shouted.

"Of course he's fucking dead," the other one responded. "It's a two-hundred-foot drop."

The pair halted in disarray, uncertain what to do next. "Better close the gate," the driver shouted.

"Not if it's supposed to be an accident," the other one shouted back at him. "Why would we close it? Unhook the fucking trailer."

"What if a kid comes along?" the driver insisted. "It can still be an accident if we lock it up again. Then we go for help."

The driver moved back towards the gate. His companion took a few steps towards the car and trailer then turned around, confused.

Both froze when Andy Lock's voice rang out, barking commands in a deep, authoritative tone. "Armed officers! Stand still! Keep your hands where I can see them and turn slowly this way!"

Lock and Gwenda advanced at a crouch from the forestry edge. Their weapons were pulled tight into shoulders, eyes behind glowing red sights.

"Put your hands behind your necks and kneel on the ground," Gwenda yelled at them. "On your knees now!"

They complied, terror in their eyes. One of them yelped when his knee contacted stones hidden in the grass.

Lock continued his crouched, step-by-step advance. "Now slowly reach out with your hands and lower yourselves face down to the ground."

Gwenda searched the prone men as Lock kept his assault rifle aimed at them.

"Where are your guns?" Gwenda demanded.

"In the car," one of the Scousers told her. "Glove compartment."

Gwenda hurried to the Range Rover.

Lock glared at them. "Where's Mister Burke?"

"He's had an accident," the driver answered. "He slipped and fell down that shaft in there. We need to get help."

"And from where did you intend to get help?" Lock asked. "The auxiliaries?"

There was no immediate answer. The young men twisted their heads sideways on the ground to face each other, eyes wide, terrified.

Gwenda returned with two handguns from the Range Rover. "Down the shaft?" she asked Lock.

He nodded as he kept his eyes on the Scousers. "Come on. Who were you going to ask for help? If you go back to the auxiliaries without Burke, they will torture you until you confess to killing him. And you *did* kill him. You pushed him down the mineshaft. We saw what you did and heard what you said."

"No, sir," one of the Scousers pleaded. "It was an accident. He slipped, honest."

Gwenda peered down the mineshaft a little distance away. "Mister Burke," she shouted, leaning over. "Can you hear me?" She listened only briefly before dropping both handguns into the shaft.

324

There was a short interval before the sound of them hitting something metal below reached her. She continued listening for a moment.

The young men were still pleading innocence when Gwenda returned. One of them was crying. Gwenda frowned at Lock. "We are not going to shoot you," Gwenda told the Scousers.

Lock frowned back at her, before quickly returning his attention to the prone men. "Unless you are stupid," he said. "And believe me, I *will* kill you both if you try anything. Do you understand?"

"Yes, sir," they answered in unison.

Gwenda sighed at Lock. She went to the Range Rover and opened its back door. She returned with a tartan blanket and placed it on the ground in front of the young men's faces. The diminutive woman spoke in an almost gentle tone. "When I say so, I want you to sit on this with your legs crossed and your hands behind your heads. Can you be good boys and do that for me?"

Lock took a few steps back as Gwenda supervised the move. She crouched facing them. Lock kept his weapon aimed.

"Now then," Gwenda began, "I want to know why you killed him. Tell me why and you will live. Continue denying it and, well, my commanding officer here will shoot you."

"It was an accident," the driver said.

But the other one, who had been crying, interrupted angrily. "Because he was evil. He was in charge of killing thousands of people. We saw him smiling when women carried their babies into those fucking gas chambers. He called it happy gas. He was a monster."

Gwenda nodded. "Good boy. And now we've got that off our chests, tell me why Mister Burke was so determined to find the missing car?"

"It was his daughter's," the driver answered. "He kept it in the warehouse in Liverpool. Jampox stole it and did a runner."

"All that trouble, just for a car?" Gwenda challenged. "Surely the man could afford another one for his daughter?"

"It wasn't the money," the tearful one told her. "It wasn't even the money that Jampox collected along the coast the day he did a runner. Some of Mister Burke's daughter's stuff was still in the car."

"Even so," Gwenda said. "No possessions are that precious."

"It's because she drowned," the driver explained. "About six months ago... She jumped off the ferry to Ireland. He had to fetch her car from the terminal. We took him there."

Gwenda tilted her head to look closer at their faces. "So, he was very upset by his daughter's death, was he?"

"Mister Burke was never upset, just angry," the driver said. "He got even angrier after she killed herself, but sometimes he just sat in that car on his own. He told us all never to touch it. Jampox was crazy though. He hated Burke."

Lock shook his head in disbelief. "What were your plans after killing him? Where were you going to go?"

"To the army," the driver answered. "We were going to ask for sanctuary. Burke told us the army was in rebellion. We were going to join them."

Lock exchanged a glance with Gwenda. "Do you believe this?" he asked. "I don't."

Gwenda stood upright and took a step back, keeping her weapon trained on the young men.

Lock pulled his into his shoulder and aimed. "They're lying. I think we should just shoot them and get it over with."

"No, wait," Gwenda said as the young men flinched. "We need to know what Burke was after."

"Are you going to tell the truth?" Lock demanded, waving his rifle muzzle in front of their faces.

"We're telling the truth, honest," the driver said. "There was a photo album in the pocket behind the driver's seat. He'd sit on his own in that car and look at it for ages."

"So," Gwenda said in a soft voice. "Mister Burke was going to lower one of you into that shaft to try to get this album. Anything else?"

"Just the money Jampox collected the day he did a runner," the driver answered. "But it was the photo album he wanted most."

Gwenda looked at Andy Lock. "What do you think?" she asked.

"I think they're murderers," Lock answered.

"Even so, killing them would be messy," Gwenda said. "I don't fancy dragging their bodies to that mineshaft, getting blood all over me."

Lock stared at them. They stared back, eyes wide in a mixture of disbelief and terror.

Gwenda's face gave the impression she was calculating something. "Let them go to the army. Who knows, army might even thank them for killing Burke."

"They'd just lie all over again," Lock said.

"Not if we text the army and tell them what happened here," Gwenda argued. The young men glanced at her and then stared hopefully at Lock.

"They'd have to tell the truth then, I suppose," Lock admitted.

"We will, sir. We promise," the driver pleaded.

"Honest, sir," the other one agreed.

-o-

"You were a long time," Wyn Ellis complained when Mair came into the bedroom at the B&B. He returned his eyes to the binoculars on the tripod.

"I made her a cup of tea in their kitchen," Mair said proudly. "We had a chat upstairs while she kept watch. Emily is a really nice lady, very educated and civilised."

"You were over two hours."

"Time flies when I get talking."

Wyn sighed. "Did you ask her about all those cars on the main road? They stopped coming about ten minutes ago."

"I know, I was watching from next door. Emily told me the army has been evacuating Bangor and Caernarfon. They've got a safe zone or something to the west of here."

"So why aren't *we* being evacuated?"

"Andy Lock has other plans for the village," Mair said as she moved closer to the window and looked out. She nudged her husband with an elbow. "Look."

Wyn took his eyes away from the binoculars. Lock's 4x4 was coming along the road from the village. The silver Range Rover closely followed it, this time without a trailer.

The Ellis couple watched as the 4x4 pulled off the road at the turning point beyond the B&B. The Range Rover passed it and headed for the main road. Wyn adjusted his binoculars to keep track of it.

"I didn't see that Burke man in his car," Mair said.

"Me neither," Wyn agreed. "I wonder where he is."

Outside, the 4x4 turned around. It drove back and swiftly reversed onto the driveway next door. Andy Lock and Gwenda Evans got out with their assault rifles.

"The soldiers have stopped them at the checkpoint," Wyn said from his binoculars as he watched the junction with the main road. "They're making them get out. Tell me, did Norton say anything about when they intend to evacuate the village?"

"Emily wasn't sure. But she did say the army safe zone wouldn't be safe for very long and that we're better off following their plan."

In the front bedroom next door, Emily Norton heard booted feet thumping up the stairs. Lock arrived in a hurry and approached the window.

Norton got out of the way to let him use his binoculars. "What happened?" she asked. "Where's Burke?"

"Dead… His boys pushed him down the mineshaft."

"Good God. Why did they do that?"

"Long story," Lock answered as he adjusted the binoculars' focus ring. The magnified image of the distant crossroads and the army roadblock wobbled. The two Scousers, hands now bound behind their backs, were being bundled into the rear of an APC.

The APC jetted exhaust smoke as soldiers climbed in behind them. Others pushed the Range Rover off the road where it tilted into a ditch. More soldiers darted from hedgerows and climbed into the trucks parked in the adjacent field.

"Shit," Lock muttered.

"What?" Norton asked.

"They're clearing the roadblock and moving out," he told her.

"But why?"

"I guess they radioed their headquarters about Burke's demise. No more protecting this village. That's what Hoyland said was going to happen anyway. They've updated their timetable."

-o-

Kyle and Banes walked up a farm lane that was overlooked by tall blackthorn hedgerows. There was more grass here than tarmac.

"That's twelve people who refuse to leave," Banes announced with a sigh.

"Maybe they'll change their minds when they hear the siren," Kyle suggested.

"They'll change them when artillery shells start exploding all around here, except by then it will be too late."

Kyle's expression had some sympathy within it. "I can understand their reluctance though."

"Oh sure," Banes said as they came to the end of the track and halted on the country lane. This also had grass in its centre. "Who's going to milk our cows?" he mimicked in a high-pitched voice.

"They get attached to them, you know," Kyle told him. "All the cows have names. Then there's the cats and dogs."

"And the goat. Did you see the goat?"

Kyle nodded seriously. "And hens."

"We can't save the animals as well," Banes warned. He pointed along the lane towards the forestry. "Whose is that next farm?"

"That's the old guy with all the televisions," Kyle said. "Hefin Gwynedd. He's got a few hens and a dog."

Banes ticked his clipboard, then turned and headed in the opposite direction towards the village. "That's it. We've told them all."

Kyle looked puzzled. "What about Hefin?"

329

"He and his dog are already evacuated," Banes answered. "Let's get some lunch."

-o-

Deep underground, Caycey Jones fastened his miner's belt. The cable and helmet remained slung over his shoulder. His eyes took on a resigned look when he spotted Hefin Gwynedd and Ventriloquist Jack.

The two men were coming over the nearest duplicate bridge. Pero eagerly sniffed at the ground as he followed them.

Hardcastle was seated at the table. "I wonder if they're happy with their new homes," he said to Jones, who was standing a few paces away.

"We'll soon find out," Jones said, then groaned quietly when Ventriloquist Jack waved at him in the distance.

"Where are you going?" Hefin Gwynedd shouted out. His voice echoed in the huge chamber. The two men, and dog, were now halfway from the bridge and getting closer.

The American took hold of the miner's helmet hanging by its wire over his shoulder, sighed, put it on his head, and then waited for them reach him.

Pero got there first and sat facing Jones, who leaned over to stroke him.

"You going back to the surface?" Hefin asked as he came to a halt behind the dog. Jack stood next to him, hands in his pockets.

"I am," Jones responded.

"Good," the old man said. "I've got things to do at home."

Jones shrugged hesitantly. "It would be best if you two stayed here."

"But I can't do that, man," Hefin said, chuckling. "There's things I need."

"You've got everything you need down here," Jones told him. "Surely you noticed that?"

"Oh, everything's duplicated," Hefin confirmed. "Even the barn and that contraption Jack built."

330

"You need to stay here. It's safer. It's almost certain we'll be evacuating the rest of the village today."

"There's a henhouse here, but no hens," Hefin told him. "Who's going to look after my hens in my real home?"

"And talking about birds," Ventriloquist Jack now added. "I've got a problem as well."

Jones issued an inward groan. "You signed up to follow our orders," he warned them.

Hefin and Jack exchanged glances with each other before squaring up to commence a verbal battle with the American.

-o-

The junction at the main road was deserted apart from a fox. It sniffed at some litter the soldiers had left behind. With a mix of disinterest and caution, the animal then trotted across the tarmac and disappeared through a hedgerow.

From here, the main road meandered and rose in bends to the inland part of the mountain. On higher ground, pine trees bounded both sides for a spell, before the road climbed to its brow.

Trees gave way to an area sweeping away to rising cliffs, some created by erosion, others by past quarrying.

Two heavy tanks were dug in either side of the road. Their guns were aimed back along the coast.

Beyond them, soldiers rested on sandbags protecting a heavy mortar. Other similar positions stretched in an arc towards the cliffs. More soldiers worked on their defences here. Infantry passed between them, fanning out into the trees overlooking the coastal plain.

Further back, a tracked vehicle swung its digger over a trench and dumped soil onto a growing pile to its side.

Captain Hoyland stood near. He had an indignant, frustrated look on his face. He shook his head, muttered a protest into a microphone attached to his headset, then listened, his expression becoming more troubled by the second. He sagged then, face resigned. "Yes, sir, understood," he said into the microphone.

331

The man looked angry as he approached an APC and barked orders at soldiers waiting there. Hoyland unshouldered his bull-pup rifle as they opened the armoured vehicle's rear doors. The two Scousers were hauled out, arms bound behind their backs. Another soldier got out after them.

Hoyland pointed, then followed as the Scousers were dragged to an area behind the digger. "This will do," he shouted over its noise. "Put them face down on the ground."

Both Scousers protested and pleaded. One of them broke into tears.

"Please don't, please," the driver begged, only to be forced onto his knees, then tilted forward until his face hit mud and grass. They both howled, the beginning of a scream.

It was cut short by two bursts of gunfire.

Hoyland lowered his weapon and stepped closer, looking down at the bodies. He aimed again and fired another burst into one of them.

"Get them buried," he ordered.

Some of his soldiers aimed accusative stares at him.

"What the hell did you expect?" Hoyland demanded, shifting his facial expression as though angry with himself, not them. "Martial law... They were guilty of murder. Prepare yourselves for far worse butchery than this." He pointed at the bodies. "Deal with it, accept it, then get ready to stop the auxiliaries from doing the same to you."

-o-

Caycey Jones pulled up outside the safe house. He parked his Jaguar untidily with one of its front wheels mounted on the kerb. The American immediately got out and headed up the drive. He ignored Mair's friendly wave from the bedroom window next door and grunted when he saw Wyn Ellis peering down at him from beside the binoculars up there.

Jones sat in an armchair in the office. Gwenda Evans offered him a steaming mug. Some of the others were also gathered here.

The American looked irritated. "What's this?" he asked, pointing at the mug.

"Tea," Gwenda told him.

"Haven't you got any coffee?"

"Only instant."

"Don't you people ever drink real coffee?" Jones demanded.

Kyle looked surprised at this. He stopped swivelling the office chair he was seated on when he saw Jones glaring at him.

"How about a cigar then?" Gwenda asked Jones.

"And how would a cigar be anything remotely similar to coffee?"

"Well, you are from Texas," she told him, "but this is Wales."

Jones immediately lowered his eyes. "I'm sorry. I was rude, but those two down there… They were impossible." He accepted the mug from Gwenda.

"Which ones?" she asked with some sympathy. "Jack Thomas, Hefin I bet?"

"Both of them."

Lock chuckled quietly from where he was leaning over a desk, studying a map. "Where are they now?"

"Still down in the chamber," Jones answered. "I had to make promises, or both would have insisted on coming back to the surface."

"So why didn't you just let them do that?" Lock asked. "Why pander to them?"

Jones shook his head and stood up. "It's what that guy told me the day I first encountered him with his televisions, but more about that later. I need a pencil and paper."

Banes opened a desk drawer and produced those items. Jones positioned the paper on top of the map and leaned over it.

They huddled around him. Norton craned her neck to watch from one side. Kyle did the same from a couple of feet away.

Jones drew two lines, then two shorter ones at right angles with a circle at the end. "That's our tunnel and that's our big chamber," he explained, "complete with the White Hair thing, duplicate houses, farm buildings, and God only knows what else is in there by now."

He drew two more lines opposite, two more lines above that, and

333

another pair directly above the first. He then completed the clumsy drawing with three more circles. The result resembled a squat, inverted H with a long crossbar and circles on all four ends. "It's been very busy down there," he concluded.

Banes stared at it. "Four chambers now?"

Jones pointed at his rough map as he spoke. "White Hair put a schematic on the ceiling when the Russian and I were talking to it. Maybe these other chambers were always there, who knows. Maybe the tunnels to the others were sealed and it just decided to unseal them. It told us it is making an effort to protect us."

"Did it tell you how it might do that?" Lock asked.

"It is painfully ambiguous," Jones said. "But it kept mentioning the village, and how the people would be sheltered and provided with sustenance."

"How about defending the place?" Gwenda asked.

"We asked it that over and over again," Jones told her. "It answered the same every time, that steps were being taken to attempt to do so."

"To attempt to do so," Lock repeated.

"Its words," Jones confirmed. He stepped away from the table. "I get the feeling an ancient, unwritten history is being repeated here."

Gwenda Evans nodded as though knowingly.

Lock eyed her. "Speak your mind, please."

"It's only a matter of time, once the coming battle is over, before the auxiliaries reach the compound," Gwenda said. "If they win that is, and as things stand, it wouldn't take them long to get into the tunnels." She looked at Jones. "This transport system, the train thing you described, and the block it's put at that end of the tunnel... What material is the block constructed from?"

"It looks the same as the lining in all the tunnels and chambers down there," Jones answered. "And I get where you are going. It's the same stuff miners accidentally blasted their way through over a hundred years ago. But the duplicate buildings in the chamber seem to be constructed from brick, stone, even steel beams. I asked White Hair all these security questions, but it answered just the same every time. It's taking steps. That's all I could get from it."

"It didn't do that very successfully in the distant past," Norton said. "Missus Evans and I counted at least two hundred skeletons in that big chamber."

Kyle's eyes widened at this.

Lock shook his head. "Maybe it was caught by surprise. Maybe this time it will be better equipped."

"And maybe not," Jones countered. "They've gone, by the way, those older skeletons. It's like they vanished into thin air."

"So, if it can do stuff like that…" Banes began.

"We already know it's capable of incredible things," Jones said. "But that all depends on whether it is willing to do so, or capable of understanding precisely what we are talking about. For example, when I told it how communication with the train thing was possible via the laptop, that other forms of communication down there would be appreciated, it just went dumb on me."

"C-four explosives," Lock announced. "We've got enough to bring down part of the miners' tunnel if we need to."

Jones considered this. "Drastic… especially if we've got the entire village down there. But that would protect us for how long?" he asked Lock.

"Maybe a week. Drastic, yes, but we still have a mission to complete. Await a response to the message we sent."

Jones sighed. "How long to drill the holes?"

"No need," Lock answered. "Our World War Two colleagues prepped the whole length of it just in case the Germans arrived victorious. It'll take Gwenda maybe two hours to pack the explosives and wire them to a timer. That's after we've got all the people down to the chamber. Can't let them see we're about to trap them underground."

"Okay," a sceptical Gwenda said to Lock. "We get all the people down there, then you want me to wire it up. What will you be doing while I carry out that delightful task?"

"Watching the village from the track to the comms tower," Lock told her.

"I don't like the sound of it," she responded.

"Me neither," Lock agreed. "But we've got to know how things are playing out before we seal ourselves and ninety-plus people underground."

"That's essential," Jones said. "Blowing the tunnel is our last resort. Have explosives ready but don't place them just yet. We don't want to trap ourselves underground until we are absolutely certain we have to." The American stepped towards the window and gazed out. "But now I have to go back and try to talk some more to White Hair."

"Hang on a minute," Banes said. "When exactly are we going to evacuate the village?"

"It's the same principle," Jones answered. "There's still a faint hope peace might suddenly break out. We evacuate only when it's certain we have to." He turned to Kyle. "Young man, you must not breathe a word to anyone about what you have heard here."

"I won't, sir," Kyle said. "Not even my gran."

Jones seemed satisfied with this. He looked at Banes. "I have a big favour to ask. I'm sure Kyle will assist."

"Sure," Banes agreed. "What do you want?"

"I'll help," Kyle added eagerly.

"Those men, Hefin and Jack," Jones said, holding out two bunches of keys. "I had to promise them…"

-o-

Mair Ellis was watching from her bedroom window when Caycey Jones got back into his Jaguar. Gwenda threw a rucksack and her assault rifle onto the back seat, then got in on the front passenger side beside Jones.

Lock loaded a wooden crate into the Jaguar's boot and slammed it shut. He spoke briefly to the American through the open driver's window before heading smartly up the B&B driveway.

"Andy Lock's coming here," Mair said. Wyn took his eyes away from the binoculars and looked down. He saw the top of Lock's head approach the front door.

The Jaguar completed a three-point turn on the road before heading towards the village.

336

Mair ushered Lock into the lounge, then inclined her head towards the stairs. "Wyn," she shouted. "Andy wants to brief us."

-o-

Kyle and Banes approached the shed behind the safe house. Kyle dragged a square of hardboard out of it.

"We'll need a saw," Banes said, "and a drill." He took a bite out of a sandwich gripped in his hand.

Kyle dropped the hardboard onto the lawn. "I'll find some wire as well."

Banes followed him back inside the shed. "What about paint? Preferably black."

"I think there's some in the garage," Kyle answered as he rummaged in a corner behind the lawnmower.

Banes came out, studied a key in one hand and headed for the garage. A raven landed on its roof and stared at him. He threw what was left of his sandwich up there. The raven snagged it with its beak and flew off, pursued by two seagulls swooping down like fighter planes.

Now Banes noticed more gulls. They were swarming at a height in the direction of the beach and harbour area.

Out over the inlet to the harbour, the gulls circled in descent. Those that had landed on the water pecked curiously at dead bodies drifting in with the tide.

-o-

Beyond Hefin's farm, the American's Jaguar passed the open barrier and headed up the dirt forestry road.

Jones frowned. "They actually pushed Burke down the mineshaft?"

"And admitted it to us," Gwenda said.

"You sent them to the army. Was that wise?"

Gwenda's expression was cool but serious. "We put on a big show of indignation, threatened and interrogated them. It was better

337

they survive and report that than kill them. Andy was very convincing with his threats. I almost believed him myself when he threatened to shoot them."

"What do you think the army will do?"

"I don't know. Get the same truth we got out of them, I suppose. But we'll be in the clear as far as the matter of Burke is concerned. One way or another, the army's got them now."

Jones turned the wheel in an easy, relaxed fashion to take the bend by the turn-off to the hidden waterfall. "How long do you reckon before the auxiliaries find out Burke is dead?"

"I don't imagine it will take long," Gwenda told him as the turn-off to the compound appeared up ahead.

Jones glanced at her. "Really?"

"Army will tell their generals. One of them is bound to get wobbly and tell the new government."

"So, they might already know?"

"Quite possibly," Gwenda agreed.

The car took the corner to the compound. An electric motor whined as the security gate rattled open.

Jones opened the steel door in the rock face. He turned around to watch Gwenda.

She adjusted her rucksack then repositioned the binoculars and assault rifle hanging by straps from her neck. A green forage cap on her head completed the picture of this small, unremarkable-looking woman's preparedness.

"Be careful," Jones told her.

Gwenda smiled at the man as he went inside, pulling the thick steel door closed behind him. She adjusted an earplug and pressed a button attached to her collar. "Two… Do you copy?" The woman listened to the response and headed across the back of the compound.

A narrow track under the cliff took her to two rows of razor-wire-topped fencing. She approached twin double gates. Beyond them, a quarried gallery rose steeply towards the communications tower overlooking the village.

-o-

On the safe house driveway, Kyle twisted the last wire securing the square of hardboard to the back of the 4x4. Banes stirred a can of black paint on the ground behind it.

"Who's going to paint the words?" Kyle asked.

Banes looked up. "I'll do that. You'd better call in on your gran."

"She'll be okay," Kyle responded. He noticed that Lock was headed out onto the road from the B&B next door.

Banes spotted him as well, before dipping a small brush into the paint. Lock was going towards the village.

"Check on your gran," Banes told Kyle again. "And find some cardboard boxes or something. I'll pick you up in the van as soon as I'm finished here."

"Don't know if cardboard boxes will hold them," Kyle said.

"They will if you use masking tape on the bottoms."

Kyle nodded at this. "There's some in the shed, I think. Better put air holes in them as well."

-o-

Up in the safe house bedroom, Norton heard a beep from a speaker wired to a mobile phone on the window ledge. Gwenda's voice followed it.

"Two… In position."

Another beep preceded Lock's response over the speaker. "Copy that. Three, comms check please."

Norton lifted the phone, removed the wire connecting it to the speaker, then clipped it to a device on her jacket. She stuffed a small plug into her ear and spoke. "Three, on station. Comms is clear."

She noticed Kyle, who was now headed along the road in the same direction Lock had taken.

-o-

Gwenda Evans sat on the canvas web of a fold-out hiking stool up on the cliffside track. The communications mast towered behind her but was still a good distance further up. She was positioned close to the edge, but behind a waist-high clump of valerian. This was growing out, all green and pink.

The woman removed a bottle of water from her rucksack and took a swig, before screwing the lid back on. She placed it by her feet next to the assault rifle, then aimed her binoculars.

There were signs of life in the village below. The few people out and about were little bigger than dots from this height. The flatbed truck from the Jones Bros yard and a following yellow mechanical digger looked like miniatures. They were passing the safe house, headed towards the main road.

A white van headed in the opposite direction, turning the corner onto the farmland lane. Gwenda watched it briefly before aiming the binoculars eastwards. She stared through the lenses, adjusting focus and shifting her scan gradually before lowering them.

Something buzzed by her ear. She swatted at an angry black-and-red flying insect. It dropped to the ground, transforming itself into a harmless-looking beetle as it folded its wings and limped away.

Gwenda watched it before raising her eyes. Something caught her attention out at sea. She pointed the binoculars. There were misty but distinctive shapes on the horizon.

"Two... Interesting maritime traffic," she said, thumbing the button on her lapel. "Aircraft carrier and four escorts headed northeast. Still no sign of land activity."

Through the binoculars, the flatbed truck was now positioned, straddling the carriageway, halfway to the junction with the main road. The mechanical digger's arm was stretched out over the truck's cargo deck. Three figures walked back towards the village from this roadblock. Lock's gait identified the fact that he was one of them.

Gwenda smiled thinly, shook her head and sighed.

-o-

It sounded as though there was a chicken-war going on inside the hen hut behind Hefin Gwynedd's farmhouse.

Banes managed a grin as he leaned against the white van parked

340

a few feet from the commotion. He glanced inside the van. A cage with Ventriloquist Jack's white parrot inside it sat there, the parrot staring at him with a suspicious eye.

The hen hut door opened a crack. "Doctor Banes," Kyle called from inside. "I need a hand."

Banes approached.

Kyle was barely visible in the opening, hens shrieking alarm calls behind him. One of his feet was inside a cardboard box wedged up to block the bottom of the barely open door.

Banes pushed back a hen that was gripped to Kyle's shoulder, from where it was trying to get out. Kyle's hair was covered in white dust. A brown feather had lodged above his ear.

The scientist pressed back on the door to narrow the opening. "I can't get inside now without a load of them getting out," he warned Kyle. "You've upset them."

"I've upset *them*?" Kyle retorted as Banes shut the door so that the latch clicked.

"Try sneaking up on them," Banes shouted.

"The bloody things are fast," Kyle's muffled voice responded from inside. "Shit, now the others are escaping from the other box."

Banes chuckled. "Use the masking tape on the lids."

"I did," the muffled voice answered back. "But there's so much dust in here it's not sticking properly."

"Use more tape then. Wrap it around and underneath."

Banes went back to the white van and leaned against it as the cacophony continued from the hen hut. From here, he could see to the east over the farmland trees and hedgerows. Smoke rose in the distance over there. The smile faded from his face.

-o-

Gwenda rose from her hiking stool. The coastline was an indistinct haze, features barely visible. Binoculars raised, she saw what looked like explosions. Creepily silent, one after another, brief flashes were followed by multiple black shapes heaving violently into the air. It was repeated multiple times, some in unison.

341

She lowered the binoculars and listened: dull thuds, barely perceptible.

Gwenda gripped the instrument on her lapel. "Two… I see artillery explosions about ten miles to the east." She listened before speaking again. "It's impossible to tell. Could be one of the small towns or a village but it's too hazy. There's a bit of smoke but I can't make out whether it's from vehicles, vegetation or buildings. I can't hear much of it either. How about you?"

Andy Lock came out of the safe house and walked to the end of the drive where he halted facing east. He listened. A faint sound like that of a very distant thunderstorm reached him.

"I can hear it," he said as he squeezed his lapel. He looked up at the safe house bedroom window. Norton gazed back worriedly at him.

"Okay, copy that, listening out," Lock said.

Kyle and Banes were carrying two cardboard boxes from the hen hut to the white van when the older man's mobile beeped. Hens inside the boxes immediately clucked in response. They were placed in the back of the van before Banes answered.

Kyle shut the van's rear doors and listened.

"Okay," Banes said into his phone. "We're finished here, so we'll get back to the village." He disconnected the call and pointed at the hen hut. "Better close that door as well," he told Kyle. "Make it snappy… We've got to get into position."

Banes got in and started the van engine. Hens clucked in the back of it.

The passenger door then opened and Kyle looked at him. "You forget something?"

"What?"

"The keys Mister Jones gave you," Kyle demanded, holding out a hand.

"You have got to be kidding…"

Banes handed keys over, saw Kyle hurrying away, then turned the van around and manoeuvred to the front of the farmhouse.

Kyle came out of there with a pet carrier. Banes stared through the windscreen in disbelief. The van rear doors were opened, then slammed closed.

Cats howled; hens squawked. "Fishy fishy fishy," the parrot called out in the back when Kyle climbed into the passenger seat in front.

"There'll be trouble if they get out," Banes warned as he gunned the engine.

"No there won't," Kyle told him. "Most of them know each other."

Up on the mountain, Gwenda Evans continued watching east through her binoculars. There were brighter flashes over there now, getting closer. She reached for her lapel.

The white van halted in the village centre. Kyle got out and sprinted towards the bridges.

Banes reversed the vehicle into the space by the side of the chapel, applied the handbrake then lifted his phone. "Four... in position." He got out of the van and jogged to the village crossroads.

At the B&B, Wyn Ellis drove his car to the end of the driveway and halted. Mair Ellis craned her head in the passenger seat to watch Andy Lock hurry into the safe house next door.

Standing near the first bridge, Emily Norton waved at Kyle. He was running towards her, now crossing the other bridge by the Jones Bros yard.

"Three... in position," Norton announced into her lapel microphone before turning to face the safe house.

Some of the people in the bungalows stared out at her from their windows.

Norton listened. That rumbling *thud, thud, thud* chorus from the east was getting louder.

And now something else from behind her: it began low and quiet, then quickly rose in both pitch and volume into the unmistakable, haunting sound of an air raid siren.

NINE

The siren's hideous noise reverberated inside the safe house. Here daylight slanted into a cupboard under the stairs. Surrounded by cobwebs on the back wall in there, a red circuit breaker was in its closed position. Next to this, a clockwork timer ticked as its numbered dial advanced towards zero.

Out in the open air, the road to the bridges was deserted. A plastic bag slid across the pavement in a gust of wind. The air raid siren was considerably louder here.

But the howl was deafening at the crossroads in the village centre. It obliterated the clank of wind chimes swaying in the back yard at the post office.

And behind the chapel, atop three telegraph poles and bolted into a metal framework, noise turbines blasted out their raucous counterpoint to a lifeless street.

Normally cluttered with parked cars, now there were none in the village. A front door in one of the houses had been left open. A gate swung in the breeze.

At the same time, as though some monster had run out of breath, the siren pitched downwards and died. A continuous *thud, thud, thud* of explosions replaced it.

Wyn's car bumped over a pothole as it passed Hefin Gwynedd's farmhouse. Norton and Kyle sat pensively in the back as Wyn Ellis drove. Mair was speechless beside him in the front passenger seat.

They were following a convoy. A minibus rattled along in front of them. A motorcycle purred ahead of that, calmly pursuing an assortment of vehicles stretching beyond the next bend.

At the head of this procession, Lock's 4x4 climbed the dirt road hill into the forestry beyond the barrier. The square of hardboard wired to its back had *FOLLOW ME* painted on it in clumsy black letters. The vehicles behind were doing precisely that.

From the cliffs overlooking the village and its tiny harbour, Gwenda Evans aimed her binoculars. The repeated *crump crump* of artillery grew louder. Mountain slopes inland reflected flashes of light. Plumes of smoke rose from the coastline in the near distance.

She flinched as something brilliant streaked over the main road. The missile struck a tank near the disused service station. White-hot gasses immediately jetted from the hole in its hull. The turret jerked upwards as it detached and tilted, followed by a rush of flames. A crackle of small-arms gunfire came from somewhere near it.

Gwenda lowered herself into a prone position, stuffing her head into the valerian weed on the edge of the cliff. She peered out as a *whoop whoop whoop* noise accompanied green tracer hitting trees beyond the flaming tank and service station.

Now she saw new movement. Two light tanks belonging to the regular army raced eastwards. One of them veered off through a hedge into a field where it halted, turret rotating. Its gun fired: *whoop whoop whoop*. From somewhere to its rear, a stream of glowing tracer hurtled with insane speed in the same direction.

Up in the forestry, Hardcastle stood at the junction to the compound as villagers hurried towards him from their cars. Like some reluctant traffic cop, he waved and urged them towards the open gate. They obeyed without question, faces etched with fear as the sounds of battle grew fiercer.

On the main track, vehicles had parked nearly all the way to the next brow, where Lock's 4x4 was coming back. Lock sounded the horn. People got out of his way.

"Keep moving," Hardcastle shouted at a family.

The 4x4 pulled to a halt alongside him. Lock got out. His face was intense, worried. "Who's supervising them through the compound?" he demanded as more people approached.

"Miiko," Hardcastle answered.

"I'll take over here," Lock said. He opened the car's rear door and lifted a cardboard box out of it. "Miiko will need to watch them inside. Take this with you and supervise things outside."

The scientist accepted the box. "What's in it?"

"Handlamps… Give them out at the door."

Lock now looked horrified. His jaw dropped as a woman wearing a red raincoat approached. She was carrying a bird in a cage.

"No luggage, you were told," Lock scolded her.

"Jenny isn't luggage," the woman rebuked and hurried straight past. The man behind her lugged a wicker pet carrier. Lock was about to say something else but instead clenched his teeth in disbelief.

The next group of people came along. They were hurrying from the line of cars parked down-slope on the dirt forestry road. Kyle and his gran accompanied an old man who was wearing the makeshift uniform of a Confederate army general. Kyle carried a large cardboard box with small holes in it. Banes followed him with another one. Norton had Jack's parrot in a cage behind them. Kyle's gran gripped a pet carrier.

Hens clucked and cats howled from their containers as this group passed Lock, who merely stared. He ignored greetings from Kyle and Norton. Noticing this, Banes put his head down and hurried past.

Next up, a clearly frightened man escorted a demented woman, who had her finger shaped like a question mark and was waving it side to side in front of her face. "Get out of my chair!" she scolded invisible adversaries in her path.

In the same group, a big woman, who was wearing a flowery skirt over cuffed Wellington boots, brought a goat on a leash. Her husband, walking beside her, wore a flat cap and hugged a live duck in his arms.

The Ellis couple came alongside some elderly people with dogs. These barked at the demented woman, who was still arguing with her invisible adversary. She turned around and barked back at the dogs.

This caused Mair Ellis to flinch with alarm. "Wyn… Wyn…" Her high-pitched voice sounded like she was barking as well.

Artillery continued pounding to the east. And now there was a roar of what sounded like a steam train, accompanied by the noise of splintering timber and falling trees from somewhere closer.

"You're in charge," Hardcastle reminded Lock, then ran to catch up with the procession headed into the compound.

-o-

Jones passed through the centre of the cannon-like devices in the chamber underground. White Hair was facing away from him the other side.

It turned as he approached. Symmetrical eyes looked him up and down from a perfectly symmetrical face.

"Greetings," Jones called out. It remained silent. The American waited a few seconds. "I wish to advise you of our current situation."

"We are aware," White Hair told him in its artificial voice.

Jones considered this and moved closer. "We remain concerned about security. We feel this place is vulnerable."

"Agreed," the figure responded. "Steps are being undertaken to attempt an improvement in security."

"With the greatest respect," Jones said, "without knowing the details, it is difficult for us to determine what measures we should undertake ourselves."

"Bring your people here. Steps are being undertaken…"

"I know," Jones said in a polite tone. "We have had this dialogue before and I apologise for pressing this issue with you."

"Understandable," White Hair said, its face expressionless.

The American pursed his lips. "You must also understand that our lack of knowledge has led us to believe we may need to use explosives to collapse the miners' tunnel connecting this place to the surface."

"Futile," the figure immediately answered. "Also, such a measure

348

is forbidden…" It lifted an arm and pointed at the ceiling. A map of the tunnels and chambers appeared up there as it continued in a monotone voice. "The transport system will respond to your commands. Position one, position two, position three and position four as indicated here."

Jones studied it. "Understood."

The arm was lowered. "This interface will no longer appear here. Once your people are in this chamber, they must remain within this chamber."

"Understood," Jones confirmed.

"Your leaders will come to position four when this signal is given." The arm was raised, pointing. A fifth shape had appeared. This was further out along the diagrammatic representation of the main tunnel. Its centre flashed red as White Hair continued speaking. "And when this tone occurs…" Three rapid beeps rang out, echoing in the chamber.

"Understood."

"You must also note this carefully," White Hair said. "We are containment. Explosives must not be employed. This must be understood."

Jones sighed. "Very well, we will not use explosives."

The figure continued looking at him for a moment; then like silent magic, it turned into a glassy fluid. This shrank downwards, then merged and disappeared into the floor.

The American stared down at the featureless blue glow it left behind. Beyond, towards the far side of the chamber, grass, shrubs and small trees edged a pathway. And beyond that, under the huge dome, the ground rose covered in pine forest towards the distant but still visible outer wall. Jones heard something. It sounded like a waterfall.

He hurried back towards the duplicate safe house.

-o-

Up on the cliff edge, still prone within the weeds, Gwenda Evans reached for her lapel. "Two, receiving," she answered then listened.

She frowned before responding. "You'd better come up here first. You need to see what's happening."

Outside the steel door in the compound, Lock said, "Copy that, on my way," into his lapel device before shaking his head in disbelief.

Now only a handful of people remained waiting at the doorway into the mountain. Here, Miiko ticked a clipboard list with a pencil. Hardcastle was issuing handlamps. The scientist turned to face Lock. "Problems?" he asked, then flinched. Explosions thudded and small-arms fire crackled somewhere the other side of the forestry. It seemed to be coming from the main road inland.

Lock raised his eyebrows. "Gwenda reckons things are not going quite the way we anticipated."

"How so?"

"She won't go into detail. I'll have to look for myself." Lock seemed deep in thought for a second then pulled himself out of it. "What's the tally?" he asked Miiko.

The Japanese woman looked puzzled by this.

"He wants to know how many people on the list haven't arrived," Hardcastle explained. Lock now approached the woman. She handed the clipboard to him.

He studied it before holding the list towards her. "Are you sure this family didn't go inside?"

She looked. "Lewis? Nobody arriving here gave me those names. I was very careful."

"Okay," Lock said. "You go back to the chamber with the others. Hardcastle, wait for me here. Stay inside and keep the door closed until I come back for you."

Gwenda Evans was on her feet, watching through her binoculars, when she heard Lock approach along the quarried gallery. His head was turned to the east as he walked, taking in the scene of battle on the coastal plain below.

She spoke when he drew closer. "Seems the auxiliaries were great against unarmed civilians, but thoroughly useless when faced by regular army willing to fight."

"Are you absolutely certain?" Lock asked.

350

"I've counted eight army tanks and ten APCs all headed east," Gwenda answered, then pointed. "Those support trucks started following them a few minutes ago. I reckon the army let the auxiliaries advance, then counter-attacked in co-ordinated actions, probably right across the country."

"If that's the case here..." Lock began, then hesitated as he watched the vehicles heading past the disused service station in the distance.

"It's probably the same most places around the world," Gwenda completed for him. "What about the explosives?"

"If the auxiliaries really are in retreat," Lock said, "we might not need to do that."

Gwenda shrugged. "Okay, so what now?"

"Continue observing. Any signs of action by the Cuckoos in response to this, call me and get into the mountain."

"And what will you be doing?"

"Fetching the Lewis family."

"For goodness' sake," Gwenda said, irritated. "They didn't turn up? Anyone else?"

"About twelve others all told, but unlike Elin Lewis, Hefin and Ventriloquist Jack, the others are not on Caycey Jones's VIP list."

"And we know why Elin's on it," Gwenda said, nodding. She then pointed. "Look."

Army trucks towing artillery were now moving along the main road far below, following in the direction of the tanks and their mobile infantry support.

-o-

Caycey Jones waited at the entrance to the passage. He gazed curiously at the new opening that had appeared on the opposite side of the main tunnel.

Bicycles still littered the glowing blue floor a short space from him towards the centre of the tunnel. The thick cable still curved out of the passage, running along the tunnel side wall towards the surface.

Jones now watched in that direction as something reflected light in the distance.

As the object grew, he noticed the floor at the centre of the immense tunnel had turned red. It was shaped like a lane, seemingly along the whole of its length. The rest of the floor either side remained its usual blue.

At an incredible speed, the approaching object shot to an abrupt halt opposite Jones. This occurred in absolute silence. It looked like a long train carriage without wheels, its underside now resting on the surface.

A single set of double doors slid open in its side.

Jones heard the clamour of people. Banes and Norton were first to step out. The American's eyes widened when he saw a goat amongst the others behind them.

-o-

Hardcastle leaned up against the 4x4 outside the Lewis house. Apart from the occasional muffled sound of an explosion in the distance, it was eerily quiet. He was smoking a cigarette, which he quickly stubbed out when his mobile phone beeped.

The scientist thumbed its screen. "Four…" He listened, turning to face the east as he did so. He then paced to the centre of the paved cul-de-sac and squinted at the sky. "I don't see anything," he said into the phone. He listened briefly before putting it away.

Lock came out of the Lewis house and hurried to join him. "Did Missus Evans call you?" Lock asked, now also gazing at the sky.

"Yes, but she was kind of vague. What are we supposed to be looking for?"

Lock pointed. "Something over there, but she's being vague to avoid giving out our position. I can't see anything either."

Hardcastle shrugged. "How about this Bibby Libby girl and her family? Any luck?"

"A cat and two rabbits," Lock answered as he lifted his binoculars and peered through them.

"I beg your pardon?"

"I told them they can bring them," Lock said. "But mainly it was the mother. Real battle-axe that one. She didn't like the idea of hiding in a cave, as she put it. Changed her mind when I told them they'll all die today if they don't come with us." Lock now pointed into the distance. "I don't like the look of that."

Hardcastle stared in the same direction. "I don't see anything."

"It's right across the horizon, but way above it as well," Lock said. He handed the binoculars to Hardcastle.

The scientist adjusted the width and focus as he looked through them. "It looks a bit like the aurora borealis."

"But it isn't, is it."

"I agree. Way too uniform and organised. But either something is ionising the atmosphere over there, and from a great height, or it's purple rain from a cloudless sky."

"Not good then," Lock said.

"Probably not. It seems to be spreading this way."

A door slammed shut somewhere behind them. Bibby Libby was carrying a small cage with two white rabbits in it. Her parents and brother followed. A cat howled from a pet basket.

"Come on, we need to hurry," Lock shouted. He began opening doors on the 4x4.

-o-

Underground and below the Irish Sea, Caycey Jones viewed the villagers as they spread out seeking their duplicate homes in the dome.

People pointed, others wandered along the curving path, gazing up at the display of stars, constellations and nebulae up in the ceiling. The rectangular repeat of the laptop monitor was now gone.

A dog barked and a cat howled in the distance somewhere.

Jones stepped up to the table and looked at the laptop monitor. Kikuko was seated there watching it.

Nearby on the radial path, Banes and Norton greeted Hefin Gwynedd, who seemed pleased to see, and hear, the cardboard boxes and pet carrier clucking and meowing at their feet. Pero was happy as well.

Ventriloquist Jack and Dimitri stood a few feet away. Jones approached them, noticing that Jack had a parrot in a cage on the floor in front of him.

"Would you two be willing to accompany me for a bit of exploration?" Jones asked.

Dimitri seemed pleased with the invitation. "Yes, of course."

Jack Thomas was more laid back. "Why not, where, in here?"

Jones shook his head. "Seems there are other chambers like this one down here. I'd like to know what's in them."

"Sounds interesting," Jack responded. "Sure, I'm up for it."

"Thank you, gentlemen, I'll be—" Jones began but was interrupted by Hefin's loud voice.

"Hey, Jack, you going to give me a hand with these?" Hefin was holding one of the cardboard boxes. Hens clucked inside it.

"I'm busy," Jack answered. "Get a wheelbarrow."

"We'll help you," Norton told Hefin as she lifted the cat carrier.

Banes shrugged and picked up the other box of hens. "I've brought the things this far," he said. "Might as well finish the job."

Caycey Jones nodded patiently. He then addressed Kikuko, pointing at the laptop. "I think we may as well take this inside the house now, with all these people here."

The Japanese woman rose and bowed to him, a puzzled look in her eyes. Jones lifted the laptop. He pointed at the duplicate safe house.

"Ah so," Kikuko acknowledged.

"I'd best leave Mister Cartwright in there for now as well," Jack told Jones.

"Mister Cartwright?"

Jack lifted the parrot cage.

Jones issued a low groan before walking away towards the safe house.

"He's a busy man," Dimitri said to Jack.

354

"A husy han indeed," Jack answered without moving his lips. He headed with his cage after Jones.

Dimitri chuckled. "I'll be back in a minute." He turned up the path to the duplicate B&B. There, Mair Ellis was framed inside the bay window, peering out. Wyn Ellis was upstairs looking out through binoculars mounted on a tripod.

-o-

Gwenda Evans lowered her binoculars in the open air on the mountain. She spoke into her lapel device. "Two… Whatever it is, it's coming this way fast. I recommend you make all haste… I'm headed back down to meet you."

She leaned over to pick up the fold-out hiking stool then thought better of it. With a glance at an ominous purple haze permeating the atmosphere in the distance, Gwenda abandoned the stool and started off down the rock shelf towards the compound.

The 4x4 raced past the open barrier, kicking up dust and chippings as it roared up the first stretch of forestry road.

Behind it, the sky darkened as the purplish phenomenon drew closer.

Gwenda arrived at the compound and entered a code into the touchpad next to the steel door in the rock face. She was hauling the door open when the main gate rattled at the bottom of the track behind her.

The 4x4 swept to a halt. Gwenda immediately opened the rear passenger door. She urged the Lewis family to get out.

Lock stared at the purple haze as he emerged from the vehicle. "How long do you reckon before it gets here?"

"Twenty minutes at the most," Gwenda answered.

"Barely enough time," Lock said as he helped a frowning Missus Lewis out of the back of the car.

"Maybe we'll be okay once we're in the miners' tunnel," Hardcastle said. He took the rabbit cage off Bibby Libby. "I'll carry it for you."

Her brother had a serious look on his face as he obeyed Gwenda

355

Evans, who was urging him to go through the doorway in the rock. The mother followed, avoiding eye contact with Lock, but the husband acknowledged him with a nod of respect.

Andy Lock closed the heavy steel door as soon as they were all inside.

Gwenda handed out small handlamps in the work tunnel. "Do you think we'll be safe in the miners' tunnel?" she asked Lock.

"I wouldn't bet on it. Go on… Get moving, all of you. I'll bring up the rear and close that brick contraption behind us."

Missus Lewis glared at Lock, then grunted as her husband pulled her along.

Hardcastle hurried along the first stretch of miners' tunnel. He was carrying the rabbits, with Bibby Libby alongside him lighting the way. They were in the lead. Gwenda urged and scolded the others to hurry from the rear.

Lock finally completed bolting the brickwork door into place before following. The group was now well ahead of him, mere lights reflecting dimly from the rock walls in the distance. He pointed his handlamp and ran.

Outside, that unearthly purple haze stretched across the horizon, shimmering as it advanced. It blotted out all light behind and above it, as though a dark curtain suspended from the heavens was being dragged across the world.

Now deeper underground, Gwenda waited anxiously at the breach. Hardcastle and the Lewis family stood just inside the glassy lined tube.

"Come on," Gwenda shouted. The point of lamplight representing Andy Lock wobbled towards her.

She grabbed his arm when he arrived at a run, then pulled him across the threshold. The pair stumbled and fell onto the glasslike floor. At the same time, an intense purple glow filled the enclosed space outside.

Hardcastle passed the rabbit cage to Bibby Libby. But as he moved to help Gwenda to her feet, the young girl fumbled it, dropping the flimsy wood and mesh item onto the floor. Both rabbits got out. Her father caught one of them. Her brother grabbed Bibby's arm before she could chase the other one out into the miners' tunnel.

The purple haze enveloped the rabbit out there. Its white fur glowed with the same colour. It took a few hops forward then rested, its whiskers vibrating, nose twitching. It appeared unharmed.

And now, as fast as it had arrived, the purple haze was gone.

"What the hell was that?" Missus Lewis demanded.

Lock faced them, barring the way to Bibby Libby, who now wanted to fetch the stray rabbit.

"We don't know," Hardcastle told them. He looked out into the miners' tunnel. "It penetrated rock no trouble, but it didn't get in here." He ran his fingers along the blue, glasslike material lining the opening.

"It doesn't seem to have harmed the rabbit," Lock observed. The small white creature out there was now huddled, facing away.

"We don't know that either," Hardcastle said.

"We can't leave her there," Bibby Libby protested. She crouched down on her haunches and snapped her fingers. "Mimzy," she called.

"Mimzy?" her brother teased.

"Shut up," Bibby shot back at him.

"It glowed," Mister Lewis warned.

"So would you in a coloured light," Bibby argued as she continued snapping her fingers at the rabbit. "Come on, girl."

"We all need to get on the train," Lock said. "The rabbit stays where it is for now."

"Train?" Missus Lewis said. She looked along the tubular tunnel and saw the bulkhead. "And what's that? It wasn't here last time."

"I'm not going without Mimzy," Bibby insisted, still snapping away with her fingers. "Come on, girl."

Gwenda rested her hand on the teenager's shoulder. "It'll be alright," she soothed. "I'll bring some food and water for her. And if she still looks okay in a few hours, I'll fetch her down for you."

Bibby Libby was crying as her mother and Gwenda led her towards the train carriage. Her father eased the rabbit he had caught into the small cage on the ground.

The brother helped him before turning towards Hardcastle, who was still watching the other rabbit out there. "You reckon it'll mutate into a zombie or something?" the young man asked, grinning.

"On the train, please," Lock ordered, hands waving the young man and his father towards the bulkhead. "Hardcastle, you as well."

Lock paused at the carriage door as Hardcastle approached. "Will it?" Lock asked.

"Will it what?"

Lock whispered, "Turn into a zombie or something?"

"I have absolutely no idea," Hardcastle answered. "But that phenomenon, whatever it was, whatever its effect might be on living organisms, penetrated hundreds of feet of solid rock. Maybe we should ask White Hair if *it* knows."

"I'm sure we'll do that," Lock agreed.

-o-

Caycey Jones came out of the passageway into the main tunnel. He was followed by the Russian and Ventriloquist Jack. Jones halted and held up his hand. The centre of the wide floor was again glowing red in a channel shape.

The three watched in the direction of the surface as the train thing approached, rapidly turning from a distant blur into the object that halted in front of them. The centre doors opened. Bibby Libby and her family emerged first. Lock and the others followed them.

The Russian approached the Lewis family to introduce himself.

Jones walked to meet Lock, Gwenda and Hardcastle.

Ventriloquist Jack wandered away to let them talk. He approached the carriage and ran his fingers over its surface, inclining his head with an expression of surprise. He then walked to its end, from where he could see the opening to the other passage, before gazing upward and around.

Without expression, his eyes took in the enormous size of the main tunnel, the silvery coils running along the green walls and white ceiling. The centre of the floor had now returned to a blue glow like the rest of it.

Now he returned his attention to the others. He saw Gwenda Evans accompany the Lewis family to the passage leading to the village chamber. Lock, Jones and the Russian came towards him, followed by Hardcastle.

Jack stuffed his hands in his pockets as he waited with his feet apart. "So," he announced. "We going to get on with it or what?"

Jones frowned. He headed for the new passage entrance beyond the train.

"Where exactly are we?" Jack asked as he tagged alongside the American. "I reckon we're way out off the coast."

"You're right," Jones agreed. "About five miles out."

"How far down? Are we on the seabed itself or below it?"

Jones waved a dismissive hand and picked up his pace, as though to get away from the man. "Not sure, probably below it."

Ventriloquist Jack raised his eyes in response to this but allowed himself to drop back alongside Lock, Hardcastle and the Russian. "Our American friend doesn't seem to like questions," Jack observed.

"Weird stuff's been happening on the surface," Hardcastle said. "I think it's upset him."

"Go on," Jack coaxed. "Tell me all about it."

Slightly ahead of them, Jones entered the new passageway. The others went into single file as they followed.

Jones took in a first small chamber. It was bare and featureless with a smaller chamber just off it. He headed immediately to a further doorway. Here, the slightly larger chamber had a closed silvery door at its opposite end. It all seemed identical, yet opposite, to the now familiar layout he had left only minutes earlier. It was also featureless: glowing blue floor, green walls, and the daylight-white ceiling. No tables, no corpses, no German naval officer's skeleton grinning from a chair.

"This layout is a mirror of the other side," Jones announced to the others. He approached the closed door. It slid open without a noise.

Like the first huge chamber they had discovered days ago, this one was enormous. It was also empty.

The dome ceiling was a dark, muddy colour. A globe of white light hung magically at its crown. The glowing blue floor was bare, the circling wall a comfortable and familiar green.

Jones held out a hand to prevent the Russian from crossing the threshold.

"You worried this door might close on us?" Lock asked.

Jones turned and faced them all. "I'll try to be diplomatic because I think it listens to everything we say, but so far the intellect down here, whatever it is, has been acting a mite unilaterally."

Hardcastle frowned. "But haven't we done the same? White Hair might not be the most forthcoming communicator, but I think it's done quite well for us so far. What's it going to do, shut us all in here? Why would it do that?"

Jones smiled thinly and nodded. "Even so—" He was interrupted by three loud beeps. Up above, near the crown, a glowing rectangular window appeared, depicting a map of the tunnels and chambers. An elliptical shape at its top was flashing red.

"We've been summoned," Jones announced.

-o-

Gwenda Evans came out of the duplicate safe house and gazed around. She observed the chamber as she walked past the lawn. The copy of a street curved in both directions. To the right, it swept smoothly past familiar-looking bungalows. She headed in that direction towards what looked like a bridge.

Three children on bicycles came over it. One of them was very young and had training wheels on her small bike. The boy and girl riding slowly beside her called cheerful greetings as they passed. Gwenda returned their hellos with a relaxed smile.

She paused halfway across the bridge. A narrow river bubbled over smooth rocks. A row of picturesque cottages with hanging baskets of flowers overlooked this and made it seem familiar. But peering towards the middle of the chamber, Gwenda noticed the river started abruptly from where the manufactured rural landscape gave way to the glassy floor at the chamber centre. The cannon-like devices towered ominously over there.

With a glance towards the second bridge, she moved on. There was no Jones Bros transport and scrap yard. The post office and chapel were much closer than in the real village miles away.

Gwenda turned down towards the cottages near the first bridge.

Kyle's gran answered the door. "Ah, Gwenda, how are you?"

"Great thanks, and you? How are you getting on in the house?"

Gran looked puzzled as she answered. "Everything seems to be here, and I mean everything. Identical."

"You're okay then?"

"I think I'll be fine. What can I do for you?"

"Is Kyle here?"

"He's in his room trying to get his games console to work. I'll get him for you." Gran moved away from the door a bit and shouted up the stairs.

Minutes later, Kyle and Gwenda crossed the second bridge. They passed the post office and chapel. One or two people greeted them from doorways but most seemed to be indoors. The pair took a turn-off into a cul-de-sac further on.

"There's two houses missing here," Kyle observed.

"I can't remember who lived in them," Gwenda said.

"I think they were empty," Kyle said.

Gwenda nodded as they headed up the path to one of the houses. "That's right. The ones missing here were up for sale in the real village."

Missus Lewis answered the door with a stern face. Her son peered at them from behind her.

"I'm just calling to reassure Elin that we're about to check on her rabbit," Gwenda announced cheerfully. "If she's got some food, a spare water bowl and cage, it would be helpful."

"It'll have turned into a zombie," Bibby's brother jeered from behind his mother.

"Shut up," she scolded. "Elin's in the back garden with the other rabbit," she told Gwenda, "but she's not coming with you. I'm not letting either of them out of my sight."

"Yo, Ken," Kyle called from the doorway.

"Yo, Kyle," the embarrassed youth responded.

On the way back, as they headed for the entrance to the chamber, Kyle was carrying a small cage containing rabbit food, a bowl and a bottle of water.

"Wait here a minute," Gwenda ordered when they neared the duplicate safe house.

"Sure," Kyle said. "You forget something?"

Gwenda was headed up the drive. "Just getting my gun," she called back.

-o-

Banes and Norton watched Hefin Gwynedd release the hens behind his duplicate farmhouse.

Pero lay on the ground nearby, snout resting on his front paws. He observed the hens as they scattered. His eyes then switched to a couple of cats that were sniffing around. Pero sighed, then pricked his ears to listen to the people.

Banes looked up at the barn. Its doors were open. "You say everything is duplicated here?" he asked the old man.

"Yiah," Hefin answered in half-Welsh. "Even my fencing to keep the hens in the yard. Can I offer you a cup of tea, something to eat? Kitchen is full of food."

One of the cats moved cautiously. Sniffing at the ground, it headed away from the farmhouse across rough ground punctuated by tufts of grass and natural-looking weeds.

"Thank you, but we need to get back," Norton answered. She seemed to be watching something above the man's head.

"That's fine," Hefin said, without looking at her. "I've got things to do as well, but you know, I feel as though I've come home here. Strange, I don't know why. It's as though it was always meant to be." He faced Banes and Norton, a faint smile on his lips.

362

Banes nodded and smiled back at the man, as though humouring him.

"That's good," Norton said. "Some of the other people are a bit uneasy to say the least but it's understandable."

"Not the children though," Hefin said. "The youngsters will take to it like ducks to water, you mark my words."

"We'll leave you to it then," Norton said. Banes turned to follow her.

"Another thing," Hefin called after them. "My arthritis is gone."

"We've noticed some health benefits as well," Norton called back. She then lowered her voice. "We need to observe how other people are behaving," she told Banes as they headed for the gate.

"Why?"

"They've been living close to this thing, some of them all their lives," she explained.

"So?"

"I think Jones is onto something."

"Go on," Banes encouraged. They went out through the gate. Norton closed it behind them.

"Jones said the old man claims the mountain has been talking to him all his life," Norton continued as they walked between hedgerows towards the village. Water gurgled in the drainage ditches either side of this duplicate country lane. "The technology itself identified the Lewis girl and insisted we bring her down here."

"Then, when we brought her down here, White Hair didn't want to talk to her," Banes pointed out.

"But it may well have communicated with her in a different way. Have you ever seen light orbs?"

"Can't say that I have."

"Others have," Norton said. "The Lewis girl was explicit about seeing them, and I think I might have glimpsed them myself since I arrived at the village."

"Seriously?" Banes said as he tripped on a pothole.

"Careful," Norton cautioned. "Then there's Jack Thomas. There's something behind that act of his. Don't get me wrong, I like him. But when he did that ventriloquist thing on me the first time, I heard something above and beyond his voice."

"I suppose I should be more immune to my own surprise and disbelief by now." Banes looked at Norton's face and almost tripped again.

"And he knew it," Norton told him. "He knew I had detected something beyond his voice, said I was a very special lady."

Banes chuckled. "Maybe he fancies you."

"Be serious," Norton said. "We need to observe these people."

Banes raised his eyebrows as he walked. "Yes, ma'am."

-o-

Dimitri slid into one of the passenger seats in the train-like carriage. He looked through the window at the scattering of bicycles lying outside.

Near the double doors in the centre, Jones spoke quietly to Lock and Hardcastle.

Ventriloquist Jack dumped himself into the seat in front of the Russian. "They don't half talk a lot," Jack muttered.

"What about this time?" Dimitri asked.

"They're debating how to phrase questions to the thing running this place."

"Understandable."

"Maybe," Jack said.

Now they heard Lock's voice. "We're moving on. You two still okay with that?"

Dimitri raised a thumb.

Jack narrowed his eyes, turned his lips into a ventriloquist's slit, but his words came out with normal diction. "Let's get on with it then."

"Transport to position four," Jones announced.

Still looking out through the window, Dimitri watched the bicycles and the passage entry suddenly speeding away. "Amazing," he said to Jack. "No inertia... How is it doing this?"

"No air friction either," Jack told him as the carriage sped along at insane speed. "You can't actually touch the outer surface. It's more slippery than..."

The window suddenly turned black. A door slid open at the end of the carriage.

"We appear to have arrived," Dimitri said.

The passage beyond the door was very different from what they had become accustomed to down here. The floor was cushioned like carpet fabric and pale grey in colour. The walls were red, with what looked like glass panels at head height between four sets of closed doors. Each door displayed strange, hieroglyphic symbols. Strips of light glowed from a high ceiling.

Up ahead, a doorway was open at the end of the passage.

Jones hesitated before leading them through. A high curving wall faced them, with the walkway splitting both ways into ramps rising upward around the side of it. The American looked up from this sunken atrium. There was a dome up there, a dark muddy brown in colour. He led the way along one of the ramps. It climbed in a long sweeping curve.

They arrived at the top. Here, four huge reclining seats faced what looked like dead consoles. An elliptical dome curved over a stepped amphitheatre. White Hair waited at the bottom.

"Correct me if I'm wrong," Lock whispered to Jones as they paused here, looking down at the figure, "but this seems to resemble some sort of control centre."

"And these seats were made for people a lot bigger than us," Jones whispered back.

"People?" Hardcastle queried.

"Why don't we get on with it and talk to the bloody thing," Ventriloquist Jack urged from behind them.

Jones turned and glared at the man. "Patience."

-o-

Gwenda had an assault rifle slung over her shoulder as she and Kyle came out of the passageway and gazed into the main tunnel. "It's not here," Gwenda observed, referring to the absence of the train carriage in the centre.

"Someone else using it maybe," Kyle suggested. He was still carrying the rabbit cage.

"Caycey Jones and some of the others, likely," Gwenda agreed. "But I'm not going to the miners' tunnel to feed a rabbit without transport."

At the word *transport*, the red channel appeared in the tunnel floor. Kyle raised his eyebrows.

They were both looking in the direction of the surface, but the carriage swiftly arrived from the opposite direction and halted in the centre.

"Came the other way," Kyle said, then headed towards it. "Cool tech, but it could do with making a sound or something, so we know where it's coming from."

"Seems this place is responding to our voices," Gwenda said in a matter-of-fact tone. "Position one, please," she announced when they were aboard.

The side door slid shut. Kyle watched out through a window as the carriage sped along, the main tunnel out there quickly giving way to the narrower tubular shape. The far end door opened when the carriage came to a halt.

Outside, in the space between the bulkhead and the glassy frame leading to the miners' tunnel, Gwenda took the cage off Kyle and set it open on the floor. She reached inside it for a carrot, which she snapped in half.

Kyle followed her to the entry frame. Gwenda pointed her lamp, beaming it from side to side on the aged concrete floor out there. A drop of water fell from the rock ceiling, splashing a few feet away. There was no sign of the rabbit.

Gwenda grinned at Kyle. "You do realise we are down a hole, looking for a rabbit called Mimzy."

Kyle just looked puzzled by this.

"Lewis Carroll?" Gwenda prompted. "English literature in school?"

"Nah," Kyle said. "We did Steinbeck and that Bronte woman, boring as hell. Are we going after this rabbit, Missus Evans?"

Gwenda frowned, shining her lamp at dark gaps in the foot of the rockfall the other side of the concrete floor. "It could have gone through there to God knows what beyond it, and it's quite a hike in the other direction. We'll leave the cage and food here in case it comes back."

"Maybe we should try calling it or something."

"Go ahead," Gwenda agreed.

Kyle leaned forward at the frame. "Hey, Mimzy, yo," he shouted. "We've got food." He then stuck two fingers from each hand into his mouth and blew a piercing whistle. It echoed along the miners' tunnel.

Gwenda clenched her teeth at the noise but smiled as she shone her lamp. "It will definitely have heard that," she said. "I'm not Missus Evans, by the way… just Miss."

"But everybody calls you Missus Evans," Kyle said.

"I know, even Andy, but that's been part of our cover. If we'd had children, I would be Missus Lock by now."

Kyle's eyes widened. "You and Mister Lock? I thought you were just his housekeeper until you got me to sign that secrets thing. Then these days you've been carrying that gun, like a secret agent commando or something. Cool."

"Oops," Gwenda said. "Here we go. Over there."

Kyle's eyes followed the lamp beam. The white rabbit hopped forward then halted. It was a short distance away in the miners' tunnel, coming from the direction of the surface. "It's got red eyes," Kyle said. "I think it's mutated."

"They've always been red," Gwenda told him. She crouched down holding out half a carrot. "It's an absence of pigmentation." She waved the carrot and made squeaking noises with air through her lips. The rabbit stayed where it was.

Kyle shrugged. "Albino then. We could put out a trail of food."

Gwenda rose to her feet and handed the carrot to him. She stepped

367

back a bit. Kyle pinched off pieces of the vegetable with his thumbnail and began throwing them out into the tunnel.

Kyle had left a neat trail of carrot all the way to the cage when he joined Gwenda by the access door to the carriage. They waited quietly.

"Do you think it will work?" Kyle whispered.

Gwenda pointed.

The rabbit hopped over the threshold onto the glassy floor. It nibbled at the nearest morsel of food, then the next one, before ignoring the rest of the trail and entering the open cage.

Gwenda moved swiftly to close it. "Okay… We leave it here for now. It's got plenty of food and water. You can be the one to tell Bibby Libby her rabbit is fine."

-o-

White Hair faced Caycey Jones. "We are taking steps to improve security," it said. The eyes moved; they seemed to stare at Ventriloquist Jack, who was a few feet away, running his hands over what looked like a control or instrument console at the foot of the amphitheatre-like steps to this area. There were other similar structures, spaced out evenly, facing the dome where it curved down to join the floor ahead.

"You're wasting your time," Jack said. He continued his tactile examination of the smooth surfaces. "You keep asking it the same questions. It keeps giving the same answers."

"So how would you approach it?" Lock asked. He was standing to one side of Jones.

Hardcastle moved away and sat down on the bottom step, a look of frustration on his face.

"It has lost all memory of what happened to it when it was disabled, probably millennia ago," Jack answered. "And it's still learning and adapting to the situation as it goes."

"So tell us what you would ask it," Jones challenged in a low voice.

Ventriloquist Jack gritted his teeth and frowned slightly. "Did

368

you ever put your bare feet in the edge of a trout lake and have those baby fish nibble at your toes?"

Jones raised his eyebrows and groaned.

"What if it was their way of asking you questions?" Jack asked him. "You wouldn't have a clue how to communicate back, except by wiggling your toes. And even then, it would be pure reflex, meaningless. There's no common framework, no recognisable reference points within that manner of communication. They nibble. You twitch."

"It learned our language very quickly," Jones said.

"Even so," Hardcastle put in. "Mister Thomas has a point. Our languages give *us* a common framework. But to this entity, it might be as primitive as fish nibbling at it, even if it can nibble back at us in a similar tongue. And even now it's probably still learning, re-learning about its past, what's going on around it now, never mind using our language."

"It's all about perspective and viewpoint," Jack said. "I doubt we can even begin to imagine its perspective and viewpoint."

"We have a mission to accomplish," Jones said as he looked at White Hair. "It understood the fact we transmitted a message."

"It's told you things in your language, in a way that corresponds as much as possible to your perspective," Jack insisted. "It's told you about *hostiles* but can't explain exactly what it means by that. The same is true about their *containment* and whatever that means."

"It summoned us here," Jones said. "And it's given us instructions. To be quite frank, those instructions need to be explained and justified."

White Hair pointed a finger towards the end of the elliptical chamber, where a square area in the dome above it now displayed a coloured map of the local coastline with a yellow circle on it.

"You must observe this place and return with data," White Hair's synthetic voice droned. It then pointed at Ventriloquist Jack. "This individual must perform the task."

"Here we go again," Jones said to Jack. "No information about risk. No information about that purple haze phenomenon. No answer to whether it detected that."

369

Ventriloquist Jack smiled. "You might as well ask whether it remembers Jimi Hendrix. But it seems to know what has to be done. That should be good enough for us. So, I'm going to do exactly what it says."

Dimitri grinned at this.

"Not on your own," Lock said.

Jack shrugged at him. "I never said I would go alone."

Caycey Jones took this in. "How far away is that?" He pointed at the glowing map.

"It's an airbase on Anglesey, about thirty-five miles away by road," Lock answered. "If the bridges are passable."

"What about the boat?" Jones asked.

"Too vulnerable," Lock said.

Jones closed his eyes briefly, shook his head then sighed. "We will carry out your instructions," he told White Hair.

It remained expressionless and silent.

The map display disappeared, that part of the elliptical dome returning to the same murky brown colour as the rest of it.

-o-

A cheerful Gwenda Evans poured boiling water into a teapot in the duplicate safe house kitchen. "Here we are with all this magical technology but we're still able to make tea the old-fashioned way."

Behind her, Andy Lock packed ammunition clips into a rucksack on the dining table. Norton and Banes watched him. Caycey Jones peered into a laptop screen at the table-end.

Miiko was waiting for Gwenda to finish with the kettle. Two instant noodle containers were positioned on the worktop with their tin foil lids peeled back.

"Those are not good for you," Gwenda said.

Miiko smiled politely and reached for the kettle.

"You are not coming," Andy Lock told Gwenda.

"And you are *not* going without me," she shot back.

"One of you needs to stay here for the people," Hardcastle said. "It's only a matter of time before they get restless."

"Then the rest of you can tell them they can't leave yet because it's still too bloody dangerous," Gwenda responded. "The days of me obeying rigid orders are over. He's my partner. If he goes into danger, I go with him." She lifted one of the weapons resting on the table and held it up by the stock towards Miiko. "Have you had any firearms training, dear?"

Miiko paused halfway to the French doors, holding noodle pots in each hand. She seemed puzzled by the question but took in the gun with a knowing expression. "G thirty-six, dual sighting, scope and dot... very deadly."

"There you go," Gwenda said as Miiko resumed her departure. "Position her with a gun at the entrance to this chamber. Nobody will dare try to go out."

"That won't be necessary," Lock said, his face exasperated. "Okay, you're coming, but we need to go soon. I want to get there and back while it's still dark." He checked his watch. "Where's that bloody Jack Thomas? I told him to hurry."

At that precise moment, Ventriloquist Jack walked into the kitchen through the French doorway. "Tempers getting frayed?" He wore black clothes and a balaclava that was rolled up to his forehead. "Don't ask me to carry a gun," he added, pointing at the table.

"Have you got everything?" Lock asked him.

Jack thumbed his rucksack straps. "Fully charged camera, bottle of water and a first aid kit." He grinned at Gwenda Evans. "You coming along for the fun as well?"

"Try stopping me," she answered, heading for the French doorway. "I'll get my gear."

-o-

Rain poured as the compound gate rattled open in the dark. The 4x4 tyres splashed an arc of muddy water as it drove through with its headlights off.

At the wheel, Lock peered forward into almost complete darkness. Windscreen wipers thumped. Villagers' cars parked along the forestry track presented only dim outlines in the gloom out there.

371

Beside him, Gwenda cradled her assault rifle as she squinted ahead. Lock slowed the car to ease between a boulder and a skew-parked minibus.

"That was the last one, I think," Lock said when he completed the manoeuvre.

"Can't see a bloody thing," Gwenda complained.

"Me neither," Ventriloquist Jack agreed from the back seat. "Put the side lights on at least. You can't drive like this."

Lock issued an irritated sigh. "I can see fine." He then contradicted himself by hitting the brake to avoid colliding with a pile of stacked timbers.

The 4x4 progressed slowly, still with no lights, until it reached the open barrier at the bottom of the forestry road.

The rain eased when they passed Hefin's farm. Up ahead, over the hedgerows, an amber haze from village streetlights became visible.

Lock squinted through the windscreen. The wipers now squeaked against dry glass. He switched them off. "Turn-off to Clwyd's farm isn't far now," he announced with some relief.

The moon peeked through a gap in the clouds, lighting up the lane ahead.

"Fat lot of good that roadblock was, except to hamper us now," Gwenda said.

"What roadblock?" Jack asked.

"He put a truck and digger across the road on the other side of the village," Gwenda told him. "As though that would have slowed down the auxiliaries."

"It seemed a good idea at the time," Lock said.

"We could get bogged down cutting across the fields," Gwenda pointed out. "It's been raining. I'm sure you noticed."

Lock leaned forward over the steering wheel to check the lane ahead. "It was only a shower. We'll be okay."

The 4x4 turned down a farm track that was bounded by tall hedgerows. The vehicle progressed for about a hundred yards before halting at a gate.

Assault rifle slung across her chest, Gwenda opened the gate. The

4x4 went through. She closed it again before hurrying back to the car. There was a light on somewhere beyond the curve in the track ahead.

A rusty lighting column illuminated a rain-wet yard. The farmhouse curtains were open but its windows were dark. Three dogs came out of a kennel near the house. They barked half-heartedly, then ceased as the 4x4 came to a halt on a cobbled area in the centre of the yard.

Gwenda switched off the air fan in the car. "Phew, it stinks here."

Lock pointed through the windscreen. "They've got pigs."

There were three slate-roof pigsties at the bottom of the yard. Between these and a wooden building, cow faces stared over from the other side of a field gate. More crowded behind them. Loud moos of protest came from over there.

"Something's wrong," Gwenda observed. She looked at the house, then at the dogs who were now staring, ears cocked, at her face in the car side window. "Dilys and Clwyd stayed behind *because* of their cows, but they clearly haven't milked them. The dogs are acting strange as well."

Lock leaned over the wheel. He glanced around the yard to get his bearings. "I think it's that way." His finger pointed towards another gate beyond two barnlike buildings on an upwards slope to the right.

"Are you sure?" Gwenda asked.

"He's right," Jack said, leaning between the backs of their seats. "Hefin and I helped Clwyd once when Dilys was ill and they had a bigger milk herd. They used to take the churns up to the main road that way. Hefin nearly fell off the trailer. That's the way we should go."

"Thank you," Lock acknowledged, putting his foot on the accelerator and turning the wheel.

Gwenda looked over her shoulder at the farmhouse as they pulled away. "Don't you want to know what's up with Dilys and Clwyd?"

"No time," Lock answered. "We warned them. They made their choice."

"Poor cows though," Gwenda said. "Nobody's milked them."

373

The cows continued their protests as the car departed the yard.

The 4x4 drove out onto the main road some distance away, leaving a field gate open behind it. Lock slowed down to pass a burned-out tank near the disused service station. The car then accelerated in the moonlight.

Auxiliary trucks peppered with bullet holes littered the roadside further along. Bodies hung out from some of them. More bodies lay on the ground. The 4x4 steered to avoid one that had been squashed by tank tracks in the road itself.

"It was a massacre," Lock observed with distaste.

Up ahead, an overturned truck spanned half the width of the road. The other side, over which Lock manoeuvred slowly, was scoured and ripped where a tracked vehicle had pushed it partly out of the way.

"I wonder where the army is," Gwenda said. She glanced at a 30mph speed limit sign as they passed. It had a bullet hole in it. She then pointed ahead. "Street lights are out here."

The 4x4 passed houses along both sides of the road. There were no lights, no signs of people.

The final house at the edge of this hamlet had a gaping hole in its corner. Rows of bricks leaned out like jagged teeth. A wrecked tank stood immediately behind it. Something had flattened most of the hedgerow behind that.

Further along in a coastal countryside overlooked by mountains, a few stray sheep huddled near a wrecked personnel carrier that was surrounded by charred human bodies.

One body lay on its back, teeth grinning from a blackened face, its arms frozen in a curve above its chest. It was as though the soldier had embraced the flames that killed him.

The 4x4 sped past, scattering the sheep.

Further along, the sky glowed red. Mountains looked down on a coastal landscape where towns and villages smouldered with glowing embers.

The 4x4 climbed a deserted ramp onto a dual carriageway. It slowed as it approached a tank that was just sitting there on a filter lane. There were no scars of damage on its hull or turret, yet the hatches were all open. There were no soldiers, no bodies on the ground; its engines idled with a low turbine growl.

Lock brought the car to a halt, then opened his side window. Light glowed from the tank's open hatches.

"Looks like they abandoned it," Gwenda observed.

Lock stared at the tank, puzzled. "And left the engine running, but it's regular army. Those soldiers don't suddenly lose discipline and bail out of a fully armed tank without good reason."

"We haven't seen a single living person," Ventriloquist Jack said uneasily from the back of the car. "I've seen a lot of bodies, a few live animals, but no people, no soldiers except dead ones."

"We have noticed," Gwenda said. She pointed at the tank. "Maybe the crew are hiding somewhere."

"From what though?" Lock said as he put his foot down. The car accelerated. "There's nothing going on. No evident threat."

"Unless that purple light killed everyone," Gwenda suggested. "But somehow didn't kill animals. That rabbit we left in a cage was caught in the light underground, but with no apparent harm. The animals were alive at the farm, but no sign of Dilys or Clwyd."

"That tank crew got out alive," Lock said. "But why, and where did they go?"

"It's very strange," Jack agreed. "Maybe we'll find answers where we're headed."

The 4x4 sped over the top deck of a towering bridge crossing a tidal strait. Moonlight glistened on the waves beneath it and highlighted rail tracks on the deck immediately under the highway.

Up ahead, beyond the far side of the bridge, was a dark landscape. Something cast a purple glow into the night sky from somewhere within it.

-o-

Mair Ellis looked down at the sleeping Russian child on the sofa in the duplicate B&B. The mother was shifting to pick her up when Dimitri intervened.

375

"I'll take her upstairs," Dimitri whispered. He gently lifted the girl.

"We should all get some sleep," Mair whispered back.

"We are very grateful to you for letting us stay here," Lara told Mair.

"Where else would you go? Besides, you are our guests, even if this isn't our real house."

"I think I'll go to bed as well," Lara said as she followed her husband to the door. "Thank you, and thank you as well, Mister Ellis."

Wyn Ellis turned and smiled at her from his position at the bay window. "You are most welcome. I really enjoyed our chat."

"*Spokoynoy*," Dimitri whispered at the hall doorway.

"Good night, *nos da*," Mair called softly.

"You can't charge them rent down here, you know," Wyn told Mair when they had gone.

"Don't be stupid," Mair scolded. "I don't think like that, you know full well."

"Just kidding," Wyn said as Mair joined him at the window.

"Well, it's not funny. Anything going on?" Mair tilted and swivelled her head, looking out with curiosity. It seemed deserted out there in the huge chamber.

"Ken Lewis has had a row with his mum and dad."

"How do you know?" Mair asked.

"He went running that way. Did that regularly up top. I think he met his friends by the main road somewhere, before all this. Out all night, no doubt."

"Is there a main road over there down here?" Mair asked.

"No, it's really strange seeing it all like this. The village road curves right round to the far side to the area that looks like forestry over there. I saw young Ken go into the trees."

"Probably up to no good," Mair said.

Wyn pointed at one of the duplicate bungalows near the first bridge. "That Mister Lee came out of his house for a little while. He was wearing normal clothes."

"Really?"

"Yes, looked quite smart actually. He stared up at the chamber ceiling for a while. Seemed really interested in that."

-o-

The 4x4 crawled as it negotiated a twisting, turning lane between two high hedgerows. Moonlight illuminated mud and grass in the middle of the sunken road. Overhanging branches hampered the vehicle, scraping along its roof and sides.

"It's like bloody bocage country here," Lock said. "The hedges haven't been cut back for months."

"I told you not to come this way," Gwenda said.

"It's safer than the main road."

"But it's taking longer. It's gone three o'clock already. It'll be daylight before we get back at this rate. And this road seems to take us into a village. What if the roads are blocked there?"

"You never mentioned that earlier," Lock said.

"I thought you knew where you were going. You can't blame me for grass in the middle of the road this time."

"Hey," Ventriloquist Jack cautioned from the back seat. "Less of the domestics, please. Look yonder."

But the view was obscured as the car pulled over a brow to where the lane twisted down again. It passed between the foliage of oak trees before the gloomy landscape opened up again. Up ahead, a finger of purple light pointed vertically into the dark sky.

"Not far now," Lock said. He turned the wheel, narrowly missing a tree stump sticking out from a hedge.

"So how are we going to approach the airfield?" Gwenda asked. "Along the beach?"

"Across the golf course," Lock answered.

"But there's no cover on a bloody golf course," Gwenda protested in a low voice.

"There is on this one," Lock told her. "Stop complaining."

Dim building shapes appeared up ahead. The car slowed at a junction with a slightly wider road. More houses were visible here, all in darkness. Nothing moved.

377

The 4x4 turned away from the village. The road curved over undulating ground. Up ahead stood the elongated shape of a single-storey clubhouse. Airfield runway-approach lights, all unlit on their frames, scarred the landscape at a distance to the left of the building.

Lock brought the car to an idling halt just past a high wooden fence in the golf club car park. All three occupants immediately gazed in the direction of the revealed airfield.

Something enormous rested across the runway mid-point: a cylindrical shape lying parallel with the ground. A finger of purple light shone upwards from halfway along its top.

Lock hastily reversed the car, turned the wheel and steered it around the back of the clubhouse, finally bringing it to a halt on a sloping, gravel footpath.

"What the hell was that?" Gwenda demanded.

"I expect it's why we were sent here," Lock said as he switched off the engine. "We could maybe get a photo from the side of the building."

"And then get out of here pronto," Gwenda agreed.

"I'd love to do that and get out of here myself," Jack said from the back of the car. "But I think we have to get a bit closer to that thing, whatever it is."

"Nothing's ever simple," Gwenda complained.

They got out of the car. Lock led the way down the path behind the clubhouse. They moved silently then halted where the path passed a putting green. This was overlooked by the clubhouse bar, which was dark inside its panoramic windows.

The green itself was shoulder height from their position on the path. Lock pointed. Its surface had been scoured by something. Sods of grass were torn upwards in a line crossing it diagonally, as though something with spiked feet had dragged itself over it.

They continued down the slope. The 18th green was over to the left. Its surface was also scarred. This strange trail disappeared into a thick bank of gorse bushes. Ahead and below them, a footbridge crossed a narrow river.

Lock took them over this, then followed the opposite riverbank until they had crossed the fairway.

Here, beyond the rough, they were met by an undulating terrain of sand dunes and gorse bushes. Only the upper surface of the cylindrical object and its finger of purple light was visible.

They skirted between dunes along the edge of the fairway, until they reached more rising ground with timber steps cut into it: the 18th tee.

Lock held up a hand to halt them again and went down on his haunches. Jack and Gwenda copied him.

"We need to keep low from here on," Lock whispered, pointing. "Top of that dune there..." He looked at Jack Thomas. "Keep your head down. Follow my lead, and crawl when I do, got it?"

Jack raised a thumb.

Lock darted forward up some sloping sand. Gwenda tapped Ventriloquist Jack and moved with him, hunched over, keeping downward pressure with her hand on his shoulder as they traversed the ground.

They did the same for the next rise.

Finally, all three crawled in line abreast through lyme grass to the head of the last dune. They came to a halt in a position looking directly over a tall perimeter fence.

Beyond it, an unlit taxiway joined the end of the runway. The hangars, buildings and control tower loomed some distance away, all in darkness, no signs of life.

Jack Thomas gazed out with incredulous eyes. There was enough moonlight to see along the length of the runway. The cylindrical object rested with one end straddling the centre point. It stretched across the dunes with its other end elevated. This stuck out towards the sea above the inner curve of a bay.

The upper surface of the object was taller than the distant control tower. And from its mid-point, the purple light beamed vertically in a channel that tapered and faded to an enormous height in the sky.

Lock pointed. A glowing tetragonal object hovered over the runway. Vertically oriented and just above the tarmac, it rotated first one way, then the other, at regular intervals.

Jack Thomas aimed his camera. It clicked and whined. He pointed it again, then stared at the objects, both large and small. The camera whirred and clicked once more, was aimed in a slightly different direction and repeated.

"Is that enough?" Lock whispered when the camera was finally lowered.

"It will have to be," Jack said. "I'm not going any closer to those things, whatever they are."

Gwenda hunted through her binoculars. "There are no signs of life. Where's the Royal Air Force?"

"Let's get out of here," Lock ordered.

They crawled backwards down the sand dune before rising to a crouch.

On their way back across the fairway, Lock took them closer to the riverbank this time.

Something rustled the thick gorse on the other side. All three hunched down, Lock holding up a finger in front of his lips. More rustling sounds. Something moaned quietly in there. It had a vaguely human tone.

A moorhen darted out of the undergrowth and slipped into the river, where it swam downstream. It made no noise, but another moan came from the gorse.

They waited, listening and watching. Lock saw only the fronds and flowers of the thick vegetation over there. He took a deep breath, signalled to the others to follow, and edged away.

Finally, they ran at a crouch to the footbridge.

Behind them, the purple light beamed inscrutably into a night sky now beginning to show the first signs that the sun was about to rise.

The 4x4 wheels kicked up gravel as it reversed up the slope and swerved onto the edge of the car park. It pulled out onto the narrow road, heading away from the bocage lane that had brought them here. Marshy countryside lay in this direction.

"What do you think that was in the bushes?" Gwenda asked in the car.

"No idea," Lock answered.

"Could have been an injured crow," Ventriloquist Jack suggested from the back.

"Stop joking," Gwenda complained. "This is serious."

"I am serious," Jack insisted. "I've heard crows sound just like what we heard back there, almost human."

The road crossed a bridge over the same river that cut across the golf course. The 4x4 then passed under a railway bridge and took the tight bend the other side at speed.

The landscape remained flat. Stone walls separated tarmac from fields that were crisscrossed by power cables slung between timber poles.

Further on, signs warned of a double roundabout. The 4x4 turned the wrong way at the first one and came to a halt at the head of an exit ramp from the expressway below.

Trucks and cars littered both lanes down there. One car was overturned and lying on its roof. Other vehicles had collided into Armco barriers, but most were untidily parked on the carriageway with their doors left open. There were no people to be seen. And in the dim pre-dawn light, this scene of chaos stretched into the visible distance.

"Looks like a convoy all decided to crash and stall at the same time," Gwenda observed. "What the hell happened here?"

"Those trucks are RAF," Lock said. "The other carriageway seems clear though." He shifted the gear stick into reverse.

"Wait," Gwenda warned. "I think there's someone still inside that car down there."

"Which one?"

She pointed. "Overturned, bottom of the ramp."

Lock lifted a pair of binoculars and peered through them. "I can see something in there, but it's not moving. Could be just luggage."

"Don't you think we'd better take a look?" Gwenda urged.

Lock shook his head. "I thought the whole idea was that we get back before daylight."

"If anything was watching, it would have surely detected us by now," Gwenda argued. "We need information about what's been happening on the surface… what's happened to people. Look at it. Why did all those people suddenly abandon their cars and trucks? Where are they? Where did they go?"

"I'm not walking down there," Lock said.

"You don't have to," Gwenda countered. "Drive. We can turn around or reverse to come back."

Lock hesitated.

"Gwenda's right," Jack said from the back of the car. "We need as much information as possible."

"I know that," Lock said irritably. "I'd be taking more risks to get that information if I was alone."

"Well I'm okay with the risk so don't worry about me," Jack told him.

"It's not you I'm worried about," Lock answered. He glanced at Gwenda and put the 4x4 in forward gear.

The vehicle rolled down the ramp and came to a halt by the overturned car. It looked as though it had been flipped by the Armco barrier when it ran alongside it.

Jack opened his window to look out. Lock did the same. Gwenda undid her seatbelt, got up on her knees on her seat in the front, and leaned over Lock to peer out.

The side windows were open in the overturned car. Dark shapes partly filled the space inside.

"Hello," Lock called. "Anybody there?"

He pointed a handlamp. The beam illuminated something that was roughly the shape of the back of a man's head and shoulders. It wasn't moving.

Gwenda's eyes were alert and puzzled. "What is that?"

Lock eased the handbrake to allow the 4x4 to move forward slightly and aimed the handlamp again.

This time it revealed a pink ear, made of a furry cloth.

Gwenda sighed. "It's a stuffed toy monkey."

"Maybe it was driving the car," Ventriloquist Jack suggested.

"That's enough," Gwenda scolded. "There's nothing in the slightest bit funny about any of this. There were people in these cars."

Jack grunted from the rear seat.

Lock merely sighed and began turning the 4x4 around.

-o-

Caycey Jones half-dozed in an armchair at the duplicate safe house. His closed eyes faced a table, upon which the laptop repeated its rolling window of *Message sent... Listening for response.*

Jones became immediately alert when Norton came into the room.

Hardcastle looked up at her from where he was hunched over two laptops at another table. "Can't sleep?"

"Banes is snoring like a truck in his room," Norton answered. "It's actually shaking the floorboards upstairs. What are you doing?"

"It's interesting," Hardcastle said, holding up one of the laptops. The screen was glowing, fuzzy, garbled. "See this? It's a duplicate I found in my duplicate suitcase upstairs." He put it down and pointed at the other laptop. "This is a real one I brought with me from the surface. This one works, the duplicate doesn't."

Jones sat up, interested.

"Maybe it hasn't got an operating system," Norton suggested.

"Even so," Hardcastle said. "It's got enough architecture and functionality to light up the screen, even if it is nonsense." The scientist held up a screwdriver. "I'm about to do some exploratory surgery."

"Have you tried loading an operating system?" Jones asked.

Hardcastle held up a DVD. "I found it in the cellar downstairs."

"So that's also a duplicate created by the technology down here," Norton said, nodding. She went to the window and looked out.

"Did you try exploring it in your real laptop?" Jones asked.

"Sure," Hardcastle answered. "The disc has got something on it, some sort of hierarchy, but the folders are all either empty, or the contents are hidden."

"So, either the entity down here can't replicate stuff in that detail, or it hasn't bothered to," Norton said from the bay window. "Yet so much here is incredibly accurate."

"One has to wonder just how omniscient White Hair is," Hardcastle said. "And what exactly its limitations are."

Norton turned around, looking at the men. "It's sent three of our people into potential danger to gather data."

"I'm acutely aware of that," Jones said. "I'm also aware of the apparent inconsistencies. White Hair can duplicate all these houses with incredible accuracy. There's a USA Today I bought in Dallas in my room next door... a duplicate. All the print is there, pictures, adverts, everything. Yet the entity doesn't know, or doesn't seem to know, what's going on a few miles away."

"A limited zone of omniscience maybe," Hardcastle suggested as he began working with his screwdriver.

"Or a selective one," Jones said. "I've been puzzling over that and a whole list of questions ever since it started doing stuff."

"Strains the old brain, doesn't it," Hardcastle said.

"That's one way of putting it," Jones agreed, checking his watch. "And don't even mention the quantum mechanics ramifications. I've been up and down that yellow brick road in my head too many times for comfort."

"I know exactly what you mean," Hardcastle said.

Jones rose from the armchair and stretched his arms. "The others should have been back by now."

Norton watched the American lift his jacket from a chair. "You're not going to do anything reckless, are you? Like going to the surface?"

"Don't worry," Jones answered. "I thought I would go to the main tunnel and keep an eye out from there. A bit of a walk might clear my head."

"Then I'll come with you," Norton told him. "I'll just get some decent shoes." She swiftly exited the room.

Jones sighed and looked at Hardcastle, who had managed to dismantle the duplicate laptop base into several components.

"Can you take watch on this for me?" Jones said, pointing at the *Message sent... Listening for response* screen on the nearer table.

Hardcastle nodded and raised a thumb. "Sure, enjoy your walk."

-o-

384

Dawn was well established when the 4x4 passed the disused service station. It did not slow down at the junction where Burke's Range Rover remained tilted over into a ditch.

Lock turned off instead at the open field gate a few hundred yards beyond.

"I want to look around the farmyard when we get there," Gwenda said firmly as they bumped along mud tracks compressed into the field.

"It's daylight," Lock warned.

"And nothing's happened, nothing's detected us and we haven't seen a single living person. I want to know what happened to Dilys and Clwyd. We could let the calves out for the cows as well."

The 4x4 halted in the centre of the farmyard. Lock got out, assault rifle held ready across his chest. A similarly armed Gwenda hurried to a long barn.

Jack followed Lock towards the farmhouse. The dogs came out of their kennel. One of the dogs barked, but then sat down and whimpered.

Both men halted. Jack petted the whimpering dog.

Up the yard slope, calves cried in alarm as they ran out of the barn. Gwenda came out after them waving her arms. Cows returned the calls from the closed field gate near the pigsties.

Lock looked at them and turned to Jack Thomas. "Now what do we do?"

Jack grinned. "I'll get it." He headed for the cows. Two of the sheepdogs followed him. They watched with approval as he pulled the gate open.

The leading cows ran into the yard, causing Lock to step back in a hurry. The small herd then slowed to a walk and progressed in a more orderly fashion to a milking station opposite the barn. The calves followed them, bleating and nudging for milk.

Gwenda had a determined but satisfied look on her face as she joined the two men.

They approached the farmhouse. The dogs did not follow them. One flattened its ears and whined.

Lock held his gun at the ready as Gwenda tried the farmhouse door. It would not budge. She made to knock on it but hesitated and decided against that. "Around the back," she whispered.

There was an overgrown orchard at the rear. A hut occupied one side of it. Beyond that, a mess of apple trees gave way to brambles and bushes overlooked by oak trees and sycamores. Something stood swaying between the apple trees.

Jack's eyes were wide. "What the hell is that?"

Lock and Gwenda aimed their weapons at the thing.

Sods of grass had been torn from the untidy lawn. They led like footsteps to the shape between the trees. It was vaguely like a man but seemed to have no separate legs. Instead, a rough-textured and misshaped column of what looked like furry red vegetation was rooted to the ground where it squirmed.

The torso area was equally vague. Purple veins crisscrossed to a tapering crown, where something white with a face-like shape moved under a skin.

"Is that Clwyd Roberts in there?" Gwenda whispered.

The thing writhed violently, trying to uproot itself.

Lock and Gwenda backed away. Behind them, Ventriloquist Jack raised his camera. This whirred and clicked.

The uprooting attempt ceased. The thing resumed its side-to-side swaying motion.

"Back to the car," Lock ordered.

All the cows and their calves had gone into the milking station. The dogs sat sentry outside its open door, watching the people get into their car.

The 4x4 arrived back at the compound on the mountain. It halted close to the rock face.

All three went inside. Lock glared angrily at the sky before closing the steel door behind him with a clank of metal. The locking mechanism clunked into place.

TEN

Caycey Jones stood in the amphitheatre area as he studied a glowing window in the otherwise murky elliptical dome. "Is this live?" he asked.

A high-definition image of the cylinder at the airfield, with its vertical, purple beam was depicted there. A tetragonal object rotated ahead of it over the runway.

Facing Jones, White Hair did not respond to the question.

"Uh, no, it isn't live," Ventriloquist Jack answered instead. "I took still pictures only, no video." He held his camera with the viewing screen aimed towards White Hair, who seemed disinterested in that as well.

"Plus it's daylight outside now," Lock observed.

"Is that a spacecraft?" Norton asked, puzzled. "And that rotating thing... A drone maybe?"

Gwenda frowned. "Whatever they are, they're not from around here." Her eyes hinted more of murder than curiosity as she glared at the image.

"The cylindrical shape matches some past UFO sightings," Jones observed. "But that rotating thing... I don't know... All the same, I think we're looking at the Cuckoos here."

As he said this, and without warning, another rectangular screen appeared.

Hardcastle almost flinched, his face an expression of disgust as he took in the new image.

A tall, plant-like creature squirmed between two apple trees. It

387

looked as though it was attempting to uproot itself. The image zoomed onto the veined upper area where the blurred suggestion of a face moved under an opaque skin.

"*That* was what we saw in Dilys and Clwyd's orchard at the back of their house," Gwenda reported grimly.

"And again, I only took stills," Ventriloquist Jack added. "The technology here must be animating the camera data. Very clever." He lowered his camera, switched it off and went to sit on the amphitheatre's bottom step.

"Seems the world upstairs has gone to hell on a broomstick," Jones said. "And you saw no living people?"

"Not one," Gwenda answered. "But animals appeared okay."

"I don't think we've seen enough to arrive at any conclusions," Lock told Jones. "There could be unaffected survivors out there."

Jones shook his head with some bewilderment. "If that purple haze carried some sort of vector—"

"That's Clwyd Roberts cocooned in there," Gwenda said, pointing up at the image of the squirming thing. "Something vectored him alright. Look at the poor man."

"We can't be certain that it is actually Clwyd," Lock argued. "Sure, it looks a bit like a face in there, but we're hard-wired to see faces. We see them in clouds, on the moon. This thing might not have a human origin at all."

"So where did Clwyd and Dilys go?" Gwenda demanded. "They would never abandon their animals."

Jones faced White Hair and spoke. "We have complied with your instructions. Please try to help us understand what is going on."

"The data is inconclusive," White Hair responded without moving its eyes. "More data is required."

Hardcastle shrugged. "There it goes again, repeating itself."

"From where should we obtain more data?" Jones asked.

"More data is required," it answered.

"There we have it," Lock announced with an air of finality. "This time, we carry out a proper reconnaissance. I want to go west along the peninsula. Army evacuated thousands of people in that direction. The places *we* passed through had all been evacuated."

"What about the abandoned convoy we saw near the airfield?" Gwenda reminded him.

"We don't know when that happened," Lock responded.

Gwenda shook her head. "But that tank with its engine still running?"

"Mysteries, yes, but we saw nothing conclusive," Lock told her. "We need more intelligence." He pointed at White Hair. "More data, as he put it."

"More data is required," White Hair agreed in its droning electronic voice.

Jones looked at each of them in turn, then sighed. "I agree with Commander Lock. We need more intelligence, but first of all we have a village to manage."

-o-

Out in the world, seagulls circled above the sea wall as wave remnants lapped at the inner beach. Here, wading birds investigated wet sand, beaks probing as they hunted for food.

Inland, beside the deserted village street near the bridges, sparrows fluttered and argued in a hedgerow. Bees busied themselves in hanging baskets at the terraced cottages. The small river below them gurgled peacefully.

A trout splashed with a flash of silver, and a starling called from a chimney pot above. The bird chirped again, before flying away over a village devoid of human life.

Further inland, a field was populated by scattered cows with their calves. They grazed, some chewed the cud. Tails swung and flicked at pestering flies, while at the bottom of that same field two carcasses were swarming with insects. The dead cows' stomachs were already bloated from the gases of decay. A rook pecked at an empty eye socket here.

Beyond the fields, the main road junction was silent. A fox trotted across, avoiding the lifeless Range Rover still tilted where it had been pushed into a ditch. The vehicle appeared forlorn and abandoned. The fox, however, looked as though it knew exactly where it was going and why.

While deep underground, out below the Irish Sea, the people in the domed village also looked as though they knew exactly where they were going.

Kyle's gran accompanied her demented neighbour across the second duplicate bridge. The demented woman was now able to chat quite normally it seemed.

Following them, Kyle looked over at Robert E Lee. The man was wearing normal clothes, no home-made Confederate uniform today. Embarrassment flashed across Lee's face when he saw Kyle observing him.

Banes, Jones and Norton came along from the duplicate safe house. While further up along the circling street, here underground and beneath a dome of artificial stars, Ventriloquist Jack waited as he watched Hefin Gwynedd approach from the direction of his farm. Pero trotted amiably alongside him.

Young women arrived with prams and pushchairs. Teenagers detached themselves from parents to greet each other. Adults shook hands; some pointed around and upwards as they swapped their hellos and repeated astonishments at this place.

But they all entered eventually into the duplicate chapel.

Inside, Andy Lock rapped his knuckles against the preacher's pulpit. The loud buzz of chatter diminished only slightly. "Your attention, please," he shouted, knocking harder this time.

The clamour died away. A toddler wailed until her mother picked her up. The congregation was seated in untidy rows on fold-out chairs, expressions alert, curious, others impatient.

Jones sat facing them, next to Banes, Hardcastle and Norton, on the raised deacons' platform at the front. Jones, especially, studied the people out there. Gwenda Evans, seated closer to the pulpit, had her eyes fixed on Andy Lock as he gathered himself to speak.

"Thank you all for coming," Lock began. "I'm sure you've got a lot of questions, but I would ask you to be patient and listen to what I have to say first."

"When can we go home?" Missus Lewis shouted from the back. She stood up. Her husband and son lowered their eyes in dismay. Bibby Libby tugged at her arm, trying to stop her. But there was an immediate murmur of support from the other villagers.

Gwenda stood up before it grew. Her voice was sharper than the woman's. She also had an assault rifle slung across her chest. "Betty Lewis, why don't you just sit down, shut up, and listen."

Jones lowered his head and closed his eyes as though in silent prayer.

Lock shot a disapproving glance at Gwenda then held out the palms of both hands to his audience. "Let's all keep calm," he coaxed. "I know you're all worried and that you want to go home. We all want that. We all want the world to go back to normal."

This time, there was a clamour of agreement for him.

"Three of us have been out on the surface nearly all night," Lock continued loudly, determined that they hear him.

Now there was complete silence. A little girl's voice broke it. "Are we going to sing?" she asked her mother. A few people laughed. Others barely managed a smile. Most remained grimly serious.

"As I was saying," Lock began again. "Three of us have had a fairly good look around on the surface. We went as far as Anglesey, but we saw no living people at all. We saw certain things up there as well, but I don't want to go into details with children here. Let me be clear though, our assessment is that it is not yet safe for any of us to go home."

"Why isn't it safe?" Missus Lewis shouted from the back. "What *did* you see?"

Gwenda rose angrily. "Do you really want us to spell it out to you in front of children?"

"Gwenda, Gwenda," Lock pleaded from the pulpit as Jones went back into what looked like prayer.

"Because if you do, here it is," Gwenda continued, pointing a finger at the woman. "If we hadn't brought you down here, you would all be dead or worse. We've seen what's happened to those

391

who stayed behind. Do you really want us to tell you about that in all the gory detail in front of children?"

"Gwenda, please." Lock's voice had a sterner edge this time. He returned his eyes to the audience. "There are some things that need further investigation up there. And we are going back to the surface to do that today, I can assure you. So, I am asking you all, please, to have some patience."

A man stood up in the centre. "Who built this place?" he demanded. "You told us it was high-tech, but this place is way beyond that."

Lock again raised his hands to plead for calm. "We know you have questions, and yes you have had an experience of something that seems to be impossible here. But let me remind you, a new form of government was slaughtering people just a few days ago. It turned into a civil war when the army rebelled against that government. You all came down here to the sounds of battle."

There was some agreement in the audience, heads nodding, except for the man who remained standing. "What about the purple light you saw up there? Betty told us you had to get away from it in a hurry." Now the murmurs turned to consternation and grew louder. Some twisted around to look at Betty Lewis.

"I'm getting to that," Lock answered the man. "Please sit down." The man ignored him. Lock glanced over at Jones with an expression that was a plea for help. Jones merely shook his head and looked at the floor. Gwenda Evans folded her arms and gritted her teeth.

As the clamour again grew out of control, Ventriloquist Jack stood up at the end of a row near the back. He smacked his hands together. It sounded like a rifle shot.

Suddenly hushed, all eyes were on him as he strode to the front of the chapel.

"Mad Jack Thomas," a woman whispered a little too loudly as she nudged her husband.

Jack arrived at the front, stood with his feet apart and faced the audience. Eyes in a sparkling glare, he pointed a finger, first at the woman who had commented about him, then at the standing man who quickly sat down in response to it. Jack then opened his hand

and pulled it back as though completing a conjuring trick. His eyes continued to glimmer as he spoke in a piercingly enunciated tone. "I was out there all night with Andy and Gwenda," he began, "and guess what? It's a good thing they're not telling you the details of what we saw out there. Do you want to know why?"

There was silence. A little girl tugged her mother's arm. "I want to know why."

Jack swept a hand towards those on the raised area behind him. "These people are professionals," he said, voice growling. "They risked their lives to save us all from what happened up there. They're not telling you certain things because they don't want to frighten you. They're not telling you some things because they want to be certain first."

"Thank you," Lock said, trying to regain control.

"But I can tell you now," Jack continued, "that most of you would *shit* yourselves if you saw what *we* saw out there." He aimed a finger at the ceiling. "The world you knew has gone..." He paused, finger wagging at his audience. There was absolute silence when he spoke again. "Think about that... It's all gone."

"Jack, please," Lock demanded.

"No, they need to be told," Jack insisted. "This place, yes it's a miracle, technology beyond human comprehension. But up there, something really bad is going on. Like this place, what we saw up there is *also* beyond human comprehension. So be thankful you are safe, for now. Be thankful these people risked their lives to bring you down here and are still doing their best to protect you."

Jack now positively glowered at the audience. "Any questions?"

"Bloody good," Gwenda said quietly behind him as the villagers remained silent.

Lock watched Ventriloquist Jack step back to stand at his side like a guard dog.

"Thank you, Mister Thomas," Lock acknowledged. "And once again thank you all for coming," he said to the audience. "I suggest you go back to your duplicate homes or feel free to look around, but do not leave this chamber. We will get more information to you about the surface as soon as we have it."

The villagers all seemed to stare at him for a second or two. Someone stood up to leave in the middle of a row. Others took the cue. Conversations started up as chairs were scraped across the floor. There was a growing clamour of departure.

Except for Robert E Lee. The man came forward alone with his hand half raised. He spoke quietly and with a puzzled expression on his face. "Excuse me, sir, I wonder if you can help me?"

Jack lifted his eyebrows and stepped back, glancing at Andy Lock.

Lock took the cue; he prompted Lee to come forward.

Closer, the man looked at Lock with pale-blue eyes in a face framed by a neatly trimmed white beard. Equally neat hair circled a bald head. "I think I've been ill," he said in a nervous English Midlands accent. "I seem to be getting better, but I'm still confused. Can you tell me where I am and how I got here?"

"Ah," Lock said, uncertainty in his eyes. Now he saw Kyle and his gran. They were holding back with the woman who had been clearly demented during the evacuation from the surface. The rest of the village continued to leave the chapel.

"I can handle this," Emily Norton said. She stepped forward and waved to Kyle's gran and the old woman to come to the front. She took Mr Lee and the woman to one side.

Lock seemed relieved that Norton had taken charge.

"You want me at the house in two hours then?" Kyle called to him from near the entrance.

"See Doctor Banes," Lock responded. "In the meantime, go and chill with your friends or something... relax, unwind." Lock fixed his attention to the chapel entrance. Some of the villagers were still talking outside.

Jones stood up and stretched his legs. "Could have been worse. Went quite well, all things considered."

"No thanks to you," Lock answered without malice. "I hate public speaking."

"It had to be you addressing them, with a little help from Mister Thomas and Missus Evans here," Jones said with a low chuckle. "The people here don't know me." He turned to Ventriloquist Jack. "Ever thought of shark hunting?"

"Not really," Jack answered. "Why?"

"Ever seen Jaws?" Jones queried with a smile. "All you needed was a blackboard to scrape your fingernails across."

Jack frowned. "Considering I'm going to the surface again, I'm not sure if I like that comparison. The man who did that got killed in that film."

"Then we'll have to make sure that doesn't happen," Gwenda told him as she tapped her assault rifle.

To the side of the chapel, Emily Norton spoke quietly to a woman who, apparently, was now not demented, and to a man who no longer believed he was a Confederate general.

Lock sighed as he observed this, then returned his attention to the others. "We'd better get ready then."

"Hefin's waiting for me," Ventriloquist Jack said. "It's my turn to cook dinner."

"Two hours," Lock warned.

"I'll be back," the man called out as he headed for the door.

-o-

The train carriage flashed along the main tunnel in silence. Its end door slid open, facing the breach area mere seconds later.

Gwenda went to the rabbit cage, crouched down and checked inside. "Still healthy it seems," she told Lock.

Lock adjusted her backpack as she stood up.

"Stop fussing," she complained gently. They had travelled here alone.

He looked into her eyes. "I worry about you."

"Well don't. Worrying never accomplished anything. I've got a job to do. That means I go wherever you go."

He leaned forward to kiss her on the forehead but gave up on a hug when the guns and binoculars slung at their chests got in the way.

They went out into the miners' tunnel, handlamps lighting the rock bore ahead as they began their walk to the surface.

Bright sunshine dazzled them when Lock opened the steel door to the compound a little later.

Gwenda waited as Lock worked at the transformer outside. Behind an open panel, eyes protected by goggles, he pumped a lever with his gloved hands. There was a brief blue flash before he came out of there, dumping the gloves and goggles.

The pair headed along the cliff face behind the line of trees. They had not gone far before Lock lifted his binoculars and aimed them out to sea. Gwenda did the same with hers.

Very distant, a hulking ship was tilted over on its side. Dozens of containers had spilled. Some had piled up. Others were afloat.

"It's stuck on a sandbar," Gwenda said.

"No sign of the crew, not from this distance anyway," Lock added. He continued walking. His eyes scanned downwards towards the gradually revealed village as they gained height over the trees on sloping ground below.

They passed the forest boundary dividing the mountain. Part of the valerian weed at the edge of the rock shelf was still flattened where Gwenda had concealed herself only a day ago.

Binoculars were raised again. Both scanned the village and the roads.

Gwenda's attention stayed on Dilys and Clwyd's farm for a while. It looked toy-like from this height.

"Nothing," Gwenda commented. "No sign of human life at all. But most of the cows seem alright. They're back in the field with their calves."

"What about Anglesey?"

Gwenda aimed her binoculars. "I can see Paris Mountain, but not the airfield."

Lock took off his pack and lowered himself to sit cross-legged. He checked his watch. "I'll observe the farm for a while. You watch the main road."

Gwenda sighed and sat close beside him. A flying insect buzzed past her ear as she did so.

-o-

Ventriloquist Jack seemed on edge as he walked up the latter part of the miners' tunnel. "You didn't have to come all this way, you know. I'm perfectly capable of getting to the surface on my own."

Banes and Kyle were following behind him. Their lamps scanned the rock floor and walls.

"Best not to be alone in these old mine workings," Banes said. "We try to stick to the buddy system."

Jack laughed and pointed his lamp. "You my buddy, Kyle?" he teased, dazzling Kyle.

Kyle grinned. "Absolutely, Mister Thomas. But I had to come up here for the rabbit anyway. We'll be taking it on the way back so Miss Norton can do blood tests on it."

"Should have sent her then," Jack said as he continued walking. "She'd be better company than you two."

Kyle flicked his lamp beam at something that had glinted in the tunnel crown. A drop of water fell and splashed into a puddle. "You like Miss Norton then?"

"You mind your own business," Jack retorted. "And behave yourself with that Elin Lewis whose rabbit you're so keen to fetch."

"Bibby Libby?" Kyle scoffed. "She's way too young for me."

Jack shielded his lamp for a second. Up ahead, the first hint of electric light glimmered in the distance. "Last I heard she was seventeen. How old are you?"

"Nearly twenty."

"Elin Lewis would be much better for you than that Sharon you were knocking around with," Jack said. But when Kyle remained silent, the man took on a regretful tone. "Sorry, kid. I shouldn't have said that."

397

"She went to stay with relatives in Wolverhampton," Kyle said. "She was a right mess, but I do wonder what happened to her. Do you think everyone is dead except us?"

That question remained unanswered as the trio continued in silence, the electric lighting visible in the tunnel bore ahead growing larger as they neared it.

"I've got a sister, you know," Jack said. He switched off his handlamp. "Married an Irishman and moved to Australia. I haven't spoken to her in years. Shame that... She's a good kid."

"How about you, Doctor Banes?" Kyle asked. The toothy steel and brickwork door was a few paces away. "Have you got family?"

"Just my mum and dad," the scientist answered. "I was never able to tell them where or what I was doing. Secrecy has its price."

"You've done a good job," Jack said, "and you had to do it in secret. None of what happened out there is your fault."

-o-

Kyle watched the 4x4 roll down towards the automatic gate, which opened with a shaking rattle. It closed just as noisily after the car had gone through. He turned to Banes who beckoned him to go back into the mountain.

Banes hesitated inside, looking up at the sky with a touch of sadness before closing the steel door with a dull, metallic clunk.

The farmyard was completely deserted when the 4x4 arrived there. Even the dogs were gone.

Lock and Gwenda got out first. Ventriloquist Jack followed them around the back of the farmhouse. The thing that had squirmed and tried to uproot itself between the apple trees was gone. A purple crater of what looked like a mixture of molten plastic and vegetable leaf scarred the ground where it had stood. Lock opened his pack and removed a small aluminium case.

"Let me do it," Jack volunteered. "I've got more lab experience than either of you."

Lock shrugged and handed over the case.

Jack pulled on surgical gloves before leaning over the purple

398

mess with a scalpel. The material was tough, but he managed to cut a small piece loose before lifting it with the blade into a Petri dish, which he immediately closed and slid inside a plastic bag. He discarded the scalpel and gloves.

Lock returned the case to his pack.

"How were you planning on getting a sample if that thing had still been here?" Jack asked him.

Before closing the pack, Lock pulled out a telescopic metal walking stick with a looped strap at its handle. The other end had a knife attached to it with ducting tape. He removed a sheath to reveal its serrated blade.

"You were going to stab Clwyd Roberts with that," Gwenda said, "just to get a sample?"

"It was *not* Clwyd Roberts," Lock told her as he put the device away. "Maybe, just maybe, it used to be Clwyd Roberts and no longer was."

"Well I reckon it was Clwyd," Gwenda insisted as she headed back to the 4x4.

"Handy device that," Jack said to Lock as they followed her. "If we do find one of those things intact, we'll have to try it."

"You can try it," Lock said. "I'll be covering you with my gun."

Sparrows flitted in and out through an open barn door as the 4x4 departed the farmyard.

The main road climbing west inland up the mountain pass had been scarred by tank-tracks. The tarmac was lifted in sharp ridges where the army had commenced their pursuit of the auxiliaries.

Further up, Lock had to slow the car to avoid lumps of mud in the road. Here, flattened hedgerows revealed a muddy mess of a field. Scattered sandbag walls of abandoned positions stretched across it to some cliffs. Forestry towered above them where the mountain rose and meandered from here towards the sea.

The car crossed the peak of the pass. The road began descending in blind hairpins. Each lower leg ahead was hidden by dense woodland and bushes. Black-and-white chevrons attached to Armco barriers signalled each turn.

They passed a dilapidated house, empty windows blackened from a long-ago fire, with a rotting *For Sale* sign hanging, tilted, from its soot-stained render.

The next bend revealed the road curving more gently ahead across lower ground. There were occasional isolated houses along its sides.

"Why don't you stop at the next house," Gwenda suggested.

"Why?" Lock asked as he drove. "We haven't seen any signs of life in any of them so far."

"It was just a thought," Gwenda said. "There could be people in some of these houses. How far do we need to go to get more evidence?"

"What do you reckon the population of Nefyn Ystod was before all this started?" Lock asked her.

"Two, maybe three thousand," she guessed.

"More like four thousand," Ventriloquist Jack contributed from the back.

Gwenda pointed a finger. "What about here?" There was a turn-off ahead. A brown tourist attraction sign with white letters marked a road headed into an area of dense woodland on rising ground.

"That's where the regular army set up their local headquarters," Lock answered.

"So?"

"They would have moved up with the advance."

Gwenda grunted something unintelligible.

"There'll be nobody there," Lock insisted as they passed the turn-off. "Nefyn Ystod isn't far now."

"The further we go, the greater the risk," Gwenda warned. "You do know that, don't you?"

"The more we know, the better," Lock countered. "There could be people out here."

"Then why didn't we stop to check any of the houses back there?"

"Because the bloody army officer told us they were evacuating everyone this side of Nefyn Ystod."

"So why didn't you remind me about that earlier then?"

"Hey," Ventriloquist Jack warned from the back of the car. "I'm scared enough as it is without having to listen to you two bickering."

"We're all scared," Lock told him. "But Gwenda here is more scared for us than she is for herself."

"Tosh," Gwenda said, but she rested a hand on Lock's arm and gazed at his face.

He glanced at her and briefly placed his right hand over hers while he steered the car with the other.

The 4x4 sped along the deserted road between hedgerows and fields of sheep. The ground rose to a moderate height ahead. Road signs warned of a 30mph speed limit.

Partly obscured by Mediterranean pines, a church and its spire topped a hump behind high stone walls.

Lock pulled the car to a halt beside a medieval arched entry. A black notice board announced worship times in flaked gold paint.

"Feel like praying then?" Jack asked.

"Risk reduction," Lock said. "We might be able to observe the village from here."

The trio approached the church. A crowbar ripped the twin leaf oak door open at its latch. Stained-glass windows streamed dim light inside.

Booted feet drew hollow sounds from bare floorboards as they walked the midway gap between the pews. They halted at the centre aisle and looked towards the front of the church and its altar. Organ pipes flanked a circular stained-glass window behind it. The vestry door was slightly ajar beyond the choir pews.

"Nobody here then," Ventriloquist Jack observed.

"Hello," Gwenda called out. Her voice filled the empty interior with a dampened, hollow echo. There was no answer.

Lock approached a door at the back of the church. He lifted a drooping sheet of paper barely attached to it with adhesive putty. A marker pen scrawl in capital letters warned:

DANGER KEEP OUT

A turn of the handle failed to open it. The crowbar in Lock's hands elicited a sound of ripping, splintering wood as it was forced open.

The interior of the spire base was a mess of builders' materials, planed timbers freckled with mildew, and scaffolding poles. A dirty bell rope was coiled on the floor, covered in dust. It looked as though it had been like this for years.

The trio gazed upwards. Most of the wooden stairway spiralling up the walls was missing.

"We're not getting up there then," Gwenda said.

"So it seems," Lock agreed. "There might be a viewpoint from the edge of the graveyard instead." He went back through the door.

Gwenda and Jack continued peering at the slanting daylight up there for a moment before turning to follow him. They found Lock halted just inside the church, one arm raised. He lowered the arm, put a finger to his lips, then bent over to place the crowbar quietly on the floor.

Gwenda's eyes questioned him. Lock pointed towards the open vestry door at the far end. A shadow moved in there.

The trio had moved a few paces forward when a dark figure appeared at the door frame. Lock and Gwenda raised their weapons to the ready as it passed behind the choir pews.

Now it came into full view, turning towards the far end of the centre aisle. The figure was dressed in black clothes that were matted with dried gunk of some sort. In profile, its head was only vaguely human in shape. Where a nose, mouth and lower jaw should have been, a cone-like shape jutted out.

It reached the centre of the aisle in front of the altar and turned to face them. A dirty white rectangle was visible at its collar.

"Is that the vicar?" Gwenda whispered.

Lock aimed his assault rifle. Gwenda moved sideways and did the same. The figure began walking in a normal human gait towards them.

The feet were bare. Black trousers, jacket and bib shed flakes of the dried gunk as it moved. The face, distinctly inhuman, was caked with something grey. Opaque skin shimmered beneath it.

402

Above the pointed snout, two circular eyes were a dark purple-red with no whites. It was also breathing with an asthmatic wheeze as it now advanced more purposefully towards them.

"I don't like the look of this," Jack warned. The figure reached the midway gap in the aisles and turned its strange face towards the open entrance door. It then continued walking in their direction before halting about ten paces away. A loud wheeze, a deep intake of breath.

Both weapons were now aimed. Two red dots wobbled on its forehead below a matted hairline. The snout opened into a black, toothless circle as its neck undulated and swelled out on both sides. With a *whoop* and *plop* sound, it spat out something towards Lock.

A white thing the size of a man's fist landed and wriggled on the floor a few feet short of him. A black needle stabbed out from it, unfolding long barbs as the thing elongated into the shape of a worm. Two pairs of insect-like wings flicked out of its sides and buzzed. Then the worm's eyeless head arched upwards like a snake about to leap.

Lock pulled the trigger, disintegrating the worm into splashes of goo with two rapidly fired rounds.

Gwenda's weapon coughed twice, taking off the top of the vicar thing's head. It collapsed to the floor, wriggling, arms flailing to its sides. The neck undulated once more, starting a repeat process.

Swiftly, Gwenda and Lock thumbed switches on their weapons, before aiming again. Both fired. It was a rapid, short-lived *brrrrr* sound that emptied the magazines. Bullet cases rattled onto the wooden floor.

Ventriloquist Jack removed his hands from his ears. "Jesus Christ," he complained as wisps of gun smoke drifted towards him.

The neck and head area of the thing on the floor was now a streaked pulp, which extended in spatters radiating away from it. A mix of clear and purple ooze had splashed over a wider area.

"I told you it was Clwyd Roberts back there at the farm," Gwenda said. She reloaded her weapon, moved a pace forward then aimed it again. "But I didn't realise he was turning into one of these. I thought he might have been trapped. I was wrong. You were right, sort of."

Lock snapped another magazine into his weapon. "We were both wrong," he said quietly through gritted teeth.

"What the hell was that worm thing going to do?" Ventriloquist Jack asked, still stunned.

Lock kept his eyes and weapon firmly on the remains of the smaller creature. "I wasn't about to find out... There's no visible movement here."

"None in the vicar either," Gwenda said as she watched the man-shaped corpse a little further along the aisle.

"Keep your distance and keep your eyes on them," Lock ordered. He lowered his weapon and hurried around the back of the pews, before heading down the side wall to the entrance. "I'm going to fetch some kit from the car. Back in a sec."

"Must have been some sort of metamorphosis going on when we saw that cocoon at the farm," Jack said. He now had his back to the rear wall of the church.

"Don't distract me," Gwenda cautioned. "Stay where you are and keep watching them."

Lock returned with an aluminium case. "It's clear outside. Any sign of life from those things?"

"Nothing so far," Gwenda answered. "I think they're dead."

Lock hurried to their position and opened the case on the floor. He took out a clear plastic helm, which he placed over his head to shield his face. Thick gauntlets were pulled onto his hands before he slid a box of Petri dishes towards Jack Thomas.

"Put the bases on the floor just there, please," Lock instructed. "You can colour-code the lids."

"I could get the samples if you want," Jack volunteered.

"Just do what I tell you," Lock said. "And use your camera to record what I do with the samples." He pointed. "Take some shots of what's left of that worm thing there as well."

Outside the church, ancient windows flickered white from the rapid flash photography going on inside.

A squirrel hesitated as it came down the trunk of one of the trees. It then bounced and scurried into a thicket of rhododendrons. A crow squawked somewhere.

The trio came out. Lock hurried to the 4x4, carrying the aluminium case. Gwenda closed the church door. Ventriloquist Jack checked his camera then looked up as Andy Lock returned.

Lock pointed through the trees. "That way."

The others followed him along a narrow path. Beyond the trees and bushes, they reached the edge of the main graveyard. They gazed with deflated expressions at a high stone wall guarding the furthest gravestones. It ran the entire length of the grounds.

"We're not going to see anything over that," Lock said.

"That means we're going back, I hope," Gwenda told him.

Lock turned around and headed for the churchyard entrance. "We have to see the village."

"Why?" Gwenda complained. "Haven't we seen enough? Clwyd Roberts in a cocoon, and now a worm-spitting vicar with purple eyes."

"But they could be isolated cases."

"Rubbish," Gwenda said.

"I hate to say it, but Andy's right," Ventriloquist Jack said as they approached the car. "We need to observe a bigger population before we can draw any firm conclusions."

"A bigger population of those bloody things might get us killed, or worse," Gwenda muttered.

They got into the 4x4.

-o-

Norton was watching through the office window. A few children passed along the duplicate road outside. Parents followed some of them.

"I think next time, we need to organise supervision for the children," Norton said. "Then the adults can be properly briefed in the chapel, no holding back."

Jones raised his eyebrows where he was slumped in an armchair, trying to relax. "Tell them everything, you mean, full disclosure?"

"Why not," Norton said. "Transparency is the best cure for suspicion. Suspicion can lead to dissent, even rebellion."

405

Jones squinted at her. "Do you think they would believe us? Hey folks, guess what? Millions of years ago a bunch of hostile aliens were imprisoned on this planet. They were allowed to mess around with genetic engineering. Eventually, they came up with humans. Then the aliens disabled the technology that was supposed to keep them contained on this planet forever. Why exterminate us? We don't yet know, but it seems we've outworn whatever purpose the hostiles had in mind."

Jones studied his fingertips, scraped a thumbnail across his forefinger. "How do you reckon that level of transparency would go down? Us humans, we are not God's chosen after all, no manifest destiny. Just rats, created as pets by a bunch of alien prisoners."

"We could then tell them about our mission," Norton offered in a deflated tone. "To ask for help from those who put the hostiles here and created this place underground."

"And the fact our mission appears to have failed," Jones said as a doorbell rang. It was loud. "Banes and Hardcastle will have heard that upstairs," he told Norton, changing the subject. "I bet it woke them up."

"I don't know how they could possibly sleep at a time like this," Norton said. She went to the hallway.

Jones sighed. He heard the front door being opened and Norton greeting someone there.

Kyle came in. He was carrying a black console in both hands, its cables coiled untidily on top of it.

"Kyle wants to show us something," Norton told Jones.

Jones frowned. "Is that a games console?"

"Yeh," the young man answered. "It's the one I found in our house down here. I've been trying to get it to work."

"Ah," Jones said. "Our duplicate computers don't seem to do anything except light up the monitor."

"Same with this," Kyle said. "It was booting up with a green screen, but after a while it just went to the black screen of death."

"Sounds ominous," Norton said with a smile.

"Yeh," Kyle agreed. "But then I decided to leave it switched on for a while to see what happened. It's started doing something. I thought you'd better see it."

Jones was now mildly interested. "Is it actually running computer games?"

"No, sir… You need to see it. It's got stuff to do with this place on it."

Jones stood up. "Have we got somewhere to plug this in?" he asked Norton. "What does it need, TV or a monitor?" he asked Kyle.

-o-

The 4x4 came to a halt a few car lengths short of a corner of the high stone wall surrounding the church grounds.

Up ahead, there was a small roundabout interrupting the road before it progressed through terraced houses and small shops on both sides. A brown tourist signpost at the roundabout urged a right turn to a *Historic Village Centre* in both Welsh and English, together with accommodation and restaurant symbols.

Beyond the roundabout, the deserted road was so packed with parked cars, they were in tight rows, taking up a whole side of the badly littered carriageway. The stationary vehicles on the other side straddled the pavement.

Further on, a primary school building. Beyond that, the road entered countryside once more. Nothing moved, other than plastic bags and scraps of paper drifting occasionally in a breeze amongst the litter.

"Deserted," Gwenda observed.

"That's only a fraction of the place," Lock told her as he began turning the car around. "We'll proceed on foot." He cocked his head as he put the gear stick into reverse for the second manoeuvre. "Did you hear a noise?"

"Only the engine," Gwenda answered as she twisted to look out the back.

"Didn't hear anything," Ventriloquist Jack said.

"Probably nothing then," Lock said. "Might have been the power steering whining a bit."

Lock parked the 4x4 in the centre of the road, facing the way they had come. The church steeple was partly visible over the wall and between the trees in its grounds.

They all got out. Lock led them towards the roundabout. To the right of it, there was a gap of open ground beyond the corner of the church wall, then a used-car showroom, its forecourt packed with cars.

A gentle downward hill beyond it swept between terraced houses in a curve to a junction. Again, parked cars took up half the street. Nothing moved.

Keeping low, the trio kept between the cars across the centre of the forecourt. Lock then took them along a gravel footpath. It curved through some rough ground, sloping down to a stream.

Another path from there led them behind some buildings, then to an alleyway between two shops. Green commercial bins, lids open, were packed with waste bags, with more of the ugly black shapes, bloated and torn, piled on the ground beside them. Another parked car blocked the alleyway entrance from the street.

Lock advanced slowly along the alleyway. Gwenda crept along behind him. Keeping his head low, Ventriloquist Jack readied his camera.

A side window allowed them to look through the shop display window and into the main street. Empty cake stands stood on low shelves, facing out at a scene that caused all three to gasp. Lock's jaw dropped.

"Jesus," Ventriloquist Jack said, alarmed.

"Shush," Gwenda cautioned, whispering. "Keep it down."

The village square, clearly visible through the two panes of glass, and only a short distance beyond their position, had an ornate clock tower in its centre. This was surrounded by what looked like a mass of people, all standing still, all facing away. The square was packed with them.

A uniformly crystalline shape, as big as a house and identical to the one they had seen at the airfield, hovered low in the air above a visitor centre roof on the far side. It rotated, first one way, then the other, alternately presenting white and black facets. The white seemed to flash light; the black gave the impression it was sucking light in.

"Don't look at that thing," Lock warned. "Makes your head hurt... This does *not* look good. Not good at all." He pointed at Ventriloquist Jack's camera, then through the shop windows.

The man took the cue, aimed the camera, which whirred and clicked. He almost dropped it, startled, when a deep sound came from somewhere. It was a sort of electrical hum, followed by a massive thump, then silence. The shop window shook in response to the low-frequency sound waves.

Gwenda's binoculars were up at her eyes as she hunted through the windows. The magnified image halted and focussed briefly on the backs of the nearest figures in the square. Their clothes seemed matted with something. Their feet were bare. Now the binoculars tilted upwards.

Whummm... clunk... A huge cylindrical object was drifting in just above the rooftops in the middle distance.

"Let's get out of here," Gwenda whispered to Lock.

"Hush, wait," he whispered back.

The *whummm* sound started again as the cylinder drifted closer to the square. A narrow beam of white, coherent light reached out from the object's circular face. It flickered around with a distinct end to its reach. This swiftly touched dozens of the figures in the crowd in turn, seemingly at random, and did this so rapidly it was impossible to follow. Then that deep, gut-vibrating *clunk* sound emitted once again.

Those figures the beam had touched simply exploded in puffs of white dust. Skeletons collapsed to the ground in now loose, dust-covered clothes. Dust spread over the ones still standing.

Now another sound bellowed from the cylinder: *Aaaaank*!

The crowd in the square all turned in unison. They began walking up the street in the direction of the bakery concealing the trio.

At the same time, above them, the huge cylinder swivelled along its axis. It flashed upwards, instantly dwindling to a point that vanished into the sky.

"Go go go!" Lock urged. They ran.

With Gwenda taking the lead and keeping low, they quickly made it up the gravel path. She then took them between the cars on the showroom forecourt.

Ventriloquist Jack was badly out of breath when they reached the 4x4.

Lock thrust the key fob into Gwenda's hand. "Get in, start the engine and wait for me," he instructed.

"Don't be stupid," she warned Lock, then issued a snarled "Get in" to Ventriloquist Jack, who was almost doubled over trying to catch his breath.

Ignoring Gwenda's protest, Lock sprinted back to the corner of the high wall, where he crouched and peeked around it. He could just about see the short curving street beyond the car showroom.

They came in a column from around the bend down there: figures of all heights, some the size of children. They walked normally, heads high, snouts extended, seemingly alert with their circular purple eyes.

Lock pulled his head back. He crouched lower but kept watching.

The barefoot column was moving in ranks of three. Although out of step, they looked as though they were in a march, purposeful, determined and orderly.

This line of walking things headed past the far side of the roundabout and proceeded away along the stretch of road packed with cars.

With incredulity, Lock saw some of them opening car doors while others waited in groups of three. A starter motor coughed and whined over there as the column now split.

A new procession of marching things came across the roundabout in Lock's direction.

He sprinted to the 4x4. Multiple car engines revved into life behind him.

"Drive," he ordered Gwenda as he clambered in on the passenger side.

-o-

With her attentive hostess smile, Mair Ellis approached the table in the duplicate B&B dining room. Here Dimitri and his family were eating and in conversation with Miiko.

"How are your fish and chips, dear?" Mair asked the little Russian girl, disturbing the quiet chat going on there.

"Delicious," Marina answered.

"The food is wonderful," Dimitri told Mair. Lara and Miiko both nodded in agreement.

"The kitchen is a miracle," Mair said. She beamed huge smiles at them, delighted with their compliments.

"But Lenin operated contrarily to Marx," Dimitri now said to Miiko, continuing their interrupted conversation. Mair relaxed her smile but listened.

"And took the gold from his Wall Street masters," Miiko agreed.

"Therefore true socialism never had a chance," Dimitri said, voice hinting challenge.

"But there are other examples of its failure and in purer Marxist environments," Miiko countered.

Dimitri frowned. "Not a fair conclusion when you consider capitalism was being pushed by hidden alien monsters, and every avenue of trade prohibited to those socialist countries."

"A good point," Miiko allowed. "Did you ever see the movie, They Live?"

"Great motion picture," Dimitri answered. "And closer to the truth than its makers might have imagined."

"Unless it was commissioned by Circus," Lara put in, apparently as a joke.

Dimitri chuckled at this.

"Well, I can see you're all enjoying yourselves," Mair said. She issued a parting smile then went out through the hallway door.

Wyn Ellis was at the bay window in the lounge. "Something's going on," he said when Mair came in. She hurried to join him, intense interest on her face.

Out at the end of the duplicated drive next door, Kyle was pointing upwards and saying something. Banes and Hardcastle were beside him, bewildered, looking up, shaking their heads.

Mair bent over and angled her head so she could see in the direction Kyle was pointing towards. She saw nothing but the domed ceiling and its display of stars. Mair straightened up, puzzled. Now Kyle again jabbed his finger at some unseen object above his head. With evident frustration, he mouthed something at the two scientists.

Some children passed on their bicycles. They too looked up, apparently saw nothing, and continued pedalling with smiles on their faces.

Banes and Hardcastle both looked defeated; their hair was uncombed, faces unshaved, as though they had just got out of bed. They stared, eyes squinting as though myopic, angling their heads first one way, then the other towards Kyle's still jabbing finger.

All three now suddenly stopped and turned to face the duplicate safe house. Mair pressed her head closer to the window. She saw that Caycey Jones was out on the doorstep next door, calling them to go inside.

"Well *he* didn't come for his dinner like our other guests," Mair Ellis told Wyn. "Did you eat all yours?"

-o-

"It's definitely not a simulation," Caycey Jones announced as Kyle and the other two came into the safe house office. The American pointed at a TV screen showing an image of the duplicate driveway. "We could see all three of you outside."

"Brilliant discovery, Kyle," Norton said. "Exactly what were you pointing at out there?"

"Same thing I saw hovering outside Gran's," Kyle answered.

"We couldn't see it," Hardcastle put in.

"But it was right there, like a ping-pong ball," Kyle said incredulously.

Jones glanced at Hardcastle, then addressed Kyle. "You say you can move it around?"

"Yeh," Kyle said. "When I saw the picture outside Gran's, and after I looked out the window and saw the ping-pong ball thing just hovering there, I got the hand controller connected. I thought it was a simulation, so I moved it right through the house wall into my bedroom. Then I knew for sure it was real when I saw myself on the screen. So I switched it off straight away and brought it here."

"That was absolutely the right thing to do," Jones said. "Show me how you moved it and do the same as you did at your gran's."

Kyle picked up the hand controller. A central white light on it flashed a few times before steadying to a glow. Eyes wide and unblinking, Kyle stared at the TV screen as he moved the small levers on the controller.

The image viewpoint moved over the duplicate lawn outside and briefly darkened as it entered through the window. The screen now showed the office interior. It moved above their heads, looking down at them.

"There," Kyle said, pointing up at the ceiling. "Do you see it? It's glowing right there."

The others stared, bewildered, and kept glancing back at the TV screen as they tried to orient themselves with their own images.

"I don't see anything," Jones said.

"Oh… now I can," Norton said. "It's very faint, keeps fading out, but it's glowing." She pointed. "About the size of a golf ball, right there, next to the light fitting."

"That's it," Kyle said with evident relief. "I'm not imagining things or making it up."

"We never thought that," Jones told him. "Do you think you could take it for a bit of a test?"

"Yeh, sure, Mister Jones," Kyle answered. "What do you want me to do?"

"Let's see if we can get it to the surface and have a look at what's going on out there in the world." Jones dragged an armchair in front

413

of the TV. "Have a seat, young man. You've done extremely well. Well done."

"Well done indeed," Hardcastle said. "Way to go, Kyle."

"Let's all stay quiet and observe," Jones instructed with his deep voice.

Kyle began tilting hand controller levers with his thumbs as the others watched the TV screen.

-o-

"You can slow down a bit now," Lock said as the 4x4 sped past the turn-off to the stately home they had argued about earlier.

Gwenda gripped the wheel with white knuckles. The driver seat was racked forward so that she was close to the steering column. She glanced at the mirror.

"It's okay," Lock told her as he tapped the passenger sun guard above the windscreen. This had a mirror in its centre. "I'm watching behind us and there's no sign of them so far. There's nasty bends ahead, so slow it down."

"I hate driving this only slightly less than the bloody truck," Gwenda said. She eased up on the throttle.

"Brake," Lock cautioned as she took the next bend.

"I can only just about reach it," Gwenda complained.

"Maybe I should take over," Lock said.

Ventriloquist Jack had his head craned over, looking through the rear window. "I don't think so. I just spotted a car back there."

"Are you sure?" Lock asked him.

"Certain," Jack answered. "I think there were others behind it."

"Put your bloody seatbelt on," Lock scolded as he twisted around to look back and noticed the man wasn't wearing his. "How fast was it going?"

Jack fumbled with the seatbelt fastener and pulled it over his lap. "I have no idea. What am I, a racing commentator?"

The 4x4 sped up.

"Slow down," Lock warned Gwenda again. "Keep it below thirty for these bends. We've got at least two minutes' head-start on them."

414

"Stop yapping at me," she complained. "I'm trying to concentrate."

"Just keep cool, drive smoothly, and stay in control," Lock soothed. "And remember your training."

"I *am* remembering my training. It was drive like hell and handbrake turns, not crawl along like a granny."

Lock was about to say something else as the first of the hairpin bends appeared up ahead, but he took a deep breath and gripped a strap above the passenger door with his left hand instead.

Gwenda lifted her foot, changed down a couple of gears and applied some brake.

The car made a perfect turn, slow-in, fast-out. It then accelerated up the steep gradient towards the next black-and-white chevrons.

As they climbed this first stretch, Andy Lock and Jack Thomas were able to look out at part of the highway they had left behind. A column of traffic was coming along it in the distance. Their view was then blotted out by trees.

The 4x4 came over the top of the pass, speeding up as it traversed the short stretch of level road before it curved downwards once more.

Gwenda slowed to avoid lumps of dried mud and torn tarmac, then put her foot down again. There was a blind turn ahead.

Lock's face grimaced in horror: a red car came around the bend at speed from the opposite direction. It veered towards them across the centre of the road.

Gwenda hiked the steering wheel. The 4x4 narrowly missed the red car, but the muddy verge caught the front left wheel. It hit a rock.

The steering wheel kicked out of Gwenda's grip. A hedge filled the windscreen. A sickening bang instantly inflated the car's airbags, the one on the driver's side slamming into Gwenda's face. A fog of white dust filled the car interior.

The 4x4 tore into the field on two wheels, lurched as though it would overturn, then bounced and righted itself before coming to a reluctant halt.

Blood poured from Gwenda's nose. She looked stunned. Her trembling hands dabbed at her face, trying to stem the flow.

Lock pushed his deflated airbag out of the way, quickly reached under his seat and pulled out a first aid box. "Gwenda, are you alright?"

He tried to help her stuff a cotton-wool cylinder into one of her nostrils.

"I don't know," she answered groggily. "I think my nose is broken."

"How's your vision?" Lock asked. He glanced back at Ventriloquist Jack, who was nursing his neck with a pained expression.

"A bit blurred, but I think I'm okay," Gwenda said as she now managed to get a cotton-wool cylinder into her other nostril. Her hands were covered in blood. The deflated airbag that Lock stuffed into the steering column recess was also slick with blood.

Lock coughed from the dust as he opened his door. "Slide over," he told Gwenda.

She unlocked her seatbelt with trembling, bloody hands.

Outside, Lock turned his attention to the torn gap in the hedge and the road beyond it. There were clumps of blackthorn in the field, with some of it tangled in the 4x4 wheel arches.

As he tugged at one of these, he heard a gearbox whining in reverse on the road. The red car appeared and halted at the gap. Two faces with purple eyes peered out from its side windows.

Lock cocked his assault rifle and hurried around the front of the 4x4, glancing at its wheels. The front tyres were flat.

Stunned and uncoordinated, Gwenda had made it only halfway over the handbrake and gear stick when Lock opened the driver's door. He pushed her unceremoniously over into the passenger seat, then climbed in. Gwenda groaned, coughed, spat blood.

Two figures now stood at the gap in the hedge, purple eyes contemplating the waist-high mess of blackthorn remaining there.

Watching them over his shoulder, Lock pressed the ignition button. Nothing happened.

"Engine cut-off," Ventriloquist Jack warned from the back. "Find the reset."

Lock's hand scrabbled under the steering column. "Shit… Where's the handbook?"

Outside, one of the purple-eyed figures lifted a bare foot over into the partly flattened blackthorn. The other creature held its arm to assist it.

A groggy Gwenda Evans opened the glove compartment. She handed the car manufacturer's handbook to Lock. He twisted around and gave it to Jack. "Find it," Lock said before opening the driver's door again.

"Where's the bloody index?" Jack demanded as he flicked through the handbook's last pages.

"Try the front of the book," Lock answered. He got out of the car.

His weapon at the ready, Lock took a few steps towards the hedge.

Both pairs of purple eyes turned to face him. The first one was making no progress in its attempt to get over the tangle of blackthorn. It pulled its bare foot back, as though reacting to pain, before steadying itself.

Lock heard a car door being opened over there. A third figure came to the gap in the hedge. All three stared at him. The sides of their necks began to swell.

"I've found where it is," Ventriloquist Jack shouted from the 4x4. "It's under the centre of the dashboard."

Lock darted back and jumped in, slamming his door closed.

"It's a metal plunger," Jack said. "You have to push it back. It takes some force."

Lock reached under there, fiddled, then gritted his teeth. Something metallic clicked into place. He pressed the starter. The starter motor whined, but the engine did not fire. He looked out as he pressed it again.

Two creatures at the hedge were trying to help the first one to get over the semi-flattened part of the blackthorn. It staggered then fell clumsily into the mess of spiked branches.

Finally, the starter motor produced a cough of combustion, whined again, then the engine turned. It produced a horrible knocking sound. Amber warnings lit up the control instruments on the dashboard.

Lock glanced out of his side window. Now the two creatures that were still standing were attempting to help the other one to its feet as it tried to untangle itself from the thorny branches on the ground.

The 4x4 coughed, sputtered and pulled only slowly away, deflated front tyres making squishy noises through the grass.

"Which way? Where are we?" Lock demanded. The field rose to a brow up ahead.

"Go right a bit," Jack answered from the back. "There should be a gate to the next field."

Lock hauled the wheel, putting his foot down. The car continued ambling along in second gear as its engine coughed, knocked and sputtered. "Any other injuries?" he asked Gwenda. "Any pain anywhere?"

"My right ankle is a bit numb," she answered. "Slipped off the brake."

Lock glanced over his shoulder. "How about you, Jack?"

"Whiplash in my neck, but I'm okay."

A field gate came into sight when the car topped the brow. It was open. Lock adjusted the steering as gravity increased speed on the downward slope. He changed up into third. The engine struggled, nearly stalled, so he hastily put it back into second.

"Maybe you should have shot them," Ventriloquist Jack said from the back.

"They weren't really doing anything hostile," Lock answered. "Would have been a waste of ammunition."

"What if they get back in that car and turn off into the fields through one of the gates?" Jack countered.

Gwenda mumbled something as she pressed a dressing to her face.

"How's the bleeding?" Lock asked her, ignoring the question from Jack.

"Under control," Gwenda answered, "but I feel sick."

418

The 4x4 rolled into the deserted farmyard with a distinct clunking sound. Its deflated front tyres thumped at the wheel arches when the car began to make a turn towards the access lane.

Feeling the resistance, Lock was forced to steer wide. The car stubbornly headed for the low farmhouse wall. He halted, put it in reverse, then backed up a bit, hauling heavily on the steering wheel.

This time, moving forward, he was able to make the turn; the exit lane from the farm was just ahead. Then the engine stalled. The car jerked with a thump as it halted, still in gear.

The ignition whined. Nothing happened. It whined again for a few seconds before degenerating into a clicking sound.

Lock got out, glancing up the yard for any signs of pursuit. It was clear. He opened Gwenda's door and started helping her out. Jack Thomas jumped out of the back and moved to the rear to open the hatch.

"Just the samples in the case," Lock told him. "Dump everything else out of it, but we need those samples."

Gwenda stumbled when she put weight on her feet. Lock held her steady, his worried eyes looking into hers.

"Oh shit," Ventriloquist Jack now cursed. He pointed. "Look over there."

Above the visible horizon, a huge object moved across the sky. The haze of distance obscured its detail, but it was shaped like a sphere with its top and bottom flattened. Dozens of cylinder craft in a curved line ahead of it were dwarfed by its size.

"It's a bloody fleet," Gwenda groaned. "Which way is it headed?"

"Going inland, I think, not this way," Jack answered.

"We need to get moving," Lock urged, still holding Gwenda to support her. "How's your ankle?"

Gwenda gasped when he let go of her and she put weight on it. "I'm okay." But she leaned against the 4x4, the skin around her eyes already darkening into a red bruise.

Lock reached inside the car then handed Gwenda's weapon to her, before turning his attention to Jack Thomas.

The man had a distinctly alarmed and worried expression as he came from behind the car. He was carrying the aluminium case.

"Can you manage that, and support Gwenda?" Lock asked him.

"Sure, it's light enough, but it's a heck of a hike on foot."

"Forty minutes," Lock said as he and Jack got either side of Gwenda. She held their arms and issued a short gasp of pain as they began walking.

"It's at least an hour's walk from here, if you're fit," Jack said. "It takes me a lot longer than that with breaks. And Gwenda's injured."

Lock glanced over his shoulder as they headed up the farm lane. Now the yard behind them was no longer in sight. He heard something. "Wait," he cautioned. "Listen."

They halted. It was a distant, rattling, knocking sort of engine sound, fading out with changes in the breeze. It grew marginally louder as it revved, accompanied by a faint but distinct squeal of metal.

"What the hell is that?" Ventriloquist Jack whispered through tight lips.

"I'd know that engine sound anywhere," Lock said. "It's Maldwyn's digger, part of the roadblock on the stretch to the main road. They've got it going."

"Shit," Gwenda Evans cursed.

"Keep moving," Lock encouraged her. Both men gripped Gwenda's arms tightly to take more of her weight. She gritted her teeth and limped as they began walking again, this time a little faster. The farm lane curved upwards ahead of them between high hedgerows. Another squeal of metal scraping metal came from the distance behind them.

-o-

"I'm trying," Kyle said exasperatedly in the duplicate safe house. He held a controller, stick pressed forward, thumb-tip white.

There was an image of dense pine trees on the TV screen. Its viewpoint was moving backwards.

Caycey Jones leaned over the back of Kyle's chair. Hardcastle and Banes peered at the screen from beside him. Norton was crouched by his side.

"It just keeps moving backwards on its own," Kyle now added. "Maybe a glitch in the hand controller, I don't know. But if I turn it around and move that way, it's okay."

Now the image rotated. It moved forward through the trees until it came to a halt at what was clearly the forestry road somewhere below the compound.

"Okay," Jones said, his finger rubbing an eyebrow. "It seems there's something inbuilt putting limits on how far you can go with it. Try going vertical."

Kyle leaned forward, staring at the screen. "I'll try, but that's glitchy as well. The x-button was taking it up, but I think moving the right stick around to aim it has screwed my orientation. There's nothing to centre it against. I think I might have triggered a combo."

Now the image swayed, lurched to one side then plunged into the dirt forestry track. The screen went black.

"It's gone underground again," Hardcastle observed.

"Which is weird," Kyle said, "because it was fine when I moved it through the tunnels to get it out there." Kyle turned in his chair and offered the hand controller towards Hardcastle. "Why don't you have a go, Mister Hardcastle?"

"No way," the scientist responded. "You're the expert on that thing, but I think you might be right about key combinations. Why don't you try some?"

"I don't know," Kyle said. He glanced at Jones. "Should I?"

"Sure, go ahead. We can always reboot and start again if you can't regain control."

Kyle pressed buttons at random. The TV screen image turned from blank black to a rainbow of flowing colours, with rotating shapes moving in patterns.

"What the hell," Kyle complained, puzzled.

"Try some different combos," Jones suggested calmly.

Kyle did so. Nothing happened. He pressed more buttons, but still no change. Three-dimensional rotating shapes moved in seemingly random but complex patterns on the screen.

-o-

Ventriloquist Jack halted a few paces up from the barrier on the forestry track. Slouched over, Gwenda held his arm. They watched as Lock lowered the barrier. He moved along with the pole, sliding his hand across its top towards the receiving post on the other side.

"Keep walking if you can," he called out as he fiddled with a bunch of keys.

From a distance, there was a loud thump, followed by the sound of metal groaning as though it was being dragged across hard ground. Lock fixed the padlock into place.

"Do you think that barrier will delay them much if they come this way?" Gwenda called out. Her face was now a rainbow of dark colours around her eyes and swollen nose.

Lock hurried back to her side. "It'll slow them down if they come in cars. But they could get out and walk, or even run."

"I don't know if I could run," Gwenda said. She now had a distinct slur to her speech. Lock grabbed her arm. They got moving again. Gwenda grimaced from pain in her ankle.

"We'll just have to shoot them if they get too close," Lock said. "We'll be fine, you'll see."

The trio moved up the slope to the first bend in the forestry track. It was quiet here; insects buzzed. But there was a distant hum of noise, barely perceptible through the dampening effect of the thick trees around them: road noise, then the popping sounds of tyres against gravel.

Lock glanced back, then froze. The lead car of a line of them had halted at the barrier. Those waiting behind it extended beyond sight in a queue. It went all the way around the bend onto the farmland lane. Ventriloquist Jack and Gwenda observed this as well. Car doors opened down there.

"Keep moving," Lock said. They picked up the pace, but Gwenda took a sharp intake of breath from pain.

"They're just standing there," Ventriloquist Jack said as he glanced back again.

Four figures were motionless immediately on the other side of the barrier, staring at it. Others stood beside cars, purple eyes aimed up the forestry road.

The trio paused to look back when they reached higher ground on a bend. Lock lifted his binoculars. Jack supported Gwenda's weight.

"What the hell are they doing?" Lock muttered, baffled. The magnified image revealed that three of the figures were struggling to get something out of the back of the lead car.

A fourth figure carried some hoses to the barrier. Now Lock saw the other three finally drag a cylinder from the car. "Oh shit," Lock said. "Get moving."

"What?" Jack Thomas demanded.

"They've got oxyacetylene gear. Whatever they are, they're clever and resourceful."

"I'm getting dizzy," Gwenda complained as she limped painfully between the two men. "Something's not right."

"It's okay," Lock soothed. "Once we get around this bend behind the trees, we'll head off into the forestry."

The slur in Gwenda's speech was now more pronounced. "We'll never get to the compound that way. How much ammunition have you got?"

"Sixty rounds," Lock answered, "plus nine in my pistol."

"I'm the same," Gwenda said weakly as she struggled to walk.

Lock glanced worriedly at her. "Once we get to the top of this rise, the road gets narrow, steep slope on the left below it and a cutting on the right. We could make a stand and stop them there."

"Sounds like a desperate plan," Ventriloquist Jack responded as he glanced back towards the barrier. "They haven't got it lit yet by the looks of it. They're not cutting anything so far, at least. Barrier's still closed." But even as Jack spoke, there was a bright blue flash from down there. Sparks rained out of melting steel. Jack's face turned grim. "Now they are."

The three of them hurried up the slope, Lock and Jack virtually lifting Gwenda's feet off the ground and dragging her along. The two men were panting for breath so much, they did not hear the vehicle coming from around the next bend above them.

Lock and Jack halted with expressions of absolute horror and defeat. A minibus bore down towards them, before skidding to a halt.

Emily Norton's and Dimitri's anxious faces appeared in its windscreen. Dimitri swiftly dropped out of the passenger side with a semi-automatic rifle slung from his shoulder. Hardcastle and Banes got out of the back. Norton revved the engine.

"Oh, thank God," Gwenda whispered, before allowing her eyes to close as the three men sprinted to help them. She went limp.

"Quickly," Dimitri urged.

"How did you know?" Jack asked him as he helped to support Gwenda's weight.

"Never mind that," the Russian said. "Get in the bus."

Banes and Hardcastle grabbed Gwenda by the arms and legs either side of her. Lock supported her head as they carried her to the vehicle.

Dimitri gripped Ventriloquist Jack's arm and hurried him along with his aluminium case.

The Russian turned when they reached the minibus, eyes fixed and alert down the sloping dirt road, hands holding the assault rifle at the ready.

Lock finally let go of Gwenda as Banes and Hardcastle pulled her up into the vehicle. He quickly raised his binoculars. He could just see part of the barrier down there.

"They've cut the wrong end," he told Dimitri. "Not so clever then. Now they're trying to lift the heavy part of the barrier with the padlock still attached to the post the other end of it."

"They've cut the barrier, but how?" Dimitri asked.

"Oxyacetylene."

"Okay, get in the bus," Dimitri said. "Let's get out of here."

Norton reversed the minibus on the sloping bend. She narrowly managed to make enough of a turn to be able to drive back up it.

In the rear, a worried Lock supported Gwenda's sagging form on a passenger seat. Her eyes were closed.

"Stay awake," Lock urged. He patted her cheek.

"Who or what were you running from?" Dimitri demanded from the front. He was holding his rifle cowboy-style, its stock resting on his upper leg.

In the passenger seats, Banes glanced at Lock, expecting an answer, but the man was preoccupied with Gwenda. The skin either side of the bruising on her face was now a deathly grey pallor, between streaks of dried blood.

Ventriloquist Jack glared from where he was nursing his neck in the back. "Whatever they once were, they're not human," he told the Russian. "There's thousands of them and apparently they can drive cars and operate machinery. There's also a fleet of alien craft, headed God knows where."

"We saw those," Norton commented as she drove, "just before we spotted you on foot. How's Gwenda?"

"Not good, barely conscious," Lock answered, gently shaking his partner's shoulder. "Stay awake."

Gwenda groaned but her eyes remained shut.

"*How* did you spot us?" Ventriloquist Jack asked. The minibus was now climbing the bend beyond the turn-off to the hidden waterfall.

"Kyle discovered a new trick from the technology down below," Norton answered as she steered. "We've now got limited but useful surveillance of the surface. How are *you*, Mister Thomas?"

"I'm fine," Jack answered. "But do any of you have medical training? It's Gwenda that's injured. She took a heck of a bang to her face."

"How did it happen?" Dimitri asked as he looked back at the woman. "I've got some paramedic training."

Lock studied Gwenda with tears in his eyes, his face close to hers as he held her. Yet his voice remained calm. "She's drifting in and out of consciousness. Severe concussion at the very least. But she might have worse. She was way too close to the steering wheel when the airbag went off."

Jones sat forward in his chair in the duplicate safe house office. Kyle eased the thumb-stick on his controller. The image on the TV screen rotated smoothly to follow the minibus up the compound track. The security gate closed behind the vehicle.

"Okay, they're safe for now," Jones said. "See if you can get it back along the forestry road so we can take another look at that barrier area."

Kyle's eyes were wide, unblinking. The image swiftly moved down the compound, rising over the gate, then banked over to the left. It then swooped downhill along the track.

"You seem to have the hang of it now, but take it steady," Jones warned in a soft voice.

"Ah, sure," Kyle responded, easing back on one of the controls.

The barrier area at the bottom of the forestry road became distantly visible as the image halted.

"That as far as it will go?" Jones asked, leaning forward.

"Yeh," Kyle answered, "which is strange because it went a lot further before."

"Indeed," Jones said, now getting off his seat and easing closer to the TV screen on his knees. "It might be something to do with the proximity of those people, if they are people."

"Well they're not zombies," Kyle said seriously. "Not if they can drive cars. Now look at them, they're lifting something from the ground."

"That's the barrier, I think," Jones agreed. "They must have cut it somehow. And what's that group doing?" He pointed a finger close to the screen.

Kyle tilted his head. "Three, maybe four of them carrying something to the first car. Maybe what they used to zap the barrier."

Both stared at the screen. The American looked distinctly worried.

Kyle appeared calm but puzzled. Then his eyes widened. "Here they come." The first car was moving forward. The screen image backed away from it. "I'm not doing that," he told Jones. "It's moving on its own again."

"Okay," Jones said. "Let's get it back inside the compound and facing the gate. See if that's where they're headed."

"Don't like the sound of that," Kyle said. The image turned. It sped above the ground back up the forestry slopes. "If they can zap that barrier, they might be able to zap their way in here. Who or what are they, Mister Jones? And those ships we saw in the sky earlier... Have they come from those?"

"We'll find out more when Mister Lock and the others get back," the American answered. "But try not to worry. This place is very secure."

"I hope so," Kyle said, raising his eyebrows. "Those things seem pretty determined, if you ask me."

-o-

Taking the lead in the miners' tunnel, Ventriloquist Jack had a support collar strapped around his neck. He carried the now battered aluminium case in one hand. A lamp lit the way from his other hand.

Booted feet thumped the stone floor behind him. Gwenda was unconscious on a mountain rescue stretcher. There was a restraining collar around her neck. A clear plastic tube, held in place with surgical tape, stuck out of her mouth. Norton awkwardly squeezed the bulbous respirator attached to it as she hurried alongside the stretcher.

Wearing miners' helmets and lamps, Lock and Dimitri had the two rear corners either side of Gwenda's head. Hardcastle and Banes carried the load at the front.

"She's going blue," Lock warned. They put the stretcher down. Jack halted up ahead, looked back worriedly, shining his lamp at them.

Now Norton was leaning over, pumping the respirator as hard as she could. Lock's hands interrupted hers. He took over. "She needs oxygen."

"She could do with something like propofol to reduce cranial pressure," Dimitri advised.

"She should also be in hospital," Lock said grimly. "But we have neither. Hyperventilating her is all we've got." He was pumping the ventilator as fast as it re-inflated.

"Your hands are stronger than mine," Norton told Lock. She eased between him and the tunnel wall. "You do that. I'll help with the stretcher."

"Okay, lift," Lock demanded. "Let's get moving again. Her colour's a bit better."

Weapon slung over his shoulder, Lock walked crablike but rapidly alongside the stretcher, pumping at the ventilator with both hands. Covered in sweat and bright red, his face bore an expression of fear and hopelessness.

"Not far now," Ventriloquist Jack called from ahead of them.

The breach area, with its aged concrete floor, rusted bolts, and the old rockfall, was dimly illuminated by the high-tech wall glowing through the shaped entry.

Echoing footsteps and lights approached along the miners' tunnel. Ventriloquist Jack arrived. He turned around, then kept to one side as the others arrived breathlessly with the stretcher.

They eased it through the shaped entrance. Lock continued pumping air into Gwenda's lungs.

Dimitri and the others set her down on the glassy floor in there. The Russian then went down on his knees to take Gwenda's pulse from her wrist. "Very weak and irregular."

Lock continued pumping the ventilator. "Put something under the head of the stretcher. Keep it elevated."

"We need to get her on the train and back to the village," Norton said. She lifted and held the end of the stretcher a few inches from the floor. Banes helped her. "There must be an oxygen cylinder down there somewhere," Norton added.

"Wait a minute," Lock said. "Look at the floor."

The blue floor around the stretcher had changed colour. A faint circle of green swiftly turned yellow, before settling into a dark, almost red circular shape.

Lock inclined his head and nodded at the others. "Now lift it and see what happens."

The others complied. Ventriloquist Jack stared with a mix of wonderment and concern as the coloured area appeared to react. It tracked the movement of the stretcher when it was lifted from the floor. Then he noticed a yellow glow around his own feet and those of Andy Lock's.

"I think this place is trying to heal her," Lock said, now with some hope in his face. "Let's get her on the train thing." His hands were still busy with the plastic bulb, squeezing air into Gwenda's lungs.

-o-

Hefin Gwynedd walked along the circular road under the huge dome of stars. Pero trotted cheerfully beside him.

Up ahead, a group of people were gathered at an area that approximated the village centre in this environment of duplicated buildings.

As he got closer, Hefin noticed it was Betty Lewis who was the object of attention. She seemed to be pontificating to a dozen or so people. Some appeared to agree with whatever she was saying. Others shook their heads.

Bibby Libby looked close to hanging her head in shame at her mother's behaviour, but she perked up when she spotted Hefin and his dog. Bibby snapped her fingers; Pero galloped eagerly towards her.

"What's up?" Hefin asked when he reached the small crowd.

"What's it to you?" Betty Lewis shot back immediately. "You seem to feel right at home down here along with all them in that house, and your pal Jack Thomas. We, on the other hand, have no intention of staying here any longer than we have to. We want to know what's going on."

"So why don't you just go to the surface on your own and have a look for yourself," Hefin said. "That broomstick of yours should get you there as quick as you like."

"And that's the best we should expect from a nutter like him," Betty Lewis told her small audience. "So, let's go and knock at their door, shall we?"

Half of her tiny audience cheered agreement; the others demurred. Some glanced at Hefin.

"I'm so ashamed," Bibby Libby quietly told Hefin. She was still crouched, stroking Pero's head. "But she can't help it."

"I know," Hefin said. He watched Betty Lewis, followed by her husband and son, together with four others, as they marched over the first bridge. "But I shouldn't have been rude to her. I'm sorry about that."

"So he should be, shouldn't he, Pero?" Bibby Libby answered brightly to the dog. Pero gave a woof of agreement.

Hefin allowed the corner of his mouth to crease into a contemplative smile. His eyes were fixed on the group of seven militants, now crossing the second bridge. "Let's see what happens," he said, then set off at a brisk pace in pursuit.

Some of the bungalow inhabitants were out in their duplicate front gardens when Betty Lewis strode past. She noticed they were looking towards the dome entrance. Responding to this, the woman halted where the glassy blue path joined the duplicate village street.

Ventriloquist Jack was coming along the path, neck support elevating his chin, aluminium case bumping his legs as he walked. He looked exhausted.

Behind him, four people carried someone on a stretcher, with a grim-faced Andy Lock hunched over it as he walked alongside, pumping at a respirator with both hands.

Now Betty Lewis froze as she saw Gwenda's unconscious form: the bruised, bloodstained face, clothes matted with blood.

Betty stood aside without a word as she watched them hurry the stretcher into the safe house. She stared with what looked like disbelief at the still open front door when they went out of sight inside.

"Maybe we should leave it till later," her husband said. He took hold of her hand.

"Oh my God, poor Gwenda," Betty Lewis whispered as her internal anger transmuted into something else. "I think she's dead."

Betty had begun crying in the short time it took her husband to get his arm over her shoulder. "Let's get you back to the house," he coaxed.

Hefin Gwynedd's face was fixed in a glum seriousness as he saw Bibby Libby hurry over to comfort her mother. Pero looked up at him and issued a quiet but distinctive whine from alongside his feet.

The man and dog watched the Lewis family head back towards the duplicate bridges.

ELEVEN

Caycey Jones caught his breath as he topped one of the ramps into the elliptical dome. Close behind him, Hardcastle carried the battered aluminium case. Puffing worse than Jones, Ventriloquist Jack arrived last. He was still wearing a support collar, face haggard and exhausted.

Like the others, Jack's eyes hunted for something or someone. He glanced at the oversized seats and dead consoles, before joining the American at the top of the amphitheatre steps. There was no sign of White Hair down there.

Jones frowned, rotated his bulky form, eyes scanning other areas. But it was Hardcastle who pointed a finger. "I think it might be over there."

Jones led them back past the barrier protecting the drop into the sunken atrium. Here the floor extended on the same level towards the rear of this place. Dim light and rows of what looked like control banks with fixed chairs combined to obscure that area.

Ventriloquist Jack stared at one of the console positions as he passed it. "Whoever used these seats must have been ten feet tall."

"We have noticed," Jones agreed without sarcasm, before pointing. "Over there." Still some distance from them, White Hair stood alongside a chest-height barrier.

"Remember that getting it to help Gwenda is our first priority," Jack said.

"Absolutely," Jones agreed.

The trio continued. But as they passed more consoles and oversized seats, White Hair moved around the other side of the barrier and began to descend.

"Oi," Jack shouted. "We need to talk to you."

But the thing ignored him, its head disappearing downwards.

When they reached the barrier, they found a ramp behind it to a level below. Jones picked up his pace. At the bottom was a wide corridor, with three pairs of closed doors either side along its length, before it hit a dead-end with another door in its centre. White Hair was halfway along. The figure turned off into a doorway that slid open.

"Don't let him get away," Jack said.

"I don't think it's trying to escape us," Hardcastle told him.

"Gwenda's dying, if she isn't dead already," Jack argued. "And she's like that because of him and his selective myopia. For goodness' sake, the technology Kyle discovered... If it can do that, why wasn't it gathering the information itself?"

"That might be a valid question," Jones said. "But let's try to keep it calm and diplomatic."

They found White Hair inside a chamber that could have housed two tennis courts. The humanlike figure turned to face Jones and held out both hands. Jones promptly took the aluminium case off Hardcastle and delivered it into the thing's grasp.

The longest wall was lined with metallic, vertically oriented cylinders. Each had a seam running down its centre and was taller than a man. The end wall, towards which White Hair turned with the aluminium case, had a line of metal drawers. There were blank, screen-shaped indentations above each of these.

"We have urgent need to communicate with you," Jones told White Hair as a drawer slid outwards. "One of our companions is severely injured. Can you help her?"

"We are aware," it replied in its monotone, electronic voice. "Our systems are attempting to repair her, but she requires more information."

With a fluid motion, White Hair placed the aluminium case inside the drawer, which then immediately slid shut.

"Do you mean *you* require more information?" Jones asked, puzzled.

"Negative," White Hair responded. "It is the injured entity that requires more information."

"This is bullshit," Ventriloquist Jack said. "You can duplicate things from the surface in detail and we *know* you can heal us. I can feel my neck injury getting better every minute since I returned to this place."

"Your individual entity has sufficient information for repairs to be effected," it blandly told Jack.

Turning to Hardcastle, Jack said, "What the hell does it mean by that?"

Hardcastle shook his head. "I have no idea. The only thing that comes to mind is the fact you said the mountain has been talking to you all your life."

"Your friend with the old televisions told me the same thing," Jones added. "But I've never heard anything like that from Missus Evans."

Jack considered this. Then, with a puzzled face, he said, "I wonder… Maybe it's something like the primer effect."

"Like on your generator and those copper coils of yours?" Hardcastle suggested.

Jones raised his eyebrows. "Quantum physics?"

"Observation and intent," Ventriloquist Jack muttered, still thinking, still puzzled. "Maybe this technology's abilities to heal are not on a biological level at all. Maybe they only work if quantum conditions are favourable."

"Or adjusted to be favourable by observation, maybe," Jones said. Now the American turned to face White Hair. "What measures are required in order for our injured companion to be healed?"

White Hair lifted a hand and pointed at the wall. One of the indented screen shapes glowed into life.

Ventriloquist Jack stared at it for a moment. Realisation animated his eyes and forehead. He turned and hurried to the door, ripping off and discarding his neck support collar as he exited through it.

Some of the villagers had gathered on the chamber's circuitous road outside the duplicate safe house. Small groups conducted hushed conversations, their eyes observing the open front door.

Heads turned to watch when Banes came hurrying along from the first bridge. He carried a canvas shopping bag stuffed with something, including cables sticking out of it, a flat-screen TV slung awkwardly under his other arm.

Three people at the end of the driveway stood aside to let him pass.

Banes went into the safe house and paused in the hallway, looking into a rarely used lounge.

Lock and Norton, together with Mair Ellis and the Russian, were by the side of Gwenda's unconscious form. She lay on a thin mattress on top of a dining table pushed up against a wall. Chin held up by a neck brace, Gwenda's head and shoulders were propped up on several pillows. The ventilator and its tube had been removed. Her mouth was open, lips flecked with vomit. A blood trickle had coagulated on an earlobe. Under the table below her, the carpeted floor glowed red.

"Any change?" Banes called from the doorway.

Lock remained crouched over Gwenda's side, holding her hand. He did not respond. A yellow glow surrounded Lock's feet and overlapped the red below the table.

Nearby, Dimitri shook his head towards Banes.

Norton also shook her head.

Mair's face was streaked with tears as she wobbled her hands at him in a signal of pessimistic uncertainty.

Banes sighed and went into the office across the hallway.

Here Kyle's unblinking eyes stared at the TV screen. It showed an image of the compound gate on the surface. The viewpoint was from somewhere near the door into the mountain.

Miiko sat next to him, assault rifle cradled in her arms.

"Anything?" Banes asked.

"Nothing so far," Miiko answered.

Banes placed the flat-screen TV on the floor. He then dragged a work table to a wall near the duplicate grandfather clock.

"You got one then," Kyle said, eyes still fixed to his screen.

"Yeh," Banes answered. He pulled cables and a games console from the canvas bag. "Kid didn't want to part with it, even though it doesn't work. But I managed to convince both him and his mum." Banes commenced plugging cables into the console.

Miiko stood up. "You two okay now?"

"Yes, thank you," Banes told her.

"I will go back to Kikuko then."

Outside, the concerned villagers had grown in number. Three children came to a halt on their bikes. They fired questions at some of the adults.

The children's eyes suddenly lit up in fascination. They had seen Miiko coming out of the safe house, carrying her weapon. All eyes tracked her as she headed towards the dome entrance.

She was halfway along the blue glowing path when Ventriloquist Jack came jogging in an ape-like gait from the entrance. He panted and wheezed, face crimson and covered in sweat.

Miiko stood aside to let him pass. He did not return her polite greeting.

Jack's anxious eyes were fixed on the villagers up ahead. He began a hoarse shout: "Has anyone..." But this immediately degenerated into a low-pitched groan as he halted and bent over, coughing. Clasping his upper legs for support, Jack fought for breath.

Still some distance away, the villagers stared at him. It was a few seconds before Jack was able to recommence towards them. This time he walked.

"Has anyone seen Elin Lewis?" he shouted, triggering another coughing fit.

Heads shook; some faces were puzzled.

"Someone go fetch her," Jack demanded between coughs. "It's very important."

"If you mean Bibby Libby, she's over there," a boy called back, pointing.

Elin Lewis was on a bike, pedalling furiously as she came over the bridge.

"Good girl," Jack whispered to himself, then got back to simply breathing.

-o-

In the room under the elliptical dome, multiple screens lit the wall above the drawer shapes. Jones and Hardcastle studied them with baffled expressions but ignored a screen showing an image of Elin Lewis.

"I have no idea what to make of this," Jones said.

An image resembling a multicoloured, tightly coiled pipe cleaner with clusters of spikes rotated on one of the screens. Symbols, almost hieroglyphic in shape, cascaded by its side.

White Hair faced another direction entirely, head tilted upward as though gazing at the ceiling. "It is information from the biological samples," it answered in its dull, electronic voice.

"Here we go again," Hardcastle said. "Repeating itself. Seems to need a question with a format and precision we can only guess at before we get anything sensible out of it."

"You try," Jones told him.

Facing White Hair, Hardcastle asked, "What conclusions have you drawn from the biological samples we gave you?"

"Analysis is required," it answered.

"How long before analysis is complete?" Hardcastle pressed.

"Analysis has been completed," it immediately responded.

"Contradicting itself again," Jones said. "We're going in ever decreasing and conflicting circles." He pointed at one of the screens. "That one looks vaguely familiar, but I can't fathom why."

"We need a biologist," Hardcastle said. "I think we can assume we're seeing something microscopic, maybe a cell or even smaller. Maybe it's DNA."

438

Jones looked dubious. "Not my field. For all we know, it could be a chemical compound or even an energy signature. The imagery is useless to us unless we know how to interpret it. And those symbols are completely alien."

"You asked us for more data from outside," Hardcastle said to White Hair. "Do you now have sufficient data?"

"Analysis has been completed," it responded.

"Contradicting itself yet again," Hardcastle observed.

Jones's baffled expression suddenly eased and his eyes lit up with a thought. "Ah... Have you completed *interpretation* of the data analysis?"

"No," White Hair said.

"A straight answer at last," Hardcastle muttered.

Now White Hair abruptly paced towards the door. "Your attention is required," it announced, moving with a curious fluidity. "You will follow this interface."

Jones raised his eyebrows. The two men followed the humanlike figure through the doorway.

"We'd better ask it about security again," Hardcastle said. "We're blind down here. No idea what they're observing from the house."

"I'm acutely aware of that," Jones agreed. "They'll send Banes or Norton to fetch us if those things show themselves."

"Might take them a little while to find us," Hardcastle pointed out.

"True," Jones said, "but I'm pretty certain that our friend here sees whatever we see on the gadget Kyle discovered. And if we can send an invisible golf-ball-sized camera out there, then it's probable White Hair can send out a whole bunch of them."

The door at the end of the corridor slid open. The interior beyond it was small and circular in shape. Hardcastle followed White Hair inside, but Jones hesitated on the threshold.

With some anxiety, Jones pointed. There was a vertical column of symbols on the inner wall. "Looks like an elevator."

"And ten levels," Hardcastle observed, mentally counting the symbols. He took a mobile phone out of his pocket and aimed it at them. The phone simulated a camera shutter noise.

439

White Hair faced Jones.

Jones took a breath and stepped back outside. "Before we go any further, we need to talk to you about the creatures on the surface."

"Proceed," White Hair responded.

"They appear able to operate machinery," Jones began. "We believe they could operate equipment to gain access to this place."

"This is known to us," White Hair said. "Continue."

"We alone cannot prevent that access," Jones told it.

"This is known. Steps are being taken to attempt an improvement in security."

"Are those steps likely to be successful?" Jones asked.

"Unknown at this time," the thing answered.

Jones now looked keenly into its glassy eyes. "We have discovered an ability to remotely observe what is going on outside. Are you aware of this? Are you also monitoring what is going on outside?"

"We are," White Hair answered. "The radius of monitoring is locally restricted to avoid potential detection. At the present time, no approach to your surface entrance has been observed."

"That's good news, so far at least," Jones said to Hardcastle.

"We will proceed," White Hair insisted. "You will enter this vehicle."

Jones hesitated, clearly reluctant, but stepped back inside. The door slid shut behind him.

The bottom symbol on the curved wall lit up, followed almost immediately by the door sliding open again, this time to darkness. Light from the elevator illuminated an area of metallic floor outside.

The darkness was short-lived. The walls and ceiling of a cavernous space suddenly glowed with light.

White Hair stepped out onto a gangway suspended across the ceiling. It approached a waist-height barrier at the edge. The two men followed.

Jones and Hardcastle both took a short intake of breath as they looked down from the barrier. "We haven't even begun to explore this place," Jones said.

Hardcastle took in other gangways deep below. These crisscrossed spaces between gigantic, clear-sided tanks. The tanks were full of what looked like water.

Jones observed this, then gazed along the gangway. It stretched a length equivalent to two football pitches, before going through an opening in a bulkhead.

"Must be a three-hundred-foot drop," Hardcastle said, still looking down from the dizzying height. "And there are nine other levels above us."

"You will pay attention," White Hair announced in its expressionless tone. "Energy storage is now complete. Power from the planetary magnetic field is no longer required."

"That's good, I think," Jones said.

"You will accompany this interface," White Hair then told them, before it headed back towards the elevator.

Jones and Hardcastle exchanged puzzled eye contact with each other as they followed.

"At least we can now decipher numerals," Hardcastle said inside the elevator as the door slid shut. He pointed at the symbols. "If we live long enough, that is."

When the door opened again, they found the machine had brought them back to the elliptical dome. They stepped out onto a previously unoccupied space overlooking the amphitheatre.

The elevator just stood there, a metallic tubular shape, with no observable moving parts. Jones studied it with curiosity.

"You may now return to the habitat area," White Hair announced. "You will select leaders of your choice. Those chosen must return to this interface when required by us to do so. That is all."

"We *must* talk to you some more about the potential threat from the surface," Jones told it, now with a stern edge to his voice. "You cannot ignore the possibility this threat will occur very soon."

"We are not ignoring it… Steps are being taken in an attempt to improve security."

A clearly frustrated Jones looked at Hardcastle.

"Exactly what steps are you taking to improve security?" Hardcastle asked White Hair.

441

The thing walked away without answering.

Hardcastle glanced questioningly at Jones, who groaned as the two men headed down one of the access ramps into the sunken atrium. "Explosives in the miners' tunnel?" Hardcastle prompted.

"If it's still an option, we seriously need to consider it," Jones answered glumly.

-o-

Ventriloquist Jack leaned forward on a chair in the duplicate safe house lounge. He was seated near the door, eyes pensive but observant.

Her back to him, Bibby Libby stood at the foot of the table. She stared at the unconscious Gwenda Evans lying upon it.

The floor still glowed red below her as Gwenda took shuddering gasps for air. Her body shook. Her mouth opened and closed like a fish out of water.

Desperation in his eyes, Lock eased her to recline more to her side. Gwenda's body relaxed. Her breathing resumed, but it was shallow.

Bibby Libby was nearly in tears. "I knew I had to come here to help her, but I don't know how. It's something to do with the angels... those light orb things."

"Are they here now?" Norton asked.

"Sort of," the girl answered. "But they seem confused and erratic."

Turning his ashen face towards Ventriloquist Jack, Lock asked, "And that's all you got from White Hair?"

"Yeh," Jack answered. "We asked it to tell us what we had to do to get the systems to work for Gwenda. Its response was to show us an image of young Bibby Libby here. Don't give up, kid. Keep trying."

"I am," the teenager said as she tried to remain composed. "I'm picturing the angels healing her, but it's not working."

"Why don't we give Elin some quiet," Mair Ellis suggested in a low voice. She had her hands together as though in prayer.

"We've been doing that, but clearly it's not working," Ventriloquist Jack said. He stood up and approached Bibby Libby, reached out and held her hand, then inclined his head to look into her eyes. "Listen," he said softly. "I'll try to help you, but I think you have to talk to Gwenda, not the light orbs."

"*Talk* to her?"

Jack tapped the side of his head. "With this," he said, then patted his upper stomach. "And this."

Lock's eyes were wide and white as he stared at them. He then watched Emily Norton take Elin's other hand.

"I'll try to help as well," Norton said.

Now Bibby Libby, frail as a bird, changed the expression on her pretty face from despair to determination. She gripped the hands holding hers, then closed her eyes and tilted her head forward.

Gwenda was beginning to go into convulsions when a brilliant white light erupted from the floor. It passed up through both the table and Gwenda's form. She shuddered, her whole body illuminated, facial features reduced to a blur. A desperate wheezing intake of breath, as though surfacing from near-drowning, came from her chest and throat.

White light also passed through Andy Lock. Unaware of this, he gazed desperately at Gwenda, clinging to her hand, as though trying to stop her from leaving this world.

-o-

The carriage centre door slid open. Jones and Hardcastle disembarked into the main tunnel. They were immediately alert.

High on the wall above the side passage entrance, a silvery coil was on the move. It was gradually sliding along, away from the direction of the surface, and above a coil that remained stationary in its original position.

The two men gazed along the tunnel. The stationary coil terminated some distance from them. It seemed the detached part had lifted upwards and was now sliding along the wall, emitting a faint humming noise. The same thing was happening up on the ceiling and on the other side.

Miiko was at the passageway entrance, watching.

"When did all this start?" Jones demanded as they approached.

"About five minutes ago," Miiko answered. "I heard a noise, so came to look. What is it doing?"

"I have no idea," Jones said. "Please continue to observe it." He glanced up at the moving coils before going into the passage. The two men hurried through the first small chamber.

"Maybe it's something to do with improving security?" Hardcastle suggested.

"Let's not go into all that again," Jones said. "I've given up trying to figure out how White Hair thinks and works. Victorian miners accidentally managed to blast their way into this place. Thousands of years earlier, the hostiles somehow disabled it. We need to take action."

Kikuko greeted them at the dome entrance. She was standing sentry with an assault rifle slung over a shoulder. "They happy," she said, pointing a finger.

Villagers, some of them still in groups, others now walking away from the duplicate safe house, seemed to be in cheerful conversation, their demeanour animated.

Jones and Hardcastle hurried in that direction.

Gwenda Evans was sitting upright on the edge of the table when the two men arrived at the safe house lounge. Lock was supporting her shoulders.

"We heard you were better," Hardcastle said. "But I wasn't expecting this. It's amazing."

Jones remained silent, eyes taking in Gwenda's miraculously healthy appearance.

"I need a shower," Gwenda said, voice a low growl. "But they won't let me off this bloody table."

"Her own angels healed her," Bibby Libby told Hardcastle.

Now Gwenda turned, as though noticing the teenager for the first time. "Come here, girl," Gwenda demanded. She had tears in her eyes.

Lock stepped aside. Bibby approached, arms held up as though for a hug. Gwenda clasped the teenager's hands and gazed into her eyes. "No hugs just yet. I stink of puke and sweat but thank you. Thank you with all my heart."

"You're welcome," Bibby said. "But really, it was your own angels that saved you."

A smile lit up Gwenda's wet eyes, cracking the streaks of dried blood below her nose and either side of her mouth. "No, dear, I didn't use my angels. They would have taken me to that other place that's beyond here." She looked at Andy Lock with an expression that seemed apologetic. "I nearly went, you know. It would have been so easy and so wonderful. I actually wanted to go."

"But you didn't," Lock said. "That's all that matters."

"You all called me back," Gwenda said, looking around the room and meeting their eyes with affection. "So I listened to my demon, not my angels. We all need our demon from time to time." She shrugged and let go of Bibby's hands. "But enough of this, I need a shower."

Lock tried to stop her, but she pushed his hands away and got onto the floor, where she stood upright, though unsteadily.

"Take it easy," Lock warned. She now allowed him to support her arm.

"Get me to the shower," Gwenda demanded.

Bibby Libby smiled. She watched Lock escort Gwenda to the hallway. Jones and Hardcastle stepped aside to let them through. Hardcastle patted Gwenda on the shoulder as she passed.

"Well done, kid," Ventriloquist Jack told Bibby Libby.

"And you, Mister Thomas," Emily Norton said.

"That's right," Bibby agreed, looking at Jack. "We couldn't have done it without you."

"But now you can," Jack told her.

"Now we all can, I think," she replied. "Is Kyle here? I think I heard him talking."

Out in the hallway, Lock and Gwenda were climbing the stairs when Kyle called out from the office doorway. "Yo, Missus Evans, glad to see you're better."

"Yo, yourself," Gwenda dismissed, waving her free hand over her shoulder without looking back at him.

"Glad you're better," Banes added, as he appeared at Kyle's side. Gwenda raised her arm again in mute acknowledgement.

"How's monitoring the surface going?" Jones asked them.

Banes and Kyle hurried back into the office.

-o-

Ventriloquist Jack walked alongside Bibby Libby as they went down the driveway outside.

Most of the villagers had dispersed and were headed back to their duplicate homes. Bibby's mother, father and brother, however, were waiting for her on the road.

"Why don't you head home?" Jack called out to them. "Elin will be along shortly. I need to talk to her for a minute. We'll be right behind you."

Ignoring him, Betty Lewis looked at her daughter. "Are you okay?"

"I'm fine, mam," Bibby Libby answered. "You all go ahead. I'll be home in a minute."

"But there's still danger, isn't there, Mister Thomas?" the mother asked with a remarkably polite tone.

"Unfortunately, that's true," Jack answered. "But the people in there and the technology in this place are working on it. We'll be okay, you'll see." He then nodded in a friendly fashion and motioned with his hands for her to move on.

But the woman did not budge. She lowered her head and averted her eyes as though ashamed. "I was hoping to talk to Mister Lock, and to Gwenda if she's well enough. I feel I owe them both an apology…"

Tears came. Her husband put his arm over her shoulder. The son, Ken, raised his eyes in irritation.

Jack smiled. "There'll be plenty of time for that when things have settled down. Go to your duplicate home and try to relax. Ken will make you a nice cup of tea, won't you, Ken?"

446

"Sure," the teenager said. "Let's go home, mam."

Betty Lewis looked up. Her demeanour altered, eyes narrowing when she saw Wyn Ellis watching from the B&B bay window. Mair Ellis arrived beside him and peered out at her as well.

Betty turned around, extricating her shoulders from her husband's arm. "Right then," she said haughtily. "Home it is."

The husband sighed. He followed her as she marched away towards the bridge. Ken reluctantly went after them.

"What you did in there was very important," Jack told Bibby Libby as they strolled in the same direction.

"It wasn't just me. It was all of us."

"Most of the rest of them are not aware of it," Jack said softly. "But you are. You were the channel for what happened. I couldn't have done it. Even if you don't fully understand it, you're awake to what we really are, aren't you?"

"What we really are is maybe a toe in the water that thinks it's all there is," Bibby said with a grin.

"That's a good one," Jack said. "A toe that falsely believes that it's autonomous. I use foot analogies myself."

Bibby looked up at him. They were now crossing the first bridge. "I didn't know you were spiritual, Mister Thomas."

He issued a subdued laugh. "I wouldn't describe myself with that word. But do you know what I think? I think our minds are just part of a quantum universe, but you can call it spiritual if you want. Do you sometimes wake up from a place where you knew everything, and it was so simple it made you want to laugh?"

"Wow," Bibby Libby responded. "All the time. Trouble is, as soon as I wake up, it sort of vanishes, and a split second later I've forgotten it all."

"What about your hands when that happens?"

"You really do know this stuff," the teenager told him. "My hands are the first things I can move when I wake up from something like that."

"It was the same with Gwenda when she came back," Jack said as they crossed the second bridge. "I was watching. First hint I had she was going to be okay was when she gripped Andy Lock's hand."

Bibby halted. Up ahead, at the radial turn-off, Betty Lewis waited, watching them from outside the duplicate chapel.

"What does all of this mean, Mister Thomas?" Bibby asked. "Is there something I'm supposed to do?"

"You know that there is… I'm the same," Jack answered. "We just don't know what it is yet. You'd better go to your mother."

"Okay," the girl said casually, as though dismissing their entire conversation. "Thanks for the chat, Mister Thomas. Be seeing you…" She jogged away towards her waiting mother.

Jack paused for a moment, thinking deeply, before going in the same direction and taking the turn-off towards his house. He glanced up at the huge domed ceiling, the crystal-clear but artificial panorama of stars and nebulae, then put his head down and walked a little faster.

Up ahead, in the distance under the same dome, Hefin Gwynedd sat cross-legged on a patch of grass outside the duplicate *Ponderosa*'s high wall. Pero was by his side.

-o-

"How about you, Kyle?" Norton called from the French doorway in the duplicate safe house. "I could make you a sandwich?"

"No thanks, Miss Norton," Kyle answered without taking his eyes off the TV screen. He was staring, wide-eyed, at an image of the security gate to the compound on the surface. Either side of the track, pine trees swayed gently in a breeze. It was silent; no sound came from the television.

Next to him, Banes watched a blank screen, listening to a second games console hooked up to it. This was buzzing away in fits and starts, its hard drive performing some mysterious process.

"I could do with food," Banes announced; he looked at Kyle. "Could you keep watch on this as well? Let me know when it boots up?"

"Sure," Kyle answered without taking his eyes off his screen.

"Remember to blink," Banes warned.

"Uh, oh, sure." Kyle blinked twice, then went back to his fixed stare.

Banes allowed himself a slight grin at this before he went into the kitchen.

Gwenda Evans was seated at the table. She was eating as though starved. Jones sat on a chair at an angle where he could keep an eye through the French doorway into the office. Lock, Hardcastle and Dimitri sat around the same table watching Gwenda.

Norton checked a frying pan on the cooker hob. "Do you want me to put more eggs on for you?" she asked Gwenda.

"I've had three already," the small woman answered, between chewing, "but I'll have more bacon when it's ready if you don't mind. I've never been so hungry in all my life." She looked around at the others. "Will you lot stop staring at me. I'm trying to eat."

"Seems you're back to normal then," Lock said. He leaned back in his chair, rubbed his shoulder and looked at Caycey Jones. "Still no sign of monsters at the compound?"

"Appears so," Jones answered.

"Hardcastle tells me you might want us to use explosives to collapse the miners' tunnel after all."

"I think we have to be ready to do that if time permits," Jones answered. "Means moving right away, if we're going to do it. Where are the explosives?"

"I stowed them in the LPG compound up top."

"Jesus," the American said, frowning.

"It's okay," Lock told him. "The gas tanks were just for show, for spy satellites. They're all empty."

Gwenda put down her knife and fork. "I'll get ready then."

"Stay where you are," Jones warned. "You're not going anywhere."

She glared, frustrated, but Lock held up a hand. "If anyone's going to do this, it will be me."

Banes sat down with a plate of food. "If anyone is interested in my opinion, I think blowing the miners' tunnel is a really bad idea."

Jones looked at Banes for a moment, then at Lock. "How long would it take them to cut through that steel door with oxyacetylene?"

449

Lock tilted his head, calculating. "It's four inches thick, with ten interlocking frame bars. If they get the oxygen mix right, probably less than half an hour."

"That fast?" Jones said, raising his eyebrows.

"If we do this," Banes put in, "it will be final. We'll all be trapped down here. There'd be no way out if we needed to escape."

"There's nothing out there to escape to, except worm-spitting monsters," Lock quietly told the scientist.

"But White Hair forbade the use of explosives," Banes argued. "It might have very good reasons."

"It also can't or won't tell us how it is trying to make this place safe," Jones pointed out. "There again, it's rearranging the tunnel coils between here and the steps."

Lock sat forward. "Really?"

Jones nodded. "Yep, sliding along nice as pie without any observable mechanism."

"Then maybe it can make other structural adjustments to secure this place," Banes suggested.

"I tend to agree with Banes," Hardcastle said. "Blowing the miners' tunnel poses too many variables. What if there was some sort of chain reaction in materials and structures in the rock that we don't know about? This place is massive. From what I've seen today, the level we're on represents probably less than five percent of the structure. How do we know it doesn't also extend into the mountain in ways beyond what we have seen?"

"How about setting up explosives outside in the compound?" Norton suggested. "Take out these creatures if they look like trying to cut through the door."

"That might delay them a bit," Lock said. "We'd need to find something to use as shrapnel."

"If you don't mind me saying," Dimitri now interjected, "I know I'm a newcomer, but using explosives in any situation that is not strictly planned, assessed and controlled will too often result in unintended consequences."

Jones was pondering this when Kyle's voice rang out from the office: "Heads up. Second console is online."

Gwenda carried on eating as the others went through.

Jones viewed the image on the second TV screen. It showed the front lawn and part of the duplicate safe house from outside. "We appear to have a second drone," he said. "Kyle, I want you to take control of it. Someone else keep watch on the other screen."

Kyle got up from his chair. He glanced around, then back at the TV screen, but none of the others seemed eager to take his place.

"Okay, I'll watch it," Banes volunteered.

Jones shifted a chair. Kyle sat with the second controller gripped in his hands.

Gwenda Evans came to the French doorway, eyes observant, plate in one hand, fork in the other as she continued eating.

"I want you to try something different this time," Jones told Kyle. "Can you go vertical?"

Lock watched the second TV. The point of view on it rose upwards in the dome, quickly passing through the ceiling into a brown murk. Something caught his attention: a hint of movement through the office bay window. They all heard someone shouting from outside. It was Kikuko.

"Mister Jones!"

Jones and Lock were about to head for the hallway when she ran into the office, out of breath. "Something else happen in tunnel," she said between gasps.

"What?" Jones demanded.

"Big wall," she answered. "Big wall coming from floor. You need come and see."

Jones glanced at Lock, then back at the TV screen. Kyle now had the image slowly rotating above the sea. A heavy swell rolled across it. The coast and village were visible in the distance.

At the same time, Banes became animated. "I've got movement. Something's approaching the compound gate."

Now they all looked at that screen.

There was no sound. Through the mesh security gate on the surface, something angular out there grew bigger, before the gate simply disappeared in a blast of white smoke: an explosion without

451

flames. Then the shape came through where the gate had been, quickly becoming clearer in a fog of dust.

It was a flatbed truck. It reversed up the compound track at speed. A black cube the size of a refrigerator rested on its cargo deck.

They saw all this only briefly on the TV before the image pulled back, then blurred as it passed through solid matter. They were left viewing the inside of the steel door from the work tunnel.

"I never touched the controls," Banes said.

"Turns out we didn't have time for explosives after all," Hardcastle observed drily.

Kikuko's eyes widened as she and the others in the office now witnessed another event on the screen. A white flash, another explosion, the brief spectacle of something big, black and circular spinning into the tunnel. Daylight then slanted through a haze of dust. The steel door was gone.

Humanlike silhouettes immediately came through the opening. Then the screen broke up into garbled lines and colours. It went blank.

At the same time, red light pulsed across the office ceiling, accompanied by three loud beeps.

Astonishment turned to anger on Lock's face. He gritted his teeth. "Get the guns."

But Gwenda was already at the kitchen table gathering them.

"Hardcastle, you're with me," Jones instructed, finger pointed at the flashing ceiling. "We've been summoned."

Gwenda thrust a belt and holster at the American. Dimitri accepted an assault rifle from Lock. Norton nervously took hold of one as well.

-o-

Outside, people came from their duplicate bungalows between the safe house and bridge. The dome ceiling was now a murky brown, intermittently flashing bright red.

Mair and Wyn Ellis emerged from the B&B. Lock and Dimitri, followed by Gwenda and Kikuko, sprinted along the short stretch of

452

road in front of the safe house. They then cut across the corner onto the radial path towards the dome entrance. Norton came out next.

"What's happening?" Mair Ellis demanded from her duplicate front lawn.

"Stay inside and lock your doors," Norton called back. She cradled her weapon as she ran along the curving road towards the first bridge, barking the same instructions to those now gawking outside their bungalows.

The red light continued flashing in the dome ceiling as Jones and Hardcastle came out at a slower pace, Jones fastening the buckle on his side-arm belt.

Inside the safe house, Banes patted Kyle's shoulder. "Go look after your gran," the scientist ordered. "Go now... Go on! She'll be scared."

Kyle wrenched his mesmerised eyes away from a TV screen. It showed bobbing waves in the foreground, the real village beyond. And above it, a huge cylindrical object moved in across the sky. An arc of smaller crystal shapes preceded it, rotating first one way, then the other, alternately flashing white and perfect black.

Norton crossed the second bridge. "Go back inside and lock your doors," she shouted at the people outside the chapel. Stunned and bewildered, they were staring at the pulsing red light above them. Norton continued running and turned along the next radial path.

Jones and Hardcastle reached the main tunnel. Miiko and Kikuko had taken up crouched positions against the wall, weapons at the ready.

Up ahead, in the direction of the surface entrance, Dimitri sprinted across the tunnel at an angle. Lock and Gwenda jogged back in the American's direction.

And beyond them, under the flashing red from the ceiling here, a grey wall across the width of the tunnel was rising slowly from the floor. It had already reached the height of a house.

Above it the detached parts of the silvery coils on both walls continued to slide along, as though retreating. The one on the ceiling did the same.

"How thick is that wall?" Jones called to Lock.

"Can't tell," Lock called back. "It's about a quarter of a mile away. There's no point getting any closer to it."

"How long before it's completely closed?"

"Probably hours," Gwenda answered in a shrill voice. "Go and talk to that bloody White Hair thing."

"Yes, ma'am," Jones muttered under his breath. "Okay," he said to Hardcastle. "Let's go."

Both men headed for the waiting train-like vehicle in the tunnel centre. Jones hesitated at its side door as it slid open.

Now Lock and Gwenda had reached the bicycles close by. Dimitri was also returning at a comfortable running speed.

"If we don't make it through this," Jones called to them, "it's been an honour to serve with you."

"Go talk to the bloody thing," Gwenda scolded him. "We'll make it fine, you'll see."

Jones and Hardcastle stepped into the carriage.

"Those things might not be able to get over that rising wall or bulkhead, whatever it is," Hardcastle told Jones inside. "But—"

"I know," Jones said. "Judging by what they did so easily to that steel door and solid rock, they might well be able to blast through it."

The carriage commenced its silent transit. Its ceiling, like every other ceiling in the place, flashed an urgent red warning above their heads.

-o-

Controller gripped in his hands, Banes watched the blank TV monitor as the games console booted up once more. At last the green screen faded to show video from the front of the duplicate safe house.

Banes tilted the control sticks with his thumbs.

Like some smoothly moving aircraft simulation, the screen image turned over a wall and sped above the radial path to the dome entrance. It slowed to pass through the first smaller chamber, then into the next.

Banes raised his eyebrows in puzzlement. He saw that the German naval officer's skeleton had been dragged out of the side room on its chair. It was sitting up against a wall. The blanket had slipped off, as had its hat, which was resting on its lap.

Dimitri appeared from the adjoining room, dragging out an ammunition crate.

Banes nodded at this and manipulated control sticks. The image rotated and moved into the access passage.

At its end, Lock was issuing instructions to Gwenda and the two Japanese women. Lock's hands were animated, weaving in the air. His lips moved, but there was no sound from the TV. They all appeared oblivious to the fact that they were being watched.

Now the image sped along the big tunnel. The floor was still blue, the walls green, but the ceiling pulsed red. Silvery coils moved along beside their static counterparts on the walls and ceiling. Up ahead, the grey wall was now at a quarter of the tunnel height. The TV image climbed and came to a halt above it, tilting to view the top.

"How thick is that?" Banes whispered to himself.

He then flinched, startled, at the sound of a voice behind him.

"You haven't got any perspective." It was Wyn Ellis, standing at the door to the hallway.

"You gave me a fright."

"I did knock, but the front door was open so we came in."

Mair's face peeked around the door frame as her husband spoke.

"Don't distract me," Banes warned. "But how thick do you reckon that wall is?"

"Can you make whatever it is you're controlling go upwards a bit?" Wyn asked. He and Mair now came into the room. They sat down, as though joining someone watching TV.

Banes pressed buttons on the controller. The image moved slightly up and away from the top of the new wall. Now it could be seen against a background of the tunnel floor below it. "I don't know," he said, "maybe ten feet thick, maybe more." The view rotated and tilted to show the silvery coils along one wall.

"I'd say fifteen," Wyn Ellis said.

"You're both wrong," Mair cut in. "It's much thinner than that."

"Anyway, I don't have time for this," Banes said. "Don't distract me."

Mair was about to say something, but Wyn held up his hand to warn her not to.

On the screen, the image raced along the tunnel. "I'm barely touching the trigger," Banes said quietly, "but this drone technology can really move."

Wyn was about to speak, but now Mair held up her hand to warn *him*, raising her eyebrows.

Up ahead, the gigantic stairway grew bigger. The pace slowed, now climbing to keep above the steps as the viewpoint made its way to the top, doing this faster than any human on foot.

It swept along the narrower tubular tunnel.

The image halted at the breach, then eased out slowly at mid-height into the miners' tunnel and darkness.

"Now we wait," Banes said as he relaxed his hands on the controller.

"No night vision then?" Wyn asked.

"Probably is," Banes answered. "But there's no instruction manual."

On the screen, the miners' tunnel was visible for a few feet, lit only by the soft glow from the breach.

"I didn't know there was a stairway in the big tunnel," Wyn said in a hushed voice. "Did you? It was huge."

"It was totally dark when we first came down here," Banes explained. "We had to walk down those stairs with bikes and crates and all sorts."

"Ah," Wyn said, nodding. "I thought you were all mad when I saw you at the house with all those bikes and things. So that's what it was all about. What was the grandfather clock for then? You took it out on a truck then brought it back."

"That was for an arty photo session for Hardcastle," Banes answered awkwardly as he stared at the screen.

Something flashed in the miners' tunnel. There was a brief image of something cube shaped, and the distorted figures carrying it on their shoulders before the screen went blank. The console whined as

456

it immediately began booting up again.

"My God," Mair Ellis said. "Monsters, Wyn. Is this real? Please tell me this isn't real." She stared at Banes.

Banes did not respond. He moved in a hurry, picked up an assault rifle and slung it over his shoulder. "You'd better go back next door and lock the doors," he told the couple. "Keep yourselves, the little girl and her mother out of sight. Keep the curtains closed. We'll all be back as soon as it's safe."

"And if you don't come back?" Wyn asked, coaxing the now tearfully frightened Mair from her chair.

"Then God bless and keep you both," Banes muttered before he hurried from the room.

Outside, he crossed the duplicate lawn, stamped through a duplicate flower bed and vaulted the side wall. He was about to run up the radial path to the dome entrance when he saw something. Banes halted in disbelief.

Coming towards him under the flashing red light from the dome, Ventriloquist Jack was dressed in what looked like an old fireman's outfit, a leather hood tilted back on his head. He had a triangular butterfly net sloped on its stick over one shoulder, two thick bamboo poles over the other.

Alongside him, Hefin Gwynedd pushed a battered supermarket trolley that was crammed with what looked like junk. Baseball bat handles stuck out, together with a tennis racket, the double barrel of a shotgun, and two more bamboo poles that were part-balanced over Hefin's shoulder behind the trolley. These swayed above and behind him as he pushed it all along. Pero trotted amiably beside the two men.

"Where the hell are you two going?" Banes shouted. "Go back indoors and lock yourselves in."

"No can do," Ventriloquist Jack called back.

"He's thought it all out," Hefin Gwynedd added. "You're going to need our help."

"*And* we've got a plan," Jack told Banes.

Banes almost tripped over his own feet as he tried to absorb the sight of them and start running at the same time. "Suit your bloody selves then."

He sprinted up the radial path.

"He means well," Hefin Gwynedd observed. He fumbled with the bamboo poles to keep them balanced over his shoulder.

"I know," Jack agreed. "But I'm not going to die all cooped up down here. Whatever he and Lock think, I'd rather put up a fight."

"Me too," Hefin said. "You feel the same, don't you, Pero?"

Pero woofed his agreement and wagged his tail.

This strange trio proceeded up the radial path, supermarket trolley wheels squeaking in a steady rhythm.

-o-

Lock and the others stood in a circle in the main tunnel. Lock spoke; the others listened. Dimitri was about to say something when Banes emerged from the side passage.

"They're on their way," Banes warned. He was out of breath.

"What's their position?" Lock demanded as the group broke their circle.

Banes inhaled deeply before he spoke. "They've got to the breach in the miners' tunnel. They're bringing that black cube with them."

"Christ that was quick," Gwenda said. "At that rate, they'll reach the wall in less than an hour."

They all looked at the rising face of grey metal along the tunnel. It had nearly reached the coils. The far ends of the coils that were moving were now visible, coming closer at a steady pace.

Banes diverted his attention back to the others. "Jack Thomas and his friend are on their way here with a trolley full of junk."

"We have to take cover inside the passage," Lock said to Gwenda and Dimitri. Then he shook his head, looking at Banes. "What did you say?"

"Jack Thomas and his—"

"For goodness' sake, go tell them to go home and lock themselves in."

"I already told them, but they say they've got a plan."

"What plan? And what sort of junk?"

Banes issued a puzzled frown. "Just junk. I saw baseball bats. They've got bamboo poles, and Jack Thomas has a butterfly net."

The two Japanese women glanced at each other. But Dimitri's expression was serious as he addressed Lock. "We should at least listen to this plan."

"Really?" Lock said.

"Remember that worm thing you shot at the church?" Gwenda put in. "It had wings. Unless they are purely for decoration, maybe they could fly over that wall."

"The vicar thing walked up quite close before it spat it out," Lock responded.

"But what if the worms *can* fly *and* travel some distance?" Dimitri asked him.

In the furthest small chamber, Ventriloquist Jack put down his bamboo poles and leaned the butterfly net against a wall. He then helped Hefin with the other poles. Pero went to the doorway and barked into the next chamber.

"There's a bloody skeleton sitting on a chair in there," Hefin said as he looked through. "German officer, looks like."

Pero sniffed curiously at the blanket draped over the skeleton's legs. Jack joined Hefin, eyebrows lifting to a curve when he saw it.

The others emerged from the passage to the main tunnel, with Lock and Gwenda in the lead.

"I won't ask," Ventriloquist Jack said. He pointed at the skeleton and smiled thinly at Lock.

"I hear you have a plan," Lock responded. "Spit it out."

Jack stuffed his hands into the supermarket trolley and pulled out a folded lump of mildewed cloth. "Mosquito net," he announced as though holding up a bargain. "Perfect duplicate of the real one I bought on holiday in Hong Kong years ago. Seems to me you are preparing with all your guns, all modern like, but what we really need to do is think like the ancient Greeks."

Lock glared at the man. "Ancient Greeks? Those bloody things are on their way and they're bringing a device that blew a steel door and its frame through solid rock like it was popping a lid on a yoghurt carton."

-o-

In the elliptical dome, Caycey Jones sat on the bottom step in the amphitheatre. His face was weary. Hardcastle sat next to him with an expression that looked fatalistic and resigned.

White Hair stood a little distance away, facing them. Behind it, the lower part of the curving, murky brown dome was partly lit up with rectangular screens.

Jones and Hardcastle listened as White Hair spoke in its dull electronic voice. "We have concluded that the entities observed on the surface are an intermediate species. They are unable to reproduce and have a predicted lifespan of less than four of your days."

"The situation is urgent," Jones interrupted. "Those creatures have breached the entrance."

"We are aware," White Hair responded. "We are attempting to take steps to improve security. Continuing with our report of our analysis, it is our conclusion that the smaller creature expelled by the entity you encountered is an invasive vector, designed to commence the evolution of a new species. We have also concluded that the entities currently on the surface, together with those bringing a device to this place, are directly controlled by the hostiles."

Jones sighed and looked at Hardcastle, then fired a question at White Hair. "Can they breach the wall you are installing in the main tunnel?"

"Unknown," it responded. "We require more information about the hostile device. Remote analysis is not possible."

"We might as well go back and help the others," Hardcastle said to Jones. "This thing summoned us here just to give us a biological lecture."

"You are required to remain here for contingency purposes," White Hair told them.

"Why?" Jones demanded with a touch of anger.

"We are containment," White Hair said. "We are calculating new options and consequences. All options will have consequences for you."

Jones frowned. "Consequences? What consequences?"

"Observe," White Hair answered.

More screens, larger this time, snapped into glowing rectangles higher up in the dome.

Jones and Banes craned their necks to look up at them.

On one of the screens, a sunlit New York was deserted; corpses littered the streets. The image rotated to show thousands of purple-eyed creatures milling aimlessly in Central Park.

Other screens showed other cities around the world. London was partly a smouldering ruin. The Shibuya Crossing in Tokyo was littered with corpses, the advertising screens and neon clusters on the towering buildings above them equally dead and lifeless. Creatures with alien snouts and faces shuffled across Red Square in Moscow.

And on the largest screen, dangerously closer and of much greater concern to Jones and Hardcastle, an army of humanlike creatures with pointed snouts, torn clothes and bare feet was making its way along the main tunnel.

At their head, like funeral coffin carriers, six of them were bringing the black cube on their shoulders. Their pace was fast.

-o-

The German officer's skeleton now wore its peaked hat again. This was tilted sideways at a cheeky angle on a skull leaned against the wall behind its chair. Socket eyes seemed to be watching the repeat of the laptop screen glowing on the opposite wall of the small chamber. A window within the rectangle continued to flash *Message sent... Listening for response.*

The laptop itself rested on the floor alongside some junk. The trellis table, upon which Dimitri stood, had been dragged to the doorway of the passage to the main tunnel. The Russian was busily sticking the top edge of a length of dirty mosquito netting to the wall

461

above the opening. Duct tape made ripping noises as he worked his way along it.

Standing on the floor behind him, Lock watched, weapon ready in his hands.

Behind Lock, Hefin Gwynedd steadied a bamboo pole, the centre of which was suspended between two chairs. Ventriloquist Jack was cutting through it diagonally with a handsaw, creating a rasping, splintering sound.

Gwenda Evans stood on a chair to the side of the doorway. She was using duct tape to secure the dropped edge of the mosquito net to the wall there. Norton held the net steady below her.

The two Japanese ladies were on the other side doing the same.

Banes arrived back at the duplicate safe house office. He immediately sat down at the TV. His thumbs moved on the hand controller, eyes wide and unblinking as the screen displayed something causing him some horror.

The image kept ahead of the black-cube bearers as they came along the main tunnel. The cube rocked on their shoulders alongside pointed snouts and purple eyes. Bare feet progressed them with speed and determination. Behind this vanguard, an army of these creatures marched out of step.

Banes thumbed one of the sticks. Keeping the image moving, he rotated it to look in the other direction. The rising wall was now visible in the distance. Banes sighed, put down the controller and grabbed his weapon.

Lock and Dimitri dragged the trellis table away from the passage in the smaller chamber. The mosquito net was now draped loosely within the opening from top to bottom, with spare material crumpled on the floor.

Ventriloquist Jack arranged four sharpened bamboo poles near the German skeleton's feet. He then lifted two others with flat ends and approached the net-shrouded opening.

Lock helped him wedge the top of a pole into an upper corner of the door frame, carefully lifting and crimping that part of the mosquito net into it. Jack used his booted foot to tap the other end into the bottom, then lifted the next one ready. "Anyone here good at tennis?" he asked as the second pole was pushed into place.

"I played a bit when I was younger," Norton answered. She patted Pero's head. The dog looked alert and interested in what was going on.

Hefin Gwynedd conducted a practice swing with a baseball bat towards the wall behind her.

"We won't be swinging the bats," Jack warned. "It'll be best to tamp down and crush the worms when they get trapped between the netting and the floor."

"So," Gwenda announced as she went to the doorway and lifted the loose mosquito netting. She was able to get it to waist height before meeting resistance. "Two of us will keep watch from just inside the passage. If they get through that wall in the tunnel, we retreat back here pronto and slide under this."

"That's when it gets a bit tricky," Dimitri said.

"Not really," Jack countered as he held up a shorter length of bamboo. "But we'd better test it." He looked at Norton. "Maybe you and Hefin should be the lifters."

"Okay," Lock agreed. "Let's try it."

Hefin and Norton positioned themselves either side of the doorway and crouched down.

"Now lift," Lock instructed.

They did so, holding up the loose mosquito netting so that there was a waist-height opening.

"I'll do it," Dimitri volunteered. He moved towards it, gun in his hands, then dropped to his haunches and quickly got through under the gap. He came back just as easily. "Now the trickier part," he said to Ventriloquist Jack.

"Again, not really," Jack said as he slid four poles, pointed ends first, along the floor into the passageway, then another four, before holding up a shorter pole with flat ends. "It's simple folding surface geometry. You stop the first walking things by holding up four of these pikes at an angle. But you hold the bamboo through the netting because the poles are already positioned on the other side of it."

"Okay, let's say you manage to impale the first creatures," Lock said. "What then?"

Jack shrugged. "If the ones behind them behave like I think they will, they'll be pressed up and skewered, maybe four or five rows of them. When they get too heavy, we let them drop and we lift the next four pikes. We kill them until they are piled up blocking the passage."

"And if they launch those flying worms?" Gwenda asked him.

"Using the bamboo this way means the netting will still be in place," Jack answered. "The worms will likely drop and try to crawl under the netting. So that's when you get them with the baseball bats. Miss Norton plays tennis with any stray that manages to get through and airborne in here. Plus, someone can use the butterfly net. Catch one in that, you can just rotate the net to the ground and stamp on the thing."

Miiko's eyes widened with realisation as she heard this. She picked up the butterfly net and said something in Japanese to Kikuko.

"I must admit this is a better defensive plan than just shooting them," Lock said. "But bracing these bamboo pikes in place with weight and pressure on them is going to be tough."

"I know," Jack agreed. "Floor is hard and smooth, nothing to brace them against, so we have to counter that." He grabbed a pole, arranged his booted feet with the inside of one up against the heel of the other, then cuckooed down. He lodged the flat end of the pole into the angle between his boots and elevated its pointed end to waist height.

Jack looked up at the others. "If we can't hold them back with these, you'll just have to shoot them."

"Which will put holes in the netting and us back to Plan A," Lock said, now turning as an ashen-faced Banes arrived from the dome.

"They're not far from the wall now," Banes reported as he looked at the clumsy bamboo and mosquito net barrier. "There's a whole bloody army of them and they're bringing that cube thing, easy as pie."

"I don't suppose you've got a duplicate flamethrower tucked

away somewhere as well?" Lock asked Ventriloquist Jack. "Or something to counter that cube thing?"

"Afraid not," the man answered. "But at least we won't go down without a fight."

-o-

It began: *Thump... thump... thump...* The sound was deep, almost below the pitch audible to the human ear, more felt than heard.

Reacting to it, Kyle leaned forward in his chair, eyes anxious. His foot tapped a nervous arc on the carpet.

Ornaments rattled in the duplicate cottage lounge.

Looking quite relaxed in her armchair, Gran was knitting. "So, it's started then."

Thump... thump... thump...

"Yeh," Kyle agreed in a low voice as he listened to it. His foot trembled faster, moving the knee above it up and down like a piston. He glanced around the room.

"Your nerves are bad," Gran said.

"I know."

"It's because you're just sitting here waiting and doing nothing about it."

"I can't leave you alone," Kyle said.

"Course you can, I'll be fine," she said casually, then looped wool over a needle. "Go on. Go and help your friends."

"You sure?" Kyle asked with wide eyes.

"Go," Gran insisted. "We'll both be better off if you're doing something."

Kyle hurried towards the front door, halted, took something off the wall there and faced his gran. "Can I borrow this?"

She looked. Kyle held up an antique wicker carpet beater.

"Sure," Gran told him. "It's not the real one anyway."

"I'll lock the door behind me," Kyle said. "Love you, Gran."

"Love you too, son," Gran responded. *Thump... thump... thump...* She put down her knitting and dabbed her eyes as soon as he had gone out.

465

It was louder outside in the dome. Kyle could feel it through his feet when he paused on the bridge. Some people had opened the front doors at their bungalows and were peering out.

Ignoring them, Kyle ran to the duplicate safe house.

Next door to it at the B&B, Mair and Wyn Ellis sat facing Lara, who was holding tight to her daughter. The little girl's face was pressed into her mother's ribcage.

"This is what living in a war zone must be like," Wyn whispered to Mair. "First you get the news war is coming, then hear it approach."

"I think I preferred the sounds of normal war on the surface before we came down here," Mair said. Her worried eyes watched cups and saucers as they rattled rhythmically on a nearby coffee table.

"We will be okay," Lara said from the other sofa. "You will see."

"Of course we will," Wyn agreed, trying his best to sound positive.

Thump… thump… thump…

Kyle picked up the hand controller in the safe house office. The image on the TV showed a halted column of creatures with snouts and purple eyes. Their lines extended back to an unseen distance in the tunnel. They were paused, some shuffling bare feet, others swaying, looking ahead as though waiting for something to happen. Kyle thumbed a stick.

The image rotated to face the grey wall. The wall's top edge was now closing a small gap to the ceiling.

Tilting the image downwards, he saw a black cube resting at the floor centre. A white haze flashed from it into the wall, then another and another. *Thump… thump… thump…*

The TV picture now blurred through the wall and emerged the other side. It tilted again. Down below, the wall was misshaped and bulging at its foot. Flakes of metal fell from it. The bulge was being punched outwards.

The image zoomed along the tunnel. Small at first, then becoming clearer, Andy Lock and Dimitri crouched with their assault rifles at the passage mouth.

Kyle grabbed his carpet beater and hurried out.

Thump… thump… thump…

In the tunnel itself, a white flash was followed by the sound of a massive final thump. Rotating chunks of grey wall blasted out and flew through the air. Others squealed along the floor.

Lock and Dimitri ducked back into the passage entry, covered their ears and faced away. A pressure wave tugged at their hair and clothing.

Then all was silent.

Both men eased back to the edge. Lock lifted his binoculars. A gaping hole interrupted the otherwise smooth wall. Packed shapes with purple eyes jostled through it and began to fan out.

Dimitri lifted his weapon. The telescopic scope picked out the black cube as it was brought through. "Shall we open fire?"

"No point," Lock answered as he watched the creatures. It looked like some sort of pageant over there, the cube bobbing along, carried on shoulders as others continued coming through the hole. "There's hundreds, possibly thousands of them. We'll hold here and observe till they get within two-fifty yards. No firing… It would be useless."

"Be on the alert for flying worms," Dimitri cautioned.

"Of course."

Kyle arrived at the first of the smaller chambers. The door to the next one was shrouded by a sheet of material suspended by adhesive tape.

Hearing hushed voices through there, Kyle approached. "Hello?" he called out.

Norton's face appeared on the other side of the material. "What are you doing here? You should be with your gran."

"I was driving her nuts," Kyle answered. He peered through the dirty mosquito netting. "She told me to come and help you."

"Well, okay then," Norton said. "But stay in there. If we retreat, we'll be coming under this. You can lift it up for us if that happens. But don't detach it from the wall. Lift it carefully if you have to, but *only* when we tell you, okay?"

"Okay," Kyle confirmed, eyes growing wider as he spotted the German officer's skeleton. "But I also came to tell you what I just saw on the TV in Mister Lock's house."

"Go on," Norton encouraged.

Banes, Gwenda Evans and Ventriloquist Jack's blurred faces now turned towards him beyond the net screen. Pero woofed. The dog was a vague shape on the floor.

"There are thousands of them in the big tunnel," Kyle told them. "And more are coming along it all the time. There's no end to them. I mean, seriously, no end to them, like ants."

-o-

Jones and Hardcastle stared, horrified, at the screens in the elliptical dome ceiling.

On one of them, a wide column marched along the main tunnel towards the side entrance. A black cube rocked on shoulders in the crowd, getting closer to the entry every second.

But there were also video streams from the surface on other screens up there.

An aerial view showed the village and adjacent fields. Humanlike figures filed along the street past the real safe house. This column stretched unbroken over the bridges, along through the village, and up the farmland lane to the forestry track, where it was joined by streams of figures crossing the fields.

Scattered across these masses, black cubes bobbed along on groups of shoulders.

On another screen, a cylindrical craft hovered in the distance. Rotating crystal shapes flashed white and black in a line ahead of it. They were moving slowly through the air, as though directing the creatures below them on the ground.

White Hair seemed to be looking at Jones. The American was about to speak when Hardcastle pointed. "Shit... Look."

On the first screen, white flying things swarmed above the heads of the parading figures in the main tunnel. They circled erratically, wings glinting.

Jones glared at White Hair. "You must help," Jones said angrily. "Our people are in there, ready to defend themselves. But they cannot possibly hold back all those things."

"We will shortly take steps to counter the activity," White Hair responded. "But those steps will have consequences for you and your people."

"You keep telling us that," Hardcastle said. "But you're not telling us what you are going to do, or about the consequences."

"You must give us more information," Jones demanded.

White Hair turned and raised an arm to point at the ceiling. Another screen appeared there.

Jones and Hardcastle stared at new images. Coloured light flickered across their stunned faces.

White Hair now faced them. "Do you grant your consent to this?"

-o-

Lock and Dimitri sprinted back along the passageway.

"Coming through," Lock called out.

Gwenda and Hefin hoisted loose mosquito netting from the floor to create a gap. The two men emerged from the other side.

As they got out of the way, Ventriloquist Jack quickly slid four sharpened bamboo poles through into the passage, then four more. Gwenda and Hefin then dropped the loose netting.

"Flying worms on their way," Lock warned.

Gwenda grabbed a shorter pole, quickly slid it under and wrapped some of the net gather around it, before angling the pole across the floor inside the passageway. Ventriloquist Jack slid and kicked the other end firmly into the opposite bottom corner.

"Into position," Lock ordered. "Remember, don't hit the netting."

Hefin, Banes and Jack positioned themselves with baseball bats; Norton did so with a tennis racket. Lock, Gwenda and Dimitri crouched with their assault rifles ready.

Behind them, the Japanese ladies got into position: Miiko with a baseball bat, Kikuko holding the butterfly net.

469

Pero retreated to a corner and sat down, nervously licking his lips as a rasping, buzzing noise came from the passageway.

It grew rapidly louder; a mass of white flying things hit the mosquito net and ballooned it out.

Lock glanced up at the top edge of the net where it was taped above the doorway. It was holding.

The flying things stayed airborne only briefly. They slid down into a squirming heap enclosed in netting on the floor.

Hefin, Banes, Jack Thomas and one of the Japanese women repeatedly jabbed down on them with the ends of their baseball bats, eliciting squelches and popping sounds. Jack quickly gave up on his baseball bat and turned to stamping the squirming things in an insane dance. Lock and Gwenda joined in.

Two worms flew up into the chamber from the netting edge, rasping loudly. Norton volleyed one with her tennis racket. Miiko stamped on it. Kikuko flailed with the butterfly net at the other one.

More worms squirmed through and buzzed into flight. Norton swung at one and missed. Dimitri swung with his gun and missed. Miiko took a wild swing with a baseball bat.

Norton then managed to strike one of them. Kikuko caught it with the butterfly net, swung this over onto the floor, then stamped on the wriggling thing trapped inside it.

Dimitri stamped another one that hit the ground. Norton twisted around, looking for a worm that had flown behind her. It hovered towards Pero, black sting probing in the dog's direction. Pero growled. Norton took a swing. The worm rasped as it dodged the tennis racket.

The others were busy stamping their boots to prevent more crawlers from getting under the net when Norton took another panicked swing, this time losing her balance. She went into an involuntary backdrop, racket and empty hand breaking her fall. The worm buzzed towards her horrified face.

She flinched when something swished past her nose, sending the worm into a splash on the nearby wall. Kyle looked down at her, carpet beater in hand. He helped her to her feet.

The others swatted and stamped.

470

And at last a booted foot stomped a single worm. The buzzing noise ceased.

"I think that's all the bloody worms for now," Ventriloquist Jack said. He took a few precautionary stamps with his boot at the mess under the loose netting.

"Get your pikes ready," Lock instructed in a low, encouraging, but almost growling voice. "Remember, if we have to start shooting them, the rest of you retreat to the main chamber and get indoors."

Ventriloquist Jack joined Banes, Hefin and Dimitri to gather up some of the netting with gloved hands. Goo slithered on the other side. "Carefully," Jack warned. In unison, they lifted two bamboo pikes each from those lying in the passage. They pulled back the blunt ends as far as the netting would permit, then each lifted and held one pole so that four sharp ends were angled to waist height in the passageway.

Lock and Gwenda squinted through the filthy netting.

"Here they come," Gwenda warned.

"Any sign of that cube?" Dimitri asked. He was hunched below her. Wrapped in loose mosquito netting, the blunt end of his bamboo pole was jammed into the angle between his booted feet.

"Not yet," Lock answered. "Get ready for pressure on those pikes."

There was a growing sound of asthmatic breathing; multiple pairs of purple eyes approached.

Jack and the others peered through the netting. The first creatures shuffled ever closer to the sharpened poles.

Jack gritted his teeth. "Get ready."

Dimitri braced himself.

But instead of walking into the pikes, two of the figures in the passage stepped nimbly between them. Hefin Gwynedd and Banes swiftly drew their poles back and stabbed. The figures parried them. Other creatures grabbed the poles, wrenching them out of the men's hands. Jack almost fell over as his slipped from his grip. Hefin tried to grab his pole again but failed.

"Shit, they're wise to it," Dimitri warned. "We've got to get out of here."

Lock aimed his weapon. "Pick your target. Aim at their throats and fire on my command." He stared with disbelief as the creatures in the passage handed the poles back between themselves in a grotesque pass the parcel. Purple eyes were alert. There was co-ordination to their movements.

Now the heavy breathing in there rose in an intense chorus. Necks began to swell alongside throats. Alien hands reached towards the mosquito netting as they moved towards it. Purple eyes gleamed.

Lock had opened his lips to issue the command to fire when there was a vibration under their feet. The passageway floor suddenly rose up like a cylinder being thrust upwards. A torrent of murky fluid gushed out as the floor thumped the passage ceiling. Solid metal now miraculously blocked the way.

Kyle and Norton avoided it. But the others were immediately covered in the slime that spurted out.

Now there was no passageway. It was plugged solid. Mosquito netting slid down its face. Shards of bamboo stuck out from its edges.

"Well thank God for that," Banes announced as he wiped slime from his face.

"Thank White Hair, more probably," Lock said. Goo dripped from his head, arms and weapon. "But it remains to be seen how long this barrier stands up to that cube device they've got."

"You're not an optimist, are you," Dimitri commented. "Was it the whole length of the floor that rose up?"

"I think so," Lock said, then spotted Kyle, who was holding a carpet beater poised ready to swing. "What are *you* doing in here?" Lock demanded softly.

"He got one of the worms," Norton said. "It would have got me if he hadn't come through."

"Well done, Kyle," Jack Thomas said from where he was bent over, catching his breath. Hefin Gwynedd stooped nearby, an arm around Pero, holding the dog as though for dear life.

Lock slapped his gloved hands together. "We've got to get as far away from this barrier as possible. When they get that cube thing on the go again, the shock waves this side will be absolutely deadly."

472

"Do you think it will hold them?" Norton asked, pointing back at the plugged passage as Lock urged them away from it.

"Only for a while," Lock answered grimly. "Judging by what they've been able to do so far, they *will* get through eventually. We have to be ready for that."

The group hurried along the radial path towards the safe house. Norton's eyes were fixed, as though in shock. Ventriloquist Jack walked beside her without speaking. Banes and Dimitri followed Lock and Gwenda, with Dimitri repeatedly checking the safety catch on his assault rifle as he walked. Pero kept close to Hefin's feet.

The dog was first to hear something. He stopped, raised his head. Kyle noticed this and shifted the carpet beater in his hands.

Lock raised an arm to halt them. He turned around and tapped an ear, signalling them all to be alert.

They listened. A faint sound, something ghostly and intangible to begin with, but it grew.

Pero issued a sharp woof to Hefin. Kyle looked at the floor as though he had felt something there.

Instead of the crunching thumps that they had heard and felt earlier, the floor began to vibrate.

"What the hell?" Lock demanded angrily. He set off towards the house again.

As the others followed, the vibrations rose into violent tremors. Kikuko tripped and fell. Gwenda and Miiko immediately helped her up. Pero barked. Ventriloquist Jack grabbed Norton when she lost her balance.

It subsided quicker than it had begun, as though going through some sort of frequency shift. The shaking ceased and the noise steadied into a low, throbbing and continuous *whummm... whummm... whummm...*

"For Christ's sake, what now?" Gwenda protested. "Haven't we had enough?" Her eyes widened when she saw movement.

The cannon-like structures rotated in the chamber centre. Like production-line robots, their barrels tilted to vertical. Then, together with a circular area of the floor beneath them, they rapidly sank down.

Whummm… whummm… whummm…

People came out of their duplicate houses. Heads turned to face the ceiling. Lock and the others also stared.

Up above, the display of stars was gone. Instead, the dome swirled with murky shades of brown and green.

Whummm… whummm… whummm…

-o-

Out on the surface, purple-eyed creatures marched along the real village streets. Others crossed fields. Where cows had grazed, big lumps with horn shapes sticking out of them lay scattered on the grass. They were encased in purple fur. A smaller shape squirmed as walking creatures passed it.

At the end of one field, a cornered calf backed into the angle between two hedgerows. A group of snouted walking things wheezed towards it, necks bulging. Flying worms swooped on the terrified animal.

On the mountain, creatures carrying black cubes slouched up the forestry track in an unending stream. A raven crashed through pine branches, wings spraying black feathers.

Birds careened, screeching as they fled. A white worm plunged through tree branches. The crow it struck screamed like a child. It fell out of the tree as though shot. The worm, nearly as big as the crow, swiftly burrowed into its body on the ground.

Some of the monsters paraded along the beach road, passing Ventriloquist Jack's real *Ponderosa* yard and home. Beyond it, others reached the car park above the tiny bay. Purple eyes watched seagulls circling crazily over the sea wall.

It looked like an aerial dogfight up there. White buzzing things swooped through the gulls, which in turn dodged and yawed, while others tried to catch the worms in mid-air. But one by one, the gulls were spiralling limp-winged to the sea below. Others crashed into the sea wall.

Now, something appeared out at sea. A black object broke the surface midway to the horizon. The sea foamed around it as it rose.

Here and there, walking creatures' heads turned to face this growing noise. It sounded like a gigantic waterfall.

The black shape was already hundreds of feet in the air but incredibly still emerging. It was as though a submerged mountain had decided to surface. Torrents of water cascaded from its sides.

An elliptical dome punctuated its upper end. Explosions of water accompanied a pair of larger domes as they appeared. Two more followed, spilling silt and water as the emergence gathered speed.

Now, finally, the rear end of this mountainous object broke free. It continued rising, angled upwards into the air, still spilling torrents of water.

And then a sound, as though a sea god had smacked its hands together. The surface of the sea rushed and slapped, producing a huge waterspout.

The bay inside the sea wall emptied, leaving a surface of slime, silt and seaweed. Fish flapped and struggled.

The purple-eyed creatures turned and aimed their eyes at the object as it continued rising impossibly. Even as the waterfalls spilling from it began to ease, the acceleration became exponential. It rose effortlessly through the clouds, splitting through them before diminishing into a dot that disappeared high in the sky.

A pillar-like vapour trail appeared behind it. Like some sort of atmospheric afterthought, this streaked upwards, puffing out white rings.

The first tsunami wave hit and leapfrogged over the sea wall. It swept the walking things from the car park and dragged them inland. A foaming wall of water and debris ripped roofs off houses in the village, then continued in over the fields.

-o-

Whummm… whummm… whummm…

In the dome, Lock and his group stared at the ceiling with mesmerised eyes. A darkness on one side faded into browns and greens. A vivid blue grew brighter on the side opposite.

The blur reduced. Eyes began to focus on detail. The Earth's horizon moved across the dome crown, shrinking more and more into a curve. Within seconds, the entire planet was revealed, half in darkness, the other half a blue jewel.

Now the Earth halted, remaining visible above the roofs of duplicated houses, hanging there like a blue half-moon.

The *whummm* sound issued once more, then ceased.

Banes held out his thumb and forefinger at arm's length and squinted through them, as though trying to grip the image of Earth.

As he did this, brilliant light from the sun flared from the other side of the dome before swiftly dimming into a disc. It seemed the dome material had darkened there to filter out its harmful rays.

Distant shouts came from villagers towards and beyond the two bridges.

"Is this real?" Kyle asked in a low voice. "Are we in space?"

"It certainly looks that way," Norton answered. She smiled thinly as though half in relief, half in trepidation. "Who would have thought..." But then Norton noticed her hands were shaking. She gripped them into fists and looked around at her companions.

Dimitri headed shakily for the duplicate B&B, where his wife and daughter were out on the lawn. They were staring at the distant Earth, together with the stunned Mair and Wyn Ellis.

Gwenda lowered herself to the floor and just sat there. Lock went through something similar to Norton with his own trembling hands.

Ventriloquist Jack finally got his breathing under control, glanced at a similarly recovering Hefin Gwynedd, before looking up at the astounding view. Pero was quite relaxed, tail wagging at their feet.

Miiko and Kikuko held up their mobile phones. Simulated shutter sounds clicked away. Their hands did not shake.

Ventriloquist Jack was now able to move his lips instead of them being drawn back over his teeth. "I always dreamed of something like this, but I never..."

"Me neither," Hefin promptly agreed. Pero glanced at him as he spoke.

"What now?" Gwenda asked Lock. Over towards the bridges, some of the villagers were headed in the group's direction.

"I have no idea," Lock answered.

A confused Mr Robert E Lee was the first to get close enough to speak. "Excuse me," he said. "I was just wondering whether this is real, or if I'm having hallucinations again?" He pointed at the Earth.

But even as he uttered his question, that *whummm* noise sounded out again, this time brief and not repeated. The Earth swung upwards and veered to the side. Another object rose into view below it.

The moon looked as though it was the same size as the Earth. Like the blue planet, it was half in darkness. Craters were visible but patterned like nothing ever seen from Earth.

"Over three hundred thousand miles," Banes announced.

"Pardon?" Robert E Lee asked.

"That's roughly how far we've travelled from Earth in less than a minute," Banes told him.

Lee still looked puzzled. "Is all this real then?"

-o-

The train carriage centre door slid open above filthy water in the main tunnel. A slotted ramp descended, bottom part disappearing into the murk.

Jones walked down the ramp without hesitation and waded up to his waist. He aimed for the passageway. After a few paces with his lower half under water, he turned around. Hardcastle was still at the doorway on the carriage, wrinkling his nose.

"It's just silt and seawater," Jones told him.

Hardcastle looked in his direction. Beyond Jones, the top surface of the plug that had slammed into the passageway ceiling was now lowered to just above the water line. A faint humming sound came from somewhere, as though pumps were in action.

Jones watched Hardcastle descend tentatively into the water, grimacing when it reached his waist.

"It's only seawater," Jones insisted.

Hardcastle gave Jones a sickly smile as he waded towards him. "Well, considering you and I both gave consent to White Hair to open the sluices, then watched on the screen as that army of monsters

477

got flushed down the toilet, I sort of knew that already, don't you think?"

Jones raised his eyebrows. "You believe you have a pretty sharp sense of humour, don't you?"

"I do my best," Hardcastle responded primly as he faced the American. "It's my way of coping with stress."

"Well then," Jones said. He then froze, his expression changing to one of rapid horror. "Watch out, behind you! Shark!"

Hardcastle twisted and lurched sideways through the water in panic. Jones caught him before he fell.

"Where?" Hardcastle gasped.

Jones pointed a wet finger at Hardcastle's face. "Gotcha."

"Jesus Christ... You frightened the living daylights out of me. What the hell did you do that for?"

"You've got your sense of humour," Jones said in his deep voice as he waded along once more. "I've got mine. It helps me with my stressful moments."

Hardcastle helped Jones clamber onto the raised floor in the passageway. Jones reciprocated to haul Hardcastle up. Both men were able to walk stooped under the ceiling to the drop into the first small chamber.

Here the German naval officer's skeleton was still seated, hat sitting prettily on its skull, apparently untouched by the mayhem that had generated the mess in front of it.

Hardcastle dropped down, then turned to help Jones lower himself. They then stepped through lumpy slime, splinters of bamboo pole and crumpled mosquito netting. Both men eyed splashes of gunk on the walls and the crushed pulps of worms on the floor.

"They had one hell of a fight," Hardcastle murmured.

"We really have to do something about him," Jones said, pointing at the German skeleton.

"He's not doing any harm," Hardcastle said.

"I know," Jones agreed. "But it's disrespectful to use what's left of him like some sort of totem on display."

"I've always spoken to him with the utmost respect," Hardcastle said. "But I agree. He deserves a decent funeral. Same for the British guys in that side room there. We never had time, maybe now we do, but where do we bury them?"

"Maybe our first burials in space?" Jones suggested.

Hardcastle raised his eyebrows. "Do a Captain Kirk and torpedo them out of an airlock?"

Jones grinned. "There's that sense of humour again. Not everything needs to be related to Hollywood movies or TV."

"Like Jaws?"

"You got me there, fair and square," Jones admitted with a broad smile. "Let's go see how the others are faring." He patted Hardcastle on the shoulder in genuine friendship.

Hardcastle patted him back.

-o-

The villagers came in ones and twos. Some came in groups. The teenagers peeled off from their parents, walking together and chatting. Most had serious expressions on their faces.

Some stared at the distant Earth and Moon through the side of the dome.

Others gazed in different directions, taking in the three other circular domes outside their own. Visible also out there in the vacuum of space, the elliptical shape of the control area where White Hair resided. Its dome shimmered green like a cat's eye against a background of stars.

But the villagers were headed as though keeping a collective appointment. They converged on the circular area in the centre of their dome.

Waiting there, Jones and the others watched them arrive. Hands were shaken; hugs were exchanged.

Close by, Emily Norton supervised children to some outdoor toys at the edge of a duplicate field. Mair Ellis placed a food hamper on a picnic table. She then shooed a couple of teenagers away. "Children only here. Go and listen. It's important."

Men and women waited in the centre, together with youngsters who were old enough to comprehend. They wore expressions of anticipation, mixed with the relief of survival.

It was Jones who addressed them. The American's deep voice seemed to fill the dome.

"Thank you all for coming," he began. "I know that Emily and Gwenda and some of the others have briefed you about our current situation, but I will say a few words…

"Most of us have lost people, friends, relatives, close family. There will be a time to acknowledge that grief and to mourn. There will be a moment when we give voice to the billions who have died, but not now. Today, at this moment, we must all make a collective decision. In order to do that, let's reflect upon why we are here and what we few represent.

"We humans, those of us who have survived, have emerged from millennia of belief that we were at the centre of God's universe. Now, suddenly, we face the knowledge that we were never alone. Not only this, but we must accept the uncomfortable fact that we are the genetic creations of alien entities of extraterrestrial origin."

Jones paused as some in the crowd murmured to each other. From the adjacent field, not connected to his words, there was gentle laughter, a few oblivious hoots of joy from the children playing there. Emily Norton's and Mair's voices also sounded out from over there. Jones smiled. Some in the crowd acknowledged this with smiles of their own before reverting to their attentive seriousness.

"To us," Jones now continued, "those aliens have unfathomable minds and hostile intent. Hostiles who consider us to be their property to do with as they please. They are an alien race who, after millennia of hidden manipulation and abuse towards us, ultimately and most recently marked us for complete extermination."

There were no murmurs from the crowd at this. Hushed, some faces reacted with glints of anger as they listened to the American.

"Why did they create us? We do not know. Who or what are they? We do not know that either. But we do know that they were imprisoned on our world millions of years before humans existed."

480

Even Betty Lewis remained silent as Jones spoke. She stood close to her husband with an affection that appeared only recently remembered; they both clasped the shoulders of their son and daughter in front of them.

Husbands and wives held each other. Young mothers cuddled their babies as though they had never before been so precious. Other parents glanced over at the children playing under Emily Norton's and Mair's supervision in the field.

Jones looked around at his friends from the safe house and the group that had defended the access to the dome. Andy Lock's arm firmly held Gwenda's shoulders; hers held his waist.

Hardcastle and Banes stood side by side. Ventriloquist Jack, hands stuffed in his pockets, was next to Hefin Gwynedd and his dog Pero.

Kyle was also there. The Russian family stood nearby with Wyn Ellis.

At the sight of them, Jones took a deep breath to compose himself, then faced his audience again. "Today we are all that is left of humanity." He pointed at the ceiling, to the field of now real stars crystal clear above it. "Our future, whatever lies within it, is out there…"

Behind Jones, Hefin Gwynedd turned to Ventriloquist Jack, looked up at the stars, and whispered, "There'll be trouble out here in space, you mark my words."

Pero woofed his agreement.

Jack smiled thinly. "Biggest trouble is going to be the entire village arguing endlessly about what we do next. *You* mark *my* words." His whisper was a little too loud.

"Thank you, Mister Thomas," Jones called to him with a raised eyebrow and a smile.

Ventriloquist Jack shrugged with an expression of denial.

"He's a brave man," Jones said to the crowd. "They are all brave and we owe them our gratitude for our continued survival. But Mister Thomas is right. We cannot talk endlessly here and now." He pointed at the distant Earth. "We can't go back there. We cannot stay here. I therefore seek your consent to a proposed course of action…"

-o-

Space… Absolutely silent…

There, a gargantuan vessel, with its pristine domes, its bulkier mass half gleaming brightly in the sun, half in darkness.

It moved now, rotating smoothly. Then without flashes of light, no roar of engines, no blasts of flame or plasma, it simply disappeared, leaving behind something that looked as though a wisp of light had drawn a line towards the stars.

THE END

For information about forthcoming books from this author,
follow him at:

rmhughesscifi.com

Made in the USA
Middletown, DE
30 November 2021

53783070R00288